P9-APD-166

THE HUNDRED PERCENT SQUAD

THE HUNDRED PERCENT SQUAD

A NOVEL BY E.W. COUNT

A Warner Communications Company

This book is a work of fiction. Names, characters, places, and incidents are either the product of the author's imagination or are used fictitiously.

Grateful acknowledgment is given to quote from the following: "Sorpresas" by Rubén Blades. © Rubén Blades Productions Inc. 1986.

Warner Books, Inc., 666 Fifth Avenue, New York, NY 10103

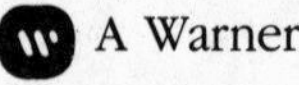 A Warner Communications Company

Printed in the United States of America

First printing: August 1990

10 9 8 7 6 5 4 3 2 1

Library of Congress Cataloging-in-Publication Data

Count, Ellen.
The hundred percent squad / E.W. Count.
p. cm.
ISBN 0-446-51471-3
I. Title.
PS3553.O854H8 1990
813'.54—dc20 89-40471
CIP

Book design: H. Roberts

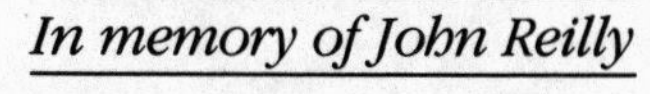
In memory of John Reilly

ACKNOWLEDGMENTS

To those finest of the Finest who inspired me in the first place, and to all those who stuck with me no matter what damn question I asked—all my thanks. Captain Stephen P. Davis was among those who shared the biggest burden, as were Philip Friedman, Mel Parker, and Sonia Pilcer.

This is a work of fiction but one that I hope achieves a measure of authenticity. If I succeeded in that, it is thanks to the help of indulgent friends: Lieut. John Doyle, Det. Michael Sheehan, Lieut. Anthony Di Chiaro, Det. Evrard Williams, Det. John Hartigan, Det. John Collins, Det. Thomas N. Ullo, Det. Bernard J. McCrossan, Det. Kenneth Bowman, Lieut. Patrick Picciarelli, Det. Fred Elwick, Det. Augie Jonza, Det. Jean A. Lettieri, Capt. Harvey Katowitz, P.O. Ron McNair, Det. Tom Natale, Det. Charles Butera, Lieut. Jay Kosack.

Assistant District Attorneys Sarah Hines, Patrick Dugan, Harvey Rosen, Dan Castleman, Steve Saracco.

Peter DePasquale, Emily Smith, A. A. Ryan, Jr., Peggy Dye, Robert Aviles, Amy M. Kates, Joseph F. Hayes, Kathryn Gillespie, Diane Cardwell, John O. Philips, Diane Tarnay, Henry Montalvo, Kitty Brazleton, George Ingraham, Mary Ann Jung, Ernestine Bugbee.

Special thanks are due Cummington Community of the Arts, Palenville Interarts Colony, The Wertheim Study—New York Public Library, and Derrick Duncker and Clarence Hambrick at Wolff Computer.

THE HUNDRED PERCENT SQUAD

PROLOGUE

Wednesday night, February 23, 1972

Cops—even plainclothes cops like Andy Flynn and his partner—were supposed to stay out of places like the Cocodrillo except on a raid. But Flynn and Nolan believed that when the stakes were high, you did what you had to do.

Since midnight, they'd been at the bar in the notorious after-hours club. They were waiting for Perez, the stoolie who would introduce them to Jorge Martín as members of the Westies, the murderous Hell's Kitchen crew, out looking for an arsenal.

In northern Manhattan in the early seventies, any bad guy who wanted an illegal gun went to Martín. You didn't have to be Spanish to walk into the Cocodrillo and buy a gun from Martín —street name, "Blanco." You could be black, white, or purple, as long as Blanco didn't make you for a cop and you had his price.

No police officer in the Fifth and Sixth Divisions could forget the springtime week in 1971 when weapons bought from Blanco had slaughtered two cops and maimed two more. The survivors wondered who would be the next target for one of Blanco's guns.

Flynn stared gloomily into his scotch, a lock of straight, dark hair shadowing his high forehead. "Perez oughta be here by now."

"We got nothin' on him and he knows it," Nolan pointed out. "Maybe he changed his mind about givin' up Blanco just to be Señor Nice Guy."

"Forget Señor Nice Guy. Perez is the type to turn Blanco in and disappear for a few months—when he comes back, *Perez* sells the guns around here. Sooner or later, he'll show up with Blanco; it's just too cold out tonight." Flynn took another hit of his fourth J&B and soda.

Or maybe his fifth—Kenny Nolan had lost count. His demon-rum sermons didn't seem to touch his partner's problem. Anytime Kenny told him to take it easy on the booze, Andy would say you only live once. Right, Kenny would answer, and with a little luck maybe you'll make it to thirty.

The two good-looking cops were twenty-nine years old. They

had been promoted at the same time from uniformed patrol in different parts of the city to Fifth Division plainclothes. Both of them loved the street and working it together. They'd been a team for almost four years.

Nolan figured he'd forget the sermon this time and stick to the subject of Perez. "Too *cold* out tonight? Very funny."

"Listen, these tropical products can't take twenty-degree weather."

"Oh, yeah? Every one of these mutts waded through the slush for their booze and their dope, not to mention their guns." Nolan scanned the crowd of Hispanics of all shapes, sizes, and Latin origins. "What would you call this crew—Spanish Eskimos?"

"I'd call 'em good customers. The kinda money they spend in here, Viera let's 'em sleep on the floor anytime it goes below freezing outdoors."

"Now when did you ever hear of Irish Viera doing *anybody* a favor," Nolan scoffed. "That's a helluva frozen banana back there." Both cops glanced across the room at the door with the NO ENTREN sign.

"Uh-uh," Flynn said, "you're forgetting Viera's one true friend—Blanco."

"Who knows if Blanco is really the true-blue friend Viera thinks."

"Let's do a test and find out." Flynn narrowed his eyes. "Say we peel Blanco's banana *good.* Will he give up the real shit on his pal, Irish—a dude who's got more goin' in this town than just the worst bar north of Forty-second Street? What am I bet?" Flynn downed the last of his scotch.

"For a Public Morals cop, you do a lot of gambling. *Dónde es Perez?* It's four-thirty."

"Screw Perez. Let's get outta here."

As Flynn and Nolan moved toward the exit, their other partner, Robbie Rivera, came down the stairs into the basement club.

"Hold on." Rivera sounded serious. "Hope you guys pass the breath test. The night is young and Perez didn't stand you up after all."

Nolan saw Flynn try to shake off his J&B fog as Robbie went on.

"Perez and that scumbucket, Blanco—sittin' on you, down the block on Columbus. Armed."

"Holy shit," Nolan breathed. "Another five minutes, they'da fuckin' had us."

"Have a drink," Flynn told Rivera. "No inspectors' funerals this week, thanks to you."

"It's not over till it's over," Rivera warned. "Fuckin' Blanco looks lean an' mean." Rivera told them which dark tenement doorway harbored a gun dealer and a stoolie waiting for a pair of tipsy plainclothes cops to pass by.

What with the booze and the messy sidewalks, the partners had to concentrate on each step. But in any weather you had to watch yourself around these worst blocks in the Two-nine Precinct. Flynn and Nolan turned east on 107th Street, walking away from Columbus; then south on Central Park West and westward again, toward the ambush.

"You don't suppose Irish Viera had anything to do with this?" Nolan asked.

"Like Irish knows what I'm thinkin' before I do?" Flynn said. "He ain't *that* smart." He and Nolan strained to sight any movement in the midblock doorways.

Blanco and Perez would be expecting the cops to come from the other direction. They poked their heads out the doorway, looking anxiously to the north. The cops had the whole thing under control. They kept their eyes on the men's hands. Nearing the northeast corner of 106th Street and Columbus, they saw Blanco reach into the pocket of his ski jacket. Then Perez dropped his pack of cigarettes and bent to get it. As he straightened up, he spotted the cops, forty feet away on a diagonal.

"Stop, police!" Flynn yelled, his breath streaking the dark air. Blanco took off eastward across the avenue and uptown. Perez followed as far as the corner of 107th Street, then ran west. The cops split up, too, Flynn racing after Blanco, Nolan chasing Perez. "Careful!" Flynn yelled.

Nolan felt totally sober; he almost enjoyed the cold air on his face as he ran down the middle of the empty side street, his .38 in his hand, closing the distance between himself and the short stoolie. Perez failed to notice a wooden skid lying on the sidewalk in front of a warehouse. He tripped and fell frontward across the skid. He rolled over, trying to yank something out of his waistband. Nolan aimed at the stoolie's midsection: *"Drop it,* Perez!"

But Perez cocked his weapon. Nolan pulled the trigger and Perez's gun clattered on the pavement. Perez fell back, Nolan's bullet in his chest.

"Andy—I'm okay!" Nolan shouted, but his partner was nowhere in sight.

* * *

Blanco ran with his hand still in the ski jacket pocket. He was about five feet nine—a little shorter than Flynn and thinner—but the cop's physical advantage was useless from here. Flynn figured the gun dealer for a good shot, too.

Manhattan Avenue, a few blocks of drug-ridden slum, hadn't been sanded. Dirty snow crusted the sidewalk. Around here, people didn't get up in the morning and shovel. Now Blanco was running with a big automatic in his hand, probably a foreign job, and he kept looking back at the cop. Flynn saw himself laid out in the big room at Matthew Bell's funeral home in the Highbridge section of the Bronx—the room where his father's wake had been held.

They took a left into 105th Street—Blanco in the road, Flynn on the sidewalk. Suddenly the gun dealer dropped to the ground. The cop kept running till he could see over the row of parked cars. Near the corner of Central Park West, a car-wash place had made the sidewalk a sheet of ice. Blanco had slipped—hard—and dropped his gun. Flynn put on a burst of speed, trench coat flapping, gun ready. He saw the son of a bitch on all fours on the sidewalk, reaching for that big foreign gun.

Flynn skidded to a stop, crouched next to a parked Jeep, and sighted along the barrel of the .38 Smith & Wesson he had won for scoring first in physical fitness in his Police Academy class. Until Blanco's bullet whizzed close to Flynn's shoulder, the cop didn't move. Then he pumped out three shots. None of them missed.

Patrol cars were already racing to the corner from all over the precinct. An EMS ambulance pulled up and paramedics rushed to the man on the bloody patch of ice, but in seconds they knew he was DOA. The patrol sergeant shook Flynn's hand when Flynn told him who the dead perp was. With Blanco gone, though, Flynn's bet with Nolan was off—they'd never know if the gun dealer would have given up his pal Viera. Flynn cursed himself for missing his chance to let the air out of Viera's tires now—before the bastard really got rolling.

Suddenly, the cops' car radios crackled with a 10-13: officer in trouble—One oh eight Street and Columbus. Flynn jumped into the back of a radio car. The siren wailed as the uniformed cops sped him to the scene, arriving just as another EMS crew loaded Kenny Nolan into their bus. Ten minutes earlier, as Perez lay on the pavement with Nolan standing guard, the half-dead stool had pulled a second gun from an ankle holster and emptied it into Nolan's left leg.

Flynn and Nolan were written up three weeks later in the

Daily News "Hero of the Month" column, for eliminating a major source of illegal guns in the city. With the column, the *News* published NYPD head shots of both cops, in uniform.

The day the story came out, Flynn brought coffee containers filled with scotch to Nolan's room in St. Luke's Hospital and the partners did their best to celebrate. Although Nolan would eventually walk again, his knee joint would never be completely normal. If he should need to run more than a block or so, the joint might not hold up. The street-crazy cop had no choice but to retire.

On Rikers Island, where prisoners have plenty of time to read newspapers, Perez clipped the "Hero" article, wrote *Interesantisimo* across the top, and sent it to Irish Viera.

Viera read the article twice, underlining the names *Jorge Martín* and *Officer Andrew Flynn*. He added the story to other clippings in a folder marked ARCHIVO CONFIDENCIAL.

Friday night, March 15, 1985

Detective Lieutenant Flynn's newest squad member, Ron Pastore, rushed through the squad room so fast that he left a jet trail in the air. His sharply creased, perfectly aged blue jeans probably bleached out another shade. He found his boss in the coffee room, filling his oversize mug from the glass pot.

Pastore had made a name for himself in the precinct's anticrime unit, where his only problem had been converting his fresh-scrubbed look into that of a shady street person. He still had a little trouble believing his promotion, just a few months old, to Flynn's celebrated command. No squad except Flynn's had ever racked up a hundred percent homicide clearance, let alone racked it up two years going on three. And Flynn had only been commander of the Twenty-ninth Precinct detectives since '82.

"Double stabbing." Pastore's voice came out louder than he intended in the cubbyholelike space. "One twenty West One oh five Street."

Flynn squinted at him with a half-smile, like he knew a secret. "Who's catching?"

"Holy shit—I am." Pastore now had a homicide of his own to investigate for the first time. He'd have settled for just a plain single, especially with the squad going for their third hundred percent. All the same, he hoped to hell Flynn wouldn't reassign the case to a more experienced man. "There's always someone dealing outta that building," Pastore volunteered, "terrorizing the regular tenants. Narcotics can't keep up with it. Uniform does vertical patrol in there all the time."

"Back when I was in plainclothes, that was a decent place to live," Flynn said. Wisps of steam rose from his mug of coffee, abandoned on a desk as he and Pastore shrugged on their trench coats and slammed out the squad room's swinging door.

By now Pastore knew that, unlike your standard-issue NYPD lieutenant, Flynn didn't make his men play chauffeur. "Boss," the young detective said as he got into the blue Chrysler on the passenger side, "the patrol sergeant said his cops stumbled on the DOAs themselves—nobody called 911."

In the hall outside the apartment on 105th Street, two uniformed cops huddled with their sergeant. They looked relieved when Flynn and Pastore emerged from the stairwell onto the third floor.

As the detectives approached, they saw for themselves what had tipped off the vertical patrol team: a minicascade of fresh blood still dripping off the apartment's doorsill onto the filthy tile floor of the hallway.

Before Flynn could inquire why the cops were just standing there instead of doing a preliminary crime-scene search, Sergeant Deegan beckoned. "Crime Scene's notified; Emergency Service, too," he said. He managed to push the steel-plated apartment door wide open without stepping inside. The two victims had fallen near the middle of the smallish room, and streams of blood flowed from their slit throats, merging to form a broad, treacherous puddle that lay between their bodies and the detectives in the doorway.

Flynn whistled.

A fortune in coke lay strewn around, under and over the pair of Hispanic drug dealers—or maybe drug customers; whatever they were, their heads were cut almost off their necks. In Pastore's seven years on patrol, he had never come upon such a scene. This event—not the gold-shield ceremony at headquarters—seemed to be his initiation into the Detective Bureau. The usually businesslike cop let his mouth fall open, skewed his jaw, and rolled up his sincere brown eyes for a total effect horrible enough to rival the dead mens' faces. The cops' guffaws broke the tension in the hallway.

"Emergency Service better bring the skyhooks," one of Sergeant Deegan's men said. He meant that if you tried to leap the puddle of blood and slipped, you'd not only destroy the crime scene but you'd probably land on top of one or both of the gory bodies, with blood and cocaine powder all over you.

Upon arrival, the ESU team took one look and went back down to their truck for a ladder. They poked it through the apartment doorway on an angle, avoiding the corpses; then they turned it flat, making a walkway on which the detectives stepped gingerly into the nearly bare studio apartment. An armchair and a nightstand stood right behind the bodies in the center of the room; a cot was set up at the far end.

Pastore followed Flynn, who squatted to inspect the victims' wounds: savage cuts that spiraled down the necks from behind one ear. "Fancy," Flynn commented. As he stood up, his eyes came level with the top of the nightstand. *"Very* fancy."

"Un-fucking-believable," Pastore said, catching sight of the six hacked-off fingers, neatly arranged three and three on the nightstand. To top it all off, the nightstand drawer had been left open just enough for the detectives to see a stack of cash and what looked like a .357 magnum inside.

"Dealers," Flynn said.

Pastore wondered when Crime Scene would show up and dust that nightstand for prints.

"You search Groucho," Flynn told him, "I'll do Harpo." The dealers had no ID on them. Pastore knew he would be elected to roll those chopped-off fingers in ink.

"Some fuckin' *robbery,* boss," he said. "The perp leaves behind a shitload of coke, an expensive gun, and a wad of cash."

"Nothing missing but the beepers; they might've helped us."

"Oh, right." Next time, Pastore would think of that himself.

Two Crime Scene Unit guys tiptoed in on the ladder and opened up their kits.

"Some modern artist could have a ball with this tableau," one of them muttered. Pastore winced inwardly, glad that the CSU detective—rather than his boss—had reminded him. He turned over a fresh page in his notebook and began to diagram the chaos.

Flynn made sure the fingerprint guy started on the nightstand. The guy sprinkled white powder on the surface, trying to avoid the fingers. "I don't get it," he said. "The perp chops 'em up like bad boys who stole, but he don't bother to recover the cash?"

"Robbery ain't the motive," Flynn said casually.

The CSU guy, like a lot of people in the NYPD, knew Flynn and the reputation of Flynn's "hundred percent squad."

"Okay, Lieu—what's the motive?" The CSU guy held a strip of clear fingerprint tape poised above the patch of white powder.

"I'd say it was a lesson. Seventh Commandment."

The CSU guy lifted the powder with the tape and stuck it on a black card. Then he jabbed a finger at the corpses. "'Thou shalt not steal'—got that, boys?"

Pastore saw what his boss meant. "A lesson for the *living,* huh?"

"Exactly. Groucho and Harpo ain't no independent businessmen. They gotta be examples—the others in the organization gotta get the message: These mutts didn't get ripped off—they got punished."

Pastore thought of the only bad guy in the precinct big enough to walk away from fifty thousand dollars' worth of coke, not to mention an expensive gun and enough cash to feed a family of four for half a year. A bad guy who had gotten away with murder time after time. Pastore looked at Flynn, who seemed temporarily lost in thought. When their eyes did meet, Pastore said, "Hadda be Viera, right?"

"Way back when, I used to call him 'the banana.' Y'know, I put his best pal underground—real dirty guy. I kinda figured Irish would get back to me on that someday. I was just thinkin', the clever son of a bitch certainly timed it right—"

"Lieu," one of Sergeant Deegan's uniformed cops yelled from the bathroom, "I think I got somethin'."

Pastore followed Flynn across the rungs of the ladder to the bathroom door.

"How about that." The uniformed cop pointed excitedly under the radiator. "I guess the cleanin' lady don't do radiators."

Pastore saw an empty plastic Baggie with a white label marked IRISH LUCK in kelly green. "That's him—the big one."

"Great!" Flynn looked at Pastore with that infuriating half-smile. "Hope you like banana daiquiris, pal, 'cause this time we are gonna make some."

Early afternoon, Friday, August 9, 1985

Five months after the still-unsolved stabbing of Viera's dealers, Flynn parked the squad's beat-up Plymouth in front of the familiar gray stone church on Amsterdam Avenue and sat there sweltering. He pictured in his mind the curly-haired, eight-year-old boy who used to sit on the floor of the Rio Piedras Bodega playing the bongos. Felipe's sister Carmel used to say he had played the drums almost before he could walk. He could play, all right. People would come into the bodega to place a numbers bet, or maybe buy a can of *habichuelas,* and go out wiggling to Felipe's beat. "Gonna be a *salsero,*" everybody predicted, and he got to be called Salsa.

That was eleven years ago, when Flynn was still riding with Nolan in plainclothes. Salsa should be about nineteen now. What kind of a witness would he make—if in fact Flynn could get Salsa to give a statement and testify in the 1982 homicide of his friend Pichón.

Salsa—it had to be him—came bopping across the avenue, unaffected by the noontime sun. Seeing the kid, Flynn thought of Sean, the younger brother whose memory was like a bruise in the back of his mind. Sean's looks were pure mick and Salsa's were pure spic, but the cocky tilt of the chin was the same; the don't-mess-with-me gleam in the eye, too. By age twelve, Sean had already been coming on like that. "Buzz off," his big brother had told him once, and Sean did. For good. The two boys never fought, they just led separate lives.

By the time Sean was shot dead at seventeen, he had achieved the tough image he'd always wanted, and the muscular build to back it up. Flynn wondered what his brother would have been like if he had lived to be nineteen.

Here was skinny Salsa—as skinny now as ever, only taller by a good two feet than when Flynn had last seen him. The Hanes T-shirt was a grown-up size and he wore it with khaki pants instead of shorts. And no more bongos. Salsa was packing a Walkman; earphones stuck out from under the curly black hair.

"Hey, that you, Officer Flynn?" Salsa peered over the car windowsill. "You been lookin' for me, huh?"

"Yeah. It's *Lieutenant* Flynn, these days. How's it going, Salsa? Hop in."

"Lieutenant! I never met a lieutenant." As he got into the car, Salsa slid his earphones down around his neck.

"Your sister didn't say how you're spending your time lately," Flynn said, shifting his body on the car seat so that he could face the kid, "but you get your messages at Irish Viera's Tabu Club, so I don't really need to ask, do I? I remember a long time ago, you told me you wanted to be a cop."

"'Cause you helped me out and I thought you was a big hero."

"Thanks for the compliment, even if you don't think so anymore," Flynn deadpanned.

"No"—Salsa laughed—"I mean all little kids wanna be cops, don't they? I kinda got over it."

"I never thought I wanted to be one, but I'm hooked."

"On lockin' people up."

"Not 'people'—scum. Killers." Flynn's tone was no longer light; he paused till Salsa looked over at him questioningly. "Like that creep Rico who killed your buddy Pichón."

"Rico!" Salsa's happy-go-lucky air vanished.

Carmel must have been afraid to tell her brother why Flynn had tracked her down after eleven years and why he wanted to get hold of Salsa. "Yeah, Rico. That lousy junkie should've been in jail for murder three years ago—*you* are part of the reason he wasn't, Salsa. Did you know that?"

"No, I—"

"A material witness and you leave a murder scene. I should have you subpoenaed. Your boss Viera would really have you dancin' around the club over that, wouldn't he?" Flynn raised his heavy black eyebrows and looked coldly at the kid. Irish Viera's people rarely got arrested, much less subpoenaed to a witness stand. According to precinct lore, even Viera's lowliest lookouts had it drilled into them that the boss didn't want anybody giving the cops excuses for nosing around.

Salsa hardly breathed. Out the window on Flynn's side of the car, a life-size stone statue of the Virgin Mary stood in a niche at the corner of the church. The statue's lips curved gently but the eyes saw nothing.

Now Flynn softened up; he smiled at Salsa. "Listen, I know—Carmel *told* you to disappear off that roof before the police came.

Okay, nobody's blaming you for doing what your older sister said."

"They ain't?" Salsa looked incredulous.

"Not if you do the right thing *this* time, like I'm gonna give you a chance to do. If I was you, I'd be pretty glad to get that chance. We got another shot at Rico—and this time we ain't gonna miss."

Salsa looked at Flynn, trying to read the cop's intense hazel gaze.

"Rico's back in town," Flynn told him.

Salsa nodded. He didn't appear surprised by the news.

Flynn reached over and put a hand on his shoulder. "You had a clear view of Rico that day on the roof. Nothing in your way—right?"

"Sure!" Salsa started breathing again. "And I knew him from the neighborhood anyway. Always flashing money that he makes dealing. He's still like that now."

Flynn pressed the glove-compartment button, took out the photo array, and flipped it open for Salsa to see. "Which one's Rico?"

Salsa looked briefly at the six round cutouts, each framing another neighborhood desperado. "Here, number five."

"Does he look different? This picture goes back."

"I—I don't think he's wearin' that earring."

"He's back dealing for Carlos Luzan, we heard."

"Yeah. But Carlos promoted him. Now Rico's the one goes around delivering."

"Good man, Salsa."

Basking in the praise, Salsa continued, "They ain't selling powder no more—Carlos, he's into that new product, crack."

The marketing jargon made Flynn smile again. Where did that come from?

Flynn put the car in gear. "Let's go back to the squad—we can get this all together, nice and neat for the DA." They already were halfway there; the Two-nine Precinct was four blocks uptown from the church. "Besides," Flynn changed the subject, "you gotta meet one of my men, Detective Taylor. Came back from vacation today just to hook up with you. He's a Spanish guy; knows Latin music A to Z."

"Taylor?"

"Yeah. His *mom* is Spanish, see?"

"He's a detective..." Salsa was getting his bounce back. "What's that make you?"

"The squad commander."

* * *

Flynn ushered Salsa into the captain's office and made a little bow toward the couch. "You got the luxury suite," Flynn said, "the captain's in and out. He's the detective captain in charge of all northern Manhattan—four precincts."

"He's your boss?" Salsa wanted to know.

"Yeah. So make yourself comfortable, okay? As soon as Detective Taylor gets here, I'll bring him in to meet you."

The door to the captain's office closed and Salsa stretched out on the dull-green leather couch. He'd seen one like it a long time ago in a school principal's office. In a quick glance, he inventoried the bookcase, the TV, and the wood desk with two telephones: some luxury suite. Was this the best a big-deal cop could do?

Salsa closed his eyes, adjusted his Walkman earphones, and as he often did, daydreamed about *his* boss's office... better than any of those power suites you saw on TV. Irish sat in a black leather chair behind a big slab of black marble. You couldn't call it a desk because Irish did even less paperwork than the honchos in the power suites. A tape system recorded all his meetings, Salsa had been told. Instead of cluttering up the marble with a regular telephone, Irish had the push buttons built into a panel in the gleaming slab and he talked into the speaker.

The only things that stayed for long on that slice of marble were crystal glasses for the Irish whiskeys that Ramón fixed for the boss and martinis for Monte, the boss's lieutenant. How'd you like an office like that for your own? the Tabu's bartender had asked the first time Salsa ever came out of there.

"I'm gonna have an office just like it," Salsa promised him.

Ever since Irish opened the club back in '78 when Salsa was twelve, Salsa had been hanging around there. Because of the music, at first. For years, he'd run errands for Ramón and the doormen; he got his first Walkman with their tips. But from the beginning, Salsa was convinced that the future held more for him than errands. Much more. Today he was making good money as a steerer on the street. Doing better by miles than a Puerto Rican guy his age could do in any straight job.

And now this Rico break! Salsa could help the cops hang Pichón's killer. That was good—a little like being a cop. But best of all, thanks to the lieutenant, Salsa would get credit for the arrest of an important guy in a rival organization. Irish Viera would really *notice* Salsa for the first time—and reward him for his good work—Salsa was sure.

Midafternoon, Friday, August 9, 1985

"Estos novatos que creen? Sí—éste es mi barrio, papá!" Jesse Taylor sang under his breath as he hurried into the station house and up the dank stairway to the squad room. A vacation—that's just two weeks you *miss,* from his point of view. Andy had called when Taylor still had three days to go, and Taylor had put on a show of being upset, but Estrelita knew her husband—he was just being polite. As much as he loved his family, he was delighted to leave them at the beach and go help his boss deal with this unpredictable Puerto Rican kid.

From the time Taylor began as an undercover at the age of twenty-three until Andy Flynn had come on the scene nine years later, Taylor had never got anything but a hard time from squad commanders. He never had buddies among the men either. Maybe it annoyed them that the big black guy didn't adopt the detective's standard-issue cigar when he got into the Bureau; didn't take to wearing a proper hat on top of his Afro either. Some of the men respected him but found him distant; others were envious and cynically wondered how come information flowed so easily to him through his Harlem network. As for the bosses, Jesse Taylor had never toed the mark the way they seemed to expect from a half-black, half-Latino detective—and he had more under that Afro than they were comfortable with. But the picture had changed when Sergeant Flynn transferred into the Sixth Homicide Squad in '73.

Flynn was Number 2 in the handpicked squad that investigated only the crime of crimes—the neighborhood drones had to deal with the little shit—and he only cared about how useful a detective you were. Nobody had to draw him any diagrams to explain how a black detective who spoke Spanish could be real useful in upper Manhattan.

From the beginning, Flynn admired Taylor's work and gave him the recognition he never got from his old bosses. Out of that businesslike relationship, a friendship slowly grew. For Flynn, Taylor was just what the doctor ordered; for the first time since Kenny Nolan had to retire on disability, Flynn had somebody to team up with. On the job, Flynn and Taylor depended on each other a lot like partners, despite the difference in rank. None of that had changed when Flynn passed the lieutenant's test and took command of the Sixth Homicide.

When Tracy Flynn threw her husband out, Jesse and Estrelita

even gave Andy a bed till he got himself together. And finally, when the NYPD scrapped the homicide squads and reassigned Flynn to the Two-nine Precinct detectives, he brought Taylor with him.

Now Taylor breezed through the squad room's swinging doors, the only ones like that he'd seen in the borough. He opened the trick latch of the low gate and crossed into the detectives' exclusive space. Billy Reynolds and Paul O'Brien were both on the phone; Obie's two C Team partners must be in the field already. Taylor winked at Betty Dominic, the police administrative aide.

In the bosses' office, Taylor signed the logbook on the table next to the door. "How's it goin', Sergeant?"

Marty Carlucci's desk stood on the left of the small room, catercorner to Flynn's. Taylor could only see the top of Cooch's expensive haircut. The stocky supervisor bent over his pile of papers, his shirt cuffs neatly rolled out of ink's way. He looked up.

"Jesse—couldn't stay away, huh?"

"That's the truth."

"Plenty for you to do here. We still got nothing on that double homicide—'Frostbite.' "

If it was a homicide, it was Taylor's job. Flynn had taken Taylor and Bill Reynolds off the regular duty chart in mid-'82 and put them on permanent "special assignment"—working homicides only, with whichever detectives caught those cases.

"That Frostbite's gotta break one of these days." Taylor sighed. He glanced at the big chart above Flynn's desk. 1985 HOMICIDES—29 PRECINCT. He knew the tally: Thirty-one murders had been committed through August 8, and the squad had cleared thirty. "Frostbite" was the nickname Billy Reynolds had given the homicide of the two drug dealers who'd died in a snowbank of coke with their throats cut and fingers missing. The squad laughed at Billy's wit, but mostly they cursed the double homicide. Especially Ron Pastore, who had caught the frustrating case.

Flynn and his men *had* to solve the double murder—or blow the only perfect homicide clearance record in the history of the NYPD detective division. Flynn, the homicide ace, had taken a bunch of bored neighborhood detectives with almost no experience investigating murders and made them the best unofficial homicide team in the city. He worked with them and they rose to the challenge. The police brass did not—Flynn put in for a unit citation in '83 and again in '84, but nothing came back from downtown, not even regrets. The squad firmly believed that the chief of detectives could not fail to acknowledge three hundred percent years in a row, and they were going for it.

Taylor knew that the hundred percent goal was less an ego thing to Andy than what got him up in the morning. Because outside the job, Andy no longer had much of a life. When he wasn't working or sleeping, he headed for the gym to coach budding PAL boxers. He still went drinking in the family bar—the squad had adopted Flynn's as their place, too—but now he only drank soda. Some Wednesday nights he'd drop in at an AA meeting.

Sergeant Carlucci shook his head dubiously at Taylor. "Even if we came up with an eyewitness on Frostbite, no mope in this precinct's crazy enough to rat on Viera."

In the years before Taylor came with Flynn to the precinct, murder after murder had been linked to Irish Viera. Among the bad guys of the Two-nine, he had no equal for ruthless, efficient vengeance. Nobody had ratted on Viera in the past, either, so when Flynn took over, the squad had all Viera's unsolved homicides on the books.

"Hey, Jesse!" Flynn appeared in the doorway. *"Qué tal?"*

"Just wondering where you was hidin' out. What's happening yourself, Lieutenant?"

"Remember that '82 homicide? Pichón, age sixteen, on the roof at Columbus and One oh nine? Well, I got an eyewitness in the captain's office now, waitin' to meet you."

"Pichón . . . ?" Taylor shook his head. "I gotta admit, I almost forgot about that one."

Taylor marveled at Flynn's recall—Andy could come up with the name of a Chinaman he met five years ago for ten minutes—but Taylor wouldn't have wanted such a memory for himself. He purposely erased the details of old tragedies to make room for the current ones. Flynn kept careful track. He could just about recite all the Two-nine's old unsolved homicides by heart. Whenever the squad got another shot at some murderer who had got away, Flynn jumped in.

That must have been what made him think of the novel hundred percent concept that balanced each old case the squad cleared against a new one, like Frostbite, that wouldn't budge. That was how they had been able to clear exactly the same number of murders in '83 as occurred that year—and again in '84. But unless some madman did rat on Viera, Frostbite would stay uncleared. And between now and New Year's, there'd be plenty more betrayals, lovers' quarrels, and other motives for murder in the precinct. Without old cases like Pichón in the bank, Flynn and his men could just kiss their third hundred percent good-bye.

"This kid Pichón got mowed down with a .22," Flynn reminded Taylor. "Perp shot at two other kids, too, but missed 'em, fortunately. Danny Doherty had the case, and when he transferred out, it kinda got lost in the shuffle."

Cooch frowned. On Marty Carlucci's watch, nothing got lost in the shuffle, and he had been in charge of the squad then. But Cooch, very much the old-style sergeant, let you know that homicide was not the only crime in *his* book—it was his job to see that the men worked *all* their cases. The two bosses' styles also were completely different. Flynn never pulled rank on his second-in-command. Carlucci, on the other hand, kept aloof from Flynn's team; a sergeant was a boss, not a squad member. Period. Taylor bet that Cooch wouldn't shed a tear if the squad blew their third hundred percent.

"There was only two suspects on that roof, Lieu," Carlucci said patiently, "and by the time we figured out which one was the shooter, he was in the wind; down in Santo Domingo, we heard."

"Right, but now Rico Nuñez is back from Santo Domingo. An old 'friend' of his up and dropped a dime on him the other day, from Attica. Sounded like the friend is looking forward to welcoming Rico to that big happy family upstate."

"Maybe, but the only other kid on the roof was a female—I remember."

"Doherty only *knew about* the female, but according to this inmate's information, there was two boys with her. Doherty's report says the female witness is Carmel Delacruz, Manhattan Avenue address." Flynn nodded at the sergeant. "Doherty's file is right up-to-date." Cooch looked appeased.

"Turns out I knew this Carmel Delacruz ten, eleven years ago when I was workin' plainclothes; she had a brother she was very close to—it's gotta have been him on the roof with her and the victim. Well, I found Carmel last week, up in Washington Heights with her mother. Great reunion! 'We never forget you, Officer Flynn,' the mother says. I got the boy out of a burglary jam back then. So I take Carmel for coffee. She turns on the charm and lies to dear old 'Officer Flynn' just like she lied to Detective Doherty, who she never laid eyes on before the day Pichón got shot: *No-o-o-body* else on the roof but her and Pichón."

"You expect her to help *you* if she thinks it means hurtin' her brother!" Taylor said.

"I saved her brother's ass once. You'd think I'd get the benefit of the doubt."

Taylor shook his head. *"I* wouldn't think so in a million years, but you're like a goddamn rookie—still runnin' on trust and dreamin' that other people do, too." In Taylor's opinion, Flynn had a blind spot about what Taylor considered a major survival issue. Taylor harped on it all the time.

"Well, she came around though, finally." Flynn neatly avoided the issue. "Her brother's in the captain's office as we speak—name's Salsa."

"The name, I like."

"I had a feeling you might. He lives in abandoned buildings but Carmel said he gets messages at the Tabu Club."

"Uh-oh."

"Uh-oh is right."

"Irish has him pushin' something, of course."

"Of course," Flynn had to agree. "Never mind that the kid is tryin' to make me think he's just a gofer...."

"I don't mind what he calls himself, long as he knows what goes on over at the Tabu when the music stops. Think he'd be willin' to share as a regular thing?"

"Dependin' on how deep he's into Irish Viera's garbage, I guess. Y'know, thirteen years ago, when Irish was still running that Cocodrillo sewer, I had a feeling he was headed for the top of the whole rotten heap—"

"Hey, wait a minute!" Taylor rooted around in the wasteland of his long-term memory. "Yeah! Viera's only buddy—that cocksuckin' Blanco Martín—*you* took him out." The demise of that infamous gunrunner had earned a place in Taylor's fickle memory.

Cooch, buried in a deskful of papers, seemed to take no notice of the conversation.

"I was sorry then that I had to total Blanco," Flynn said.

"Sorry!"

"Yeah. Wanted to take him alive, charge his ass, and get him to give up Irish. I was shit-faced at the time—but even sober..."

"It hadda be a fatal shot or you wouldn't be here talkin' about it. Besides"—Taylor had never been surer of anything in his life—"no way Irish was worth that scum Blanco coppin' a plea. Not then, anyway."

"If I'd locked up Irish back then..." Flynn smiled the half-smile that the journalists always called his trademark.

"He'd be out by now—and you'd be on top of his hit list."

Taylor didn't let Flynn reflect on that at great length. "Tell me somethin'—where the fuck did he get 'Irish'? I always wondered."

"His mother's Irish, I heard. Father was a big plantation owner in Ecuador—probably with some Indian blood not too far back. Anyway, this girl from Dublin or someplace goes to Ecuador as a mother's helper for another rich family and there you go—that's where he gets the name. Dennis Viera Kelly, I think it says on the immigration papers."

"Indian blood on the father's side—"

"Just a guess, but check out his hair next time and tell me what you think."

"I bet you're right."

"Now I want to know what you think about Salsa. One way or another, unfortunately for him, he's close to Viera's operation. Wouldn't you suppose—"

"I sure would suppose he either knows something about our Frostbite casualties and how they died—or could find out. Before we go talk to your boy, lemme have a look at that perfect file of Danny Doherty's."

The case folder told the story of the end of Pichón's life. On the night of the shooting, Doherty had interviewed Carmel Delacruz, who gave a detailed account of the last half hour she had spent with her friend Pichón, the pigeon keeper. She told of a "game" invented on a barrio rooftop in the boredom of a hot night and of a mishap that ended in murder. "A window broke," Doherty wrote, "and two Dominican males with a large dog came to the adjacent roof...."

Carmel described Rico's screaming at Pichón; the other Dominican's throwing a brick at the pigeon coop where she was hiding—and his later handing Rico a rifle. Carmel said she heard about five shots from inside the coop. She told Doherty about Rico's shooting at her when she left the coop to look for Pichón, and about finding Pichón lying faceup on the roof, bleeding from his head.

"She describes Number 1, known as Rico: M Dom., 21, brown skin, 6′, slim, small Afro, mustache, wearing an earring in one ear, wearing black pants, Hawaiian-type shirt, black shoes.

"Number 2: M Dom., 30, black skin, 5′7″, heavy set, mustache, wearing blue jeans, short-sleeved, vertical-striped shirt, black shoes."

Carmel's account lacked only one minor detail: her brother, Salsa.

The folder held CSU's pictures of the roof with the pigeon coop and the roof just across the air shaft on Columbus Avenue.

Lodged in the east wall of the coop, the cops had found part of a slug—.22 long, according to the Ballistics report—and on the other roof, five shells.

The autopsy report showed Pichón's height and weight: 5′5″, 135 pounds. "Pigeon" was a good name for him.

The other Dominican with Rico—Arturo Zueca—lived in the Columbus Avenue building when he wasn't in jail. In an interview with Doherty's partner late on the night Pichón was killed, Zueca maintained that he had been eating dinner in his apartment at the time of the shooting. He gave the names of half a dozen dinner guests, but "did not know" anyone called Rico, the partner's report said.

Doherty had obviously talked to someone who knew Rico by more than his street name—the folder contained Rico's arrest record and his picture. Also a photo array and a report dated several days after the shooting, in which Doherty said Carmel had picked out Rico's picture from the array and positively identified him as Pichón's killer.

So, Taylor thought, a week after this homicide went down, the detectives had a fresh eyewitness and a case that was ready for the DA; all they'd been missing was the perp. But now, two years later, the perp was within reach and Flynn had *two* eyewitnesses—Salsa and Carmel—from the sound of it, a pair that even a Manhattan jury could love.

Flynn opened the door to the captain's office. "We're gonna put up a plaque," he announced. "'Salsa slept here.' The private bath is at your disposal, sir." He gestured around the corner of the room.

"Just like the Waldorf," Salsa said, over his shoulder, as he disappeared.

"I'm sure glad vacation's over, Lieutenant." Taylor made himself comfortable in the captain's chair. Flynn liked to do interviews standing up. He leaned his muscular torso against the four-drawer file, resting his elbow on top. Despite the relaxed pose, you could tell who was in charge.

"Meet Detective Taylor," Flynn said when Salsa returned.

"Hi, *papá,*" Taylor said. "Ever *been* to the Waldorf?"

"Not yet."

"Since you came to the States, you ever been outta Manhattan?" Taylor wanted to know how deeply Salsa might be involved in Viera's drug business.

"Yeah."

"Where to?"

"Vineland, New Jersey, where my sister is."

"Lieutenant Flynn went up to *Washington Heights* the other day to see your sister." If the kid had to lie about something so trivial, it would not exactly build Taylor's confidence in him.

"No, the other sister, Rosita."

"But Carmel is the one who was with you on the rooftop, when your buddy got shot?"

"Yeah."

"We're gonna get the motherfucker who did it—*por fin.*" Taylor smiled a wide, satisfied smile. "You know we *always* get our man, sooner or later. Lieutenant Flynn probably didn't tell you—he's too modest—but this is the *hundred percent squad* he's the boss of."

"Verdad?" Salsa's eyes got wide.

"Sí-í-í, papá! But tell me, how come you didn't come forward before on this horrible case?"

"Carmel, she said I'd get in trouble."

"There's your friend Pichón, lying on a roof with his brains blown out and the cops are lookin' for the shooter—and you run away. *That's* how you get in trouble." Taylor jabbed a finger at the kid. "That and lies."

Salsa looked at the floor.

"You ready to help the DA put Rico where he belongs?" Flynn chose his moment and jumped in. His tone made clear there was only one possible answer.

"You gotta *get* him first—how're you gonna do that?" All of a sudden Salsa was in the middle of a real live TV cop show.

"You know someplace he hangs out?" Flynn asked.

"Easy! Las Flores."

"The all-night coffee shop on Amsterdam?"

"Yeah, where the taxi drivers stop."

"Fine. We'll pick him up before his beans have time to get cold," Flynn said. *"If* your information is good."

"It's good," Salsa protested.

"Oh, yeah? Why should I trust you? How do *you* know?"

Flynn got up and walked to the window. He stood there for a while, his back to Salsa.

"Listen, I know."

"Lieutenant Flynn just wants a little somethin' to go on, *papá, entiendes?"* Taylor coaxed. If Salsa had no credibility on this, he'd never have any.

"First of all, I seen Rico plenty—I know him years before he shot Pichón, okay? And the other day—maybe a week ago—I happened to hear Monte tellin' Irish, Rico's back in the neighborhood workin' for Luzan; he's sellin' this new product, 'crack.' Sure enough, I go by Las Flores for coffee and I seen Rico myself—two times. He don't see me, not yet anyway. I'm gonna eat my breakfast some other place for a while."

"Irish and Monte talk in front of you?" Flynn asked casually.

"Sure they do. I'm always around there."

"No, I mean, do they talk drug *business?* Customers? Competitors?"

"Sometimes they do. See, if I'm around, that don't stop them."

"Okay," Flynn said; he had planned a little test for Salsa. The cop took a couple of pictures off the top of the file cabinet. "You know these two mutts?" He held out the two ID photos, each with a front face and a profile of a tough male Hispanic.

Salsa studied the pictures one at a time, saying nothing, keeping his eyes down in a way that didn't inspire a cop's confidence. Finally, he shook his head and looked up. "You lookin' for *them,* I can't help."

"They got business with Irish," Flynn pressed.

"Well, I never seen 'em anyway. I could've heard the names, though."

"Herrera and Hernandez, they're supposed to be cousins."

"Oh! Could be Los Primos. Maybe that's them. I heard Monte sayin' somethin' about 'em once."

"What?"

"Honest, I don't remember. I think it was last year sometime. He was making a joke about 'em or something. Irish didn't laugh, but he don't laugh too much anyway."

"As I remember, he never did," Flynn said.

"You *know* him?"

"I know everybody in this precinct, startin' with Felipe Delacruz and family, right?"

"Guess you do."

"So you're gonna ride with the hundred percent squad when we get Rico—we need you to positively ID him. What time you been running into Rico for breakfast?"

"About six—after I get done at the club."

"Detective Taylor will call the Tabu and leave a message for you: '*Papá* wants to see you,' with a day and a time—like 'Tuesday, five o'clock'—you think you can get over here bright and early?"

"You bet!"

"See you soon, pal." Flynn gave Salsa a friendly punch on the shoulder and left the captain's office.

Taylor put his feet up on the captain's desk and leaned back. "So the Tabu's your headquarters—"

"For a long time. They got all the crazy music, you know? The disco—people all dressed up, dancin' all night. I like it."

"You like Rubén Blades's music?"

"Número uno!" Salsa snapped his fingers to a beat.

"New album's comin' out, you know. I got it."

"You got it already? How come? What's the name?"

"Escenas, it's called. I got a friend at the record company."

"All right!"

"You know what's on it? The second part of 'Pedro Navaja.'"

"You serious?"

"Of course—'Sorpresas,' Rubén calls it. Good title, huh? *'El barrio estaba dormido,'"* Taylor sang, *"'llena brillaba la luna. De pronto...'* Well, you gotta wait and hear what happens with Pedro. *'Sorpresas: verdad!'"* Taylor got up and opened the door for Salsa.

"I got one for you," Salsa said as they walked together to the squad-room gate.

"Let's have it."

"Rubén's father, he was a cop for a while."

"Verdad?"

"Sí, señor."

Taylor gave Salsa the palm-slapping ghetto handshake. "I'll leave you the message, okay, *papá?"*

"Leave it with Ramón, Detective Taylor."

"Te veo, Salsa."

As Taylor came back into the squad room, Paul O'Brien from the eight-to-four tour, Franco Levy from the incoming four-to-one, and Billy Reynolds had their heads together with the bosses.

"Join the party, Jesse," Flynn said, "it's just getting good."

"According to the kid," Reynolds was saying, "Rico Nuñez is back dealin' for Carlos Luzan?" As a hell-raising, baby-faced street cop, Reynolds had won his gold shield with the off-duty arrest of a brutal rapist. Four years in the squad hadn't cooled him down a bit. "Seems like Viera and Luzan are workin' the same turf, doesn't it—and nobody got whacked?" he wondered.

"Nobody got whacked *so far,"* Obie said in his brogue. "It does make you wonder, now doesn't it." Obie, tall and white haired, was the squad's first-grader—the highest you could go in the Detective Bureau; he earned a lieutenant's pay, like Flynn. Obie and Flynn had taught Reynolds the basics of detective work and Reynolds was good—when he felt like buckling down, which was less often than anybody would have liked.

"Suppose Viera and Luzan *ain't* competing—suppose they're sellin' to different junkies," Flynn suggested. "Salsa mentioned that Nuñez is pushin' some kind of 'new product.' "

"Betcha it's that dreck they call crack." Franco Levy snapped his fingers in keeping with the fifties hipster image he cultivated. "I was havin' a few beers at Flynn's the other night and Katz, the Street Narcotics boss, comes in. He tells me about this stuff his guys have been makin' collars on down around Amsterdam in the high Eighties, low Nineties. First pusher he collared with it last spring, Katz had no idea what it was, except he knew it was drugs. The collar told him it's *crack;* comes in little crystals. It's like 'prepared freebase,' the guy said—all ready to smoke, so you don't have to blow yourself up like Richard Pryor."

"What's it cost, Franco? Did Katz say?" A question from Cooch, the squad's consumer expert.

"He says they sell it in these dinky plastic vials with different color tops. The first ones he saw, they were all premarked—ten bucks," said Levy, the would-be actor and fan of the fifties. One night at Flynn's he'd talked about the *Guys and Dolls* production he'd starred in as a high school kid in Brooklyn, the experience that must have changed his life and his look. The perfect accent, he was born with. "You can make a shitload of this crack out of a kilo of coke. Say you buy a key for forty-eight thousand dollars—"

"Cost you more, if you're from Jersey," Taylor heckled.

"I don't even *know* nobody from Jersey. Stop breakin' my balls, will ya? Besides, if I'm big enough to buy a key, I'm gonna get a good price no matter if I'm from fuckin' Maine."

"You're from south of the border"—Taylor again—"you get a *real* good price."

"I'm tryin' to tell ya"—Levy sighed—"these crack guys can get a hundred-twenty-five-thousand dollars' worth of those little crystals out of a key."

Cooch whistled. "I don't suppose you got an idea what a key of coca paste'll run you in Bolivia?"

Cooch's brain was a biocomputer as intricate as the global phone system and probably more efficient; Levy didn't expect to wait long for the figure.

"Five grand."

"That crack garbage," Obie said, "they're selling it right in the Two-nine? I'd say business will be pickin' up around here."

"There goes our fourth hundred percent." Reynolds didn't see the crunch coming till *next* year.

"We ain't got number three yet," Franco Levy pointed out.

"Well," Flynn pursued his train of thought, "assuming Luzan is buying his coke from Irish and makin' those profits, how long before this marriage bombs?"

"Long before anybody here retires," Taylor said.

"Speak for yourself." Obie's steel-rimmed glasses glinted when he was indignant. He had thirty years on the job and no intention of putting in his papers anytime soon, but he liked to threaten Flynn that he might change his mind.

"When they get their divorce," Levy said, picking up where Flynn left off, "we'll get a shot at Luzan, maybe—and *he*'ll rat on Irish."

"Oh, yeah"—Reynolds laughed—"when they get their divorce, we get another homicide—Luzan."

That was all Obie needed to set him off. He slumped in his chair and groaned. "Where's my papers?"

"Uh-uh, pal"—Flynn pointed his finger at the fatherly looking detective—"when you go, I'll be next, and I ain't got a nice colleen and a little castle in County Cork to hole up in like you do. So never mind the 'papers' blarney! Anyway, the fun's over for C Team today—why don't you beat it. Give Maureen my best." Then he looked at Carlucci. "Who's workin' days Tuesday?"

"A Team."

"Okay," Flynn went on. "Tell 'em we're gonna pick up Rico at oh six hundred hours. Two hours of overtime, right, Marty?" Cooch usually leapt at the chance to supervise overtime work.

Levy, a B Team member, complained that he wanted to change teams. "We're always in the wrong place at the wrong time."

"Don't worry, O'Levy, pal," Flynn soothed, "you'll have somethin' to tell the grandchildren." Levy's name satisfied everybody—Cooch called him Franco.

"O'Levy" did not appear reassured.

"I'll let A Team know about the arrest," Cooch said.

"Tell 'em to take their vitamins, work out, and sleep tight—here in the dorm; no side trips." Flynn grinned at Billy Reynolds. "That means you, too, son." Reynolds had a girl on Central Park West and a girl on Eighty-sixth Street, and probably a few other girls that Flynn wasn't caught up on. Reynolds said okay but warned the boss not to be surprised when the Civilian Complaint Review Board called.

"What'll they call you on?" Flynn wanted to know.

"Neglect of duty." Reynolds might infuriate the others by taking every possible investigative shortcut—but he kept them laughing, too. All except the Cooch.

Flynn put away the Pichón folder and cleared his desk, leaving Carlucci to attack the paperwork he thrived on and Flynn happily delegated to him.

"Friday night!" Taylor noted as he and Flynn walked out through the squad room, "Goin' dancin'?"

"Gotta stop by the gym, first." It had been some time since Flynn did any dancing.

Monday afternoon and evening, August 12, 1985

From the moment he made lieutenant, Flynn knew he'd be down the tubes in six months if he couldn't be out in the field, investigating. He'd call a meeting about once a week and sit behind his desk for an hour. Maximum. Managers sat behind desks, cops went out. And Flynn wanted to collaborate with his men, not "manage" them.

The homicide chart, hanging on the wall above and to the left of his desk, was the only piece of paperwork Flynn had ever relished; he had ruled and lettered the prototype himself soon after the hundred percent clearance idea came to him. What looked like mere record keeping actually was a scoreboard that displayed the squad's goal where he and the men could see it, especially him.

Depending on the time of day and the season, Flynn always drank coffee or tonic water during meetings. He broke out a bottle of tonic from the six-pack under his desk as Freddy Urquhart, Larry Mazocek, and Ron Pastore—"A Team"—pulled their chairs into the bosses' office. Flynn, with his precise Irish bone structure and fair skin, was never as comfortable as when he was surrounded by his ethnic rogues' gallery. Of all the men, he was the most colorless dresser. Urquhart alone among them could pass for a WASP: clotheshorse build, smooth features, classic wardrobe, but he was Catholic like all the others except Franco Levy, and a graduate of Fordham, not Yale. Mazocek—florid, potbellied from too many Heinekens—contrasted sharply with his partners. He dressed like the Prince of Polyester, according to Reynolds.

The three of them sat down with Taylor, who kept his Afro

short and went around in baggy, K-Mart–style sportswear until it came time to go to court and then he cut quite a figure in rich tweeds.

Even though Cooch's day tour was over, he had remained behind his desk for the meeting. His favorite blazer hung on the coat-tree hanger, within easy reach. Navy blue with gold buttons, the blazer set off the sergeant's perfect iron-gray hair.

Freddy Urquhart pointed at the new entry on the homicide chart. "Somebody snitch on this Nuñez?"

"Somebody who's in Attica 'cause Nuñez snitched on *him,*" Taylor answered. "What goes around comes around."

"In those circles, anyway," Flynn agreed.

Taylor persisted, "I never saw any circles where it didn't." He believed the vengeance motive was as common as cold germs.

Ignoring his friend's moral, Flynn went on, "Jesse's been following up on the case. We located two eyewitnesses and we're ready to grab Rico—oh six hundred hours tomorrow.... Okay, let's take another look at Frostbite." Flynn glanced at the homicide chart. Other neighborhood squad commanders copied the chart, hung up the copies in their squad rooms, and wondered why they didn't get results like Flynn's. But even if they had understood how he worked, they wouldn't have had the nerve to try it. He and his methods definitely didn't fit the NYPD command mold.

The case of the 'frostbitten' cousins affected Flynn like a pebble in his shoe. He and Taylor and Reynolds all had spent tour after tour working with Pastore on the double murder. Flynn's boss had insisted on bringing in the borough task force to help. Frostbite managed to drive them crazy, too.

"Not a fucking thing new." Pastore looked depressed. "That case is frozen solid. Fucking Irish is immune."

"Well, this is the squad that's gonna melt it down." Flynn looked at him and at the others in turn. "And when Frostbite goes, we'll have witnesses on eight other homicides comin' out of the woodwork."

Pastore's depression showed no sign of lifting. "Hector and Geraldo had both been dealing Irish Luck for years. For a drug operation, Viera's is pretty stable."

"Anybody who's 'unstable,' Irish just takes 'em out," Billy Reynolds announced as he walked in the door, twenty minutes late. Cooch gave him the evil eye; Reynolds winked. He drew an X in the air. "That's Irish's personnel policy."

"What did you get from Narcotics?" Cooch asked Pastore, shifting attention from Reynolds.

"Plenty of mopes who knew the whole story but nobody who's gonna fuckin' *testify*. They'd rather go to jail where the survival rate is better."

"You did voucher those fingers?" Reynolds razzed Pastore. Weak laughter. Like a good partner, Mazocek had helped Pastore roll the victims' chopped-off fingers in fingerprint ink and print them. Because the skin on the fingers had loosened, Cooch made them call Detective Defina at the morgue for special instructions on getting clear prints. She had reminded them that when the body was released to the driver of the morgue wagon, all the loose digits must have their own tags.

"What about Los Primos' relatives?" Flynn suggested. "Don't somebody want to avenge the brutal murder of these two mopes?"

"There's a brother in the Heights. He practically never heard of Hector the first time around, but maybe we can get him to give it some more thought."

"Maybe bring the brother in—tell him the lieutenant wants to say hello in person."

"Good idea." Pastore jumped up. "Let's go, Freddy."

About an hour after the meeting broke up, Flynn got a call. A DOA at Henry Hudson Parkway and 107th Street, where the highway runs between the western edge of Riverside Park and the Hudson River.

"Looks like somebody dumped one on yuh," the highway cop told Flynn when he got there. "We saw this shoe stickin' out and we thought it was kind of a funny place to take a nap. Though you never know—could be a homeless. But it ain't your homeless-type shoe. Whoever dumped this guy musta swung him good to get him over the bushes. Male Hispanic—no ID that we could find. Sorry."

"Just what we want on a Monday, a DOA from God knows where with no ID." A murder could be committed in Kalamazoo, but if the body turned up in the Two-nine, it was Flynn's squad's problem. A dump job was a dirty trick to play on detectives.

Urquhart and Pastore got to the scene a few minutes later.

"Gunshot wound—plenty of blood, Lieu—" they heard one of the highway cops say. "Got your gloves?" Flynn went to the Plymouth. The gloves that cops kept in their glove compartments were now made of disposable latex; in the age of AIDS, you no longer touched bloody bodies with your bare hands. All the detectives looked grim as hell. "I'm up," Urquhart said. The dump job became his case.

A radio car from the precinct arrived and then another with the patrol sergeant, Deegan. Everyone parked near a paved playing field and followed the highway cops toward some scraggly bushes next to the road.

Sergeant Deegan's men stretched a barrier of neon-yellow crime-scene tape to keep passersby about ten feet back from where the police were working. But few curiosity seekers showed up; the vast park was all but empty at dinnertime.

The shoe that had attracted the highway cops was a pointy, tan loafer, right foot; the corpse was still wearing the left one, too. The victim's thin nylon socks matched his sky-blue polyester three-piece suit. His body had landed twisted, assuming it hadn't been disturbed, with the chest toward the ground. Flynn put on the gloves and turned the stiff torso upward. Dried blood covered much of the sky-blue vest, which had what looked like two small-caliber bullet holes where the topmost vest buttons should have been. The clothing also bore some dirt and grass stains. "They couldn't have dumped him in broad daylight, and the guy's dressed for a night on the town," Flynn said, "so he's gotta be layin' here at least since last night, maybe even Saturday night." He rechecked the pockets, finding a hundred dollars and some change in the pants, but no papers. "Well, money no object, hm?" he said to Deegan. "The perps just wanted to make sure somebody hadda write some vouchers. How about we go over the area, see if they dumped anything else. Like maybe their business card. Got a minute?"

"Good luck." The sergeant laughed. "You want another car?"

"I figure you and your driver, the radio team, and the three of us are enough, that is if Highway will stop traffic while we check out the gutter."

"Sure, boss," the highway cop said.

Nothing found in the gutter for fifty feet in either direction except a few soft-drink cans and a lot of twigs. On the park side of the curb, nothing but dog shit and more twigs. As the search continued, the Crime Scene Unit car arrived. Slow night up to now, they said, explaining their prompt appearance.

They measured distances from the body to the edge of the paved playing field and to the two nearest lampposts; the serial number from the base of each lamppost went into their notes. If and when the case came to trial, the DA would order a diagram of the crime scene based on these measurements. One CSU officer took photos of the body from several angles. The other one cut swatches of the pants material with the dirt and grass stains, as well as pieces of the bloody vest; he sealed the swatches in envelopes made of special paper that would not contaminate blood or other substances.

With the murder a day old—at least—Flynn knew he was already behind. The first few hours, the first day... if you didn't get it together then, your chances deteriorated quicker than the corpse.

When the cops had finished the roadside search and the late, irate commuters were back on their way to the northern suburbs, Urquhart wrote down the highway cops' account of their discovery of the body, and their names and shield numbers. The highway cops wrote the detectives' names in *their* memo books. Flynn thanked the cops and sent them back on patrol.

Urquhart, Pastore, and the precinct uniform guys gathered around the lieutenant. Sergeant Deegan ordered his radio car team to guard the body till the morgue wagon came.

Flynn turned to Pastore and Urquhart. "How's Herrera's brother doin'?"

"We never made it, Lieu." Pastore said unhappily. "Got as far as the Bridge when this call came over."

"Tell you what—why don't you and Freddy stay on that. Run up there for dinner; maybe they're having roast pork. Bring a bottle of wine, like good guests—the brother might still get sentimental about dear ol' Hecky. Never can tell. I guess we'll have to postpone breakfast with Rico—but not the overtime. We'll start canvassing here tomorrow at oh six-thirty. Good enough?"

"Good enough, Lieu."

Flynn knew that Freddy Urquhart had no investment in the dump job—it wasn't even going to make the eleven-o'clock news. Besides, Freddy was a tenacious detective, proud of his reputation for following up the slim leads and tiresome details that made you grit your teeth but that could surprise you and break a case like Frostbite.

As Flynn drove out of the park, he caught sight in his mirror of the two patrol cops with their radio car, silhouetted against the brassy river and the smoggy August sunset. The dead man they guarded lay next to the scrubby border of the park, invisible from the detective's vantage point, and anonymous.

Monday night, August 12, 1985

Before Flynn could even begin to look for a homicide suspect, he had to find out who got killed. For a start, the medical examiner would provide a rough idea of the time of death; would recover the bullets from the dead man's body—and maybe other evidence that would help steer Flynn and his men in the right direction. But none of that could happen until tomorrow.

The more ground Flynn could cover now, the less chance the trail would get cold. He wanted the deceased's fingerprints—the quickest route to an identity, *if* the man had an arrest record. The problem was to get the body on its way to the morgue to be printed ASAP. With any luck, Joe Mahoney would be the morgue dispatcher on duty; Flynn and Mahoney had gone to Bronx Catholic together.

Back in his office, Flynn started to call the morgue, then hung up and dialed the duty captain first. Homicide, no matter whose, is the crime of crimes; each police level must promptly notify the next one up. If the death has news value, the bigger the supervisor's ass, the more cover it requires. Just below Headquarters brass came the Zone commanders in each borough. Tonight that would be Captain Lang from Manhattan South, not Flynn's boss, Joe Zachs.

Lang wanted to know if the dump job was Fidel Castro's nephew.

"Nope, not the Guatemalan delegate to the UN, neither. You ain't gonna hear from Channel Two on this one." The Borough brass competed with Headquarters for media attention.

"Okay, keep me advised, Andy. By the way, hope this don't kill your hundred percent," Lang bullshitted. To a man, the city's detective captains—and most of all, Zachs in Manhattan North—were rooting against Flynn's team. With the average squad's homicide-clearance rate running less than seventy percent, the Two-nine made the commanders' other squads look sick. Flynn hadn't figured on that when he dreamed up the hundred percent idea, but if he had, he would probably have gone ahead anyway. If he presented his men with a challenge and it woke them up, who did that hurt besides the perps? Was there such a thing as locking up too many murderers?

"Thanks, Cap," Flynn bullshitted in return. "I'm gonna check Intelligence. If the deceased turns out to be a Puerto Rican terrorist, I'll be sure to get back to you." He couldn't resist reviving Lang's hopes of calls from reporters.

The Manhattan morgue couldn't afford enough big black vans

or medical examiners for all the people in the borough who died under suspicious or violent circumstances. No corpse could be moved until the ME had examined it at the scene, but Flynn was in a hurry to move this one so the fingers could be printed. He was relieved to hear Joe Mahoney's voice. No problem, Mahoney said; one wagon just pulled in and the team would like nothing better than a nice ride in the park on a humid night. They'd go on up there and wait on the ME. The minute the exam was done, they'd take off back to the morgue.

"I'm on my way down there," Flynn told Mahoney. "What can I bring?"

"Ham and cheese on rye, coffee regular, and a few dancing girls. Not too many."

"Ah, self-denial."

"When and if the ME opens up *my* head, Sister Gabriel-Marie is gonna pop right out," Mahoney said, bragging, not complaining, about this effect of his Catholic boyhood.

Flynn stopped off at the big newsstand at Seventy-second Street and Broadway and bought four skin magazines for Mahoney. When he delivered the goods, he and Mahoney had time to take their sandwiches out of the deli bag and schmooze a bit at the dispatcher's desk before the wagon came back with Flynn's DOA.

"Thanks for the rush job, pal," Flynn said, and Mahoney responded in his good Irish tenor with a few lines from the Bronx Catholic anthem about "brothers loyal and true."

The sign on the wall of the morgue detectives' basement office said, "Don't take life too seriously. It's only a temporary situation." The corollary, according to Detective Irene Defina, was, "Don't think of the DOAs as people, only as bodies." Keeping that thought in mind, she circulated among the oversize stainless steel lab tables where naked bodies lay with masklike faces peeled down and male cadavers' pricks standing straight up, wrapped in brown paper deli bags. She could calmly turn over the bloated carcasses of drowned "floaters"; open up corpses' mouths, hold their hands, and take their fingerprints.

Irene, a girl so thin you could almost see through her, went about all the grisly chores with skill and poise, but she had once told Flynn that in the beginning she'd had nightmares for several weeks. In the dreams, she saw herself and the other cops in her family riddled with the bullet holes that were a routine sight in her new job. Her father had retired as a lieutenant; her younger brother was a rookie.

With less than five years in the police department, Irene still had a cop's "white" shield—silver metal, not the gold one she would get in the Detective Bureau. Nevertheless, she was a full-fledged member of the Missing Persons squad, doing the work of a detective. And doing it under difficult conditions. She was called upon to work the morgues in several boroughs; here in Manhattan, the sour smell of decomposition even seeped up the stairs to street level. But Brooklyn was worse, she assured Flynn.

"I think you got a great job," he kidded while she prepared the fingerprint ink. "Nobody talks back to you, right?"

"Yeah, but if I hear that line *one* more time..." She scornfully shook her ponytail of wavy brown hair. "I'm surprised at you, Lieu, I thought you'd do better than that."

Flynn flashed his famous half-smile. "I'll keep trying."

The deceased lay on a gurney in the hallway outside the lab, still wearing the blue polyester suit. Before an attendant placed the body in one of the stainless steel "boxes" that lined both sides of the hall, he would remove the suit. In Manhattan, the attendants sorted the garments and sent them, tagged, to the building where evidence is stored—but in Queens, Irene had to do that along with all the rest. Handling the piles of often filthy, bloodstained clothing was the part of the job she complained about.

"All right," she said, rolling the last digit on the paper, "that's it for Mr. Blue Polyester."

"Señor Blue Polyester," Flynn corrected. "Come to think of it, he needs a third name—Spanish people like to use the mother's name at the end."

"Well, it's probably 'Blend'—I mean, 'Blend*o*'." They both laughed till they were laughed out. "I don't speak ill of the dead," Irene said, "but nobody said anything about not making a little fun, right?" She handed Flynn the sheet of prints, which he safeguarded in a folder he had brought for the purpose.

"Wish I could ask you out for a beer," he said, "but I gotta go wake 'em up over at BCI. But how about tomorrow—when I come down for the autopsy, we'll go for lunch. How's that?"

"Good." Irene smiled. In her line of work, it never hurt to have lunch with someone with a sense of humor. "That'd be nice."

When detectives from the Two-nine investigated a homicide, they rarely sent their requests to BCI by interoffice mail. They phoned ahead to the criminal identification section at police headquarters, then jumped in a car and rode downtown to 1 Police Plaza. The BCI men knew the Two-nine squad and admired their "pursuit of excellence," as someone in the unit had once jokingly put it. The officer on duty this Monday night looked mildly shocked, nevertheless, to receive the squad *lieutenant*—any squad lieutenant—at 2355 hours. The officer searched the files but nothing came up; he would instantly transmit Blue Polyester's prints to Albany. He told Flynn to call BCI in the morning—the subject's criminal record and pictures should be back before noon.

At the crime scene, Flynn and the men had performed a set of small essential steps; finding the identity of the dump-job victim would be a big leap. Provided the victim had a criminal record, technology would help. But until tomorrow, Flynn would have to think about something else.

Cops usually do their thinking about something else in bars, and Flynn had not given up bars when he gave up booze—least of all the family bar, F. X. Flynn's. He had quit drinking alcohol when Father Joe Dunne, the NYPD chaplain, collaborated with Tracy Flynn to push him into sobriety.

Tracy had threatened to divorce him if he didn't get clean. He laid his recovery at Tracy's feet, as he had brought many other expensive, hard-won gifts to the sophisticated blond model he considered himself lucky to have married. She praised his self-control—and congratulated herself on her power over him.

But the day came when she learned of his brief affair with a policewoman in his AA group. Tracy found her power wanting after all—and at the same time, it occurred to her that, through her real estate job, *real* power could be hers. Wondering why she hadn't understood that sooner, she wasted no time in ending her marriage of ten years. Flynn never knew what hit him—especially since she had left him right before the NYPD decided to trash the homicide squads and make him play major league ball with a farm team. With so many strikes against him, only his alert AA friends had prevented him from ending up in the gutter.

After the divorce, his life consisted of the job, his hours at the boxing club where he coached kids who loved boxing just as he had when he was growing up, and his hours with the crowd at Flynn's bar. When he was a kid, his father Francis and his uncle Jack owned and ran the family bar in Inwood at the northern edge of Manhattan—Jack worked behind the scenes, Francis at the bar. Cops from all the surrounding neighborhoods drank in the place, including a big, barrel-chested detective second grade named Jimmy Sullivan, who became a regular.

For years, Sullivan heard the bartender boast of his elder

son's boxing triumphs in the PAL, but Sullivan and Andy never met until Andy graduated high school and began helping out in the bar.

Sullivan did know the bartender's younger son, Sean, however. Fifteen-year-old Sean was really looking for trouble—the detective had unsuccessfully tried to make Francis Flynn understand that. When Sean was caught in a stolen-car caper with some older kids, Sullivan cut him loose with a warning. A year and a half later, Sullivan decided he'd better talk to Andy about Sean. "Where'd your brother get the funds for that Honda cycle? The kid's gonna have real problems any minute. Your dad goes blank when I bring up the subject. How about your mom, can't she see the handwriting on the wall?"

"Sean's her baby. He just pats her on the head and gives her a kiss and she melts."

Detective Sullivan didn't ask how come Andy hadn't acted like a big brother is supposed to act. The cop just said, "Why don't you get him down to the gym, away from those creeps he's travelin' with?"

Andy said he would try, and he did try. But Sean just grinned and said he knew how to fight pretty good, thanks.

"Great! C'mon down and work out, then," Andy urged, praying that it wasn't too late to start over.

"You got it," Sean said—but Flynn never followed up and it didn't happen. At the age of seventeen, Sean took three bullets from a .357 magnum in the chest and abdomen when he and two friends guessed wrong about how easy it would be to hold up a twenty-four-hour bodega. Sean died before the EMS crew could get him into the ambulance.

Flynn thought his mother would never survive, yet somehow she made it through the tragedy. But he was convinced that his father's fatal heart attack three years later had been connected to Sean's death. Francis, who could talk about his customers' problems for hours on end, had never opened up to anyone about Sean. And even while Andy brooded painfully about his brother after he died, somehow he couldn't bring himself to broach the subject with his dad.

Things would have come out differently, Andy believed, if he'd done whatever he had to do to get hooked up with his brother—even if it had meant knocking the kid silly first. Around the time Andy graduated from the Police Academy, he finally felt ready to talk to his father about Sean, at least to try—but then Francis Flynn died.

Francis's wake filled the whole first floor of Bell's funeral parlor. And Bell's came up with the top-of-the-line coffin for bartender Flynn, who had buried more than a few customers at his own expense and buried them at Bell's.

After Francis died, Uncle Jack ran F. X. Flynn's by himself. Andy almost always went there after the gym. He and Uncle Jack got to know each other better. Physically, Jack was bigger than Francis, but somehow he didn't have the same presence; he wasn't the born bartender Francis was. That didn't bother the old customers, though; their devotion to Flynn's and the Flynn family never wavered. They always liked to see Francis Flynn's cop son, Andy—and he liked to see them.

"Hey, it's Lieutenant Andy!" It was going on two A.M. on the night of the dump-job homicide, but Uncle Jack was still serving some customers when Flynn walked in. Andy bought a couple of rounds and nobody noticed that Jack didn't pour any gin or vodka into Andy's tonic.

Flynn unwound a little, doing more listening than talking. He was not in a war-stories kind of mood. As the hour passed, the customers faded away; the two Flynns had the place almost to themselves.

"What's the news from the gym?" the bartender asked his nephew.

"Terrific—great bunch of kids and they work real hard in the summer."

"So why doncha look happier?"

"You really wanna know?"

"No, I'm just makin' like a bartender, for chrissake."

"The squad's headin' into the fourth quarter with two cases down as of tonight—and one of those two is a double. Now to tell you the truth, Jack, those two drugmongers' deaths don't mean nothin' to nobody except maybe some junkies who can't see straight anymore. Not even the relatives give a shit. But we're pullin' out all the stops to clear the case anyway, just like they was a pair of saints that got butchered."

"I don't get it then." Jack poured his nephew a refill. "Why bother?"

"First, because the guy behind the job is public enemy number one. If we locked him up, we could all die happy. The other reason is, if we don't clear the case, we can forget our third hundred percent—and the men want that, too. They was goin' along, livin' the life of Riley—and they traded it in for a lotta sweat the past couple of years. I guess maybe I gave them the idea they could win. . . ."

"The PD sent you a mixed bag and you turned around and sent back a winning team." Jack stopped drying glasses and looked proudly at his nephew the detective boss.

"Well, they're a team, for sure—and they want the recognition that comes with three wins—that magic number."

"Why can't you clear this double? You know who did it."

"Everybody in the precinct knows, but nobody's gonna say so in court. Rattin' on this particular buzzard is an infallible way to die."

"It's true, that don't sound too good. But if I know you, you got some kinda ace in the hole. Right, Andy?"

"We got an old case that looks like it'll break, which would help. But even that's only a maybe—the whole thing's ridin' on a nineteen-year-old Puerto Rican witness. He's a good kid, bright; wants to come through for us on the case. But outside of that, he's walkin' a dicey line—just like Sean did. Every time I see him, I think about Sean, too. Kinda shakes me up, y'know?"

"Kids are tough," Uncle Jack said. "I guess if anybody learned that the hard way, you did."

Flynn went out into the humid night thinking about Salsa. About Viera—and Luzan. If Viera and Luzan's relationship had soured, as Salsa said, Viera would probably give the kid a medal for turning Rico in. Salsa knew what he was doing.

Late Tuesday afternoon, August 13, 1985

The fingerprints that Irene Defina had pulled from the corpse were those of Juan Rosa, DOB 4/10/50; born, Vieques, PR; last known address, West 130th Street, according to the rap sheet that came back from Albany on Tuesday morning. Rosa had a record of seven arrests for receiving stolen property.

"A fence from Harlem," Cooch said, looking over Flynn's shoulder at the printout.

Jesse Taylor poked his head into the bosses' office. "A fence from Harlem who likes Eddie Eldorado music," he said with a grin.

"Wiseass," said Carlucci, who was not amused by Taylor's riddles.

"What did the ME say this morning?" Taylor wanted to know.

"No surprises," Flynn said. "Gunshots to the left lung and

heart at close range, one exit wound in the back. Two .25-caliber slugs recovered. Stomach contents was spicy meat of some kind—you could still get a whiff—and black beans."

"That last meal fits. Did he say when Blue Polyester died?" Taylor persisted.

"Probably Saturday, maybe as late as Sunday—any special reason you're asking?" Knowing Jesse, there would be.

"Because in the not-so-wee hours of Sunday—something like five-thirty A.M.—a male Hispo, about five eight wearing a light-blue three-piece suit, was observed leaving the Tabu Club. The mope was in 'very bad shape' and being 'assisted' by two other male Hispos. Eldorado's band played the Tabu this weekend."

"I don't wanna jump to any conclusions, but the description fits," Flynn said.

"When I came in, I found a message from this limo chauffeur I know," Taylor said in a can-I-help-it-if-God-loves-me voice. "I just spoke to him now."

Flynn turned to Carlucci. "What happened with the canvass?"

"The four of us got out there at oh six-thirty hours, talked to twenty-three joggers and cyclists. Zip. Nobody remembered noticing anything out of the ordinary over the weekend."

"What about that Club de Amigos?" The words *Club de Amigos* were professionally sign-painted on the paved playing field that directly overlooked the dump location.

"Urquhart called the Parks Department. The Club is defunct but there's a group of Frisbee maniacs that uses the field most days in the late afternoon. Not after dark—there's no lights. But you know those steps along the east side of the field? Mazocek—who else?—said, 'Wouldn't that be a nice place for the amigos to sit and drink beer and watch the cars go by late at night.' C team should go down there tonight," Cooch suggested. "Find out if someone hangs around in the wee hours and if so, what they saw."

"Right." Flynn nodded. "Obie'll have a swell time down in the park, tonight. He's a nature lover."

"Guess you put the Nuñez collar on hold?" Cooch's tone was neutral.

"Not for long. Rico's scheduled for breakfast tomorrow. Jesse's gonna play reveille for A Team at oh five hundred. Stay over and start the day right, why don't you."

Cooch was tempted by the overtime but not by the rice and beans. "I just remembered, Claudia invited somebody for supper on the patio." Cooch went over to the logbook and signed out. "I better go make the drinks."

* * *

Flynn double-parked in front of the Tabu Club and walked with Taylor to the club entrance. Through the smoked-glass facade, they could see someone working at the end of the bar. "Must be Salsa's answering service—Ramón," Taylor said. The bartender, a slight man with an old-fashioned waxed mustache, came to the door.

"Qué tal?" Taylor smiled. "We'd like to talk to Irish for a few minutes." He and Flynn opened their wallets, showing their gold badges.

Ramón looked at his watch. "Maybe he's not here yet." He went behind the bar and picked up the intercom.

"You hit it lucky. Señor Viera came in a little early." The bartender escorted Flynn and Taylor down the thickly carpeted stairs and along the corridor lined with slick black paneling. He stopped at a black door with a polished bronze handle and knocked. "Monte, *policía* to see the boss."

Flynn remembered having seen Viera's lieutenant once before, almost five years earlier in Harlem. Luis Almonte still had a taste for shiny shirts and big rings. He maintained a poker face as he admitted Flynn and Taylor, who also showed no expression. Irish Viera sat behind a bigger piece of black marble than you could find in most banks. The desk was clear of papers. Nothing but a glass of whiskey and some tape cassettes. Viera was talking on the phone, a headset clamped over the straight, heavy black hair that had no trace of gray. The headset left his hands free to fiddle with the tapes. Flynn noticed the phone itself—a push-button panel built into the marble. Taylor's gaze went to the musicians' autographed photos on the office walls.

Almonte lounged in one of three black leather chairs arranged in front of Viera's desk, letting the cops wait standing up until Viera hit one of the buttons on the panel, took off the headset, and looked up at the visitors.

"Mr. Viera," Flynn shaded his tone with contempt, "Lieutenant Flynn and Detective Thomas of the Two-nine Squad." He noticed that the drug kingpin's brown eyes had gold flecks that glinted like the mica in rocks. The eyes lingered an instant on Flynn's face.

Viera waved absently at the empty leather chairs.

Flynn and Taylor chose to remain standing. Viera had to keep looking up at them. "A man was shot last weekend and the police found his body in the western part of the precinct. However, we believe he was here at the Eldorado show until shortly before he died."

"What makes you think he had some such happy hours before the sad end?"

"His brother, for one thing," Flynn lied. "The brother told us the deceased almost never missed an Eddie Eldorado performance. The brother said the deceased loved the Friday show at the Tabu and said he definitely was gonna come back again Saturday. We believe he came back." Taylor opened the manila envelope he was carrying, took out a folder, and handed it to Flynn. Flynn shuffled the papers and came up with the police ID photo of Juan Rosa. "This is the victim—"

"The guy had a record? Nobody gets in here with a gun—"

Flynn returned the folder to Taylor and slid the picture across the black marble.

"Monte, do you remember seeing this man?" Viera shared the picture with Almonte.

"We had a full house, boss, and even if I saw him, I might not remember." Monte looked at the picture and frowned.

"He was wearing a light-blue three-piece suit," Taylor said. "He probably stuck out."

"The face don't look familiar to me."

"I don't recall him, either. I wish we could help, Lieutenant, but..."

Flynn looked at his watch. "I'd like Detective Taylor to begin meeting with each of your house staff people—the waiters, everybody—and see if this photo rings any bells with them. Okay with you?"

"We'll make it fast, before we start getting busy." Viera looked at Almonte. "Tell Ramón to help Lieutenant..."

"Flynn. Thanks for your cooperation." Flynn looked at Taylor. "I'll meet you upstairs in a minute."

Alone with Viera, Flynn smiled the half-smile that the media loved. "It's hard to believe this place is 'son of Cocodrillo,'" he said. "Your business has grown, Irish."

"You knew the old bar."

"It was my job to know it."

"That was my trial balloon, where I made all my mistakes. I closed Cocodrillo in '75. I took my time putting the Tabu together—three years—but the result is exactly what I had in mind. I hope your last ten years left you just as satisfied, Lieutenant Flynn."

"Well, it's sort of pineapples and oranges, I guess."

Viera smiled. "Yes—hard to compare. Because I have something to show for my efforts, while you..."

"I can't really see or touch what I accomplish. My 'results' usually sink back into the mud. Like Cocodrillo." Flynn almost said "Blanco."

"Well, good luck with your investigation." Viera stood up. "If that fellow was here, at least he enjoyed his last night."

"Do you think he was here?"

Viera folded his arms and closed his eyes, concentrating as if mentally scanning a crowd. He opened them and said, "No. On Saturday night, especially, I always walk around the house and say hello to people. I would remember a light-blue three-piece suit." One eyebrow went up in distaste. Flynn understood that Viera-the-fashion-snob wanted to rewrite his dress code, banning light-blue polyester suits forever from the club.

"You'll find my memory is good, Lieutenant Flynn."

"Thanks again," Flynn said.

When the office door had closed, Viera used a remote device to lock it. Then he reached under the marble slab, pressed the rewind button, and began to play back the last minutes of the tape: his conversation alone with Flynn. While he listened to the tape, he released a section of black wall paneling and pulled the ARCHIVO CONFIDENCIAL folder from a hanging file. He opened it and turned over the yellowed clippings from the social page of *El Universo*. There were only a few: The marriage of his father, Jaime Viera Ceballos, to Margaret Evelyn Kelly of Dublin. His own marriage to Manuela De Soto Bonifáz, and the obituary of Manuela, aged twenty-two.

No one but those three had meant anything at all to Dennis Viera—until Blanco. Jorge Martín. Blanco had been a clever businessman with a reckless streak that Viera admired. And Blanco had once done time rather than finger Viera in a deal they'd been partners in together. Viera unfolded the 1972 *Daily News* clipping and looked at a photo of two cops. One was Officer Andrew Flynn. Andrew Flynn, thirteen years younger, but with the same little smirk on his face as now. Before replacing the ARCHIVO, Viera slipped the tape cassette inside it.

Monte knocked and Viera buzzed him in. "The cops left," Monte said; "they got nothin'. Ramón is fixing fresh drinks."

"I heard from El Grande," Viera announced. "He wants to know where's his Miguelito?"

"Like I said, boss, Panama was the best I could do." Even in the air-conditioned office, Monte sweated at the thought of his Sunday morning at Kennedy airport. "The Bogotá plane didn't leave till five-thirty that night, but there was seats on a noon flight to Panama City."

"I told El Grande the son-in-law got in a little trouble. I did not lose my temper and inform him that Miguel Inoa Lopez did a stupid murder in *my* club—and the cops are running around here like *cucarachas.* Looks like Miguelito is screwing off in Panama and hasn't bothered to call home. El Grande swore to me the new shipment is on its way—this time, it's coming in watermelons—but I know we won't see a gram till Miguelito is home with the wife and kids."

"Meanwhile, boss, nobody's holdin' up Luzan's shipments. This down time is bad for us—upscale customers are only brand loyal up to a point. If Luzan is ready for them, he could be grabbing our market as we speak."

Salsa knocked and came in with two drinks on a Lucite tray.

"Ready! That Dominican deadhead and that pack of jokers he calls an organization? He belongs in the sugarcane fields back where he came from. I heard he does twenty-five, thirty thousand bucks a day with his two-bit crack crap!"

"Like the old saying, 'It sells itself'; this fuckin' product does," Monte said. "That's the thing, you don't have to be smart and well organized to make it with crack."

Viera knocked back his Irish whiskey on the rocks. "What's this shanty-Irish 'Flynn' all about?"

"Just another precinct cop as far as I know. He *was* a homicide cop but they buried those homicide squads a few years back."

"How come? Do you know?"

"Nobody knows why those dumb fuck cop bosses do what they do."

Salsa had paused to look again at all the photos of Latin music greats on Viera's wall. "I heard something on the street, though."

"What's that?" Monte asked.

"I heard that his squad has a perfect record on homicides. They always get the killer."

Viera startled Monte and Salsa with a real laugh. "Yeah? Los Primos have been dead since March, the whole neighborhood knew about it, and no arrest yet—"

"Salsa"—Monte held out his glass—"bring this back to Ramón—too much vermouth."

Salsa left the office and Viera continued, "So how the fuck will they solve a shooting that happened in an empty men's room at five in the morning? No witnesses and the killer's out of the country." Viera raised his almost empty glass. "To Andrew Flynn and his squad of clowns. A laugh a minute."

Monte leaned forward in his leather chair. "We got Luzan tryin' to grab our market with that powerhouse new product. We got nine big new accounts comin' to town to look us over—you don't want anything extra on your mind. Who needs this cop trouble, boss—why don't we take care of it right now?"

"Because I gotta have some fun with this guy. I waited a long time; I'm not just gonna order a pair of cement shoes and be done with it, that's why. I want something slower... more painful. Wait awhile. You'll see."

Wednesday morning, August 14, 1985

For the arrest of Rico at Las Flores, Flynn had decided to recruit an anticrime cop to pose as a taxi driver. Anticrime, Pastore's old unit, cruised the precinct in an authentic yellow taxi, following street criminals and grabbing them in the act. Pastore had recommended his buddy Vic Espinosa. Wednesday at 0500 hours, Espinosa, medium height and chunky, came to the squad dressed in cutoff jeans and sandals. His loose, short-sleeved sportshirt billowed over the revolver stuck in his waistband. He would blend right in with the Las Flores crowd.

Flynn handed Espinosa the ID picture of Rico. "This is the geek that blew away not only a kid, but a kid who raised pigeons?"

"Took him out with a rifle, split to Santo Domingo for a long vacation. We're the welcome-back committee."

"It'll be a pleasure." Espinosa stared at the picture. "How's this cocksucker built?"

"Tall, thin. Oh, yeah," Flynn added, "we think he eighty-sixed that earring. Must be tired of the hippy look."

"Got it," Espinosa said. "I'm h-u-u-u-ngry and the taxi's all gassed up."

Flynn introduced Salsa, who had showed up without his Walkman, Flynn noticed, but with his chin at the usual cocky angle.

"This is the victim's buddy—he witnessed the shooting. Salsa's gonna positively ID the perp."

Salsa did a good job of looking cool as he got in the back of the maroon Thunderbird with Taylor. Urquhart drove. Flynn and Pastore took the blue Chrysler. Espinosa's taxi came last. At 0600 hours, Flynn parked on the side street around the corner from Las Flores, and within sight of the Thunderbird in the uptown bus stop across Amsterdam.

Taylor stepped out and hesitated for an instant, listening for a "thunk," Flynn figured—Urquhart's locking the car doors from the front seat. Salsa would be sitting on the floor, waiting for Freddy Urquhart to give him his cue. As Espinosa drove the taxi up in front of the coffee shop, Taylor went over to the newspaper store next to Las Flores and began browsing through the headlines.

Flynn and Ron Pastore watched the taxi back into its corner space and Espinosa hop out, but then he left their line of vision. If Espinosa immediately reappeared, it would mean that Rico had skipped breakfast today. Everyone waited.

From across Amsterdam, Urquhart kept his eyes on the stucco-faced coffee shop with its curlicues of white metal grillwork over dusty windows. Several minutes slowly passed.

"Looks like our pal is chowing down, Salsa," Urquhart said over his shoulder. "Get ready now, and when I tell you, just lift your head up enough to see out. See if they got the guy who killed your buddy." Urquhart backed up the Thunderbird till it was across the avenue from Las Flores.

Urquhart saw Flynn and Pastore get out of the Chrysler and walk to the corner opposite Las Flores.

0621 hours. Espinosa ambled out of the coffee shop carrying a paper bag. He jerked a thumb back toward the door. *He's in there.* Jesse Taylor quit "browsing," came around the newsstand and walked toward Espinosa; Flynn and Pastore crossed the side street and paced around right next to Las Flores.

When the coffee shop door swung open again, the suspect all but tripped over Flynn and Taylor.

"Police," Flynn barked. "Freeze, Rico."

"You're under arrest," Taylor said in Spanish. Rico's right hand dropped toward his ankle.

"Taxi!" Pastore yelled; he and Espinosa converged on Rico. With four pairs of unfriendly eyes staring at him, Rico knew enough not to resist Flynn's handcuffs. Flynn removed a .25 Titan from under Rico's black pants leg.

Espinosa took off in the taxi. Pastore brought the Chrysler around, ready to take the prisoner. But Flynn and Taylor just stood there with Rico between them.

Taylor pretended to complain to Flynn. "Hey, I didn't have no breakfast. I'm gonna get somethin' to go, long as we're here..."

Flynn and Taylor kept up the "argument" for a couple of minutes, each of them holding on to the guy in handcuffs with one hand and waving or pointing with the other. From where they stood, Flynn could see Salsa peering over the windowsill of the Thunderbird.

"That tall guy in the middle," Urquhart said, "You know him, Salsa?"

"That's Rico."

"Abogado!" Rico shouted as they led him toward the cell behind the squad room. His English had deserted him about the time Taylor read him his rights in the backseat of the Chrysler.

Flynn took the hefty, old-fashioned-looking iron key off its hook above the 1984 files and unlocked the cell for Rico.

"Abogado!" the perp repeated for the ninth time, including once before and once after Flynn had handed him the telephone so he could call a lawyer.

Flynn shut the barred door and turned the key. "Your lawyer must be on the way, and so is the DA." The phone rang and Taylor went to answer it.

"K. Patrick for you, Lieu."

Flynn looked at the time as he hurried into the squad room and picked up. "Kev, hope we didn't wake you."

"The office says you got a homicide—this is that old one you mentioned the other day?" asked Flynn's friend, the assistant district attorney.

"Right. The '82 case. I know your watch is almost over—you comin' up?"

"Of course. I already called for a radio car. Is your defendant talking?"

"Like a broken record: *'abogado, abogado, abogado . . .'*

"Shit. He's asked for a lawyer—I'll just be wasting my time up there."

"Hold on," Flynn said. "This thing's three years old—maybe he figures he can beat it. But I got an eyewitness—a friend of the victim's who was there. And he positively ID'd the perp when we did the arrest half an hour ago. He's feelin' brave right now—all ready to testify. We could do a video and lock him in."

"Yeah, we better do that. Nobody'll be able to say, 'Oh, the cops read him his lines.' I'll give the video unit a shout right away."

"Dynamite."

"Listen," Patrick's voice was warm, "when the top squad in the city calls, we don't fool around, you know that. How's your body count, anyway?"

"We're a little behind but we'll catch up—we got a title to defend."

"Hey, the doorman's buzzing; must be my ride," Patrick said. "See you soon."

As Flynn hung up the phone, Taylor came out of the captain's office, shutting the door behind him.

"Patrick's on his way," Flynn said, looking relieved.

"The star witness claims Rico had breakfast and *he* didn't."

"Ain't it the truth. We let the perp stuff his face before we take him but the witness goes hungry. Did Salsa say what he'd like to eat?"

"Rice and beans and sunny-side up."

"Protein—great! It'll help him get through his interview with the DA." Flynn looked at Taylor. "Come to think of it, I'm gonna have some, too. What about you?"

At about seven forty-five, Assistant District Attorney Kevin Patrick sat down at Flynn's desk to read the case file that the lieutenant gave him. He felt rested and glad to face a challenge. Ex-Marine Kevin Patrick believed he had not left the warrior profession behind when he joined the Manhattan DA's office a decade before. Nobody understood better than he did Andy Flynn's drive to destroy the enemy.

For Patrick's money, Flynn and his squad deserved their reputation; they rarely stopped at the basic requirements for homicide clearance but worked to come up with what a DA needed for *conviction.* But with so much at stake for the squad right now, even Flynn could have slipped. Patrick would be the one to fight the case in court—he had to have live ammunition. Especially on a case with a three-year-old ID. Everything would have to be carefully analyzed.

Flynn headed for the far corner of the squad, to the two-by-nothing coffee room. He detoured to walk by Rico's cell. Never fails, he thought: the deep, peaceful sleep of the perp who knows that *you* know he did it.

"Andy," the DA said when Flynn returned with their mugs of coffee, "how about this detective who interviewed the sister—Carmel—and supervised Crime Scene, can we get him for trial?"

"No problem—Doherty's in Manhattan South. And Wolff, the first patrol officer on the scene, he's still here in the precinct."

"I see that Carmel's count of the number of shots corresponds to the casings found—nice going. But why did she lie to

Doherty that she and Pichón were the only ones on the roof? What's the story?"

One day Patrick might have to persuade a jury of that story; right now it was up to Flynn to persuade *him.*

"She and her brother, Salsa, were very close. And he was the one who started this nail game that touched off the dispute—the kids throwin' nails across the air shaft at the wall of the other building. She thought that if Salsa hadn't started the game... if Rico's window hadn't busted... Pichón would still be alive. So she figured because it was Salsa's game, the cops would blame him. I think a jury would believe her anxiety."

"Does he have a sheet?"

"No arrests."

"What about Family Court—any history there? Delinquency?"

Salsa's only youthful indiscretion that Flynn knew about had been the disappearance from his family's Rio Piedras Bodega and numbers depot of $1,200 in customers' winnings when Salsa was eight years old. Flynn had managed to resolve that burglary—the brainchild of an older kid who Salsa hung around with—without the criminal justice system *or* the numbers bosses coming down on Salsa. The stepfather had made up the stolen money and Salsa slowly worked off his debt. Salsa had never had any juvenile charges brought against him in Family Court, Flynn told Patrick.

"What about drugs?"

"Some involvement, probably," Flynn hedged. "He spends too much time around the Tabu Club for there not to be."

"Well, I gotta talk to him about it."

"Right."

"Back to Carmel," the DA said. "A defense lawyer could have a ball with her prior inconsistent statement, you know."

Flynn did know. He tried to emphasize the positive. "Did you get a chance to read her description of Rico?"

"Yeah."

"Take a look at Sleeping Beauty in the cell."

"Okay," Patrick said when he came back, "her description was accurate and the squad had his street name. I don't get why there was no arrest *then.*"

"They held the heavy-set guy, Zueca, here overnight—by the time they realized he didn't do it, Rico was in the wind."

"Oh. That was before you took over the squad, Andy?"

"Yeah, but those things can happen."

"So, Carmel had no trouble describing the guy who tried to kill her—at the time. But can she ID him *now?*"

"She picked him right out of a photo array last week, same as Salsa did."

"Salsa left the scene...," the DA mused.

"She told him to book," Flynn explained. "He would've hung in."

"Either one of them could get cute again, couldn't they? Let's bring Carmel in here for a lineup now—and while we're at it, she and Salsa can act out the whole thing under the lights. That way they're *both* locked in."

Flynn checked the time. "That would be ideal but I don't think she could make it on this short notice. I can bring her down for a lineup this week, though—no problem."

"We got till Monday to do the grand jury presentation. The sooner the better, before Rico shaves his head or something."

"I'm sure I can work it out with her for tomorrow or Friday."

"Sounds good." Patrick pulled the autopsy report from the file and handed it to Flynn. "The ME talks about possible gunpowder residue on the dura around the wound. Now that doesn't support a rifle shot from across the roof."

"The ME said 'possible.' I'll ask her to take another look at the slide."

"We'll get into that distance thing with Salsa, too," Patrick added. "How's he doing—ready to start?"

"You want to warm up a little before the video?"

"This is the DA, Salsa." Flynn, Taylor, and Kevin Patrick walked in, leaving the office door open. "Came up here before breakfast to see you." The star witness took his feet off the captain's desk and the earphones off his head. Salsa arranged his earphones atop the Walkman unit and set them aside on the desk.

"My name is Mr. Patrick," the assistant district attorney said after Salsa thanked Flynn for the mug of coffee. "I brought a video crew with me to record your account of this horrible murder. While the crew's setting up, we can talk a little bit. I'll let you know when you're gonna go on."

Salsa had trouble ignoring the video camera on its tripod, just a couple of feet away from him.

Flynn and Taylor sat in chairs to one side of the desk, and Patrick leaned against the desk, arms folded, looking steadily at Salsa with blue eyes as inscrutable as the camera's lens.

"Where do you live, Salsa?"

"My mother's in Washington Heights."

"Well, is that where you live?"

"Not really. I stay in different squats around here."

"Sealed-up buildings, like the one where your friend was killed on the roof?"

"Yeah."

"So how will I find you when it comes time for the trial."

"Lieutenant Flynn, he knows how."

"Do you have a girlfriend?"

"Nobody special—playin' the field."

Patrick changed the subject abruptly. "Lieutenant Flynn tells me you saw a good buddy of yours get shot to death three years ago. You didn't have anything to say to the police back then, but now—everything's different."

"Right."

"How do I know you're not gonna cut out on us this time, too?"

"I wish I didn't run away, Mr. Patrick. I wanna see that guy locked up tight for what he did."

"You work, Salsa?"

"Yeah."

"Doing what?"

"Odd jobs around the Tabu Club. Whatever they need."

"Ever been arrested?"

"No."

The DA came on strong even if he was young looking, with his straight blond hair and light build. Salsa was impressed by the gravel in Patrick's voice, the tough way he didn't open his mouth too much when he talked.

"Take drugs?"

Salsa looked at Flynn.

"Gotta tell the truth, man."

"Pot."

"Were you smoking anything that night?"

"No. Didn't smoke with my sister around."

"Do you use coke?"

"Maybe Sunday, sometimes."

"That stuff is death, Salsa, one way or another. If *it* doesn't kill you, somebody'll kill you to get it. Or they'll kill you because they were usin' and got paranoid. Isn't that the way it came out for Pichón?"

"Yeah."

"Okay, we're gonna do the tape now. All set?"

Salsa nodded. Patrick knocked on the wall and Salsa heard the camera click on.

The interview started with Patrick asking for Salsa's full name and date of birth. "The guy who shot your friend Pichón," the DA went on, "do you know his real name?"

"No."

"What's his street name?"

"Rico."

"How long do you know him?"

Salsa thought for a minute. "Since I was about twelve—so, seven years anyway. Maybe more."

"When's the last time you saw him, and where?"

"A couple of hours ago, outside Las Flores."

"What's that?"

"The coffee shop, about four blocks up on Amsterdam. Rico walks out after breakfast"—he laughed—"they"—he nodded at the detectives—"snap him up just like that." Salsa looked right into the video camera, like a pro. "And I'm watchin' the whole scene from a car across the street."

"He's the same guy who killed Pichón?"

"Yeah."

"Anytime lately, did he come looking for you?"

"I sure hope he didn't come lookin' for me."

"You got it in for him?"

"He shot Pichón! He shot at me and Carmel, too, but he missed."

"About what time did this incident happen?"

"Something like seven at night."

"Was it dark out?"

"No. It was August. Plenty light."

"When Rico came up to the roof, did he come alone?"

"No, with a fat guy and a dog."

"Did the fat guy have anything to do with the dispute or the shooting?"

"Well, Rico made him go get the rifle."

"Where was Rico standing when he started shooting?"

"By the ledge on his roof, the next one over from ours."

"How far away? Like from where you're sitting now to where?"

Salsa pointed out the captain's office doorway to the far side of the squad room. "At least as far as that wall."

"What if I heard somewhere else that Pichón was shot from close up?"

"That ain't how it happened."

"It could have happened that way and you could be blocking it out—not on purpose," the DA persisted. "Think back."

Salsa shook his head and pointed across the squad room again. "He shot from that far away, maybe a little farther."

"Maybe he shot from that far and missed Pichón—like he missed you and Carmel. Maybe you started to run before the whole thing ended and you didn't see that Pichón got shot from up close. *By someone else.*"

"No, I know it happened like I remember."

"What was Rico wearing?"

"Jeans and a red T-shirt."

"All right." The DA finally smiled. He signaled the crew and the camera clicked off.

"We can wrap it up there. Salsa, you'll be a good witness at Rico's trial. Your sister's gonna be a witness, too. I'm gonna tell her just what I'm telling you now: The shooting went down three years ago, yet you're still clear about it in your mind today. It could be another seven, eight months, maybe even a year, till the trial—you gotta *keep remembering* all that stuff, keep the pictures in your mind, as unpleasant as it is." The DA sat down on the corner of the captain's desk. "And whatever you do, *don't get arrested.* The jury doesn't believe witnesses who commit crimes. Pay your fare on the subway and everything. Got me?"

"Yeah, Mr. Patrick."

"Rico's in a cell back there." Patrick jerked his thumb. "We're gonna *keep* him behind bars for twenty-five to life. For Pichón and for you and Carmel."

Salsa looked drained. Flynn started to tell him to go home, then remembered he didn't really have a home. "Take it easy now," Flynn said, giving Salsa his business card. "Hold on to this, okay? Nobody knows you're here—but still, things happen. Somebody could threaten you. I want you to keep in touch with me. Now get some sleep."

"Okay, Lieutenant Flynn."

"Remember my name, too," the DA said, writing it on a piece of paper and giving it to Salsa.

"You want a lift?" Taylor asked. "We'll put you right in a radio car."

"No, *gracias.*" Salsa collected his Walkman, gave Flynn a little salute, and disappeared out the squad room's swinging doors.

Late Wednesday afternoon, August 14, 1985

"Buenas tardes!" Ramón said to Salsa. "You look like you're only half out of bed." The Tabu didn't open till seven-thirty but Ramón

let Salsa into the club's mirrored-all-over entry at about five on the muggy afternoon. Salsa's disheveled images and Ramón's dapper ones surrounded them, reflected back and forth countless times. "Monte's looking for you—"

"Irish here yet? I gotta tell him some good news."

"Yeah, what?"

"I better tell *him* first, you know. Is he—"

"Here, you can take him his drink, he just called up for it before you walked in. If I was you, I'd make a pit stop on the way. I'll tell him you'll be right down."

"Okay, but Ramón, what's this fuckin' drink?" Salsa took the crystal old-fashioned glass, gently shook the ice cubes, and sniffed the opaque liquid. "Looks like you put some Fudgsicles in the blender."

"No, it comes like that." The bartender showed Salsa the bottle of Bailey's Irish Cream. "Somebody gave him this as a joke and he liked it. Right away, 'Ramón, order a case!' Hey, I thought you're in a hurry."

Salsa left his Walkman behind the bar and ran downstairs to the black marble men's room, washed his face, and combed his hair. He also combed the little tuft of chin hairs he'd been growing. On the way out, he noticed that the damaged marble wall tiles had been replaced.

"Mr. Irish," Salsa said as he put down the glass and the Tabu Club coaster next to a small stack of cassette tapes on the desk, "lemme get some more ice for this." He went to the built-in refrigerator behind one of the shiny black wall panels and opened it by pressing the corner of the panel near the "ice cube" made of real-looking plastic.

"Salsa, I think Monte wants to see you."

"I'll go find him right away. I just got one thing to tell you first. It's important."

Irish looked surprised but motioned to a black leather sling chair. Salsa had never sat down in Irish's office before. "Rico, you know? The—"

"Yes, that *cucaracha* of Luzan's."

"The cops got Rico for murder. He won't be selling no more crack for a long time.... He's in jail." Salsa saw that his boss was really pleased.

Viera smiled. "Where did this good news come from?"

"The police station. Three years ago, Rico shot my buddy, you know? And I was a witness. They just reopened the investigation now, and this morning, when they picked him up, I was with them—to make sure it was him."

Never before had Salsa held the boss's undivided attention. The dark brown eyes with gold flecks looked only at him. Irish raised his glass toward Salsa. "It's smart to rat on a *cucaracha.* We should drown Luzan's whole mess of *cucarachitas.* They're all over the neighborhood. They even have the nerve to stand around outside *here* and hustle that cheap crack to Tabu customers." Irish pushed the intercom button on his desk and used the speaker phone to call Ramón. "Beep Monte. I want him in here right away."

Salsa stood up, but Irish waved him back into the chair. "What do you want to drink?" Irish asked.

As Irish pushed the intercom button again, Salsa wondered where you could buy such a perfect shirt as the boss wore, white with skinny blue stripes and initials on the pocket.

A minute later, Monte came in carrying three drinks, including Salsa's Mexican beer. "Salsa! *Here* you are. My car—"

"Forget that dusty Chevrolet for a minute," Irish cut him off. "Poor Carlos has had bad luck with that *cucaracha* of his—Rico."

The story knocked Monte out. *"Fantástico!"* he said. "Now the city cops got Rico—the feds should get whoever's supplying Carlos Luzan with his coke."

"Somebody will have to set up Carlos like Salsa set up Rico. But that might not happen this week," Irish said. "In the meantime, Carlos is minus a lieutenant—Rico's in for murder; the judge won't set bail. I want to be aggressive while they can't fight back. Turns out we timed our 'new accounts' meeting right. Luzan will be too busy this weekend to pay much attention if any of the new prospects decide they want to do some comparison shopping." He fiddled with the cassette tapes.

"To service the new business, we need men we can trust. I want to promote from within." He looked at Salsa. "Salsa's known in the precinct, now—he can't keep steering, working the *street* all night. If he gets picked up, the detectives might help him—but then he'll owe them favors. Right now, *they* need *him.* Salsa's an MVP. So, find him an inside location, Monte... or use him as your assistant." The boss flashed a smile. "Yes! Salsa can free you up to work on the new business. Just what you need. Salsa, did you ever use a gun?"

"A couple of times."

"Get him a .38 and a beeper and train him."

Irish took a cassette from the stack on his desk, put it in the tape deck next to him, and put on a pair of huge, black earphones. Salsa remembered that Ramón had his Walkman at the bar, but he waited for Monte to stand up and followed him out of the office, not knowing where they would begin.

Thursday, August 15, 1985

"Read all about it," Flynn said when he reached Carmel uptown at her mother's bodega. *"Daily News,* page three—Rico's in jail."

Carmel was so excited that she spilled a roll of quarters all over the floor and swore into the telephone. Flynn stifled his laugh and just said, "Pardon?" as if he hadn't understood her Spanish. When Carmel recovered, he told her that her brother was cooperating with the cops—and they would need her help in the case, too.

"You saw Salsa? When?"

"Just the other day."

"How *is* he?"

"Terrific!"

"Really?"

Flynn knew that Carmel worried about Salsa's getting in trouble. *"Verdad,"* he said reassuringly. "Now we're doing a lineup tomorrow, downtown in the DA's office. About this time. I want you to come and view it, okay? I'll come and get you myself."

Sudden silence at the other end of the line.

"Don't worry, Carmel—nobody will be able to see you or even know that you're there, understand?"

"Really?"

"Of course. I'll be at the store by one o'clock. Good enough?"

"Bueno."

Later that afternoon, Flynn and Taylor were sitting at the ancient wooden table in the squad's retreat—a room big enough for a witness, a detective, and a lawyer to stand in and look out the one-way glass at a lineup. That was the room's primary purpose, but it also held the squad's TV set, fastened high on the wall, and their coffeemaker, on top of a file cabinet.

Taylor kidded Flynn about the *Daily News* story, "Good thing you only made page three. Your face ain't in the photo—and the *Times* didn't run it at all. Maybe it won't get anybody's balls in an uproar downtown."

Flynn had attracted a lot of media attention in his Sixth Homicide days. Taylor knew any number of big bosses who would just as soon Flynn never got any more press; after all, there was only so much to go around, and the brass considered it rightfully theirs.

"They got plenty of 'paper' to worry about besides that," Flynn said. He switched to the dump job. "Well, since the Tabu Club staff stonewalled, we got no choice—we gotta ask the customers. There's no other way, is there?"

"If there is"—Taylor shook his head solemnly—"I never heard of it." They agreed that a nice busy Saturday night would be an ideal time for the canvass. Flynn paused in midsentence when they heard the phone ringing in his office.

Obie grabbed it. "It's Parkin—Community Affairs, Lieu."

Thursday evening, August 15, 1985

With the dull roar of precinct business as background, the Precinct Community Council executive board meeting came to order in the muster room. The din was music to board members' ears. A chance to soak up the atmosphere of police work was what kept most of them running for reelection, year after year. And brought them to the poorly air-conditioned precinct on an evening when the temperature was still in the eighties.

Because of the *Daily News* article, the board invited Flynn to their meeting. For backup, he brought along Carlucci. When Community Affairs Officer Parkin introduced the detectives, citing the squad's best-in-the-city homicide clearance record, the board clapped loudly.

More applause for the arrest reported in the *News.* Flynn smiled his half-smile and casually shared a detail or two that hadn't been in the newspaper. When he made a point of crediting "someone in the community who wanted to see the killer caught" for helping the squad, a board member asked who. Flynn reminded him that detectives always protect their witnesses with confidentiality. The group nodded approvingly. But then a well-dressed senior citizen stood up, fists on her hips.

"You obviously know that there's a dreadful *burglary* epidemic on West End Avenue this summer." She glared from Carlucci to Flynn. "People have told me that the detectives call and ask a few questions—but do they come out and make a real investigation?

Never! Well, I consider that a *scandal,* and I'm sure I wouldn't be alone in that opinion for one minute if I chose to raise the issue in the right places." She glanced meaningfully at the door of the precinct captain's office.

Flynn's "backup" rushed aid and comfort to the enemy. Cooch promised to *personally* review the burglary file "tomorrow," his voice sounding as if he were steeling himself for the horrors he would find. Flynn was considering how to get the hell out of there when he noticed a honey-blond board member in a skimpy red T-shirt dress eyeing him coolly. Finally, the senior citizen accepted Cooch's business card and sat down.

"Lauren Daniels." Red T-shirt dress raised her hand. "I live on Ninety-second Street between Amsterdam and Columbus. Last spring, when that special task force was on the block, we felt safe, but since they pulled out, the dealers are back again. It's so open, it's like they're selling popcorn. We have a strong block association and we do more than complain—people have been trying to help the police. But your 'confidentiality' doesn't work." Lauren Daniels looked at Flynn accusingly. "Word gets around somehow and the dealers have threatened these people—who now live *in terror.* I believe you're wrong to encourage this kind of 'help' from the community. You're paid to protect—but you're jeopardizing peace of mind and even lives."

Flynn loosened his tie. Whatever had made him think that she'd be on his side?

"I can't deny that there's an element of danger for witnesses, ma'am," he answered quietly, "as hard as we try to keep it to the minimum. And it does put us in a tough position. We're not Superman; if people didn't help us—if we *didn't* encourage that—then crime would be a lot worse even than it is now and everybody would suffer. All I can promise you is that there's really no other way." He tried the half-smile. "Sherlock Holmes is a fantasy. Like Superman."

Friday afternoon, August 16, 1985

"Bing bing, bam bam." "Boom boom ba boom." "One more!" "Unh!"

The voices got louder, the sounds more distinct, as Flynn and Salsa climbed the stairs to the Clinton Boxing Club. "I'm going to *my* club—the boxing club," Flynn had told Salsa casually. "You want a taste of life in the squared circle, you can come along. . . ." Salsa was casual right back, but he went along; he was more interested than he let on.

They climbed past the gym entrance, up the second flight of stairs to the locker room. Salsa just kept on his same T-shirt and jumped into a spare pair of Flynn's sweatpants. On Salsa's long legs, the pants didn't bag properly at the ankles. "Next time you come," Flynn promised, "we'll fix you up with some Everlast gear."

"Hey, Andy!" A tall, broad-chested guy called out to Flynn as he and Salsa entered the gym itself.

"Salsa, meet my pal Charlie, he's a cop in Brooklyn. Myself and Charlie got a couple of PAL kids comin' in after school a few times a week. Whichever one of us is here trains 'em—we take turns."

" 'Salsa'?" Charlie said. "You got your nickname already, huh? When Andy was fightin', he was known as Andy *A-Train* Flynn."

"A-Train!"

Flynn laughed. "In Brooklyn, cops don't know how to keep their mouths shut."

A black kid with a flattop haircut and compact build walked across the crowded room toward him. "This is Jemal," Flynn said. "He's comin' along great."

Jemal grinned and Charlie began to wrap strips of gauze and adhesive tape carefully across Jemal's thick hands, around his thumbs and wrists.

"This place is *busy.*" Salsa's glance took in the body at rest on the massage table, the rope skippers skipping fancy steps under the display of bold yellow, red, and black fight posters. Farther down the room to the left stood big mirrors and guys boxing with their reflections, guys doing sit-ups or knee bends, a guy slamming a punching bag almost as big and heavy as a man, and another guy rat-a-tat-tatting on a small, fast bag. And in the front by the big window, two guys sparring on the square of dirty gray canvas with the ropes around it. Salsa tried to catch the trainers' words as they yelled out moves. He asked Flynn, "What do I gotta do first?"

"Well, this time . . . mostly you watch. 'Cause to actually learn this stuff, you gotta get in shape. Build up some endurance, or as Charlie says, 'insurance.' "

"Like how?"

"Run," Charlie broke in. "Roadwork. It ain't hard—unless you're smokin' something. And you really need that strength in your legs when you're dancin' around the ring for two minutes straight. Two minutes is a *long* time in there."

"I thought it was three minutes," Salsa said.

"Not till you fight five fights," Charlie told him. "But look, I'm gonna work with Jemal now—he's gonna shadowbox. Just keep your eyes open and Andy'll explain what's happening."

With Charlie's help, Jemal put on the bulky red gloves. Then he went into a slight crouch, the upper body turned just a little, and began boxing the air. Charlie stood a few feet in front of him.

"Y'see," Flynn began, "Jemal's got the opposite build from you. More of a heavy-hitter type, where you'd be fast—dancin' around, like Charlie said. On the order of a Hector Camacho—what they call a 'classic boxer.' Either way, a fighter's gotta have good *balance.* That's why the basic thing is the stance—the right position—so a little shove don't knock you over. The reason you turn your body like that, it makes you a smaller target, right? We can start on the stance today. Now this shadowboxing, it's to develop your technique, sharpen your combinations. He's gettin' the rhythm good, see?"

"Step forward when ya jab," Charlie bellowed at Jemal. "Bend your body. Bring that other foot up. Chin down. Elbows in."

"You can't tense your hand when you punch," Flynn added. "Keep loose."

"Come back with your left or get hit!" Charlie yelled.

"Besides stamina, strength, and balance," Flynn said, "you gotta have speed—especially a boxer type, like you." He squinted at Salsa. "Then there's one more key thing. People don't always realize it if they're not into this sport: A boxer's nothin' without *brains.* You're about the same weight as the other guy—you get the advantage by out*thinkin'* him."

Salsa got absorbed in the sparring match.

"Look how Jemal tries to come right back to that stance," Flynn said, "after every punch. See that?"

"Yeah," Salsa said, "you gonna teach it to me—the stance?"

"Right now." Flynn put his arm around Salsa's shoulder and guided him to some free floor space by the mirror. The lieutenant gave him all the pointers and Salsa followed till he had the stance. He looked in the mirror as Flynn said, "Looks nice—how's it feel? Comfortable? Balanced?"

Salsa checked it out—it felt natural. When Flynn suddenly gave his shoulders a solid push, he kept his balance.

"Great," the cop said, "maybe this is your sport—think so?"

"May*be,*" Salsa said. He thanked Flynn for bringing him to the gym. "I'm gonna come back here and try it. Soon."

"Great." They headed for the locker room stairs. "Do me a favor in the meantime?" Flynn said. "Keep those eyes open around the Tabu and... keep me in mind."

"No problem," Salsa answered. Since the Rico arrest, Salsa was like teacher's pet to his bosses. If not for Flynn, he wouldn't be on this fast new track.

Saturday night, August 17, 1985

An electric sign with moving letters, Times Tower–style and not much smaller in scale, ran around the wall of the Tabu's private party room, about two feet below the high ceiling. More elaborate than the sign in Times Square, the one in the Tabu Club's inner sanctum sported multicolored light bulbs to dramatize parts of the moving message. The sign read, IRISH LUCK, in green lights... CHRISTMAS IN AUGUST, in red lights... IT'S SNOWING PROFITS, in white. Pulsing in the large, indirectly lit, matte-black room, the lit-up marketing slogans mesmerized; the flashing phrases repeated themselves backward in the mirror behind the bar.

Viera had hired an Andean Mountain octet of *zampoñas* pipes, *bomba* drums, and guitar to play background music for the cocktail party. The musicians had shamrocks tucked in their hatbands. Waiters circulated through the small crowd, offering tall, thin glasses of champagne. Waitresses carried mirrored trays of caviar on toast and lines of coke. In the center of each tray stood a bud vase of shamrocks.

Monte helped Irish chat up the prospective new accounts from Chicago, Detroit, Houston, Los Angeles, Philadelphia, New Orleans, and Phoenix. All the drug lords and their assistants were Latins, and except for Dalia Diaz from Philadelphia, all were men. The men wore expensive, sharply cut silk suits; Diaz, a red lace cocktail dress. Viera admired her body but thought it would look better in a Carolina Herrera style. Well, he reminded himself, what he needed were good businesspeople who could dominate their markets by promoting and selling his material. If they were less than elegant, he could live with that.

The musicians played a fanfare and the guests turned around expectantly as Viera walked up the steps to a platform at one end of the room. The lights on the moving sign above him flashed off and on, and IRISH VIERA traveled around the room, repeated in green, red, and white. The company laughed and stamped.

"I'm not going to make any speeches," the host said in his lavaliere microphone. "Welcome to a long weekend in New York City as the guests of Irish Luck, a product that has no equal. A product with—flash." The moving lights pulsed excitedly once more and displayed the original messages once again. The host continued with the script that the expensive consultant had written for him. "Irish Luck will perform for you as brilliantly as our great stars this evening in the Tabu Club—Cheo Novente and Tonia Reyes!" Clapping and stamping. "Irish Luck can do the impossible." Now came the part the consultant said would blow their minds. "Do you believe it can snow in this town in August? Wait and see! Dance till dawn in the Tabu disco—I swear to you it will snow before the sun comes up. Enjoy yourselves and thank you again for being here."

One floor down, in the club dining room, the Tabu's maître d' escorted Viera's guests to their tables where handpicked dinner companions waited.

Monte went up the hidden stairs to the now-empty private room and found Viera at the mirrored bar, accepting a whiskey from a waiter. *"Fantástico!* You blew them away, boss. They never heard nothing like it."

"If I never see another microphone, that'll be soon enough." Viera held out his glass to the waiter for a refill.

"Believe me, boss. They're sold and they ain't even got to the *paella.* Come on—you got a place at La Dalia's table."

"Dios me ayude."

In the squad room, everybody was dressed up better than if they had to go to an affair at their in-laws, tugging furiously at the knots in their ties on the August night. Taylor had no complaints—he had conned Flynn into redesigning the whole operation so he, Taylor, would get to hear a Tonia Reyes set. "She's the queen bee of salsa," he crowed to anyone who would listen. "She released her *fiftieth* album this year."

"What name is our reservation under?" Flynn, preoccupied with logistics, wanted to know.

"Suarez," Taylor said.

"And how did you explain a stag party of seven on Saturday night?" Taylor and Reynolds, Pastore, Urquhart, and Mazocek, plus the two bosses, would do tonight's canvass at the Tabu.

"I said we stayed in town for the weekend to work on a crash project; we're just taking a break to hear Tonia. I told 'em to give us a table for four, the other three can sit at the bar. Otherwise I figured we'd attract attention."

"Right," Flynn said, "and we can spread out around the room faster if we're not all sitting in one place."

"What business are we in?" Carlucci asked. He had volunteered to come and help supervise.

"Contabilidad—accounting. Oh, I forgot to tell you, Billy and I parked the Chrysler and the Thunderbird around the corner there on Nine-seven, so we got the return trip covered."

"Your pal with the stretch limo gonna be on time?"

Taylor looked at his watch, "Twenty-two forty-five—he's probably—" At that precise moment, a rookie uniformed cop walked into the squad room, looking a little dazed. "Which one is Cinderella?" he said. "Your pumpkin's takin' up the whole fuckin' front of the house."

"Who're you?" Reynolds said. "The wicked stepmother?" The rookie retreated.

Flynn issued a flashlight reminder: "There's no candles on the tables in there." As the men went through the swinging doors, Cooch handed out ID pictures of Juan Rosa, the homicide victim.

Cooch had escorted his dress-buyer wife to many garment-industry functions over the years, always in fashionable places. He was familiar with the best of them, but he was still dazzled by the richly done-up Tabu Club. With its sleek, glossy interior, it compared to some of the best places in town. Black lacquer panels, bronze lighting fixtures, rosewood bar...as Cooch genteelly sipped his glass of Spanish champagne, he scribbled numbers on a napkin, trying to come up with a dollar amount that he thought would cover the cost of putting together such a place. As he took care to point out to Flynn and Taylor, the crowd included quite a few expensive dressers.

"Yeah, fancy dudes," Taylor agreed, "but a lot of 'em look to me like out-of-town fancy dudes. Oh, boy," he said, "here she comes!" The lights came up on the bandstand; Cheo, looking distinguished and simpatico, led his all-stars into action and an exuberant Tonia Reyes in strapless blue satin zoomed up through a trapdoor in the floor to meet her cheering audience. She tossed her black hair, threw open her arms to embrace the crowd, and began to sing.

After the encore, as waiters moved about the room, collecting orders for fresh drinks, Flynn and his men also fanned out among the tables. Courteous and attentive though they were, nobody could mistake them for waiters. "Excuse me"—each detective would start by showing his badge—"sorry to interrupt—"

A bouncer stationed near the bar noticed the cops first and headed toward Viera's table.

Next, the detective would pocket his badge and shine his flashlight beam on the picture of Rosa. "Maybe you know this man, Juan Rosa. He was here in the club a week ago, but now he's missing. We're trying to find out what happened to him..." "We're looking for this man—he was here last Saturday night, have you seen him since? Thank you; enjoy your evening." If no one at a table understood English, the detective would call Taylor and he would do the spiel in Spanish.

As the bouncer approached Viera's table, Dalia Diaz was whispering flirtatiously to her host. The bouncer stood between Monte's chair and Viera's. "Boss—" Dalia's assistant looked up. The bouncer was too big not to be noticed, but Viera chose not to respond. The bouncer looked at Monte, who shrugged helplessly.

"Boss, uh..." The bouncer cleared his throat.

Viera waved as if there were a fly near his left shoulder and kept his attention fixed on his potential Philadelphia market. The bouncer appealed to Monte, who glanced around the room and abruptly stood up.

As the detectives approached a table, customers would put their heads together over the picture of Rosa, look at one another, and murmur, *No, no conozco*—sorry—and go back to their conversations. The fancy out-of-towners acted jumpy and hostile, while the New Yorkers took the detectives' visit in stride.

By the time Monte got Viera's ear, most of the detectives were moving to their second table. Viera stood. "All right, stay here with our guests," he told Monte. "I'll take care of it"—he put a hand on Dalia's shoulder and smiled down at her—"and be back before you know it."

Flynn was a few tables away, showing something to Figueroa, the new account from Detroit, and Figueroa's assistant. Viera watched as the men eyed the cop suspiciously and heard them tell Flynn that they were not from New York and couldn't possibly know the man in the picture. Viera stepped up, apologized to his guests for the disturbance, and recited a little commercial for the Tabu disco. He urged them to discover the unique environment—unlike any other dancing scene in New York—as he shooed them off with their companions toward the disco entrance.

Viera reached for the photo that Figueroa had hastily dropped on the table and made a show of studying it as he snarled at Flynn in a low voice, "What the fuck do you think you're doing?"

"The same thing I was doin' last time we got together—investigating a homicide. We didn't get any leads from your staff that day—which seemed strange. The victim sat in your club for a couple of hours, at least, and the service here is attentive—somebody must have brought him a drink. But"—Flynn sighed—"since nobody on the staff remembers him, the next step is to ask the customers."

"You don't have a warrant."

"I don't need one—there's no search. This is an investigation, not a raid."

Viera watched six detectives lean down to talk to people at tables scattered throughout the room—in full view of Irish Luck's new accounts from out of town. Dalia Diaz bit her full, red lip and glared at her assistant, who waved his hands as he pleaded with her in rapid Spanish. Monte tried to distract her with the offer of a tall, frothy piña colada.

"I only hope we learn something tonight," Flynn told Viera, "otherwise we'll just have to keep comin' back till we get a break."

"What you're doing is nothing but harassment—unjustified interference with my business. I strongly advise you to stop."

"What I'm doing is investigating a homicide; I would be neglectin' my duty if I stopped."

"Believe me, you'll stop."

"When we arrest the killer."

Sunday, August 18, 1985

Viera faced a double challenge: to rid the visitors' minds of the police image, while at the same time keeping them out of reach of Luzan and other competitors. Instead of spending this warm, windy Sunday racing his catamaran, *Irish Luck,* on Long Island Sound, Viera accompanied his guests and their expensive escorts as they circled Manhattan in a luxurious rented yacht at a lazy five knots an hour. The cruise featured a lavish Caribbean buffet—and great music, of course. Viera even went so far as to invite La Dalia to dance a nostalgic cha-cha or two.

In this carefully planned setting, the genial host made the most of his time and his captive audience. He explained to Diaz and Figueroa and others who asked that the cops' visit was routine. "Their bosses order them to harass us now and then, so even though they never find anything, they show up and go through the motions." The guests, seduced by Viera's extravagant hospitality and the Manhattan views sliding hypnotically by, accepted his story. "But I don't get uptight," Viera went on, "so the cops have no excuse to get violent." He boasted about his long-held policy of avoiding open war with the police. *"Discretion...,"* he counseled the group of new accounts seated around him on the yacht's aft deck, "covert action with no witnesses. That's the way to go; it always works for me."

Monday morning, August 19, 1985

Viera wanted to send signals of outrage, not panic, to City Councilman Oscar Rafael. Calling the politician at his City Hall office on Monday morning meant Viera's getting to the Tabu Club at an hour when he usually was still in bed. A small sacrifice, considering the ultimate goal. When the dispatcher at Luna Car Service heard his voice at eleven A.M., she nearly fell off her chair.

Traveling in the car from his Riverdale apartment, Viera went over the wrap-up message he would deliver to the new accounts at the grand finale luncheon that afternoon. He would say just enough to close the sale. Then Monte would collect a signed letter of agreement from each new account, and the precedent-making three-day meeting would close with champagne toasts in honor of Irish Luck.

Comfortable despite the early hour in his leather chair behind the black marble slab, Viera pressed the two-digit speed-call number for Oscar Rafael's office—the discreet first step in his strategy for dealing with Lieutenant Flynn.

Viera, the Latin music mogul and campaign contributor, traded complaints with Rafael, the politician, about the New York August heat. "How come you haven't wandered in here, where it's air-conditioned every night," Viera said, "and the *music* is hot!" He raved about the top talent booked into the club all summer. "You missed Tonia and Cheo on Saturday. Come to think of it, if you'd been here, you'd know what I'm about to tell you. Strange as it might sound, Oscar, we're having a problem with police harassment. Somebody in the precinct must have it in for the Tabu. Sorry to say this, but they don't seem to appreciate a Hispanic-owned business making it big like we have."

"What happened?" Rafael asked. "What's the story?"

"The detective lieutenant over there—the name is *Flynn*—came by my office last week and told me they had a homicide under investigation and they believe the victim spent the evening at the club before getting killed. On that basis, I said okay, you can talk to the staff. Well, naturally the staff doesn't know anything, so the next thing—he shows up here in the middle of Saturday night with ten detectives! Shoving a picture of the homicide victim under my *customers'* noses, looking for who-knows-what. To top it all off, he threatened to keep coming *back* if he didn't get what he wanted on Saturday."

"Did he get what he wanted?"

"He hasn't favored me with the results—big surprise. Now, as you of all people know, Oscar, these blocks around here are coming up fast. When we moved in seven years ago, we did market surveys—this area was sixty-five, seventy percent Hispanic. Am I right?"

"Very much so."

"Well, the whites are pushing uptown, of course, and now they're the majority. The Tabu hasn't been affected because we draw from all over the city. Whoever thought they could gentrify us out of here finally woke up—it'll never happen; so they're looking to work another angle. The police. And I'd say they knew what they were doing with Flynn and his bunch. My customers were very shook up at the way they were treated—verbally. Under the circumstances, the cops couldn't very well get physical. The house was full of well-dressed, well-behaved people. So let's put it this way, they did psychological damage—a quiet outrage. But I don't intend to *keep* it quiet."

"Now, Irish," Oscar said, "you've got a right to be angry. Your place is a boon to the community, as any fool can see. You deserve TLC from the police, not harassment. But let me handle it my way. I'll talk to my contact at headquarters, and when the word gets around, you'll see results. If I was you, I wouldn't go public with this. You could get a pretty vocal backlash from the propolice element—they might even encourage this guy..."

"Flynn."

"Yeah, I just wrote it down: Flynn. We'll be better off going through channels on this one. Low profile—know what I mean? You have my word it'll be effective. Okay?"

"You know what you're doing, obviously. You got the ball—

run with it. I'm satisfied. Now, when are you and Francine gonna be my guests? Tell you what. I'll send you the talent calendar by messenger. Red carpet for you at the Tabu. Just say when."

"Fabulous! Francine will be thrilled. See you soon."

Monday afternoon, August 19, 1985

As usual, Flynn sat with his men in the squad room, not in the bosses' office. The phones jangled, one after another.

"Lieutenant," Taylor said, covering the mouthpiece of the one that had rung last, "it's your favorite stool—Salsa." Flynn signaled "keep him talking" and cut short his first conversation. He handed the second phone to Taylor, who passed him the third phone with Salsa on it.

Salsa wanted to know what had happened to Rico. "Nothing good. He stood in a lineup and we got a positive ID."

"Is he arraigned?"

"You bet, and he's got a new address—Rikers Island, bail denied. So no more roofs for Rico anytime soon. I took Carmel out to lunch and told her I'm keepin' an eye on you—I said you're flying' right, just like the DA told you."

"Ain't you workin' on another one now?" Salsa fished.

"Another homicide? 'Fraid so. We been by the Tabu a couple of times. How come we never run into you over there?"

"I'm in and out. Like the captain."

"You got an office, too?"

"I'm gettin' a fancy one—but right now I got a *travelin'* office, and wherever I end up, my eyes are *open.* The locker room, the pantry, the wine cellar... I'm watchin' different places and rappin' with different people."

"Been rappin' about a customer who left the club in bad condition?"

"Right."

"Want to come up or meet me by the church?"

"Now?"

"Yeah."

"I'll be up."

"See you soon, pal."

Flynn and Taylor hung up at the same time. *"Nu?"* Taylor had adopted bits of Franco Levy's Yiddish.

"Sounds like Salsa might have somethin' on the dump job. He's coming by."

"Listen, I like the kid," Taylor said, "but if I was you, I'd watch it. I don't trust him half as far as I could throw him. His sister tried playin' it cute with you, didn't she? Like sister, like brother."

"He gave us Rico. That was worth plenty."

"To him, too—right? What's he got this time?"

"We'll see. We don't wanna jump to any conclusions either way. I must say I'd love to turn him loose on Frostbite and watch him produce."

"Oh, not jumping to conclusions, huh?"

"No. Wishful thinking."

When Cooch came on for the four-to-one tour, he carefully hung his smartly tailored summer-weight blazer from a wooden hanger on the metal hat rack and went straight to his IN box. He pawed through the papers like a burglar rummaging in a dresser drawer full of costume jewelry.

Not even stopping to roll up his shirtsleeves, he marched to the locker room where metal doors banged as A Team got ready to go home. He stood in the middle of the room perspiring and, without preliminaries, started to bellow. "I got no paper—not one fucking report from anybody—on this Rosa case. The fuckin' dump job. Bad enough we get socked with this fuckin' mystery, but I got an empty file. Pastore, Urquhart, Mazocek—you was either at the scene or on the canvasses or both. What the fuck is with you guys? I'm tellin' you right now, nobody from A Team is swingin' outta here tomorrow for two carefree days unless I got my paper. And where the hell is that space cadet, Reynolds—the 'homicide specialist'?" Cooch stalked out.

"Marty," said Flynn when Cooch reappeared in the bosses' office, "I got a report for you. Should make you feel a lot cooler."

"Oh, yeah?" Cooch put Flynn's pink Detective Division form in front of him on the desk and rolled up his sleeves as he read.

On Aug. 19, 1985, at 1330 hours, Flynn had typed, *a person known to this department reported to the undersigned at the 29th Precinct Detective Squad facts relevant to the investigation of case no. 12442/2066, homicide of Juan Rosa. Informant, employed part-time at the Tabu Club, Columbus Ave. and 98th St., states that he had a conversation with the night porter of the club, Angel Nieves, in the locker room of the facility in the early hours of Fri., Aug. 16, 1985. He further states that the night porter nervously told him that shortly before leaving work at 0600 on Sun., Aug. 11,*

1985, he [the porter] assisted another club employee named Luis Almonte (aka Monte), in removing from club premises an MH victim of bleeding gunshot wound(s) to the chest. Nieves said victim was wearing light blue suit. Informant attempted to console Nieves by saying, "It's okay, you *didn't shoot the guy." However, Nieves said he was nervous because when questioned during a police canvass, he had not been forthcoming. The conversation between informant and Nieves took place in Spanish. A formal statement signed by informant is attached.*

Cooch flipped to the statement, scanned it, and looked at Flynn. "Nice break, Andy. I ran into your stoolie as I came in the house—dancin' down the steps, lookin' very pleased with himself. I figured somethin' was up."

Flynn frowned. "He better calm down before somebody at the club looks at him funny."

Cooch looked at the statement again. "What's this here Manhattan Avenue address? I thought the kid was squattin'."

"He took a room, so he has 'someplace to clean up.' Says he has to look good now because Irish promoted him for gettin' Rico locked up. By the way, he says Irish and Luzan are definitely splitsville, like we figured."

Taylor was leaning on the doorjamb. "What'd he get promoted *to?* And did you tell him we'd be headed over that way? I hope to hell we don't run into him."

"You can bet I didn't ask what his new title is—just told him to watch his step and keep his eyes open. And I didn't say we'd be over, but he can add two and two. If we do run into him—well, they know he knows us."

"Yeah, but they don't know what he's done for us lately, at least I hope they don't."

"What's all this hope all of a sudden? I know you all these years, Jesse, and I never knew you had the word *hope* in your vocabulary."

"I don't. I just ripped it off of yours."

"On you it looks good, as O'Levy would say."

Cooch's paperwork covered his oversize gray metal desk. "Marty, pack it in," Flynn said. "The Tabu party is leaving: myself, you, Taylor, and Obie. It's T minus ten—Señor Almonte's gonna be on the road if we don't get there soon."

Ramón picked up the intercom and pushed the button. When the bartender hung up and looked around for someone to escort the four detectives downstairs, Flynn thought he saw a figure move in a doorway at the far end of the dining room. Finally, Ramón left the maître d' hovering by the phone and took the cops down himself.

"You're early," Viera said to Flynn. "We don't have any customers yet, for you to hassle."

Flynn stood in front of Viera's desk and introduced the other three cops, who posted themselves between Monte's sling chair and the office door. "No canvass tonight, Irish. We're makin' progress."

"Wonderful. I assume that means you'll soon be leaving us in peace."

"As soon as we do what we gotta do. To bring you up to date: The victim's brother had it right—Rosa did spend his last night here. He must've enjoyed himself up to a point; he ate well and stayed late. Unfortunately, however, he left the club in approximately the same shape we found him in—two bullet wounds to the left chest. We learned he was escorted out of here by Mr. Almonte." Flynn nodded at Monte, whose facial expression read, "Fuckin' copper." Viera's hand strayed toward the panel of telephone buttons set into the black marble. Cooch, the gadget freak, had spotted the phone setup; he stared at it, fascinated. "So, with a half hour of Monte's time at the precinct," Flynn concluded politely but firmly, "I think we can move right along."

Viera put on his headset and pushed two buttons for a speed call. Cooch nudged Obie, who made a naive, "just-gimme-a-good-ole-rotary-dial" face.

"Yeah, Stanley—it's Viera. Look, I got some precinct cops in my office, investigating a homicide. They found this body across town and they're trying to tell me the shooting happened at the club. In fact, they're looking to pick up Monte for questioning. Talk to them, will you. I'm putting the speaker on so you'll come in loud and clear."

"Stanley Britton, Mr. Viera's attorney," said the hollow-sounding voice. "Who'm I speaking to?"

"Lieutenant Flynn, Two-nine Precinct squad commander; Sergeant Carlucci, Detectives O'Brien and Taylor."

"Look, Flynn, lemme get right to the point—are you looking to *arrest* Luis Almonte and if so for what?"

"Not at all, Counselor. We just want to clarify the circumstances under which Mr. Almonte escorted the wounded victim from the club. We're sure he can shed some light on this—and then we can move forward and not bother the Tabu folks anymore."

"Even if Mr. Almonte did what you claim he did, which we don't concede, he's a busy man. Right, Monte?"

"Around the clock."

"Got time to go to the precinct for a chat?"

"Not this year."

"Unless you're prepared to arrest Luis Almonte here and now, forget it," Britton snapped. "As you well know, no citizen is obligated to undergo police questioning. The law says that's completely voluntary. So, Lieutenant Flynn, *case closed.*" The lawyer didn't pause for a response. "Irish, does that do it for tonight?"

"Case closed. Get back to me on those contracts I sent you this afternoon, will you? Thanks a lot."

"Okay. *De nada.*"

Viera punched the button to hang up. "What I love about my adopted country"—he looked at Flynn—"is that we citizens have rights. Where I come from, people are at the mercy of our governments. A cop says 'jump' and we jump, or face the consequences. Here, our government's laws protect us from injustice. Don't they?"

"With or without Monte's cooperation, we're gonna get our man—that's the American way, too."

As the detectives filed out, Cooch brought up the rear. Viera saw him eyeballing the built-in telephone. "Glad you like it, Sergeant, I designed it myself."

Silence in the Chrysler as Obie drove it to the precinct. Finally Obie spoke over his shoulder to Flynn, "Let the bugger think he won that round. His guard will be down and we can—"

"Move right in," Flynn agreed.

"That's the spirit, Lieu."

"You see, Obie—what would we do if you put your papers in?" Flynn didn't pause for an answer. "Maybe it's a long shot," he said, "but tomorrow morning, we're takin' apart that night porter's locker. Do I hear any objections?"

Obie dropped off Flynn and Taylor at the precinct and went straight downtown to the district attorney's office at 1 Hogan Place with Cooch. They scared up a DA who was working late and persuaded her to write up a search warrant.

Tuesday, August 20, 1985

Double-parked on Ninety-seventh Street, Urquhart and Mazocek observed through a light drizzle the back entrance of the Tabu

Club. The first employee came along the side street at about 1200 hours, heading for the concrete ramp. But the detectives moved out and intercepted the assistant chef, each taking one of his arms, hustling him down to the door.

The assistant better show them the right locker, they made clear, or they'd pry open every fuckin' one. By 1300, they had vouchered a blood-stained, gray twill workshirt with ANGEL embroidered on the pocket and delivered the shirt to the police lab for blood analysis.

Urquhart would be swinging out the next afternoon; Obie said he would watch the mail for the blood report.

Thursday morning, August 22, 1985

The sun would be up by the time Angel Nieves came out of the Tabu. Nieves would probably leave through the back-alley ramp to Ninety-seventh Street, but Flynn couldn't take any chances; he had to cover the club's front entrance, too. Because of the early hour, everybody working this morning was on overtime, including O'Levy. Flynn had called him and his partner because they hadn't been on the Tabu canvass; the club staff might not make them. O'Levy couldn't believe that for once he was in on something major—until Flynn gave him and his partner their assignment: cover the front entrance. "Oy," O'Levy muttered, "always a bridesmaid."

Flynn, Taylor, Urquhart, and Cooch prepared to waylay Nieves. They approached the rear of the Tabu by cutting through the landscaped grounds of Parkton, a luxury housing development that backed up on the club. In daylight, the detectives would be able to see right down the concrete ramp to the service door. But they themselves would be just as visible to anyone who happened to come out. The nearest trees on Parkton's grounds were too far away to use for cover.

Cooch hastily cast about for another option but had to admit that Flynn's idea was the only workable one: He and Taylor would stand on either side of the alley where it gave on Ninety-seventh Street; Cooch and Urquhart would wait across the street at the apex of the triangle, in case Nieves bolted in that direction. Flynn realized he hadn't ordered his men to wear bulletproof vests—what if Monte should come out the back way?

* * *

"Amigo," Taylor said softly as Nieves got to the top of the ramp, "relax. Don't worry." The guy saw four cops and started to shiver in the balmy morning air. Nieves was so slight, it was a wonder he could even pick up the big metal garbage cans. He looked as if he was pushing age fifty and had not led a real easy life to date. Cooch crossed the street and got into the Thunderbird's backseat. Taylor had his hand on Nieves's shoulder. "Take it easy. Sit in back with me. You're safe, *entiendes?*"

"What did I do?"

"Nada. Don't worry, Angel."

Flynn drove a detour of several blocks so he could come back down Columbus, honking for O'Levy and his partner to signal the end of their assignment.

Nieves still hadn't stopped shivering when they got him up to the squad room. Flynn brought him a cup of black coffee in the captain's office. *"Con leche?"* Taylor asked.

"Sí, por favor." Flynn went back to the coffee room and brought the milk carton.

"Solamente uno problema," Taylor began, once the witness had gulped down some coffee. Flynn took a supermarket bag off the top of the file cabinet, pulled out the gray workshirt, and held it up. He pointed to the blood and shook his head, the hazel eyes looking gravely into Nieves's dark ones.

"We know whose blood this is," Taylor assured the Tabu's night porter. "And we got a good idea about the rest of the story. You tell us, and you're in the clear—even though you lied when we asked you at the club. Nothing will happen to you. *Who shot the customer, Angel?*"

"No sé."

"His blood is on *your* shirt," Flynn said.

"I don't shoot."

"You helped Monte take the guy outside—that's criminal solicitation."

Angel's shivers came back.

"You scared of Irish and Monte?" Mazocek asked.

The shivers got worse.

"Look, if you have the information we need, you'll be protected as a material witness. We'll put you someplace safe, in another borough. With a guard. Right, boss?" Taylor looked at Flynn.

"Right."

Disbelief deepened every line in Nieves's pale face. Taylor got up and took a legal pad and a ballpoint pen from the captain's desk. "We're gonna write down that if you help us, the government will protect you. We'll sign it—myself and my boss." Taylor wrote it out in Spanish and English; he and Flynn signed both versions. Flynn yelled for O'Levy, who took the papers upstairs and came back with photocopies. Rather than return to the squad room, O'Levy lounged in the office doorway.

Nieves read over what Taylor had written. He rubbed his face wearily and crossed himself. "A friend," he blurted, "a friend was shooting."

"Your friend?" Taylor frowned.

"Friend of Irish," Nieves whispered, "not from New York."

"Spanish guy?"

"Sí."

"Did you see him?"

"Sí."

"Why did he shoot? An argument?"

Nieves nodded.

"They argued about drugs?"

Nieves crossed himself again. "No drugs. Music. The friend and the guy in the blue suit argue about *music.*"

O'Levy, standing in the doorway, rolled his eyes.

"Big argument—the waiters talk about it."

"You heard the argument?"

"No—only the waiters."

"Where did the shooting happen?"

"No sé."

"What did the waiters say?"

"The friend follows the guy in the blue suit downstairs."

"Where did you and Monte go get the guy in the blue suit?"

"Downstairs."

"Downstairs where?"

"Señores."

Flynn looked at Taylor. "No wonder nobody saw the job. It went down in the men's room."

"Exacto."

"Irish's luck."

Thursday afternoon, August 22, 1985

Like a cardsharp, Taylor fanned out the batch of car-service call slips and riffled their edges. "Now any of these four *could* be our guy," he said to Flynn, "but this one here was a Waldorf round-trip. Apparently, the Tabu usually calls El Exigente service, not Luna, when a customer decides he wants to ride a limo home. Anyway, the chauffeur dropped this fare at the Waldorf at oh six-ten hours. Whoever wrote this thing has a handwriting worse than mine, but the passenger name starts with *I,* so it shouldn't be that tough to find."

"It'll come right up on the Waldorf computer," Flynn said.

"Freddy counted—two hundred and thirty-six slips we went through. And that was just Manhattan. El Exigente's got some fuckin' big fleet." Taylor shuffled the slips. "The aces was either on the bottom of Freddy's deck or the bottom of mine. Where else?"

Flynn knew that without Freddy, all would probably have been lost. Taylor hated nothing so much as a paper chase, whereas Freddy relished such jobs the way Obie did. Nothing in detective work fazed Obie; like most first-graders, he was solid as a rock and no fireworks. In time, Freddy would turn out to be another Obie.

The boss at El Exigente Car Service, Ralph Delgado, had only allowed a detective in the door because Taylor's friend the limo driver vouched for him. Taylor's friend was no longer driving for Delgado, but that was not a problem. The problem had come up when Delgado saw Freddy; Taylor had to lecture for twenty minutes on the sterling character and trustworthiness of the gringo detective before Delgado had let the two of them get started on the call slips. They'd examined every slip from Saturday, August 10, the night of Blue Polyester's demise, to noon Sunday.

"El Exigente had four calls takin' Hispos from the Tabu to the Waldorf that night; and one from the Tabu to the Omni."

"Irish's friends don't stay at the Omni," Flynn said with finality.

Friday, August 23, 1985

"You comin' on this Waldorf paper chase," Flynn asked Taylor over coffee, "or you got better things to do?"

"Who, me? Pass up Salsa's favorite hotel?" Taylor's enthusiasm surprised Flynn. "It's been a while since I was over there."

"I think they're doin' some heavy-duty renovating right now, puttin' back the original twenties stuff."

"Twenties in, sixties out, I bet."

"Now that you mention it, that'd be right up O'Levy's alley.

He's workin' days." Flynn started to go to look at the log to get an idea of O'Levy's whereabouts.

"Franco's tied up, Lieutenant Flynn," said Betty, the police administrative aide. "Before they went home yesterday, the sergeant handed him and his partner a whole bunch of closed burglary cases; told Franco to reopen them."

Taylor chuckled. "O'Levy's day may come, but it hasn't yet."

"Don't laugh," Flynn said. "When we got 'invited' to Community Council board meeting the other night, a rich old lady from West End read us the riot act about how the detectives don't come out and investigate burglaries over there. Cooch did a whole number—calmed her down, told her he'd personally take care of it and report back—"

"Would this be the kind of rich old lady who'd put a hardworkin' detective sergeant in her will?"

"I wouldn't put it past the Cooch."

"So if Levy's not available to go to the Waldorf, Urquhart's on his swing, who are we gonna take?"

"Where's Reynolds, Betty?"

She looked at her watch. "He should be back any minute. He said he was going across town for an hour."

Flynn knew that Reynolds's next-best haunt—after F. X. Flynn's and one or two other favorite bars and the bedrooms of his five best girlfriends—was the steam room at the East Side Y. Even in the summer, he loved going there. Sometimes he overheard stockmarket tips in the steam room, and he had once graciously passed one on to Cooch; the tip didn't pan out, though, and it didn't improve the Carlucci-Reynolds relationship at all.

"Well," Flynn said, "one of our young fashion heads would be a real help on this gig, but it looks like we're on our own, Jesse. Straighten that tie." As usual, Taylor wasn't wearing a tie.

The Chrysler had just rolled out of the precinct parking lot and paused for traffic when Reynolds sprinted around the corner. He popped into the backseat, but not before Flynn noted his lack of tie. "I don't know what the problem is with you guys—it ain't even that hot today. You can never tell what'll come up on a high-class job like this. Someday the mayor's gonna walk in the squad and your commanding officer is gonna have to explain all you tieless wonders. Sergeant Carlucci will be busy with some urgent paperwork. I can see us all now—back in the bag. That'll solve the tie problem, all right. Any color you want, as long as it's NYPD black."

"We're goin' to the East Side anyway," Reynolds cajoled his fuming boss, "we could stop by my place for a minute."

"Good thinkin', Billy. The steam must've cleared your head."

Reynolds came out of his towering red-brick apartment house wearing a blue-and-white-striped seersucker suit, blue shirt, and Madras tie. Flynn said Reynolds must've gone shopping with Urquhart at preppy headquarters. Taylor had borrowed a white shirt and solid-green tie. The shirt strained a little over the gut, but if the tie stayed in place, he could get away with it. Reynolds had also supplied him with a dark-green corduroy jacket that was definitely too small; Taylor left it folded on the front seat between himself and Flynn.

Like most cops, Flynn always got a little bit of satisfaction out of driving up to a fancy hotel, stopping just past where the taxis pull up, slapping his police ID on the dashboard, and breezing through the polished-metal revolving doors.

Taylor flipped Reynolds's green jacket over his shoulder as casually as possible, a gesture that displaced the carefully positioned tie. "I'm gonna look around," he said. "If you need me, check over by Peacock Alley in twenty minutes."

"The day manager?" said the tall female clerk with the curtain of straight blond hair and the sharp nose. "That would be Mr. Hasp. Did you have an appointment?"

"A police matter." Flynn showed his badge. "Just came up. But we won't keep him long."

"Who shall I say is calling?"

The tall blonde went away with Flynn's business card and returned with Mr. Hasp, who looked enough like her to be her father.

"How can I help, Lieutenant?" Hasp glanced curiously at Billy Reynolds's unpolicelike attire.

"Myself and Detective Reynolds are trying to locate one of your recent hotel guests; I could tell you in detail if we had some privacy."

Hasp sighed and led the detectives through a mahogany door and down a carpeted corridor to his office. Everything in the room except Hasp's walnut desk was light gray, including the couch that Flynn and Reynolds sat down on. Hasp's paperwork came in hard-edged stacks on the polished desk.

"Thanks for your time, Mr. Hasp," Flynn began. "Late on the night of August tenth, a Hispanic visitor got in some trouble—serious trouble—in a nightclub on the Upper West Side. In the early hours of the eleventh, several Hispanic customers of the club—four of them, to be exact—separately used a car service to come back to the Waldorf, where presumably they were guests. The visitor we're looking for should be one of those people. We'd simply like to search your computer in that time frame for those four names. Obviously, we're lookin' for the home addresses."

"Are these people Latin American?"

"They could be."

"If they are, doesn't that put them rather out of your jurisdiction?" Hasp objected.

"We have resources in other agencies that can assist us, when and if it becomes necessary."

"Frankly, Lieutenant, management hasn't forgotten the 'Waldorf Murder,' and all that negative publicity we had. My superiors don't want to hear about this kind of thing in any way, shape, or form. I'd have to suggest a subpoena."

Flynn and Reynolds looked at each other. "You're concerned about news coverage, down the line," Reynolds said, "when we make an arrest. Is that correct?"

"As I said, management's very touchy on the whole subject of crime and any connection with the hotel's name."

"We could lose a *lot* of valuable time getting a subpoena," Reynolds said.

"Which would seriously hinder a *homicide* investigation. But," Flynn pointed out, "the Waldorf would still be connected to the case. I'm the news source on the story, of course." He and Reynolds got up from the couch.

"Lieutenant," said Reynolds, like the voice of sweet reason, "if we didn't have to go the subpoena route, you could..."

Flynn frowned thoughtfully. "I could tell Public Information, as well as all the press people who ask me personally, that the suspect was stayin' at 'a midtown hotel.' That would be simpler for everybody, I think."

"Now that you mention it"—Hasp touched the knot of his Countess Mara tie—"I can see that it would. If I can arrange it, what time frame exactly would you like us to print out for you?" He held out his desk diary for Flynn to consult.

"Your checkout records show guests' addresses, don't they?"

"Yes, because that's the bill."

"Well, then I think the checkouts for August eleventh should do it. Our subject had to be eager to get out of town at that point."

"If you work on the records here in the hotel, we'll photocopy whatever you need," Hasp said. "You can use my conference room until eleven-thirty, when I have a meeting. Follow me, please."

In the mahogany-paneled conference room, Flynn looked at his watch. "Go find Jesse," he told Reynolds. "We only got an hour for this paper chase—besides, he's got the names."

Saturday morning, August 24, 1985

Some cops might grumble or sulk—when Franco O'Levy complained, he did it on a grand scale. He plunged an imaginary dagger into the upper-left side of his summer zoot-suit jacket. "The *Waldorf?*" he yelled. "Fucked again!"

"We went down there lookin' for Blue Polyester's perp," Flynn explained. He sat at his desk, making like a lieutenant for a change.

"Since when does a Waldorf guest do a homicide in the Two-nine, or was it a Waldorf employee?"

"Hold on a minute," Flynn said. "What's with all those West End burglaries? Under control?"

"When Sergeant Carlucci started reviewing the cases, he realized that there could be a pattern. Well, a residential specialist got paroled this month. We're showin' the doorman of each building a photo array with this guy's picture. Two doormen already picked him out, but we got a couple more to go. I'd say we're doin' good."

"What about the complainants? Cooch's pal, Mrs. What's-her-name and company?"

"Mrs. Berry. As it turns out, she wasn't burglarized herself—not a good target 'cause she's a widow, doesn't work, and she's home a lot. We most certainly dropped by to see her, though. She's the type of lady everyone says hello to in the supermarket, and she knows the whole fuckin' scene around West End in the low Hundreds. Mrs. B. heard about all these career-girl types gettin' broken into, and if there hadn't been that board meeting, she probably would've called Community Affairs. Hell, she would've called the precinct commander."

Flynn underlined his mental note: Tell Officer Parkin not to hesitate to call anytime the detectives might be helpful at Community Council.

"We also left messages on the answering machines of four

complainants. Should be hearin' something today—unless they all left for the beach."

"Not a bad bet for a career girl on an August Saturday, unless maybe she thinks she stands a chance of gettin' back her VCR."

"Ten to one this perp took his collection of VCRs to the fence long since. So speakin' of fences, are we closin' in on Blue Polyester's killer"—O'Levy finally got the conversation back where he wanted it—"or what?"

"We are if Nieves is right that the perp's from out of town. That night, the Tabu had four guests that took limos back to the Waldorf and one to the Omni. According to the Waldorf computer, one of their guests who went to the Tabu checked out at oh seven hundred hours—about forty-five minutes after the limo brought him back." Flynn showed O'Levy an ID photo lent by the Drug Enforcement Administration. "One Miguel Inoa, residing in San José Guaviare, Colombia."

O'Levy looked at the picture. "They don't have barbers in Colombia?" He fondled his own late-model crewcut. "Inoa's hair looks like something off a Doors album cover."

"He could afford a good barber—the DEA says he's married to the daughter of El Grande, one of those billionaire Colombian coke exporters. Inoa may be on the payroll as an enforcer."

"Who are the other Tabu customers from out of town?" O'Levy asked.

"Well-to-do Hispanic Americans from here and there. No arrests on any of 'em."

"No down-and-dirty music lovers, huh?"

"Willing to drop a couple of bills at the Tabu on a Saturday night, yeah," Flynn said, "but probably wouldn't kill over a music dispute."

"Shows a lack of true passion," O'Levy lamented. "I sure hope Nieves can tell one hairdo from another. How about I put together your photo array?" O'Levy quickly added, "It's too early yet to wake up our tired career girls on a Saturday morning."

Flynn had already sat behind his desk too long—and on a Saturday when he could have been at the gym working with Salsa. "I'll look at the picture file with you."

Flynn and O'Levy pulled out the narrow metal picture drawers and began thumbing through the hundreds of perps. You could lose a good cop, Flynn believed, if boredom really set in. The better the cop—the bright, aggressive types like O'Levy were the best—the more boredom could be a problem. He supposed that was also true in other kinds of work, but in other kinds of work you didn't wear a gun. "When Taylor gets here," he promised O'Levy, "we'll go see Angel."

"It ain't the Waldorf," Taylor said as Flynn and O'Levy followed him to the entrance of the modest residential hotel on East Eighty-sixth street, "but Angel more or less thinks it is. He was livin' in the Grantley before now."

"Hold on, Jesse," O'Levy yelled. He dashed into the luncheonette next to the hotel and came back with the take-out menu. "A person could faint if you show him a bunch of bandits like Inoa and his look-alikes on an empty stomach."

"You're right," Flynn said.

Nieves looked a little less pale and shivery than he had fifty or so hours earlier. He smiled shyly when Taylor offered him the menu and requested Breakfast #1: scrambled eggs with bacon, orange juice, toast, and coffee—regular.

O'Levy phoned in the order, adding coffees for the detectives.

"Qué tal?" Taylor asked the witness, while they waited for the delivery. Nieves occupied the narrow room's lone chair. Taylor sat on the edge of the single bed; Flynn and O'Levy stood, each leaning against a wall—something cops learned never to do in the roach-ridden Grantley, Nieves's former home.

Angel said that this hotel was quiet—no shootings like where he lives.

"You live alone? What about your family?" Flynn asked.

"Nadie," Angel said, "only cousins in Puerto Rico." Now he seemed upset again. Flynn sensed that Angel was on the point of asking about Viera and the Tabu when breakfast finally arrived.

As Angel spread his toast with grape jelly from a foil packet, Taylor explained why the detectives had come. If Angel saw a picture of the shooter, would Angel recognize him?

Angel nodded confidently between bites. *"Sí."*

With the windowshade drawn, the room was on the dark side, Flynn noticed. O'Levy flipped on the light switch, but one of the pair of bulbs in the overhead fixture had burnt out.

The small room was silent except for Angel's enthusiastic munching. From the official NYPD folder, six different faces, each in its own circular cutout with a number printed below, glowered at the Tabu Club's ex-porter. Two rows of three pictures, each row numbered across.

Angel switched the remaining triangle of toast from his right hand to his left, stared at the photo array for one more moment, and tapped his right index finger on the frowsy hairdo of number four. The detectives let out their breaths, clapping Angel on the back. They thanked him in Spanish and English and said they would be in touch.

Flynn stepped on the gas and the Chrysler sailed through the almost empty Central Park transverse. New York was manageable on a quiet summer Saturday. "Nice work, everybody. It's all over but the Wanted Card."

"Hopefully"—Flynn grinned at O'Levy in the rearview mirror—"your complainants are still waiting by the phone."

"Hopefully," O'Levy said, "there's somebody left at the gym for you to coach."

"Hopefully," Taylor said, "Estrelita won't divorce me if I get home in time to take her to the beach."

Flynn knew, and so did the others—but nobody felt like talking about it—that there was no chance of the Colombian government's extraditing Miguel Inoa for the murder of Juan Rosa. Without Inoa's arrest, the homicide would have to qualify for Exceptional Clearance. That would depend on the district attorney, who might or might not see it their way. Flynn was ready to pick up his gym bag from the squad office, hang up his tie, and head downtown.

Saturday afternoon, August 24, 1985

In the Flynns' divorce settlement, Tracy had demanded and got the white Chevy van she'd said a million times she wished Andy had never bought. Flynn was left with the subway, which took him from his crummy Hell's Kitchen apartment to work, almost door to door, in fifteen minutes. In winter you felt colder standing on the subway platform than on the street; in summer the heat and the racket of the trains added up to a fair approximation of hell. Before making the trip to the gym, Flynn decided to fortify himself first at the ice cream store on Broadway.

Steve's Ice Cream had a bigger crowd inside than Flynn had seen in one place anytime that day. While waiting his turn, he debated several flavors with himself, knowing all the time what the outcome would be.

"Next?" asked the chubby black girl in the red-and-white-striped apron.

"Rocky road. Double scoop, please."

All his concentration was on the cold mouthfuls to come.

"Is there anything symbolic about your choice, Lieutenant?"

The blonde in the white playsuit, aka the blonde in the red dress at the board meeting; she was taller than he'd thought then—about five foot six. Lauren Daniels. He wondered how long she'd been standing there.

"I never thought about the meaning of ice cream, ma'am, but now that you mention it, all cream and no crunch ain't too interesting." He hadn't said "ma'am" to anybody since he got out of uniform. "What flavor for you?"

"Peaches 'n' cream, thank you."

"Double?"

"Just one."

The chubby black girl was busy with someone else's order. "I'm not going to ask you about the meaning of your choice," Flynn said.

"I'll tell you anyway—ice cream should be sweeter and smoother than life."

The minute they stepped outside, their cones began to drip furiously, making them both giggle and slurp. "Could I interest you in a little Riverside Drive breeze?" he suggested.

"On one condition."

"Yes, ma'am?"

"Stop calling me ma'am!"

"Cops are a little old-fashioned, Ms. Daniels. Even today some rookies say 'ma'am.' "

"Well, you're no rookie—and I notice you didn't call Mrs. Berry ma'am. So old-fashioned courtesy isn't the motive."

Flynn found Lauren Daniels pretty, rather than beautiful. A West Side sort of look—casually put together, at least on this laid-back Saturday. He liked her light suntan; it didn't look worked on. "Okay, I plead guilty to mixed motives. I did want you to think I was a true-blue type of guy, but I admit I also wanted to bug you."

"Well, you succeeded," she said without clarification.

He slung his gym bag over his shoulder. As they walked west on Ninety-eighth Street, she commented on the nice renovation of a pair of reddish-stone buildings.

"Yeah," Flynn said, "I knew 'em when."

"When what?"

"When they were some of the worst SROs in the precinct. Seven floors of felons."

"What about the elderly who lived in those hotel rooms, and

the other people who just can't afford apartments? Where can those tenants go? You know, almost half of the West Side SROs that existed in 1960 have been converted into luxury housing—"

"That sounds about right. Because something like a third of the crime up here—minimum—comes outta the SROs. Close down those hotels, the crime rate takes a nosedive and the neighborhood improves. Another deal where overall, things get better but some individuals get screwed."

"I work in City Planning," she said. "The Commission doesn't know the answers, either."

"You're a planner?" he asked as they reached the Drive.

"Press secretary."

"If we go downtown a ways inside the park," he said as they reached the Drive, "we could walk by that crazy garden." The river breeze felt wonderful.

"A crazy garden? By all means."

"You don't know the park?"

"When someone says 'the park,' I think Central Park."

"Oh, I remember. You're on Nine-two between Columbus and Amsterdam. Heavy drug traffic. D'you know someone who was actually threatened? They should definitely get in touch with the precinct."

"I don't happen to know the people personally, but I heard about it from a reliable source. I gather they're scared to go to the police. Last I heard, they were trying to find another place—which is not a nice thing to hear about your neighbors. Makes you wonder if you should move, too."

"Look, once in a while it does happen that a witness is harmed, I can't deny it. And it's tragic. But it is rare—not including the bad guys who set each other up every day of the week. Do you think people should just turn their backs if they see a crime?"

"I don't know about 'should,' but I think it's the wiser course. I haven't been in the situation, so I'm not clear what I'd do myself."

"Follow the wiser course," he repeated, keeping his facial expression neutral.

"I said—I'm not sure what I'd do."

"Do you believe this garden?" he asked. Two beautiful garden plots lay ahead, interrupting the paved promenade. Each garden was fenced around by wrought iron and lovingly planted every which way.

"The mad gardener at work." They walked down one side and around. "I guess it's everyone for himself in there," she said.

"Now just try and find something relaxed like this on the *East* Side."

"Couldn't you?"

"I doubt it. Oh, for pete's sake!" She stopped dead. "I haven't seen any hollyhocks since I left my hometown."

"Which are they? I don't remember seein' any in the Bronx."

"Those big guys over there, with the floppy red blossoms. Nice comfy flowers to grow by a cottage door—as opposed to, say, gladiola that go right out of the ground into the back of a hearse."

Flynn pointed to a nearby section. "Aren't those wildflowers?"

"Mm-hm, black-eyed Susans. Maybe whoever planted them wanted a reminder of country fields."

"Your hometown is where?" he asked as they headed to the nearest park bench. They sat facing the garden, and beyond it, the Hudson River and the hazy New Jersey shoreline.

"In western Massachusetts. A perfect little New England picture." She snapped an imaginary shutter.

"Crime free?"

"Well, it's not Naked City. People do ugly things off in the woods instead of on rooftops."

"Or in nightclub bathrooms. That's the latest."

"The latest test of your best-in-the-city squad... what's that record Officer Parkin said you hold?"

"Homicide clearances. Clearance means arresting the perpetrator. If, for instance, thirty-two homicides occur in the precinct this year and we clear thirty-two—that's a perfect record."

She looked puzzled. "Well, but what about that old case, in the *News*—the Puerto Rican boy?"

"That counts toward this year's total—it's 'in the bank.' Say we had a double homicide last March and we don't solve it by the end of the year. Hopefully, we'll have cleared two old cases to make up the difference and give us our hundred percent." Sounds easy enough, Flynn thought.

"Fascinating." Resting her elbow on the top slat of the backrest, chin on hand, she looked at him. She wore her honey-blond hair in a loose bun on top of her head, wisps trailing on her neck. "I'd call that heroic accounting," she said, smiling. "It seems pretty damn enterprising compared to some of the civil servants I've run into. I can't imagine my post office branch striving for a hundred percent anything."

Flynn liked the brown-eyes/blond-hair combination. "Detective work defeats people with its weird combination of details and horrors," he said. "I figured it might help to set it up a little like a

sport: a team, a score, a shot at 'winning'—even if the odds are outrageous." He realized he had said more about his work to Lauren Daniels in fifteen minutes than he had to his wife in ten years.

"And does it help?"

"It helps lock up more murderers; it helps the men take pride in their work. They really push themselves and pull together—even when there's personality clashes."

"So you're on a winning streak." She smiled. "For how long?"

"The past two years."

"If the other side knew your reputation, they'd be running scared. But you're the best-kept secret in town. Who the hell's doing your PR? Fire them!"

" 'The other side?' " He laughed. "You must've heard that most victims know their killer. Well, that's true. So do you think if some lady was planning to put poison herbs in her husband's soup and she saw the squad on the six-o'clock news, she'd think twice?"

Lauren looked him straight in the eye. "I think there's a much better chance the herb lady—or *whoever* is on the other side—will think twice if she *does* hear about you, than if she doesn't. If the media had no effect on people, Lieutenant Flynn, would the brass be sitting on your squad's story?"

"Try 'Andy.' "

"Okay, and you try 'Lauren.' "

"Anyway, Lauren, the herb lady only wanted to do in her husband.... The pimp cut up his pross because he had enough of her holding out on him.... Nobody was after *us*. Not even the Mafia—too busy making a good living. We did what we had to do just like they did. But the whole scene is changing now on account of drugs. One of these days, we might be up against a real opponent."

"Sounds to me like 'one of these days' has arrived."

"Let's talk about one of these nights," Flynn heard himself saying. He smiled his half-smile. "One of these nights—we might have dinner."

Sunday afternoon, September 1, 1985

When Flynn called Lauren, she'd invited him to spend the day by the rooftop pool at her girlfriend's place in Battery Park City. They had drawn breezy, cloudy-bright weather, but even if Flynn couldn't see the sun, he could feel it and that was good enough. As they lay stretched out in their deck chairs, he savored Lauren's light tan and how great it looked with her simple black swimsuit. He liked the oval neckline showing a little cleavage. Her body's gentle curves captivated him, as did the honey-blond hair pulled up carelessly on top of her head and held there with bright-red combs.

"Wasn't it nice of everyone to disappear and leave all this just for us?" Lauren cupped her hand above her sunglasses and looked beyond the green-tiled expanse of terrace and the luxurious pool with its glass roof, to the end of Manhattan Island and the Statue of Liberty, a distant miniature in the harbor. Nothing other than a lone striped towel flung on a bench suggested that they could expect company.

Liberty Vistas. Good name, Flynn thought. "If anybody had told me I'd spend Labor Day Sunday forty floors up basking by a pool," he admitted, "I'd have said they needed help." What a relief to get to know her outdoors in this nice easy way instead of being cooped up in some restaurant. "You are a genius for thinking of this."

"We owe it all to Carroll. She knows I'd rather spend a holiday weekend in the city, especially if I can spend it in this paradise of hers."

"I'm better off far away on holidays," Flynn said. "A lot of our customers uptown don't have anywhere else to go—they're just hangin' around with all this time on their hands. They start to celebrate... next thing you know, somebody's dead. Back in '82, they had *two* Labor Day shootings in the precinct. Sorry, I didn't mean to get into that."

"I don't see how you could really avoid the subject. It has to stick in your mind. Not like..."

"Plumbing? Some people actually do think of it that way—nobody in my squad. We've got good detectives."

"Which means what, exactly, since I think you said Sherlock Holmes isn't in your squad?"

Flynn considered whether she was just looking for cocktail-party stuff; he thought maybe she really wanted to know. "Just average intelligence and education. You start out on a case lookin' for the obvious, easy answer—and a lot of times, that's it."

She looked startled.

"But if it ain't, then you gotta tackle the obscure and difficult. You can gather the facts, make good judgments? Great. But most of all, you gotta be sharp about people . . . get along with 'em. And be able to keep goin' when there's nothin' to go on. So—what about your job? You like it?"

"Small-town girl falls for the Big City, wants to see it look beautiful and *workable,* too. Well—good luck." She shook her head. "It's interesting, though, to watch what goes on. Imagine being able to actually create even a little piece of this." She waved her ringless hand at the cityscape. "Nobody has impact like architects and planners, but there are so many opposing forces. Fascinating—the power politics—till it starts getting to you. The wrong side usually wins."

"That part sounds familiar. What about dealing with the media?"

"More politics. My boss and *his* boss see to that. Everybody has an agenda to hype, but not everybody gets to hype it. It helps if your agenda happens to be on the mayor's agenda. Never a dull moment."

"Just what you really need for a little variety: a cop."

"You took the words right out of my mouth."

"Don't count on a TV show."

"No—I know what you're doing is real. And there's no . . . middleman."

"Middleman? Is this the commercial break?"

"I mean, there's nothing between you and the criminal, or the victim, is there? *You* are it. Your experience, your nerve—"

"Your backup and your gun."

"Aren't those also really parts of *you?*" Lauren swept up his additions in her argument. "The responsibility is all yours."

She really did seem interested. He let himself feel flattered by that. "The brass ain't about to let us forget that responsibility—much less the media or the lawyers," he reminded her.

She rushed on. "Say anytime there's a high wind, a bunch of

windows fall out of this building—maybe the architect gets sued. If a reporter messes up, the paper might get sued—not exactly fun. But if *you* make a bad mistake—it could be life or death then and there."

"It could," he said. "That's the job—"

"It must be strange to see what the media do with the stories of your life. You could end up seeing it *their* way, couldn't you?"

"You try like hell to make *them* see it your way.... I think I could use a swim about now. Can that pretty suit get wet?"

"As wet as yours can."

The pool, inside its glittering glass shell, looked as if it had just been photographed for the Liberty Vistas brochure. Flynn and Lauren sailed off the edge of the deck, bodies slicing into the water almost in sync. She rolled into a lazy sidestroke; he streaked away, his powerful crawl churning up foam. The city went by them soundlessly outside the glass; they heard only the swish of their bodies through the water. Lauren and Flynn passed each other, going opposite ways. When he caught her heel in his hand, she folded her body and plunged under the surface, pulling him with her. He let go and slid his hands lightly along the sides of her smooth legs to her hipbones. She flutter-kicked, moving toward him. His hands traveled up her torso, touching the hollows under her arms, slipping back down to her waist, bringing her close against him. He nibbled her face and neck, leaving a trail of little bubbles. Her fingers caressed his nape, then combed through the fine, straight black hair. He grabbed her hand and they shot to the surface, gasping and laughing and shaking the water out of their eyes.

Thursday night, September 5, 1985

Customers sat or stood three deep along F. X. Flynn's bar. Flynn's uncle Jack, the bartender, was tall enough to see over their heads, and Flynn knew he watched the door like a cop. Jack saw him come in and winked. All he had to say was, "Hey, make some elbow room for Andy, okay?" and the regulars moved right over. Anybody but Flynn would just have had to stand in the back row. Jack fussed over Flynn's tall glass of tonic water, swizzled it, and added the wedge of lime before setting it down with a flourish.

"Cheers," Flynn toasted his uncle, feeling pretty good. Thinking about it now, Flynn had to admit that Jack had grown into the bartender's job over the years, made it his own. Otherwise, the place really hadn't changed since Flynn's dad died. The new generation of customers looked a lot like their fathers, outwardly at least. And the fake-pine paneling that Francis Flynn had put up had turned out to be indestructible. You couldn't nail into it, so nothing hung on the walls, then or now.

Francis used to like to display his son's boxing cards by wedging them into the frame of the mirror behind the bar, but nowadays the only decoration was Christmas lights strung over the long bar—and not till after Thanksgiving. Flynn tried to put aside the thought of the holidays, the end of the year. One day at a time, he reminded himself. Things would come out okay for the squad, they would make it through.... He really wanted to stay in his good mood.

"How's it going, kid?"

"Nice, thanks."

"Oh, yeah?" Uncle Jack paused with a glass and a towel in his hands. "Like what?"

"Like a young lady." Flynn was surprised to hear himself saying this.

Uncle Jack went back to polishing the glass as if he didn't want to make too big a deal. "Ya don't say.... Lotsa fish in the sea, just gotta get out and do a little fishin', huh?"

"Well, if I *try* to meet someone, it's always a bust. I met Lauren by accident, right in the precinct. She gave me a rough time at a community meeting, but we got things straightened out since."

"Lauren! That's pretty; she ain't a cop?"

"Uh-uh, but she does work for the city."

"Doing?"

"Press secretary for City Planning."

Jack whistled. "Smart, huh? She got any kids or anything of that nature?"

"Not even a cat, far as I know."

"Sounds like just what the doctor ordered, Andy. Guess it was only a matter of time. Can't rush these things, can ya." He glanced down the bar at a line of empty and near-empty glasses. "Hold on, kid. The night is young, right?" He poured Flynn a quick refill and hurried off to attend to the others.

When Jack came back, he asked Flynn what was doing at the gym.

"We got a new recruit—maybe the next Macho Camacho. How d'ya like that!"

Several customers who heard Flynn's remark said, We sure could use some new blood, or words to that effect.

"Well, don't lay any bets till I tell you. Right now he's still just a Puerto Rican string bean from the precinct, but we're lookin' to give him some direction—I think I mentioned him to you, Jack. He goes by 'Salsa.'"

"That the one makes you think of Sean?"

"Yeah, he does sort of. . . ." Flynn knew that was true, but he allowed the knowledge to hover just under the surface of his thoughts. Coaching Salsa, he put all he had into the work and felt kind of bittersweet about it. He understood that this was his chance to heal the bruise that always ached when he thought of Sean.

"Well, how's he gettin' on?" Jack asked.

"Goin' to the boxing club regular and working hard. If he keeps it up, boxin' could be a good thing for Salsa. Teach him discipline, how to make the tough decisions."

Jack grinned at his nephew. "I remember"—he nodded at the mirror behind him—"how tickled your dad was when he pasted up your Golden Gloves cards over here. Hell, he had *all* the cards, startin' with your first PAL match."

Tuesday afternoon, September 10, 1985

Salsa exited the park at 110th Street, the sound of Mongo jumping in his earphones. He'd run two miles in fifteen minutes flat with no breeze at all to fan him. He jogged along Central Park West, slowing his pace bit by bit, trying to cool down. Sweat was still dripping off him when he got to the station house, zoomed up the three steps, and in the door.

The place seemed pretty quiet. A tall red-haired officer stood on the raised platform behind the desk. The officer hooked his thumbs in his gun belt and stared at Salsa's bare, sweaty chest and running shorts.

Salsa grinned up at him. "Hi Officer."

"Sergeant."

"Could I go see Lieutenant Flynn, please, Sergeant?"

The sergeant looked at his watch. "I don't know. For one

thing, he could be gone already. And if he's still here, he might not be takin' calls. Does he know you? What's your name?"

"Tell him Salsa's here."

"Oh, boy." The sergeant rolled his eyes and picked up the phone. "Yeah—the lieutenant still up there? I got a kid at the desk, wants to see him.... Who? Yeah, yeah—'Salsa'! How'd you know?" The sergeant shrugged. "Send him up?"

Salsa listened to Mongo while he waited for the outcome.

The sergeant hung up and pointed at the door to Salsa's left. "One flight up, Mr. Salsa, first door on your right."

"Qué tal?" Taylor came down the aisle between the row of desks and the offices off the side of the main room. He opened the gate and let Salsa in. "This what they're wearin' at the Tabu now?"

"Nothing' to do with the club. I'm workin' out," he boasted, "doin' my roadwork. I'm out there every other day, Detective Taylor. Just dropped by to see how you was doin', you and Lieutenant Flynn."

"Lieutenant," Taylor yelled, "somebody to see you. Says he's lookin' for a good trainer." He sat down at a back desk and started to type.

Flynn came out of the last office on the right. "Cup of coffee, Salsa? Soda? Have a seat, pal." Flynn went back into the office and reappeared with a couple of bottles of tonic. "It's kinda warm but it's wet."

"How come the captain don't have a refrigerator in that luxury suite?" Salsa waved toward the captain's room.

"You been hangin' at the Waldorf too long. Not even the PC has that."

"The who?"

"The police commissioner." Flynn sat down at the desk nearest a wooden bench where Salsa already lounged. Flynn raised the bottle of tonic and took a pull. "Here's to your welter-weight title!"

"All *right.*"

"How's the roadwork?"

"Man, I seen a lot of the park I never knew about at all. Sometimes I run over to the East Side and back. It's crowded in there, even in the middle of the afternoon. You gotta watch your step."

"Well, what's your time like?"

"About two miles in fifteen minutes." Salsa grinned.

"Gimme a break! Already? How many times a week?"

"Three—and then three times at the gym, maybe even four."

Salsa bounced to his feet and mimicked punching the speed bag, making Flynn laugh. Now that he had the cop's attention, he said, "You was over at the club lookin' for Monte. He was laughin' about that—but cursin' the porter. I thought you was just goin' after the porter. Didn't know you was gonna go bother Monte." Salsa leaned on the edge of the desk, next to Flynn's chair.

"When there's a murder, we investigate *whoever* looks like they're involved. If it bothers them, can't help that. But any information we get is confidential. The informant's got nothin' to worry about—as long as he keeps his own ass covered, too. No loose blabbin'! See?"

"I still thought you was just goin' after the porter."

"What we do with information people give us is whatever we *gotta* do to solve the case. That's what makes it so important for people to cooperate. Anything else you wanna ask?"

Salsa skipped little skip-rope skips without the rope. "Yeah."

"Shoot."

"When you goin' to the gym yourself, Lieutenant Flynn—haven't seen *you* at the boxin' club since that first day you brought me there." Now it was Salsa's gym and he was doing the inviting.

"How's Saturday sound?" Flynn suggested. "Three o'clock?"

"You got it."

Tuesday afternoon, September 17, 1985

Reynolds said you could almost see Pastore's albatross, the unsolved Frostbite case, weighing the guy down. Nobody was exactly happy about the situation, but Pastore was at the point where he lost sleep over it. Flynn had run out of investigative ploys; even Cooch had nothing left to suggest. Otherwise, though, things seemed to have quieted down and the squad was grateful for that. The men almost welcomed their daily quota of ho-hum aggravated harassments. Leave it to Flynn's boss, division commander Captain Joe Zachs, to stir up the pot a little. Flynn had just considered walking fifteen feet to the coffee room to refill his coffee mug when Zachs slipped through the swinging doors. The captain's trim figure could almost fit through the space *between* the doors. The detective brass didn't have door-filler physiques to compare with the patrol division.

"How ya' doin', Cap?"

Zachs nodded and disappeared into his office, having duly

noted Flynn's base of operations in the squad room instead of in the bosses' office.

Flynn wasn't expecting the captain today but he wasn't not expecting him either. When the squad had a heavy case, something with media appeal, the bosses would descend, Zachs first; otherwise, he made unscheduled appearances. Flynn checked his watch and went back to the reports he was reading. Experience had shown that the *Post* would keep Zachs busy for twenty minutes or so. When the captain did poke his head out, Flynn was deeply engrossed in his files.

"Lieutenant, when's the last time you saw the inside of a real office? Come on down here."

Lieutenant? Something was up. Flynn noticed that Zachs's face was a shade less ruddy than normal; from a distance, he could also see the icy gleam in his boss's eye. He got up and walked to the captain's office, only regretting the empty coffee mug he had left behind.

Zachs and Flynn were about the same height; Flynn had intended to use the standing-up tactic, but Zachs motioned him to the chair in front of the desk. "Now, this hundred percent homicide clearance, Andy, that's gonna look great on your gravestone, I know. But I got a problem with it—a couple of problems."

What else was new?

"I hope those was burglary cases you was so busy readin'. That stuff's not gettin' enough attention. Burglary is way up in this precinct and most of it's big-ticket stuff, outta West End Avenue apartments. You heard all the noise at Community Council. These people are influential—*up*scale—right?" He didn't wait for a response. "Don't think the new Deputy Inspector downstairs has been lettin' me forget it. So stop spinnin' your wheels on those homicides and get the fuckin' burglars, okay? Gimme some burglary collars—*good* collars, of course." Zachs sputtered to a halt.

"The West End stuff is a solo act, Cap, we know who it is. When we grab him, we'll let PI talk it up and the council will cool off." That should satisfy Zachs, provided he could make sure that Public Information handled it to his liking.

The captain only said, "*When* are you thinkin' of grabbing him?"

"We showed his photo to a couple of doormen who ID'd him; soon as we talk to a couple more, we'll sit on his mother's place and pick him up. Shouldn't be long now."

"Is he Hispanic?"

"Jamaican, why?"

"Lucky for you."

"How come?"

"You got enough troubles in the Hispanic department already without makin' a big deal out of collarin' some Cuban burglar."

"What troubles?"

"I happened to get a copy of a letter that Councilman Oscar Rafael wrote to the Chief of Detectives about you. Not *only* you: you and your entire command. Bear in mind that Rafael just won renomination and now he's gonna step up his crowd-pleasin' campaign in the Hispanic community. Meanwhile, according to him, you are harassing the Hispanic business community's pride and joy, their numero uno success story in the whole fuckin' city. Maybe you are even shakin' him down."

"Oh, sure, the Tabu: numero uno coke supplier and direct or indirect death dispenser to Hispanic youth from here to Midtown South—to put it conservatively. There's plenty to shake down all right."

"Assuming that's true, that would be Narcotics' problem, now wouldn't it?"

"You know it's true; so does the Chief of D and the rest of the department. But Narcotics can't nail Irish Viera, and everybody's looking the other way, that's all. What else is new?"

"Rafael don't see it like that."

"Wouldn't that make you wonder about Rafael? What's Viera and company doin' for him?"

"The Chief of D sent me Rafael's letter—am I supposed to wonder about the Chief, too? Get serious, Andy. You got a problem here and you better fuckin' watch your step. If push comes to shove, the Commissioner ain't gonna ignore a City Council member, and I'd say it'll come to that if you keep buggin' the customers in the Tabu."

"Just for the record, we had a *homicide* in the Tabu. But now that's out of the way—"

"What homicide? Oh, yeah—that dump job where the perp went bye-bye to Colombia. That don't do much for your hundred percent, does it?"

Flynn displayed a confidence he didn't feel. "Sure. The DA'll give us an EC on it. Why not? It's legit—we got what we need to go to court on Miguel Inoa tomorrow, but what are the chances Colombia's gonna extradite him?"

"Listen, I don't want my detectives spendin' weeks at the DA's office on some Exceptional Clearance—on top of all this manpower you're devotin' to *old* homicides. Oh, don't get me wrong—we can't have Dominican sharpshooters runnin' over the roofs mowin' down kids and gettin' away with it. Ya gotta lock up a guy like that sooner or later. Later if necessary, I guess. But ECs, that's another story. The victim's dead *and* the perp's dead; or in Colombia—same difference. So the only reason to work on ECs," Zachs pointed an accusing finger, "is to pump up your clearance numbers. One hundred percent *ego.* And P.S., I got three other precincts up here lookin' kinda pathetic, comparatively speakin'."

"I was gonna say, the team that doesn't win the series always does look sad." Flynn became aware of a ringing phone in the squad room; he heard Jesse take the call. "But Cap, maybe these fellas need a shot in the ego themselves—then they'd give us some competition."

"Forget competition, Andy. Keep in mind that we're just here to keep the peace, serve the public, and so on."

Flynn started to wonder aloud if locking up murderers really was a disservice to the public, but Taylor appeared in the office doorway.

"Levy just called from Amsterdam and Nine-two. He was headin' for the precinct to sign out when he heard the 10-85. Shoot-out in the middle of the fuckin' sidewalk—both shooters took off. Bystander shot; Levy's pretty sure he went DOA."

Flynn flashed on the coffee machine with its glass container full of fresh-brewed hot liquid ready to be poured. He sighed and automatically patted his suit jacket, making sure he had a notebook in the inside breast pocket. "Ready to roll, Jess?"

"All set. Cooch is ready, too."

"I'll call the Chief and follow you in a minute," Zachs said.

"See you there, Cap."

Flynn headed down the station house stairs with Cooch and Taylor. "Cap's gotta rehearse that speech of his," Taylor said.

"His speech about the JFK assassination scene—even you remember that one."

"It's a fuckin' classic. You think he'll add some new lines if and when some JFK actually gets blown away in Manhattan North?"

"You're waiting for somebody like that to make a state visit around here, you'll wait a long time," Cooch predicted.

"If it ever does happen," Flynn said, "what I'd really like to know is—will Captain Zachs go to bat with the Chief and get us extra manpower for the investigation?"

"Sure he will"—Taylor clapped Flynn on the back—"more tin soldiers for him to play with."

* * *

As the first—and for the moment, only—investigator at the scene, Levy could not afford to be hypnotized by the sight of the hole in the victim's right cheek, an ugly crater the size of a quarter, in the soft place under the bone. Levy couldn't see any blood on the street under the man's head—the bullet most likely was lodged inside his skull. He looked to be in his early thirties, Levy's age.

One radio car had parked on the curb by the newspaper shop and more kept coming. Luckily, Sergeant Deegan showed up in time to discourage the civilians and the uniformed cops from tromping all over creation. The homicide had gone down at rush hour, just as the better element of the neighborhood came home from work; none of the passersby had any intention whatever of moving till they could find out about the shooting of their favorite newsdealer. Anyway, somebody in the crowd must have been a witness, so let 'em all stay there awhile. Witnesses might even come forward on their own.

While the medics searched frantically for vital signs, signs whose absence would mean that Levy had caught the squad's thirty-third homicide of 1985, the detective tried to sort things out. He talked to the first cop on the scene, who now stood as if rooted to the asphalt near the victim's feet. The cop said the shoot-out had happened right in the middle of the sidewalk, near the newsstand. One gunman apparently ran west toward Broadway, maybe toward the Ninety-fourth Street subway entrance; the other headed for Central Park. Levy thought this could make a helluva canvass—if you had a fuckin' army of detectives to cover all the territory.

The cop's partner gave Levy the name and number of the witness who had recounted the shooters' flight. "Postal worker," the cop said. "When he saw the victim, you could see he got a shock. I told him go sit in the car a minute, calm down."

"Maybe he was too upset to get the story straight."

"Naw, he had it down."

"I've seen 'em have second thoughts later when we knock on the door."

Sergeant Deegan had stationed a patrol car at Ninety-second Street and one at Ninety-third to divert traffic but Levy had to decide where the cops should stretch the neon-yellow tape—how far apart had the shooters been standing? What exactly should be the boundaries of this crime scene? He and Deegan roughed it out, and the cops strung the tape from parking meters and a lamppost at the curb to trash cans that they positioned near the storefronts.

A patrol cop came up to speak to Levy; this was his sector, the cop said—he knew the storekeeper, Abdul Mahmoud, pretty well. An immigrant from someplace like Morocco, Abdul had complained about drug activity outside his store. (Levy wrote in his notebook.) The slightly built storekeeper worried that his customers would be scared away by the tough kids who did their deals a few feet from his newsstand. They congregated next door by the corner store. The cop pointed; Levy looked at the words on the corner-store awning: CERVEZA FRIA . . . PRODUCTOS TROPICALES.

The sector cop said he had explained to Abdul that drug arrests were off limits to patrol, but he had talked up the new Special Narcotics team in the precinct. He had assured Abdul that they knew about the problem—which was the truth. "They call this 'cocaine strip' over here, from Eight-seven all the way up to Nine-six. But if you ask me, it's gettin' to be crack alley. That stuff is so cheap, any minute you're gonna get amateurs in the business. A lot of 'em. They're callin' the area 'destabilized' now"—the cop laughed without humor—"wait a few months."

The cop said he had advised Abdul to go to the precinct himself and bother the bosses, but the cop had never really expected Abdul to do it; he knew that Abdul worked alone. Until the newsdealer saved enough to bring over his wife from Morocco, it was just him in the store eighteen hours a day. "Store" was an overstatement, Levy thought—Abdul's place of business had less floor space than the precinct cage.

The blue Chrysler came down Ninety-third Street and parked by a fireplug. Flynn and Cooch got out and walked quickly through the onlookers toward the white EMS bus and the cleared area where the Emergency Service team was working. The two medics spelled each other; the one who had been applying pressure to the victim's frail, bare chest sat back on his heels and took deep breaths. He caught sight of Flynn and made a thumbs-down sign.

Just as Levy began to wonder where Jesse Taylor was, he spotted Taylor arriving on foot. Drifting along in his discount-store getup, he blended perfectly with the street element. He went through the thickest part of the crowd, stopping in the second row, right behind those closest to the body, and stood among the curious, like one of them.

Levy told the sector cop to check out Abdul's candy store, see if anything looked wrong; then to guard it. "One of us'll get back to you," the detective said, and went over to Flynn.

"That's it," Flynn told him without expression.

The young cop standing by Abdul's feet heard Flynn and looked glumly at the detective. "I gotta do the notification."

"No. No relatives in the States, looks like," Levy said. "We'll do it when we find 'em."

"You don't gotta do nothin' but ID the body at the morgue later," Cooch added.

The young cop just stood there with a stressed-out look in his eye, like a Vietnam vet.

"What've we got?" Flynn asked Levy. After Levy ran it down, Flynn turned to the still-motionless uniformed cop. "Officer, locate your partner—I want him to guard the deceased, here, till the ME shows up, and the morgue wagon. I want you to get me all the plate numbers on both sides of Amsterdam, okay? Keep goin' a couple blocks north and south."

"Right, Lieutenant Flynn." Blood seeped back into the cop's face. He tugged his thick memo book from his back pocket and marched away from Abdul's body.

Flynn opened his arms to encompass the taped-off area and started to ask O'Levy a question, but was interrupted.

"Andy," Captain Zachs yelled from a good fifteen feet away, "the scene! What're you doing there? Remember what happened in Dallas. Those cops who fucked up—the locals, the feds, you name it—to this day"—he hardly lowered his voice when he reached Flynn—"they're all spear carriers for the parks department." He imitated a porter spiking bits of trash. "The fuckin' media—"

"—'took 'em to the cleaners,' Cap."

"Yeah. So what's with this scene right here? This deceased was pretty popular. The community's gonna be heard from."

"Sergeant Carlucci and Taylor are gonna work the crowd. Patrol did a preliminary search, didn't come up with nothing. Myself and Levy are goin' over it again now."

Zachs frowned. Flynn knew that he irritated his boss by his insistence on digging into a case himself on that level—but until Zachs could find a flaw in Flynn's handling of the big stuff, the captain had no beef. Flynn anticipated the next question: "Deegan said CSU has been called." He motioned O'Levy to come with him and walked away from his boss.

The young reporter for the neighborhood weekly paper, *The Westsider,* wore his orange press ID card strung around his neck just like the heavyweights from the dailies wore theirs. Hank

Markle knew that Zachs recognized him, but the captain made a show of peering at Markle's press card anyway.

"Hiya, Captain Zachs. Who'd want to wipe out a quiet guy like Abdul, Captain? Robbers? You got a suspect?"

"The investigation just began, Hank. Now, you gotta have Abdul's background, right? Okay, Public Information will give it to you—soon as we got all the details. From the looks of things—robbery was *not* the motive. We'll be canvassing the whole area now. And that's it, kid."

"C'mon, Captain—Abdul was a 'mushroom,' wasn't he? Poor guy just had the bad luck to pop up in the line of fire."

"Some witnesses did make statements to that effect."

"The Ninety-second Street block association's been complaining about rampant muggings and drug activity around here for months. Did Abdul get caught in a drug dispute?"

"*I* don't know that but if you wanna be creative, be my guest. Okay, Hank?"

"No, sir—investigative," Markle said. "By the way: I'm aware that the murder rate has dropped off in this precinct over the past few months. With that in mind, how do you see today's incident? Is a new crime trend developing in this area now because of the surge in drug activity?"

"We can't stop and do sociology studies at a crime scene, you oughta know that. Right now, our job is to find the perpetrator—Lieutenant Flynn is in charge of that. And this is *not* the time to bother him," Zachs yelled as Markle started along the barrier toward Flynn.

Flynn's back was toward the reporter. The lieutenant and another detective squatted on the sidewalk in front of a barbershop two doors south of Abdul's. They looked completely absorbed; Markle couldn't get up the nerve to interrupt.

Flynn and Levy stood back a little as Crime Scene photographed Levy's find: a bullet that had ended its trajectory at the base of a security gate stanchion. Levy stared at the bullet, willing its cooperation. Markings that no one had yet seen must be clear enough under a microscope to link the bullet to a gun that no one had yet found. And the sides of the soft lead slug must be protected from anything that would add marks.

As soon as Crime Scene had their photo, Levy picked up the bullet, scratched "FL" into the lead base, and hefted it for a moment in the palm of his hand. Then he plucked the pocket square from his double-breasted gray linen jacket, wrapped the blue silk hanky around the slug, tied it tightly, and dropped it into the jumble of keys and coins in the pocket of his pegged pants.

The September light faded and the air grew chilly. Even so, the crowd thinned slowly. People lingered, remembering neighborly chats with a shy man who wanted only to please. For some time to come, they would pass this familiar corner and think of death.

Taylor moved about as if restless, scavenging scraps of conversation and moving again. He stood near the southern edge of the crowd, behind a pair of young Latino dudes wearing fat gold rings and chains and leather bomber jackets. Street yuppies, Taylor thought. One of them laughed about somebody's bad aim—"Guess he was cracked out and couldn't shoot straight."

"Listen," said the other, "for a short guy, José ran pretty fast; maybe the crack gave him wings. 'A pocketful of pebbles, it's your ticket to the moon.' That's what Carlos says."

The dudes remembered how José, or maybe was it *el gordito*—they couldn't see in the confusion—had bumped into *la gringa* and knocked her down; *"la gringa, she* saw him, that's for sure."

"And who cut down the mushroom? Who did it," the two asked each other, "José or that fatso coke dealer?" They talked about laying bets, but in the end, they passed; how could they bet when they would probably never know which one fired the killer shot? Then they debated who owns the corner now—Carlos or Irish? "Carlos, he's lookin' to own the *world.*"

"Yeah, he's big, he's doing okay. But Irish Luck don't have to get out of the way for *nobody*. That corner belong to him till somebody beat him cold."

Taylor spotted Flynn and Levy directing Crime Scene in front of the barbershop next to the newsstand. When Flynn looked up and met Taylor's glance, Taylor nodded toward the two gold-trimmed dudes. As Flynn and Levy moved in their direction, Taylor faded back into the crowd. He would keep his cover while Flynn and Levy grilled the dudes. Taylor mulled over the questions that the dudes had been debating and considered how to find this "white girl" based on no more description than that.

Tuesday night, September 17, 1985

Dusk had fallen by the time Flynn and Levy finished interviewing the two dudes and other rubberneckers and storekeepers along

Amsterdam Avenue. Crime Scene had long since packed up and gone. Cooch and Taylor stood talking near where the body had lain. Since Abdul had bled only internally, no trace of his body remained on the sidewalk by his shop. The incident had disappeared like the perps, Levy realized, leaving nothing but a few inches of neon-yellow tape tied to a parking meter.

"Your punks got real cute when we came over," Flynn told Taylor. "They looked just like those two monkeys, see-no-evil and speak-no-evil. You said they mentioned a fat perp and a short perp but no hint about which one is Luzan's and which is Viera's.... The perps are both Hispanics?"

"Well, the short one's name is José; 'Gordo,' we don't know for sure, but I'd say Hispanic, ninety-nine to one."

"Oh, right—Gordo. And *la gringa?*" Flynn asked. "That's the whole description: she's white."

"That's it."

Levy's hand kept straying to his pocket, fingering the bullet in its silk wrapping. He pulled out the hanky with the bullet inside. "Boss," he said, "I gotta take this baby to the lab."

"We are still nowhere with these mutts' descriptions," Flynn reminded him. "When are you gonna talk to that witness you got from patrol?"

"I'll call from downtown and go see him."

"Lieu," said one of the robbery-squad detectives as Flynn, Cooch, and Taylor entered the squad room. "How's it goin'? I just took a message for Reynolds from that pizza man down on Amsterdam"—he looked at the scrap of paper in his hand—"Mickey Krystos. He says make sure Reynolds calls me, ASAP."

Cooch said he had stopped at Mickey's Pizza, but the owner had been out. "There was nobody but a Greek counterman who speaks pizza-English only. I didn't get a lot from him."

"Krystos didn't leave nothin'," the robbery-squad man said, "just his name and phone number." He held out the paper to Flynn as Taylor watched, but somehow the paper ended up in Cooch's fist.

"I'll give him a call," Cooch announced.

Flynn folded his arms across his chest and smiled the half-smile at his sergeant. "All you're gonna get is a pizza recipe and not a great one at that. I don't know how Mickey sells that stuff but I don't care—he's got good eyes and ears and he's helped before. He knows Billy and that's who he likes to talk to; let Billy reach out for him tomorrow, okay?"

"I don't know why the fuck anybody wants to talk to that lazy bum, even on the phone. And definitely not face-to-face, for chrissake. Who the hell could put up with that wise mouth for two minutes."

Flynn reached for the message slip. "I bet that's just what they said about you twenty years ago—'wise.' Billy's kinda restless but he's smart. And people take to him—like Mickey. Details aren't his strong suit, I admit. We gotta use those people skills, give him a challenge."

"He wouldn't know a challenge if he tripped over it," Cooch grumbled on his way to his desk in the bosses' office, "unless it was wearing a skirt."

Flynn laughed. "That's what I said, people skills." He perched on a gray metal desk, reached for the phone, and pushed the buttons for Reynolds's number.

"Leave your name and number," said Reynolds's voice on the answering machine, "and your call will be returned." "Beep." Flynn's watch said 2230 hours; he wouldn't hold his breath for a call from Billy tonight. Bad luck—the sooner they knew what Mickey Krystos had to say, the more it would help. Or might. He relayed the pizza man's message and hung up.

Taylor had been listening from the next desk as he scribbled notes in a steno book.

"That business about *'la gringa,'* " Flynn said, "tell me again?"

"One of the perps knocked her down when he started running away. According to this one punk, she hadda see the face."

"Of the guy who bashed her?"

"Yeah, his face."

"La gringa—could she be white and seventy-five years old?"

"If you saw a seventy-five-year-old black lady, would you refer to her as the black girl or the old black woman?"

"I get it. That makes her somewhere between fourteen and forty-five?"

"Besides the fact that we ain't got shit to go on with this case"—Taylor looked Flynn in the eye—"what else is bugging you?"

"Okay: my friend Lauren. She lives right there—Nine-two and Amsterdam, practically catty-corner from Abdul's store."

"So she's *la gringa.*"

"Of course not. But if she was..."

"Maybe if you just give her a jingle, you'll free up your mind and all of a sudden this case'll look like nothin' but a grounder."

Taylor could see his friend's facial muscles relax. Flynn reached for the phone again but paused with the receiver in his hand. "Y'know, in AA, they got a name for somebody like you."

"Here it comes."

"Enabler."

"I know I've been called worse. What's the statutory minimum?"

"Well, it depends, see. For instance, here's a typical scenario. Alcoholic comes home around four in the morning just in time to lose it on the Oriental rug and pass out. Enabler cleans up, takes off Alcoholic's shoes, and brings the pillow and the blanket. And calls the boss the next day, sayin' Alcoholic's 'indisposed.' Alcoholic wakes up and thinks—well, this could be a lot worse. The better job of hidin' the truth Enabler does, the more likely he or she's gonna be takin' the consequences again soon."

"So what I hear you sayin' is, the young lady's got you good and hooked. It don't escape my attention that you look like you just might be enjoyin' life for a change, and boom—next thing I know, I get some phony 'enabler' rap laid on me!"

"Okay, okay—I got the wrong man. False charges. Besides, I just realized—this thing with Lauren is strictly recreational and we're gonna keep it that way." Flynn finished dialing her number.

He almost didn't recognize her voice with the unfamiliar shake in it. Lauren sounded close to the edge. She knew the murder victim—had bought her *Times* from Abdul every morning for two years; the *Post* and sometimes the early edition of the *News* in the evening. When he saw her hurrying toward the shop, he would fold the morning paper and push it through his window. She could just grab it and pay him, almost without having to break her stride.

"Look," Flynn said, "I know it's late but you could use a little hand-holding." It was true, he told himself, ignoring reasons both personal and professional that had to do with *his* need to see her. The split-second pause before she said yes, come over, didn't escape him.

For all that, he wasn't prepared for the pale person who greeted him in a red flannel bathrobe. Without shoes, she lost some of her purposeful look. And from the gingerly way she moved, she obviously wouldn't be flying by anybody's newsstand tomorrow. She sat down slowly in a chubby black velvet armchair and tucked the bathrobe around her legs. Ignoring the ottoman, she sat with her bare feet touching the floor.

"For a change, just for a change," she blurted, "I didn't work late—so I come off the subway and walk straight into a shooting! All I wanted to do was get home, but then I heard who it was..."

Flynn leaned toward her from the love seat. "Everybody we talked to said Abdul was a good guy, hard worker."

"Yes—helpful, eager to please."

"Did he get along okay with the Hispanics?"

"I think everybody liked him."

"Well, maybe not the drug dealers who hang out there, near the store," Flynn pointed out. "He was always trying to chase them away, wasn't he? Talking to them, finally gettin' upset and yelling."

"That's true—he did, but..."

"Maybe he yelled once too often, and they got tired of his attitude and this is what they did about it. Dealers buy guns like the rest of us buy groceries, except they don't put 'em in the fridge."

"Well, I don't think those two went after Abdul...."

"What did you see that made you come to that conclusion?"

"See? Nothing. What do you mean?"

"Well, some people told us this pretty blond lady ran past the newsstand right after Abdul went down; this gunman tried to get the hell outta there and he knocks over the pretty blonde."

He saw Lauren tense, trying not to wince when she changed the position of her legs. She didn't meet his eyes.

"According to what we heard, she gets a look at the first gunman. Plus, she's gotta see gunman number *two* movin' outta there in a hurry. The way these guys carry on, it looks to her like they're not on the same team. She thinks maybe they went for *each other* and Abdul got caught in the middle...."

Flynn sat on the edge of the love seat, his elbows resting on his knees and his chin on his laced fingers; he kept his eyes on her. He wanted to know what she knew about the homicide, he wanted to go over and touch her hair, he wanted to be able to separate those desires—but it was like trying to keep the cubes from dissolving in your drink. He kept his eyes on hers, wondering which of his motives she would read and how she would respond. His lack of control of the situation bugged him.

Finally, she went limp against the soft chair cushions. "All I wanted was to get home, but he just slammed into me."

"The bum really messed you up, didn't he?"

"I fell kind of hard, but I just got some scrapes; nothing serious."

"Yeah, but you don't want an infection—who did the first aid?"

She smiled. "Thank you, Dr. Flynn—I did."

"Do me a favor and go get those great legs x-rayed, tomorrow, okay?"

"If I say yes, can we stop the medical routine?" She sounded more like herself.

"Uh-huh."

"Okay, Wednesday's always a terrible day, but I'll try—but anyway, no bones broken. I'd know if there were."

"I'd like to be sure."

"End of medical routine—that was the deal."

"Okay, okay." His tone stayed casual. "Did you see the guy's face?"

"Oh—just a blur." She seemed at ease with the question.

"Really? A white blur or what?"

"N-no, I think Hispanic."

"You don't think you'd recognize him?"

"Uh-uh."

"Then there's only one small problem."

She looked at the old-fashioned clock on the mantel. "God, it's almost midnight. I don't think I'm up for even a small problem."

"Small now but could get unpleasant if ignored. And I'll help you handle it." He sure would. The personal interest and the professional duty melted relentlessly into each other. "The trouble is, the word on the street is the pretty blonde who got knocked down saw the shooter's face. In other words, from where the bad guys sit...she's a witness against at least one shooter."

Lauren curled up in the chair, hiding from this news. Again he fought his impulse to go to her.

"I'm *not* a witness," she said, her voice sounding scared again.

"Sorry..." Flynn considered how well she and that chair suited each other—and the room, too, except it was *small.* He guessed it was a New England kind of room, a version of the ones she grew up in, maybe. "Okay..." While his thoughts drifted, his mind had solved the problem. "I know what we can do."

"My brain's on a merry-go-round. Anything that requires rational thought, tell me tomorrow." Her eyelids drooped.

"Wake up, kiddo, we're off to see the wizard."

"Tomorrow." Eyes still closed.

At last he went over to her. He sat on the arm of her chair, bent down, and kissed her temple. "Put your jeans on, okay? You're really not safe around here right now. You'll be better off in my neighborhood, crummy as it is. I'm gonna give you the keys to Divorcé's Retreat and I'll stay here and house-sit for you. If anyone comes lookin' for a pretty blonde, they'll be very disappointed. How about that?"

Lauren just murmured, "I'm a wreck."

"Come on." He drew her gently out of the big, soft black armchair.

Wednesday, September 18, 1985

In the taxi, they spoke little. Flynn just kept his arm around her and let his thoughts wander. If a defense attorney ever got wind of their involvement...but no, she wasn't a *suspect.* How could she *not* have seen the mutt's face? Not remember, okay, but not *see?* Well, at least he hadn't lost his objectivity altogether. The taxi turned off Ninth Avenue and onto his street of rundown tenements. He helped her out and led her into the narrow, dingy entrance hall of his building. "Only three flights," he apologized as they started up the stairs.

"I'm okay." Flynn knew damn well she wasn't. "Did it ever occur to you"—she kept her tone light—"that when the first tenements were built, people had to haul all their water up these long flights. On the other hand, you've got higher ceilings here than a lot of the new so-called 'luxury' housing."

"I like the old houses they used to build for fancy folks—brownstones, like where you are."

"But did you ever notice that there are basically two brownstone widths; when they break up one of the narrow ones like mine, you tend to get apartments with cubbyholes for rooms. I'm not complaining, though—I love my place." She stood next to him in the darkness of his apartment, her voice faltering. "I can't believe I'm not safe there."

Flynn intended to take her mind off that. He located the floor lamp, switched the three-way bulb to low. "Ta dum—the Anastasia Suite at the Hell's Kitchen Hilton."

She didn't react to the gangster's name as a native New Yorker would have.

"Are you ready for the fifty-cent tour?"

"You mean the sixty-second tour? That's about how long I can stand up."

She suppressed a wince when he took her hand; he looked at it under the light and saw the raw scrapes on her palm. "Wow," he said, "you did get plenty of souvenirs."

"Take me on the tour?"

"Okay, where we're standing is the living-bedroom. Did you know that the futon"—he pointed to his inexpensive double-size sofa bed—"is the invention of a smart Japanese divorcé? He's a billionaire now."

She giggled.

"On your left"—he walked a few feet forward and to the left—"the dining alcove. We specialize in small parties." A pair of 1950s kitchen chairs and a tiny round table with a matte-black-painted top.

"The Informal Look," she said, "I like it. Who's your decorator?"

"Goodwill and Goodwill."

"Of course! Only the best, from every period since Louis—"

"Armstrong." He whistled a few bluesy bars.

"Well, if you say so." She leaned into his supporting arm as he steered her through a pair of louvered pine doors.

"Originally, this was the classic bathtub-in-kitchen railroad flat; as you see, we have modernized with a stall shower—but you still brush your teeth in the kitchen sink." To the left of the sink, Lauren saw a door plastered with boxing-match advertisements and a sign done in black-and-red calligraphy, *Think*.... Inside the door, nothing but a vintage pull-chain toilet to which Flynn had added a real oak seat.

"But"—Lauren looked around quizzically—"a railroad flat should have at least one more room..."

"Right you are." Flynn pushed aside a curtain at the far end of the kitchen, revealing a nice-size closet with a window.

"Great! A closet as big as the Ritz."

"Please, Albert Anastasia turns over in his grave when anybody mentions the competition. He was a famous crime boss—on the docks, you know?"

"Like in *On da Waterfront*?"

"Yeah." He put his arm around her and pointed out the window to where the shadowy piers jutted into the Hudson.

"*On the Waterfront*—scary," she sighed, "but so romantic..."

"Your hair"—he touched the blond tendril that curled on her cheek—"is kind of Eva Marie Saint."

"That's the nicest thing I've heard in I don't know when." Her voice was faint with fatigue. When she leaned against his shoulder, he felt his breath catch. He led her back to the front room.

She stepped out of her black pumps and abandoned them under the little round table.

"The futon is all yours," he said softly.

"Sure"—she looked at the Japanese billionaire's design—"and I know you're planning to sleep in the bathtub."

"No, because that's against Anastasia's house rules; but the floor's okay."

"I think," she said, holding his hand but not looking at him, "that I need to feel the strength of your body next to me. I could really use that tonight."

"That would make me…I guess *happy* is the word." He felt her hand on his. "I'm not too familiar with that word." He held her bruised palm against his cheek, then kissed the pulse point high on her neck. Her arms went around him as he undid the buttons on the back of her martini-olive-green top. He kissed her bare shoulders. As his fingers moved along the waistband of her skirt to the button, they encountered the incredibly smooth skin of her midriff. The skirt fell to the floor.

She reached over to switch off the floor lamp. "The scratches," she said, "not exactly the latest look in *Vogue.*"

"Didn't read *Vogue* this month; I guess I'll have to take your word."

She unbuckled his belt and unbuttoned his shirt. He suddenly wanted to pick her up and carry her like an injured child; her office outfit was safely out of the way.…He imagined her stretching out bit by bit on the bed. Flynn scooped her up and let her down in one swift motion.

"This is better—much better." She sighed.

"Is the sheet too rough?" He smoothed it under her. "Maybe some baby oil…?"

"Mm, that might help…"

Flynn went to get it, and when he returned, she had pulled the top sheet over her. He draped a T-shirt carefully over the lamp and turned on the light. Under the pale-blue sheet Lauren was now nude; he could see a tiny shadow by each nipple.

Leaving the sheet on her, he put his lips on one of the tiny shadows and let out his breath. His hands traced her ribs, her navel, the slight roundness of her belly, the soft thighs, and the place where the thighs parted. Her breath quickened. She reached out to touch his face, held his face in her hands, and coaxed his mouth to hers.

After the long kiss she said, "Suddenly I feel just fine."

"You sure?"

"Yes."

He kissed her again, one hand going under the sheet, repeating the tour it had taken before, this time with nothing between it and that silken skin. Her fingers played over his cheekbones and combed the gray hair at his temples. As he caressed her body, he felt her hands go to his back—stroking lightly at first, up and down; then, as she breathed deeper and harder in response to his touch, he felt her fingers' increasing pressure. He went inside her and she tilted up her hips, asking for him.

He thrived on her moves and the sounds she made. He could feel his life expectancy improving. "Still feel okay?" he asked. She smiled and kissed the cleft in his chin, his cheekbones. He moved in her, building the tempo, feeling her body answer his until he called her name and let his body relax with hers.

In the morning when he opened his eyes, a glimpse of her shoes parked under the table pleased him. He absorbed the warmth of her next to him. Then he remembered the newsdealer, Abdul, and the two gunmen, now in the wind.

"Lieu." Flynn had barely got through the swinging doors when O'Levy intercepted him. "That witness—the postal clerk—I caught up with him about midnight. Name is Leoni. He says he was coming out of the subway, starts goin' east to Mickey's for a slice, and thinks he hears a shot."

Flynn settled down on the corner of the nearest desk and listened. Taylor leaned against the wall and listened, too.

"Sure enough, when Leoni comes out of the pizza place, he sees a big crowd up the block. He decides to head back that way, and just as he's gettin' to the corner, these two maniacs fly by, goin' opposite ways. Leoni knows somethin' happened and it couldn't've been good, so he tries to check out these guys who are so busy tryin' to disappear."

"He gave you descriptions?"

"Okay, the guy going towards the park, he's Hispanic—like Jesse thought. Age maybe twenty-five. About five eight or nine, and heavy—'baby fat.' Hairline mustache. Wearin' a red sweat suit—sort of fancy, Leoni thinks, maybe with white racing stripes."

"What's he give you on the other mutt?"

"Also Hispanic; younger—twenty to twenty-two. Five foot five or six. Weight about one forty. Glasses with—like, no-color frames. Wearing jeans and a Giants jersey, shoulder pads an' all."

"So the little guy is the one that went west."

"Right. I asked Leoni would he come to the sketch unit and he's game."

"Good idea," Flynn said. "But right now, aren't you due at the morgue?"

If O'Levy dreaded the prospect, he didn't show it. "By the way," he said, his hand on the gate latch, "that slug—it's a .38."

Flynn dialed Irene Defina's number. "Hiya, pal. You know you got a treat comin' your way. Detective Franco Levy of the Two-nine."

"You must be talkin' about that gunshot case, Arab male, a name like Mohammed?"

"That's the one—a nice, hardworkin' guy gets caught in somebody else's drug dispute."

"Seems like Mohammed must've had a lot of friends in the neighborhood."

"Did you read that in his palm, or what? You got a job in my command anytime. He *was* popular and there's a lot of sentiment. It'll make a nice little human-interest piece for the local weekly. Too bad the widow can't live on that."

"When does the weekly come out?" Defina asked.

"I think Tuesday, but don't hold me to it. Why?"

"So we gotta wait a week on that. But today you might want to look at the front page of the *Times.*"

"No kiddin'! Well, the reporter must live on the Upper West Side. The *News* didn't cover it at all—not enough Moroccan readers."

"The *Times* said somethin' about two shooters, so I guess the bullet in his head could help you a lot; there's no exit wound—it's gotta be in there."

"Yeah—let's hope it's in good enough shape for Ballistics to work with. Whatever else the ME comes up with, we're grateful for any small favors."

"When are you comin' down yourself?"

"The way things are going around here, could be anytime. Thanks for watchin' out for Levy; if I know him, he'll be there in ten minutes."

Billy Reynolds had walked in while Flynn talked on the phone. Now Reynolds and Cooch could be heard going at it in the bosses' office. Cooch snarled, Billy snapped. Flynn and Jesse looked at each other and started back toward the noise.

"Billy," Flynn said, seating himself formally behind his desk, "I know you talked to your pizza guy—shut up and tell us what he gave you."

Cooch marked items on the Investigative Checklist in front of him with elaborate attention. He rifled his IN box, looking vainly for fresh paper. So far he had nothing but the Unusual Occurrence reports and the uniformed cops' list of plate numbers. He made a lot of notes on Part 2 of the Investigative Plan.

"As usual, Mickey knows his way around guns better than pizza," Reynolds said. "I told him, 'Never for breakfast,' but he wouldn't listen."

"Terrible pizza," Flynn agreed, "but try and stick up that place—you end your days a justifiable homicide like the last dummy who tried it."

"Anyway, Mickey's positive that the guy with the .38 shot first—he's in Luzan's crew. The other one, the butterball, he's the Viera man and Mickey says he had an automatic. They're both regulars around that block; Mickey knows 'em by sight."

"He knows the whole neighborhood. If he comes to a lineup, he better come discreetly."

"He can't wait for us to pick up those guys so he can ID them. He must think he's bulletproof."

Cooch had been writing busily. Now he looked up, ignoring Reynolds, and whipped out a copy of the *Times*. "Did you see this, Andy?"

"No—I just heard about it."

"Fuckin' front page for the victim's life story. Half a sentence on the crime," Cooch sneered. "Don't even say 'drug-related.'"

"Tell me this, Marty: Did they really kill Abdul by accident—or was he being set up for at least a robbery because he went to the cops?"

"And if it *was* an accident," Cooch said, "then what was the gunfight about? Some personal beef? Territory?"

"Assuming Mickey's got the cast of characters right, I'd say territorial."

Reynolds nodded.

"I'll buy that," Taylor said. "Those shitheads ain't tryin' to make it *look* like an accident if it wasn't; that's beyond their powers."

The phone rang and Cooch picked up. In the small office, everybody could hear and recognize O'Levy's voice as Cooch held the receiver away from his ear.

"Copper jacket"—the morgue hadn't toned O'Levy down—"the Ballistics detective was just here pickin' up evidence; he told me it's a nine millimeter for sure."

* * *

Flynn felt a little guilty letting himself into Lauren's apartment that night, as if it were his own. He hung up his two suits and a couple of pairs of pants in her coat closet but left his duffel, still packed with shirts and turtleneck sweaters and jockey shorts, sitting on the bedroom floor. Then he tiptoed around, switching on every lamp and the overhead lights in the kitchen and bathroom, too, as if to illuminate a crime scene.

He squinted at her possessions—looking for potential ways into the mystery. The clock on the mantel, the brass candlesticks, each book and painting must be a link to her past; he wondered about every item in the small room. She had built a window seat into the little bay. He sat on it and peered out to where he knew there must be midblock gardens, but he couldn't see much by the few security floodlights attached to backyard fences.

He moved to the big, soft armchair where she had sat the night before and sank into it, feeling sentimental about their little interlude here at her place and enjoying the warmth of the chair as if it came from her body heat instead of his own. He realized that it wasn't too late to call to see how she was doing.

"It's fun being 'on the waterfront,'" she told him. "I feel like a tourist, which would be great if I could do some touring, but I still feel like a rusty gate when I move. By the weekend I'll be ready for a stroll, I know I will. What about the case?"

"It's going good," he said, "we know who did it."

"You know who did it?"

"Well, we know the shooting was drug related and we know the two shooters work for rival drug interests, we know which side fired the fatal shot and with what kind of gun. That's all but knowing who did it."

"Oh." She sounded disappointed. "What kind of a gun?"

"Powerful. A lot more so than what we carry. Anyway, Detective Levy's doing great. When he called in from the medical examiner's office to tell us he had the bullet, I knew exactly what was going on in his head—he could already see the DA holding that bullet up in front of the jury. Don't worry, it'll happen."

Lauren sighed. "The paper said someone put a bunch of flowers in the grate at Abdul's newsstand."

"Right, they did. Everybody we canvass is outraged, too."

"Why does knowing the kind of gun help you?"

"Because the patrol cops make gun collars every day and they file a voucher every time. O'Levy'll watch those vouchers and one fine day he'll get a hit, and then we'll have a gunman who wants to talk his way into our good graces. Now—ready to give me a report on life in the halls of power?"

"Almost. Would I have heard of the 'rival drug interests'?"

"One of 'em you might have and you definitely wouldn't like him. I haven't liked him for about thirteen years. One of these days I'm gonna get a chance to do something about it."

"You at least can lock up your old enemies; I have to work with mine. Like one of our staff lawyers, Parker Graham, Esq. He'll find the wrong side of an issue that doesn't even have one. And leaks to the press are his 'secret' weapon. I *know* he was the one who told the *Post* that my boss is glad Times Square is the State's problem."

"Well, they've been talking about bulldozing Times Square for years, haven't they, and it was still there last time I looked. Graham sounds like a reporter's dream." Flynn's voice got softer. "Listen, speaking of dreams, I like sleeping in your bed. It's the next-best thing to sleeping in any bed that has you in it."

"As soon as it's safe for me to sleep in it again, we'll rededicate it together. How's that?"

"Gives new meaning to the word 'motivation.' But of course your presence in the Anastasia Suite gives new meaning to 'home sweet home,' too."

"Maybe we can arrange a visit for you," Lauren said, "maybe even this weekend."

Flynn hoped the Abdul case would be in good enough shape by then that he'd be able to duck out.

Friday, September 27, 1985

A police-artist's sketch based on the postal clerk's description of Abdul's killer appeared on page one of *The Westsider*. Hank Markle's story revealed a neighborhood depressed by the murder—but some residents he quoted charged that the community had no right to grieve because, they said, people hadn't rallied behind Abdul in his struggle with the drug dealers. "If we can lose Abdul to this madness," said one woman, "we have begun to lose our neighborhood. Soon it will belong to the drug lords, not to us." Markle noted that the police had found neither the murder weapon nor the other gun fired at the scene, but that they were actively seeking both. One of the pistols used had been a .38, the story said.

As the squad canvassed endlessly, Markle's piece helped open doors—but only in the neighborhood's gentrified buildings where people were inclined to help the police anyway. The canvassing detectives came up with another witness—a Columbia University professor who had seen the .38 shooter's face and was willing to view a lineup. The police-artist's sketch of the suspect generated nothing but a lot of false leads.

Ten days after the murder, Levy brought the latest in a series of confiscated .38s to the Ballastics lab in the Police Academy building. He drove through a downpour, and by the time he pulled up at East Twentieth Street, Levy worried that the old unmarked Plymouth was waterlogged in some vital part. He could remember having been in better moods. He paced around the lab while the Ballistics detective, Ericson, methodically sorted through a pile of reports on his desk. Finally, Ericson found whatever it was he was looking for, set the papers aside, and carefully capped his disposable pen. He swiveled his chair toward Levy.

"Charter Arms, huh? Let's go." Ericson stood up and held out his hand for the gun. Levy followed him into a smallish room off the Ballistics office. Ericson loaded the revolver from an open box of cartridges and ambled over to the nine-foot-long metal water tank. He gave Levy a pair of "muffs" to protect his eardrums and put on a pair himself before he fired two quick shots downward through a long tube. "Okay, you got time to grab some lunch"—he retrieved the bullets with chewing gun on the end of a broom handle—"while I put these suckers under the 'scope. See ya later."

Levy moaned. "I'm in Dutch with the boss already," he lied, "and he's really hot for this."

"Uh-huh, you play a good violin, Detective, but they're busy in there. You're jumpin' the line as it is. Anyways, I told you—this Charter Arms just *might* be your match. Only two other possibilities for that class of slug."

"Which would be what?" Franco asked. If he learned something, he told himself, the trip would still be worthwhile.

"S and W or Ruger."

Flynn held the phone away from his ear.

"Boss!" O'Levy yelled. "We got it—'a positive match,' the Ballistics guy says. With the kind of marks that's on our slug," he showed off, "there's only three .38 makers. Anyway, this gun they grabbed what's-his-face for—LaPaz—it matches the bullet we found."

"Nice break," Flynn said. "This thing is gonna go now, for sure. We'll be home free in a couple of days. You hoppin' over to the courthouse for a lineup order? Wish we could do it tomorrow, but the defense'll never buy it. Let's try for Monday, thirteen hundred hours."

"Somebody's gotta take a ride to Rikers to interview LaPaz, too."

"I think we'll handle it on this end. How's the Plymouth doin'?"

"Kinda iffy."

"I don't want her dyin' on you over there in this weather. I can think of nicer places than Rikers Island to spend a rainy weekend."

"Thanks, boss. Soon as I get back, I'll reach out for the witnesses—or do you by chance already have Ms. Daniels on your Friday phone list?"

"No wonder they call you the Brains from Brooklyn."

"Aka the Thinka from Tribeca."

Flynn chuckled. "But you better call her about the lineup yourself. The defense could burn us on it otherwise. We gotta watch our ass."

"You sound a little battle-weary," Flynn said to Lauren when she answered the phone. "Graham Parker been up to his old tricks?"

"Parker Graham," she corrected, laughing. "As a matter of fact, he has. We held a Times Square hearing on Thursday—"

"Another one?"

"*Emergency* Times Square hearing. P.G. was really in top form. He alienated anybody he could get his hands on; not that anyone needed *him* to sow dissension. The theater owners not only don't want the theaters landmarked, they want the air rights to be transferable so they can sell them."

"If it comes down to hiring more cops with those developers' taxes," Flynn said, "or preserving the nice old theater buildings we looked at the other day—"

"That sounds familiar, Andy; the mayor has a guy on his staff who's into comments just like that. The spokesman for the playwrights' group said that if megadevelopment takes over the neighborhood, art will die. The neighborhood residents say landlords are sending in the goon squads to harass tenants into leaving so they can do luxury conversions."

"That'd be worth plenty of cops."

"Sure would. Meanwhile, more or less everybody who spoke gave the Commission bad marks for not having a plan for the whole area—and they're right, of course."

"What did you tell the media folks when they asked about that?"

"Just the facts."

Flynn laughed. "You're a pro!"

"What about you: your nice detective called about the lineup—nice but very close to the chest. Did you get a break—what's the story, anyway?"

"I'll tell you more *after* the lineup, I promise. I'm sorry it's gotta be on a workday, but will you come?"

"If you want me to, sure; but I wish I were going to be more help."

"Like I tell the fellas, always keep an open mind—okay? We'll pick you up about twelve-fifteen."

Maddeningly, the idea occurred to Flynn that if Lauren couldn't ID LaPaz... she could still be coached to choose the right guy. He wondered how he could even think of trying to compromise her. Well, the more IDs the tighter the case, the faster it would go, and the sooner she could live a normal life again, free of any threat. What better reason did he need! Okay, he could fool the defense, maybe—but not Jesse. Somehow Jesse would catch on. That was what finally killed the idea. Of course, Jesse would stand up for him no matter what dumbass thing Flynn might do, but he wasn't about to set up his pal to perjure himself.

Monday afternoon, September 30, 1985

"This ain't gonna be too tough," Reynolds said. He and Taylor took a ride in the Chrysler to Columbus Avenue, looking for five short Hispanics to stand in the lineup with José-Maria LaPaz. "You're the only tall Hispanic I know."

"That's 'cause I'm black."

"You're one from Column A *and* one from Column B."

"Hey, my grandmother on my mother's side was Jewish—I bet you never heard about that. Anyway, there's at least one other tall Latino you forgot: Viera."

"Well, we're gonna cut him down to size any day."

"I'm glad somebody's optimistic. And even if we do inactivate him..."

"Yeah?"

"Forget it. The sun's out today, for a change—I can be

downbeat some other time. Let's drive over by the Park and back and forth in the little streets—I say we're gonna find everybody we need on the first two stoops."

"Oh, I forgot," Reynolds said, "we need short Hispanics with *no facial hair.*"

"Minor detail—we're gonna have to hit every stoop on this fool block and I'm gonna make *you* do all the askin'. In Spanish."

Later, when Reynolds drove over to the pizzeria to bring Mickey Krystos back for the lineup, the pizza man was watching an employee carefully pull a special pie out of the oven. "Wrap it up," Mickey said, "that squad's *hungry.*"

Reynolds grinned and said thank you; you couldn't be rude to a guy who always kept his eyes open and who hadn't hesitated to use his licensed pistol to save at least one cop's ass. The only remaining problem was, who would go the extra mile and actually *eat* the pizza?

Still later, the pizza man, the Columbia professor, and the postal clerk each met Flynn in the coffee room and took a turn looking out through the one-way glass at the row of six short, unmustachioed Hispanics. O'Levy shot a crystal-clear Polaroid picture of this unusual group. A budding Andy Warhol, he told himself as he expertly applied the fixative to the print.

Each witness waited his turn in a different office. Taylor kept Lauren company in the captain's, while Flynn stayed behind the one-way glass with the defense attorney, and O'Levy paraded the lineup in front of it, once for each successive witness. Mickey and the professor and the clerk each unhesitatingly picked out short, unmustachioed Hispanic Number Two—José LaPaz—as the man who'd been shooting south to north when Abdul's homicide went down and who had fled west toward Broadway. So Flynn was feeling good when Taylor brought Lauren in. Whatever she did, or didn't do, wouldn't signify that much. Or so he thought till Lauren stared blankly through the one-way glass. The defense attorney's frown disappeared.

"If I saw any of those guys, I don't remember," Lauren said. "I must have been too busy peeling myself off the sidewalk."

Okay, he *had* hoped that seeing the guy in the flesh would jog her memory, giving him four positive IDs. So much for hope. Flynn shrugged. "We tried. That's the most we could do." He ignored his queasy feeling and smiled at her.

"Boss"—O'Levy poked his head in the coffee-room door—"I

got the DA in the captain's office waitin' for the counselor." He nodded toward the defense attorney.

"I'll need some time with my client, first," the attorney said.

"Right this way," O'Levy told him.

Flynn turned to Lauren. "Thanks for showing up, pal. I bet you had better things to do." He liked her narrow skirt and big green sweater. "Jesse, help me liberate my pal from this loony bin, will you." The three walked out to the squad room. "Lauren, you got someplace to go, Detective Taylor'll give you a lift. Matter of fact, if you want to stop by your place—"

Lauren looked surprised. "Great!"

"Okay, but don't stay long. And Detective Taylor goes upstairs with you. In fact"—he looked around for Reynolds—"Jesse, Billy goes, too."

"Gotta *find* him first, Lieu."

"When it comes to a pretty girl, he can't be far away. Billy'll materialize before you're outta the house."

Lauren laughed. "Onward and upward," she told Flynn.

"Talk to you soon," he said. Before he could sit down with the DA about a deal with LaPaz's lawyer, he needed a refill on his coffee mug.

"Too bad you didn't get the fourth ID," remarked Assistant District Attorney Roberta Drake the minute he stepped into his office. This was his first encounter with her.

"Yeah—A-minus." Flynn smiled the half-smile. "The other three are ironclad, though."

A judge would have to crane his neck if she stood directly in front of the bench—she was five foot three in high heels. Tops.

"Could you be a little more specific?"

Pleasantries didn't seem to be Drake's style. Flynn responded to the question, not to the sarcasm. "LaPaz has been buying a slice at Mickey's Pizza every day since Luzan set up operations in the area. By the way, we gotta tell—Furman? that the defense attorney's name?—we gotta say, this witness has a business near the scene, never mind what kind. Plus, Mickey Krystos is a gun buff. He not only knows the perp's face, he can put the face with the gun. Then we got the professor: this ain't the absentminded type; he teaches finance up there at the business school—magnum smarts. The postal clerk—no-nonsense guy, typical man in the street. Hell, these are the kind of folks a jury'll believe. Furman's gotta take one look and talk turkey. Besides, his client was trying to *kill* the other shooter anyway. LaPaz probably can't wait to give him up!"

"Let's not forget," Roberta Drake instructed, "Furman's getting paid to restrain him." She frowned. "I wish you had that fourth ID."

Flynn tried an end run. "So do we hit him with attempted murder? What do you think?"

"Felony murder *and* attempted murder, Lieutenant Flynn."

"If he cooperates, we talk manslaughter? We gotta get him to come up with the other shooter's name," Flynn urged. "Better yet, the name and address."

"We most certainly do want the information—and if we get it, that shows his good faith. Especially if the information checks out. But the bottom line is truthful testimony at trial. LaPaz is in all the way or we don't lift a finger to lighten the sentence."

Flynn had to admit that Drake had her tough-DA act together. He wanted to see how it would hold up.

"No promises till LaPaz performs," she was saying as O'Levy ushered in Furman and his client. *"If* he comes through . . . we'll let the judge know."

Flynn seated the DA at his own desk under the homicide chart and stood on her left. He put Furman at Cooch's desk and LaPaz on a chair between the two lawyers. Drake's message ricocheted around the small office; when LaPaz's lawyer could get a word in, he translated.

José-Maria LaPaz was not shy. At the end of a stream of Spanish obscenities long enough to make the Guinness Book of Records, he uttered the word "Gordo."

"Fatso," Furman said.

When the DA asked LaPaz for "Gordo's" address, another stream of obscentities followed, and nobody regretted more than LaPaz that he had no idea where that rodent of a coke dealer could be found. "Not on Ninety-second Street—no way," LaPaz said. At least he had the personal satisfaction of removing Gordo and all Gordo's little slaves from there.

"But where does he sleep?" O'Levy insisted.

"Rodents sleep in holes," LaPaz reasoned, "so maybe he crawls down a hole somewhere. A big fat sewer pipe . . ."

"Terrific." Taylor had returned from chauffeuring Lauren just in time for LaPaz's "rodent" speech. "We ain't been knockin' on any sewer pipes in a long time."

"If you're bullshitting us about this despicable crime"—Drake pointed a sharp finger at LaPaz—"you'll find yourself at the bottom of a well."

Taylor listened attentively to the defense attorney's translation of Roberta Drake's threat.

The DA and Furman had finished up pretty fast, as such things go. Flynn figured he might even get to the boxing club in time to catch up with Salsa.

"What about tonight?" Taylor asked his friend, "After the gym, how 'bout a little Monday evenin' bounce?"

Monday night, September 30, 1985

Flynn and Taylor paid regular visits to F. X. Flynn's, but it had been quite a while since they really bounced around together. In the old days, Flynn had taken Taylor to all his favorite hideouts, which now were Taylor's favorite hideouts. Flynn waited for him at Gallagher's, enjoying the atmosphere of the big, rectangular bar that occupied the middle of the restaurant's outer dining room. Unlike Flynn's, Gallagher's had real paneling, red mahogany, which gave the place a lot of warmth.

Herbie welcomed Flynn with a bear hug, reached for the vodka bottle, then shook his head and put it back. "Canada Dry and lime, right?"

"Thanks, Herbie," Flynn said.

The bartender introduced Flynn to a martini-drinking talent manager, and the two had a good time being impressed by each other's line of work. When it came to refills, Flynn bought the round. He thought how picture perfect the freshly mixed martini looked with the beads of moisture forming on the slanted sides of the glass. The talent manager saw Herbie fill up Flynn's tall glass with tonic. "Hey, what's this," he protested, "I'm drinkin' alone?"

"No offense"—Flynn raised his glass as Taylor walked in the door—"I just like to meet my friends in bars." Herbie served Taylor his usual Rémy Martin and soda.

"Your friend doesn't drink but he bought mine," the talent manager said to Taylor, "so yours is on me."

Taylor didn't feature the "done deal" sound of this, but he also didn't feel like messing with a guy so early in the evening. "Cheers," he said; "thanks." He took a step backward, requiring Flynn to move toward him if they were going to hold a conversation in the noisy room. "How's things in the pugilism department?"

"Dynamite. You wouldn't believe how fast Salsa is coming along. Lookin' more and more like a natural boxer. If he's gonna work this hard, maybe the Tabu scene ain't such a big deal after all. He's really got a shot at straightenin' out."

"A shot, yeah," Taylor said, "but a long one. Boxin's a long haul, right? You gotta see what he's up against. Sure, you're a nice guy, but Viera makes serious money. That's where it's at for a kid that don't have nothin' and never *had* nothin' or nobody to set him an example—except a stepdaddy in the numbers racket. It's a million-to-one. You don't see it?"

"Yeah, I hear you," Flynn said, not really wanting to hear more. "How'd you like Lauren?"

"Smart, sexy—knows a good thing when she sees it, like Andy Flynn for instance. You got at least a fightin' chance with *her*. Of course, I made sure not to leave her and Billy alone."

"Very funny. You think Billy's the type to hit on the Commander's lady? He's not *that* crazy."

"Can't I push your buttons once in a while? I gotta get a *little* fun out of life. But if you're askin' me, I think he sure would make up to a commander's lady if he liked her and *didn't* like him. If Herbie'll let us out of here, how about a change of venue?"

"Like the Landmark? I'm ready for a bowl of their chips."

"Fries," Taylor corrected.

"Chips—like in a pub."

"Oh, an English pub?"

"An *Irish* pub. They ripped off that damn recipe from us."

"Blarney."

On a bleak, windswept corner of Tenth Avenue, the Landmark Tavern's three-story, red-brick row house stood alone and incongruous, the rest of its row long since torn down. Inside, the brick walls of the bar looked old and warm, the pressed-tin ceiling comfortably low. The polished mahogany bar itself was as long and inviting as any in the city and handsomer than most. Upstairs, in lace-curtained rooms that a family once occupied, lovers of good Irish fare, cops included, could eat their fill.

"Oh, yeah," Taylor said as the bartender reached for the Rémy, "and a couple of orders of fries—uh, chips?"

When Taylor's drink was half gone and Flynn's bowl of chips showed a large dent, Taylor brought up another subject. "You must've been out canvassing the other day—the day *The Westsider* came out—when Zachs came by. He was pissed as hell that the story said 'the cops are lookin' for a .38.' I swear he was all but frothin' at the mouth. He goes into his office and grabs the phone. 'No wonder we can't find that fuckin' weapon,' he yells. '*Flynn* musta told Markle. Gotta be a publicity hound, even if it means compromisin' a murder investigation, blah blah blah.' I don't know who he was talkin' to—but I can guess."

Flynn could guess, too. Every other word out of Joe Zachs's mouth was "the Chief of D" this and "the Chief" that—who else could it be?

Taylor went on, "Don't aggravate Zachs and the rest of 'em, Andy. They all got bugs up their ass these days—for a change. And by the way, I'm not helpin' your position, either. You know a lot of brass got no use for me from way back. You got a guilt-by-association rap on top of whatever else they got against you. *Lie low* for a while, you know what I mean?"

"I know what you mean and I appreciate your sayin' it. The thing is, it's all a crock—I mean if Zachs or whoever really wants my ass, it don't matter *what* I do or don't do. It just so happens I didn't tell Markle about the gun—I didn't talk to him, period. I'm tryin' hard to believe the brass got better ways to waste their time than doin' a number on me. They sure as hell better worry about this new crack garbage—the highest high ever *and* the cheapest—or we're all gonna be in deep shit. Right?"

Taylor just shook his head as if to say "I tried" and ordered another Rémy and soda.

Saturday afternoon, October 5, 1985

All week, the squad reached out to everybody they thought could possibly help, but Gordo remained whereabouts unknown. On Saturday, Flynn managed to get to the gym for a session with Salsa. By the time he arrived, all the Saturday-morning boxers had finished their workouts and gone home, leaving the big loft almost empty. Even Brooklyn Charlie had called it a day. Instead of the usual discord of boxing sounds, a crisp duet greeted Flynn: the whistle-and-snap of Salsa's skip rope, counterpointed by Jemal's strong, last-of-the-day rat-a-tat-tat on the speed bag. Salsa caught sight of Flynn, waved, and speeded up his rope work, showing off.

Feeling out of shape, Flynn got on an exercise bike and pushed the pedals, working the oxygen into his system till a satisfying sweat drenched his T-shirt. He hadn't quite forgotten Gordo, though.

A couple of minutes before Flynn would hit ten miles, Salsa bounded over. *"Qué tal,* Lieutenant?" Salsa said, bouncing and feinting next to the bike.

"Business as usual, pal—what about you?"

"In the pink." He grinned, modeling his neon-pink satin boxing shorts. "And Jemal, he's got a PAL smoker comin' up next week, fightin' a guy built like me. He sparred before when Charlie was still here, but he's askin' me would I spar a little more with him—that okay with you?"

Flynn whipped the towel from around his neck and dried his face, buying a few seconds' delay. Salsa had asked him like he would ask his trainer—but Brooklyn Charlie really was Salsa's trainer. Charlie had the time.

"Yeah, but he's gotta go light—he's an old-timer compared to you. I'll come over there and watch. Today we help Jemal train for his match; concentrate on you the next time, right?"

"Sure, I got a little while before I'm gonna actually fight anybody."

"A little?" Flynn laughed. "Don't have to rush it." He got off the bike and they walked to where Jemal was hitting the speed bag near the corner of the ring. "Hiya, Jemal—who're you fightin' next week?"

"Pete Liberato—'The Liberator.' Up at Christ Church on Park Avenue."

"Way to go, champ! Let's get some tape on you guys." Jemal stayed with the speed bag while Flynn wrapped Salsa's hands carefully with gauze and adhesive tape and helped him on with his training gloves. When Flynn had finished Jemal's hands, Jemal and Salsa climbed into the ring. As they sparred, the afternoon light coming through the big front window bleached the ring's dingy canvas and deepened the young boxers' shadows.

As Flynn concentrated on the sport, his problems took a backseat. The kids both looked fine; Salsa's progress amazed Flynn all over again. The stance worked. And Salsa was fast; despite Jemal's longer experience he had quite a time trying to use the hook he'd been practicing—which was just as well for Salsa because when Jemal did land one, it could be damaging. Flynn yelled encouragement whenever either of the sparring partners did something smart; he reinforced the good stuff, let the negatives go till after.

Salsa climbed out of the ring.

"You learn fast, Salsa," Flynn said as he handed the kid a towel, "and you definitely got the legs." Jemal had stayed in the ring and was shadowboxing intently. "These sluggers can hardly catch you, but what'll you do when you come up against a boxer like you? I bet Charlie already talked to you about that." Flynn and Salsa went around to the bench next to the front window and sat down.

"Yeah, we started working on slippin' an' blockin'."

"Terrific."

"Well, how *you* doin', Lieutenant Flynn—what about the newsdealer guy? You get the shooter yet?"

"We got a subject. . . ."

"Yeah—who?"

"Ever hear of a 'Gordo'?"

"I think I did. That's the guy?"

"Ballistics is sold on him. He's in the wind, though, as far as we can tell. Maybe you heard where he's holin' up these days."

"No, but—"

"Think you can check it out?"

"No problem."

"Be careful, now—be *very* careful about getting in touch with me."

"If I come up with somethin', I'll just leave you a note—upstairs, like usual."

"Good. That's a good, safe place." From where they sat with their backs against the front window, they could see the whole gym. At the sound of footsteps on the stairs, Flynn fidgeted. Lauren came through the door wearing something black and not really fancy, yet sexy. No sign of the limp.

"Come over here," Flynn called to her, "and meet these champs."

He introduced Salsa and Jemal. "I'm gonna grab a quick shower in honor of Saturday night; meanwhile the champs will tell you how they're gonna get to the Golden Gloves."

"Same way as you get to the Metropolitan Opera?" Lauren asked.

"Pardon?" Salsa said.

"'Practice, practice'—right?"

"I've heard that old friends are the best friends," Flynn teased, "but I never heard the same about old jokes."

"I like old jokes and new friends," Lauren maintained. "But what happened to that shower? Now's my chance to learn the difference between a jab and a hook."

If she didn't want to know about boxing, she was a good actress, Flynn decided.

As Flynn went upstairs to the locker room, he could hear Salsa holding forth on the subject of good *balance*. "The first thing a fighter's gotta get is the 'stance,' see?—that means the right position—so any little shove don't knock you over..."

Lauren sighed happily as she and Flynn settled into the window table they had lucked into at the River Cafe in Brooklyn Heights. He'd only known of the place because O'Levy kept raving about what a great spot "the R.C." was—romantic and gorgeous. "Even if the food wasn't so hot, people would pay just to come over here and look at the view," Lauren said.

"Unless of course people happen to be hungry and it's time for dinner; only a New York nut like you could eat the view," Flynn told her. There seemed to be little distance between them and the lights of Manhattan just across the East River. He wondered in passing who had taken her here before. But only in passing.

The waiter asked for their drink orders. Lauren hesitated.

"Have a drink—you can handle it," Flynn told her. When her glass of white wine arrived, she toasted "the hundred percent squad."

"Thanks." Flynn raised his glass of tonic water. "Hope it's not the *ex*-hundred percent squad. If the year ended tonight, that'd be that."

"Really? Has-been city?"

"Yup. They say you're only as good as your last arrest—and they're right."

"How did this hundred percent business get started anyway?"

"When I got to the Two-nine, I found myself with kind of a motley crew on my hands and I was looking to make a team out of 'em, that's all. They needed a bigger challenge and so did I. What's bigger than murder, the crime of crimes? Maybe not every group would have bought it; they did."

"From what I saw, you have some winners in Jesse and Billy."

"Jesse's more than a good detective. Ranking officers don't have partners, but myself and Jesse have been as good as partners since I was a sergeant. Without him and Obie, I'd have thrown in the towel when the PD junked the homicide squad. Obie's our Old Master, solid as a rock, you know? He's the one even Charmin' Billy respects."

"And what about that other charmer, Salsa?"

"We go way back to when he was eight years old. To tell that whole story, I might need more than one dinner—you better look at the menu before I get started or you'll be pretty hungry before I'm done." Menus conveniently appeared.

Distracted by the elegant dishes that were set before him like works of art, the dazzling panorama of the city, and the spell cast by Lauren, Flynn let down his guard. He told her about Salsa and the tug-of-war for Salsa between himself and Salsa's boss, Irish Viera. About Viera's cocaine kingdom and his murderous exploits. Though he skimmed over his own history with Viera, talking this much to a woman about his life on the job felt strange.

After dinner, they set out to walk across the Brooklyn Bridge, and Flynn kept right on talking. About halfway to Manhattan, he put his arms around Lauren and kissed her while hundreds of cars streamed by, their lights probing the night.

Monday afternoon, October 7, 1985

Monday—Practiced Slipping Punches.

Flynn smiled at the note Salsa had scribbled on a square of yellow paper and stuck on Flynn's gym locker. He got a real charge out of Salsa's commitment to the sport. But what about Gordo? Disappointed that the kid hadn't come through on that, Flynn dialed the combination that opened his locker door. As he pulled out his boxing shoes, a wrinkled scrap of newsprint floated to the floor. He looked down at it and saw a phone number written in the margin of the paper.

Pastore answered his call to the squad. "Ronnie, write down

this number"—Flynn read it off the strip of newsprint. "Call Cole's and get a name and address, okay?"

"What's the story, boss? Give me a hint."

"If we got what I think we got, you're gonna love it. The fat shooter in the Abdul homicide."

"O'Levy's case!"

"Yeah, *and* it turns out he's one of Viera's mutts. Think maybe he might know somethin' about Frostbite?"

"When are you comin' in?" Pastore managed a semicasual tone.

"I just walked into the guy—I'm gonna hit the bag a few times before I walk back out. If you draw a blank with Cole's, reach out for me here. Otherwise we'll put something together tonight and grab him in his pj's."

The Cole's Directory operator gave Pastore a Queens address and the name *Solano, E.,* which he wrote down on a fresh page of his notebook. He started toward the bosses' office to fill Carlucci in, then hesitated, turned back to the phone, dialed again, repeated the number to the Cole's operator, and heard the name and address a second time.

Tuesday morning, October 8, 1985

Soon after three A.M., Flynn and his detectives blasted off in three unmarked cars followed by an Emergency Service truck. The convoy took the Triborough Bridge out of Manhattan, passing through streets that Kenny Nolan, Flynn's partner from plainclothes days, had patrolled as a young cop in uniform. The neighborhood had been famous for its many bars—and some of the bars were infamous; Nolan had locked up plenty of the people who had helped give those bars a bad name.

The Queens Emergency Service truck met the convoy by the Travelers Hotel at LaGuardia Airport. Three cars and two trucks now drove toward East Elmhurst. Flynn radioed Queens Central: Keep the local cops out of the target area till the operation is over.

The vehicles paraded down empty avenues to a spot close to Gordo's address and waited in the silent, motionless night. Compared to the Two-nine, this stretch of four-story brick houses, would-be garden apartments, looked downright suburban. Not so much as a candle glimmered in any window; not even a tree branch quivered. Up to now anyone who had a mind to could easily have disappeared in this pitch dark.

Flynn sent O'Levy to scout the house and backyard. A common driveway ran behind the unit, serving it and neighboring ones on either side. Then Flynn told Emergency Service to go ahead and set up their spotlights and take positions around the house and in the driveway.

Taylor and Pastore were to drive to a phone booth a couple of blocks away and call Gordo from there. Taylor put the car in gear but idled the engine till the powerful Emergency Service beams lit up the nondescript structure like a movie set. Pastore stifled a gasp.

Taylor whistled. "Can you imagine if O'Levy had missed this production number—we woulda had to sedate him."

In a second-floor window, a hand shifted a venetian blind, but no light came on. The Emergency Service men reversed their peaked caps, visors back, and trained their shotguns on the floodlit house.

From the phone booth a few minutes later, Taylor radioed Flynn that they were ready.

"Okay—go ahead and call him!" Flynn's voice came over the walkie-talkie.

In the glare of the lights, the row of neat houses and lawns looked to Pastore more like a set for a grass seed commercial than a haven for drug dealers, but Flynn's sources had always produced before. Pastore had to believe Gordo was in there. Taylor dialed the number and firmly asked to speak to Gordo, *por favor*.

"He's sleeping—call back tomorrow," said a female voice. *Click*.

Sleeping! Through this Hollywood epic?

Taylor redialed. *"Policía,"* he told the woman. "Gordo's in trouble. Not for drugs—*big* trouble. We're coming in to get him—you better wake him up."

The woman hung up again. Taylor cursed as he redialed.

"Señora! Your house is surrounded; the men are armed. We're coming in for Gordo!"

"Please, no guns—I have a child here!"

"Tell Gordo to come out, hands up."

"Please—I'll get him. He's coming now."

"Is he out?"

"Sí, sí! Momentito!"

"What is he wearing?"

"Pantalones rojos y una camacilla roja y blanca."

"Andy," Taylor radioed to Flynn in front of the house two blocks away, "he's on the way out."

"What!"

"She says he's on the way out! He's wearing red pants and a red-and-white shirt." Taylor's radio was silent for about a minute. Then he heard Cooch's rasp.

"Jesse—nobody's coming out. What the fuck is going on?"

Pastore closed his eyes and crossed himself.

Taylor spoke distinctly. "She says he's on the steps with his hands up."

Another silence. Then Flynn radioed, "No one's out there, Jesse!"

"Tell me, *señora*"—Taylor managed to sound as if the right answer would win her the lottery—"what is your address?"

Taylor slammed the phone onto the hook. Pastore cringed as Taylor radioed, "Andy—you're at the wrong address!"

O'Levy slapped his forehead: "Holy shit—wrong address!"

Flynn, O'Levy, and Cooch looked at one another for an instant and dashed down the block. Flynn had deliberately parked the Chrysler behind all the other vehicles; no one was in the way. O'Levy tripped and almost fell as they neared the car.

Astoria Boulevard was as broad as the average highway. Flynn rocketed along the north side of it, back toward Manhattan. They'd been a good ten streets east of the right address.

"Andy—there he is!" Cooch yelled, and indeed, a tubby figure in a red-and-white sweat suit was slouching toward them on the south side of the boulevard.

Even Cooch laughed. "Un-fucking-believable! Andy—lemme out!"

Flynn was going too fast for that. They couldn't hop the wide, landscaped center strip either, not even at a lower speed, and the next U-turn was several long blocks down. Flynn finally reached the turn, but just as he pulled out of it, Gordo crossed an intersection and disappeared down a tree-lined, unlit side street.

"We lost him!" Flynn swore, but under his breath. He gunned the car to the intersection and hit the brakes hard, peering into the darkness. Nothing. He pulled the wheel over to make the turn anyway, wondering if he had the right street. Suddenly the white of the sweat suit bobbed again in the blackness.

Flynn veered to the side of the road, slammed on the brakes, and jumped out running, his grip tight on the wooden handle of the .38 he had won in the Academy.

"Halt!" he shouted several times as he narrowed the fifty-foot distance between himself and the bobbing patch of white. Gordo had speeded up but was not running as he had run from the homicide scene. He dropped something in the gutter. Now as Flynn closed in, Gordo's hands were hidden in front of him. O'Levy and Cooch were still a little way back.

"Police—*freeze!*" Flynn grabbed on to a shoulder, his fist full of fuzzy sweat-suit material. He held his gun close to his prisoner's face. After he had cuffed Irish Viera's former salesman, Flynn walked him to the nearest parked car and carefully patted him down for a weapon. Gordo had a little penknife on him, covered in mother-of-pearl and marked IRISH LUCK in green letters—but no nine-millimeter automatic.

"Andy," Cooch said to his boss, "what'd he drop?"

Gordo's little bit of cocaine just meant more paperwork for somebody—Flynn would as soon have kicked it into the sewer. He retrieved it and put it in his jacket pocket with the envelope of marijuana he had found in Gordo's sweatpants pocket. No wonder Fatso looked and sounded so spaced—must be zonked on pot.

O'Levy stuck close by Gordo's side. Taylor and Pastore walked just behind.

"Why do you do this?" Gordo griped. "I am sleeping peacefully, you keep ringin' the phone and wake up everybody. My sister's baby start screaming and never stop. I am tired."

"Then how come you went out walking? And by the way, where were you goin' when we just happened to run into you?"

"No place. My sister is having a fit—'the cops! the cops!' But I don't see no cops. The baby keep screaming so I go out. I don't do nothin'."

"Then you got nothin' to worry about. You get a free ride to the big city, how's that?"

"I don't do nothin'," Gordo insisted.

"Well, we'll just sit down and have a nice chat together."

"Too tired."

"You can sleep in the car, the lieutenant's a safe driver. Nobody'll disturb you, I promise."

The prisoner promptly nodded out before anyone could read him his rights.

Gordo cooled his heels in the bosses' office while Flynn had a quick strategy session with his men in the captain's office. When the detectives walked in on Gordo, Flynn didn't go with them.

Cooch, Taylor, Pastore, and O'Levy gathered around Gordo

as he sat in the armless wooden chair that Pastore had provided. He constantly fidgeted with the beeper he wore clipped to the bulging waistband of his red sweat suit.

"I'm gonna read you your rights, now," O'Levy said.

"No! I ain't dying—you ain't a priest! No rites!"

"You got the right—" O'Levy broke up—"to remain silent. Do you understand?"

"Yeah!"

Pastore tried to help. "You got the right to an attorney, and—"

"No! I don't do nothing! No lawyer!"

"Do you understand that you can have an attorney?"

"No lawyer!"

A high school graduate, Gordo would know enough to respect a desk and a suit, so at five in the morning, the sergeant put back on his well-tailored suit jacket. "We heard from a lot of people," Cooch began, "that you were at Abdul Mahmoud's newspaper store when Abdul was shot. These people all saw you. You better tell us everything you can about it...."

As the interview progressed, Gordo's hairline mustache glistened with moisture. He took the beeper off his waistband and played with it. Gordo opened his arms wide, palms up, and beseeched the detectives to understand that the shooting of Abdul Mahmoud, the community's favorite candy seller (Gordo related to candy more than to newspapers), had been a terrible accident. "I apologize. If Benny wasn't sick last Saturday, *he* would be shooting. Benny use the pistol; I use my brains. I am very, very sorry."

"Well, maybe we can get you criminally negligent homicide on that." O'Levy made sure to look as if he was seriously considering the possibility.

"Remorse is good," said Pastore philosophically. "The judge will go for it."

"You could do a couple of years, if we talk to the DA." O'Levy sounded sincere. "You don't have a record, until this arrest."

Gordo brightened; he looked as if he was thinking that the cops seemed to understand him.

The detectives had all been sitting until this point. Suddenly Cooch was on his feet, looming over Gordo. "We all know the real reason for this 'accident,'" Cooch growled. "You was trying to shoot José-Maria LaPaz and poor Abdul got in the way—"

"José shot at *me.*"

"Abdul was a hard worker." O'Levy stood up, planted his foot on the chair seat, and leaned toward Gordo; the gesture was pure

Flynn. "He left a wife and five little kids in Morocco with no one to support them anymore because of this terrible murder."

"José is no good." Gordo hit his palm with his fist and almost dropped his beeper. "He kill you in a minute. He need to be locked up for a long time. In my childhood, my mother taught me not to run away. 'Defend yourself, Juan-Emanuel,' she told me every day before I went to school. They picked on me because I was fat—it was always, 'Gordito, Gordito, open your lunch box!' Nobody else *have* a lunchbox.

"Do you expect me to run away or let José kill me? The streets will be much safer here when you put José in Attica. You will be heroes to these people." Damp patches on the red sweat suit showed the effort Gordo put into his speech.

"You knew that Abdul had a *clear view* of your gunfight with José; maybe you didn't shoot Abdul by accident after all. We have several witnesses to this crime who told us in detail who did what—right, Detective?" Cooch asked O'Levy.

"That's correct, Sergeant, I have all the reports right here." O'Levy opened the file on Flynn's desk.

"This shooting shows *reckless disregard for human life,* Gordo."

Gordo shut his eyes tight and uttered a little moan. "Please, Sergeant—I am *Juan-Emanuel.*" Trickles of sweat garnished his moon-shaped face.

Cooch folded his arms on his charcoal-gray flannel chest. "That's Murder Two, Gordo. Twenty-five years to life."

"Depending, of course..." Pastore reached for O'Levy's file and closed it.

"Depending how *we* present the witnesses and the case," Taylor explained.

It was 0600 hours; according to plan, Flynn passed by the partly open door of the office and Cooch motioned him to come in. "Boss," Cooch rasped, "regarding the Mahmoud murder—do you have a minute?"

"Of course—tragic case." Flynn shook his head, his hazel eyes serious. "Community wants blood."

For Gordo, Pastore thought, the world had shrunk to the size of the small room he now shared with five detectives. Outside the window, the night was black and soundless. Not even any traffic noises to remind him of the time, only a few hours ago, when he took his freedom for granted.

"Mr., uh, Concepción," Cooch went on, "is the shooter in the Mahmoud case. He claims it was an accidental shooting. Now it just so happens that he also has something to tell us about that double murder last spring—Herrera-Hernandez."

Gordo's sallow face paled.

"It happens that Mr. Concepción is an employee of Irish Viera."

"Well!" Flynn unbuttoned his jacket and sat on the edge of the sergeant's desk. In his dated three-piece suit of indeterminate color with his tie a little bit loose, he could have been an accountant ready to drive home to a Long Island suburb—except for the small .38 in the leather holster on his hip. Strands of straight, black hair fell on his forehead. His chin almost rested on his chest as he looked intently at Gordo.

Gordo paled another shade lighter before Pastore's very eyes; anxiety leaked from every pore. No one would ever consider giving up Irish Viera. If Irish ordered the fingers cut off thieves, Gordo must be thinking, what would he cut off a stoolie?

Pastore admired the way his bosses handled Gordo; O'Levy was doing good, too. Pastore didn't dwell on the near snafu caused by the wrong address he had researched; for the time being anyway, nobody else had brought it up. He could think of nowhere he would rather be than where he was—learning from Flynn and Cooch.

"Of course," Flynn said to Gordo, "we know who killed those two dummies. And you do, too. So tell us what you know and we'll see if we all agree. And we'll see if we can believe you about this 'accident.'"

"Well..." Gordo mopped his brow with the sleeve of his sweat suit top. The look on his face said he believed the cops knew the truth. "I heard that Irish did it 'cause they beat him for some coke."

"He *heard.*" Cooch spat out the word. "Forget it. The lieutenant asked you what you *know,* now didn't he. That's what we asked for—what you *know,* what you *saw*. So now let's start over, okay, Gordo?"

"I didn't see nothing."

Flynn pointed a finger. "Herrera and Hernandez beat Irish for some coke—*that* you know. Okay, how much coke?" He counted on Gordo's common sense. Even Irish did not kill you for a detail.

"Ten ounces, they say."

"Ten ounces, *you* say," Flynn corrected. "Don't even bother to tell us what you heard. *Unless* you heard it right there with your own ears."

"Irish told me." Gordo blotted his face with the sleeve of his sweat-suit jacket. Pastore opened his steno book to a fresh page and wrote the date and Gordo's nickname and real name.

"That's better," Flynn said. "So what did Irish do about these dealers stealing over half a pound of coke from him?"

"He did what he had to do."

"Killed 'em?"

"You don't fuck with Irish."

"So Irish killed them."

"Yeah."

"Did Irish do it himself this time?" The computer in Cooch's head sifted the precinct's homicide cases, marking all the other ones Viera was involved in.

"That he didn't tell me, Sergeant."

Flynn and Cooch exchanged looks of annoyance. "If he didn't pull the trigger on those two," Flynn said, "I want to know who did."

Pastore kept writing.

O'Levy reminded the suspect, *"You* pulled the trigger on Abdul."

"No—Los Primos wasn't *shot.* I heard they—"

"You what?"

"They got *cut!"*

"You didn't hear it, you *saw* it," Cooch said as confident as if he weren't making it all up. "Now, lemme ask you this: Was it Irish who cut them?"

"Look, man—Listen, ten years—whatever time I gotta do, I'll do. If Irish finds out—my time is *up,* man. I ain't rattin' on him."

"You saw it," Flynn pressed. "You were *there.* As far as we know, man—you helped *set it up.* On Abdul's homicide, we could maybe make a case that it was an accident and get you 'criminally negligent.' But killing the dealers, that's another story."

Gordo's friend Pastore had kept silent for a while. Now he looked at the suspect and shook his head. "That's gotta be Murder Two," he said.

"Exactly," Flynn agreed. Gordo had sweated off a pound, at least. He rubbed his empty belly. "We got enough here to charge you on Herrera and Hernandez and there's *no* deal on that. No way. And my men don't want to sit around here till lunchtime. So let's take it from the top, now: Who did what, who said what. From when you first walked in to Three-S, One twenty West Hundred and fifth Street on Friday night, March fifteenth."

"I think someone's going out for food, " Pastore whispered to Gordo. "You want something?"

"Chicharrones," the suspect sighed deeply, exhaling as he said the name of his favorite dish.

"Uh-huh," Pastore said. "Get started."

Gordo sighed again. "Me and Benny, we come to work that night—"

"What time?" Flynn asked.

"Seven o'clock. We always come on and Los Primos take off."

"Herrera-Hernandez—they're cousins?" Flynn had heard it from Salsa, too; he wanted confirmation.

"Cousins from a stupid family," Gordo said. "So we just walk in the door; Monte shows up with the boss. He didn't beep me or nothin', to let me know."

"You mean this guy—Luis Almonte?" Pastore showed Gordo the NYPD's out-of-date picture.

"Yeah, Monte."

"Which one cut Los Primos?" Flynn asked.

"Monte did it."

"Besides the cousins and you and Benny—who's Benny?"

"My man—Benito Silvera."

"Besides them and you two, who's there in Three-S?"

"Just Monte and the boss. They come in and first thing, the boss pulls out two guns; 'Nobody move!' he says. Monte just grabs Hector from behind and cuts his throat. Hector didn't have a chance to say nothin'."

"What did Monte use?"

"A knife for carpets—curved. In a second, he hooks into the artery, about a gallon of blood pours out."

"Then what?"

"Hector falls in the blood."

"Yeah, and?"

"Geraldo is shaking like a tree. Me and Benny don't say nothing. We don't know what's coming next. Irish goes for his briefcase and takes out a whole kilo. He starts throwing handfuls of coke on Hector, on the floor. The blood is getting it pink. He goes, 'Geraldo, next time you tell me *right away* when you hear someone is thinking of stealing from me. Don't wait. I should kill you, too.' Geraldo says, 'Well, it's my cousin'—you know, like his aunt ain't gonna take this too good. But Irish looks at Monte and his eyes say, neither is Geraldo's mother. So then Monte hooks Geraldo's neck with the knife. Los Primos are both on the floor and there's blood everywhere, except where Irish is. His Guccis are perfect.

"Irish points at Benny and me and he goes, 'You ever want some coke from me, you just ask, that's all. You can *have* it.' And he gets the rest of the kilo and starts throwing it all over Los Primos."

"Just a minute, Gordo," Flynn said, "you left something out." He waited till the suspect had to look him in the eye and asked, "Who cut the fingers?"

"Benny.

"Irish says, 'This is for thiefs.' Monte gives Benny the big clippers—like for bushes, you know? And he did it."

O'Levy had been sitting quietly, staring at the pattern in his pegged pants, but now he looked up. "Judges don't like liars, Gordo."

"It ain't a lie," Gordo protested, "Benny did Hector's fingers."

"And Juan-Emanuel did Geraldo's," Pastore said, making notes on his steno pad.

" 'Hurry up!' Benny tells me. It was hard, I can't do it fast," Gordo said. Then he muttered, *"Los stupidos—primos stupidos.* Can't do nothing right."

"Why did Geraldo rat on his cousin?" Flynn asked.

"Los Primos wanted the coke for a buyer in Staten Island—the deal was eighteen hundred an ounce. They see a quick score so they faked it that somebody robbed them of half a pound. Me and Benny come up to take over one night—they're all tied up and Hector has a black eye. But Monte knows it was bullshit."

"Staten Island?" questioned Pastore, thinking of his wife, Kitty, and his two small daughters, the nice quiet home in the borough with a reputation for peacefulness.

"Yeah." Gordo shook his head again. *"Stupidos!"* he fumed. "So the boss calls Geraldo up to the office and Geraldo says it's his cousin's idea. 'Bad idea,' the boss says. 'Business is good—tell *tu primo* Hector not to think so much,' he says. He gives Geraldo a drink and lets him go, but I heard from Monte that Irish is upset. *Stupidos!"*

O'Levy went to the supply closet and selected a fresh legal pad for Gordo's statement.

Pastore was brooding about the Staten Island drug buy. "You sure, Juan-Emanuel," he asked, "it wasn't *City* Island or *Long* Island?"

"Los primos los más stupidos," Gordo repeated his theme. "Do you believe it, the Staten Island dude was a cop anyway. I know because the guy who put the deal together, he is in jail now."

O'Levy gave Gordo the yellow legal pad. "We want you to write your statement now, about the accidental shooting of Abdul."

"I am hungry," Gordo complained. "Too hungry to write."

"Just begin," Pastore told him, "your *chicharrones* are gonna be here in two minutes."

Flynn dialed the homicide-call number for a DA.

* * *

"Breakfast!" O'Levy said as he delivered the bulky brown paper bag. Gordo stretched out his arms for it. After he had unpacked the paper napkin and the plastic knife and fork, removed the cardboard cover from the aluminum pie plate, and started munching on the fried chunks of chicken, O'Levy told him, "By the way, you're under arrest for the shooting of Abdul Mahmoud."

Gordo's appetite didn't seem to desert him and his mouth was too full of *chicharrones* for him to protest.

Pastore felt no fatigue as he went to the file cabinet to safeguard several pages of notes on Frostbite. He was itching to get Gordo on videotape, too; when the day came that the suave and personable Irish Viera got behind a defense table, the jury was gonna need to see and hear something more drastic than notes in a notebook. Flynn and the others were also walking on air. Then the desk sergeant called from downstairs.

"Counselor's here—Stanley Britton?—for that perp you're holding."

Gordo had not even asked anyone for permission to make a phone call; he hadn't quite finished breakfast. Was Viera psychic or what? the cops wondered. Where in hell was the DA, the video crew?

Britton shouldered his way through the swinging doors, his silk tie flying and his expensive leather briefcase gleaming. He looked as if he'd been up and running for hours. The attorney's belly matched his client's, except that it was better dressed. "I'm Stanley Britton, legal counsel to Mr. Concepción—bring him right out, please."

"Early bird gets the worm, all right," Pastore muttered. "You'll need to see the lieutenant, of course," he explained politely, postponing the inevitable. "Let me try and locate him."

After Britton's session with Gordo, his thick salt-and-pepper hair looked as if he'd been running his fingers through it, but his voice was calm with a steel edge. "Not only did you fail to read my client his Miranda rights, you tortured Mr. Concepción into signing his name to ridiculous statements about whatever murder cases you happen to be under pressure to solve."

"We read your client his rights, Mr. Britton. He told us he didn't want counsel. In fact, it's kind of a mystery who called you since he didn't. And nobody even raised a voice at him, let alone a hand."

"I'm referring to *mental* torture—beginning with your four A.M. terror tactics at his sister's door." Britton simply ignored that the cops had *missed* the sister's door by a good half mile. "Of course four o'clock in the morning is your usual hour for convening witnesses, isn't it, Lieutenant?"

"When necessary, it is. And I certainly agree that we're under 'pressure' to catch killers. Most people in this precinct don't like to see anyone get away with murder. That kind of 'pressure' we couldn't agree with more. But nailing the wrong man ain't the answer."

"Well"—Britton's tone warmed up about thirty degrees and he went head-to-head with the truth as he would in a courtroom—"then we can all shake hands and call it a day—including poor Mr. Concepción, because he *is* the wrong man."

"Nice try, Counselor—save it for the jury."

The steel-edged voice returned. "Mr. Concepción has consulted counsel." Britton headed for the swinging doors. "If the DA was here, I'd say it to him, too. No more questions to my client, not even 'How are you?' "

Flynn called after Britton, "Come back and join us for the lineup, Counselor."

Pastore sat down at the nearest desk and buried his face in the typewriter keys. Taylor gave Flynn a you-know-I-support-you-but-it-ain't-always-fun look.

"Ronnie," Flynn said, "where'd you hide O'Levy?"

Pastore didn't raise his head but made as if to pound a fist on the desk, noiselessly.

"Right here." O'Levy emerged from the coffee room. "Coffee's ready, gang."

"Give Ronnie a cup of that. He's got Frostbite on the brain. I can tell. Then go write on the chart: 'Abdul case cleared. Gordo arrested.' "

"Yeah, but what've we got for the DA to work with. Bupkis."

"You must be tired, pal. We're gonna have a nice juicy lineup, remember?—and we're gonna find the *gun.*"

"First we gotta find the DA," Taylor pointed out. "If he would've made it over here with the video before Britton showed up, we wouldn't be in this mess."

O'Levy brought Pastore a steaming cup of coffee. Pastore's head moved. O'Levy bent down and stage-whispered, "This is for you—if you promise never, never to call Cole's Directory again as long as you work here."

Thursday night, October 10, 1985

Viera was upstairs in the club table hopping and wouldn't be down till some time after he had introduced the show. Monte and Salsa hung out in the office, waiting for him. Salsa wanted to catch a number or two before he and Monte left to make the night's rounds.

"Whose gig is it?" Monte asked.

"A Dominican girl group—I heard they're hot."

"Dominicans? *Coño!* Watch your ass around those *campesinos.* Watch it *double* if they're women."

"I'm not doin' a deal with 'em; just wanna open my ears and see what comes in, you know?"

"Listen at your own risk," Monte insisted.

Salsa changed the subject. "What's Mr. Irish want us for?"

"He didn't say. Take it easy, relax. He'll be here any minute."

Salsa sat back in his chair, enjoying the rich feel of the leather. Even though Viera's office had become familiar territory, the room impressed Salsa all over again each time he went there: the marble and phones and everything—all of it made to order.

The boss walked in the door, wearing a dark-blue suit and a wine-colored shirt and tie. He moved as thin and graceful as a snake, Salsa thought.

As it turned out, Irish wanted to talk about sales over on Amsterdam—Gordo's territory. Usually, Salsa didn't come to these meetings; just Irish and Monte.

"The curve is still flat," Irish said, "what's the problem?—I thought Silvera and the new guy could handle it."

"Benny's still training the new guy, for one thing. The other thing is, he was kind of down about Gordo bein' gone. And that was even before the cops dumped Gordo in the can. That made it worse, I guess. Of course, I been tellin' Benny *pep up*—but now I'll tell him you don't like the figures. That'll goose him."

The intercom buzzed and Monte picked it up. "Ramón says the drinks are comin' down."

Viera smiled. "Tell Silvera that *I* said Gordo sends his best. He's comfortable—we make sure of that. He even works out in the gym over there."

"Oh, yeah—you heard from him, boss?" Monte asked. The waiter arrived and Viera buzzed him in.

"Indirectly. Gordo's gonna beat this rap—because he was smart and ditched the gun. Not like some *imbécils* who worry how much money they're throwing in the sewer. Salsa, pay attention: In certain circumstances, you and your gun are better off going separate ways." Irish turned to Monte again. "Those brilliant cops aren't about to find where Gordo dropped the pistol and neither is anyone else." He raised his glass of Bailey's on the rocks. "*Salud.*"

"Kind of a shame, though, letting it lay there and rust," Monte objected. "We're talkin' big pesos for that."

Irish looked Monte straight in the eye. "I don't care if it's a million pesos and you been getting around in sewers all your life. *Leave it* right where it is—in the sewer by the newspaper store."

"Forget it, boss"—Monte shuddered—"I can't handle no sewers. Something else you wanted?"

"Check on Benny's new guy and *make sure* he knows what's expected of him. Tell everybody else you see tonight that I want extra productivity to make up for the Gordo gap."

Monte stood up, drained his martini glass, and ate the olive. "*Vamos,* Salsa."

"Have a good night," Viera said as Monte and Salsa walked out.

Monte started for the back entrance.

"I gotta hear one number," Salsa said, "just one."

"You got five minutes—like I told you, listen at your own risk."

Monday morning, October 14, 1985

While Emergency Service searched the sewer at the corner of Amsterdam Avenue and Ninety-second Street, the whole block had to be closed to traffic and the cops who stood guard refused to let car owners take their cars out of the metered parking spaces. Faces turned as red as the expired meters. "I'm late and I'll get a ticket to boot!" fumed the owner of a silver Conquest.

"We're not writin' tickets, lady," a cop answered. "And they're gonna be done with this job in a few minutes. You'll just be a little late."

"Done with what job?"

"They didn't tell us the details."

She stuck her head out the window. "Looks like they're fishing for something."

"Could be."

It was noon when the cop got the word that the search was over. "Off you go," he said to the infuriated lady.

"Did they find what they were looking for?"

"I'm just directing traffic, lady."

She looked up the block at the knot of detectives by the Emergency Service truck. "They don't look happy," she said with satisfaction.

Flynn and Taylor watched Emergency Service lower the sewer grate back in position. "Well," Flynn said, "at least we didn't stand out here in the rain all morning."

"I'm glad you had a nice time," Taylor said. "I would've had a better time if we found the 9mm."

"Can't understand it."

"Lemme ask you this"—Taylor imitated raspy-voiced Cooch, who was on his swing and was no doubt raking leaves in his driveway—"did you make it to the boxing club on Saturday?"

"Sure did."

"And you ran into the next Macho Camacho..."

"Yup."

"...who just happened to mention something about a gun in a sewer."

"Yup."

"I never did trust that kid. His boss is playin' games with us and usin' him to do it."

Flynn contemplated the sewer grate as if he wanted to start the search all over again. "There's gotta be another reason why this didn't pan out. If Salsa gave us bad information, that don't mean he knew he was doin' it. Irish is certainly capable of screwing him *and* us in one move. Which means Salsa could have a major problem—wouldn't you say?"

"He could." Taylor couldn't disagree with a conspiracy theory just because he didn't dream it up himself.

"I'm gonna get Freddy Urquhart and Larry Mazocek to sit on Salsa's place tonight."

"Yeah—set your mind at ease." Worrying wasn't Andy's style, Taylor knew, so if he was worried, maybe he had a right to be.

Early morning, Wednesday, October 16, 1985

As the sun started coming up, Monte always drove back to the Tabu with the night's receipts. Monte would drop Salsa off at his rooming house on Manhattan Avenue unless Salsa felt like dancing the last cut or two in the disco. But today, without asking, Monte just drove straight to the club.

Salsa got along fine with Monte, especially if Salsa didn't ask questions, because Monte didn't have the patience. He let you find things out as you went along and that was okay with Salsa. If something was wrong, Monte wouldn't keep it a secret.

When Monte and Salsa got to Irish's office, Irish had his earphones on and was listening to a tape. He never looked tired, no matter what time it was. He let them sit down and kept listening. All of sudden he pushed open a wall panel behind him, took out another set of 'phones, and handed them to Salsa, who put them on. The music was good but Salsa didn't recognize the group.

"What do you think?" Irish asked when the side was over.

"Good; they sound different—where they from?"

"Colombia."

"Oh, no wonder I didn't catch it. I never heard much Colombian."

Irish held out his hand for the 'phones. "You got a good ear for the words, kid." His tone got hard as the marble slab in front of him. "But you should have stuck to *music.*"

Salsa squirmed in the leather chair. What had happened to get Irish worked up like this?

"You repeat anything you hear at the Tabu Club, it better be *music*. The words you keep to yourself. Who do you think we are"—for a moment, Salsa saw Irish as a coiled snake; then the snake began uncoiling across the marble, its fury hissing—"some moron *campesinos* who don't know what tune you're singing and who you're singing it *to?*"

Salsa flushed hot, only to feel the next instant as if he'd been hit by a blast of air-conditioning. His heart banged. All his training at the gym couldn't help him while he stayed a prisoner in the chair—yet to stand up seemed suicidal.

"You hear a business discussion about one of our dealers who's got problems with the police and throws his gun away—"

Oh, *Dios*—the gun!

"—and you dare to go running to the precinct and blab to your 'hero of the month.' What an insult! You know, your taste in heroes disgusts me." The snake swayed menacingly in front of Salsa. "Well, you won't be surprised to learn that this organization has ways to gag little squeals. You'll learn the hard way...."

Salsa sat mesmerized, his insides hollow. How could they have found out? *How?* That terrified Salsa more even than Irish's threat. Salsa had nowhere to turn for help. Out of the corner of his eye, he could see Monte sitting against the wall looking at a magazine.

"I put a lot into you." Viera's voice came back, cold and hard. "You're doing better than you ever dreamed, thanks to Irish

Luck—and you go *sing to the cops!*" He sat back, his eyes pinning Salsa. "That's what they call a swan song; the last one you ever sing. Monte, get rid of this bird. I don't want him around."

Salsa had no time—he felt his air supply close off as the choke hold clamped on his neck and his body left the smooth leather chair. In a second everything went black.

He came to with ice on his face, lying on the thick black carpet in the office. Monte stood over him.

Salsa wasn't quite sure he was actually alive. "Lucky," Monte said, frowning down at him. "Irish decided to give you one more chance. That's the only time in history I saw that happen, and I know it ain't gonna happen again. You better know it, too." He made no move to help as Salsa struggled to sit up. "Now you gotta prove we can trust you. You're on trial—and remember—this was a fluke. Next time there won't be no waking up."

Salsa managed to get to his feet and wobble out the door. He didn't go upstairs but slipped through the dark kitchen and the back door. Groggy as he was, he felt a terrible dread. For the first time since he was a kid and took the numbers money, he feared that he was in trouble he wouldn't get out of. Like Monte had said, he had to find some way to make them trust him again...how would he do it?

Viera yawned and took off his earphones. "Very nice, Monte—you handled him just right. He needed some discipline, and he needs some more. He understands now he can't screw around, but you gotta keep after him so he doesn't forget. When he has that down, he'll be useful—very useful."

"We tested him, boss, and he flunked. Zero. He ain't nothin' but a kid with big ears and a big mouth. I don't get how that's useful."

"Because our famous 'hero' lieutenant *likes* him. We're gonna teach Salsa to use those ears in the precinct and that mouth over here—Flynn will be sorry he ever had anything to do with him."

"I still don't see why you want to fool around," Monte complained. "That cop could've been in the river months ago."

"I told you—we're going to make him *wish* he was in the river. I'll give you the latest example of what I mean, and then I'm going home for a siesta."

Monte massaged his face to revive himself, feeling the severe case of five-o'clock shadow on his cheeks and chin. "What do you have in mind?"

"Gordo. He's Flynn's prize catch. We'll make sure he slips out of their net and into ours. When we get through with that fat fish, the DA won't be able to serve him to any juries. Ever...."

Thursday, October 17, 1985

Larry Mazocek had spent most of the morning testifying in a six-month-old assault case. It went well, including the cross. Now he sat on a stool in the dismal courthouse coffee shop. He was not about to *eat* anything in this place; you had to be really in a hurry to make that sacrifice. He just wanted a cup of hot coffee to tide him over. All around him, harried people were ordering factory-built sandwiches and paying too much for them.

Mazocek stuck a paper napkin under his cup to blot up the slopped-over coffee and took a sip. How could it be lukewarm already? The counterman had just poured it out of the pot. By the time he'd be able to get the counterman's attention, it'd be stone cold anyway. The detective noticed the two court officers who came into the shop, talking excitedly.

"It's so fuckin' easy, it's a miracle it don't happen once a day," the one with the blond crewcut said.

"You can't stop the defendants from havin' a conversation," said the one with thinning gray hair and glasses. "Even if they're in for somethin' big. This guy that just vamoosed was a homicide suspect, no less."

"Where did he walk out of?"

"Part Eighty-one!" The officers digressed to gossip about friends assigned to duty in that courtroom.

Mazocek hoped for the sake of the detectives involved in the homicide case, whoever they might be, that the case had at least been a grounder.

The court officers picked up the thread again. "This wasn't Mr. Nondescript, either. I heard he was fat enough to roll outta there and he was wearin' a fuckin' red sweat suit."

"Black guy?"

"Hispanic."

Mazocek remembered hearing O'Levy laugh about Gordo, the fat perp in the Abdul case, and he began to feel a little uneasy. He told himself that fat Hispanics in red sweat suits were a dime a dozen. When the court officers left with their take-out bags, Mazocek followed. He caught up with them by the bank of elevators and politely identified himself—"Mazocek, Two-nine squad. Would you mind filling me in," he said respectfully. Nothing else in the NYPD compared with the polish of these sharply pressed white uniform shirts. "Okay, this happened in Part Eighty-one, right? Are you sayin' the judge released a homicide defendant?

Where was the DA? Y'know, I just wanna make sure this ain't one of *our* perps...."

The officer with the crewcut said the judge *thought* he was releasing a shoplifter. The two Hispanic perps—shoplifter and murderer—had secretly switched IDs. Mazocek heard him through an anxious haze. As usual, the judge was rushin' through millions of cases and didn't notice that the shoplifter's picture didn't look nothin' like him. If you ask me, a murder rap was the least of the fat guy's problems. He hadda be a rat and he was scared of who he ratted on. That shoplifter musta made some piece of change.... The officers' words ran together. Drug money, what else?

Mazocek took a deep breath and thanked the court officers. He turned and walked out to the lobby where clipboards with each day's court calendars were posted on the wall. Halfway down the top sheet, there it was: *Juan-Emanuel Concepción 02899-85 Part 81 Room 1300*. The detective looked across the lobby at the row of pay phones—one was free.

"Two-nine squad, Pastore."

"Ronnie, is the boss out? It's me, Larry."

"Yeah, he's out. What's the story? You sound like you're goin' down for the third time."

Mazocek told him. "Gordo pulled a fast one—paid some shoplifter in the holding pen to switch IDs. Just walked out there when the other mutt's case was called. The judge's eyeglasses was dirty or somethin'—he didn't catch it. He ain't gonna hold no fuckin' shoplifter—so out goes Fatso, fancy-free."

"You made that up," Pastore said, "it didn't happen."

"Now who's goin' down for the third time? Get your shoes on an' hop over here—we'll put out a Wanted flyer."

Thursday night, October 17, 1985

To avoid the corner where Monday's disastrous sewer search had gone down, Flynn tried walking back to Lauren's place via Columbus Avenue instead of Amsterdam—but he could see the offending corner perfectly every time he climbed the steps of Lauren's stoop. What he needed, he decided, was a glimpse of his old homestead—and of her. When he called, she said of course, the welcome mat at the Anastasia Suite was always out for him.

She looked great in her jeans and red polo shirt and she felt great in his arms. They kissed and neither one wanted to stop.

"That's better," he said finally. "How long has it been, anyway?"

She took a step back, looking at him. "Almost two weeks."

He sat down on the futon and patted the space beside him. "Come hear my excuses."

"You don't need to make excuses." She sat down but didn't cuddle up.

He put his arm around her. "Sorry—what I meant is, lately me and my buddies just haven't been havin' our usual fun at the office, but we've been spending lots of time tryin'."

"Did you see *The Westsider* this week?"

When he said no, she went to get her briefcase. The clipping was a page-two story by Hank Markle:

Cops Search Sewer in Vain For 'Candy Store Murder' Weapon

Markle, the only press to show up at the search, hadn't been allowed near the Emergency Service truck. Instead, Flynn realized, the reporter must have wandered around listening to marooned car owners griping to the uniformed cops. Markle had managed to turn one of the overheard conversations into a story about the search. His article also noted that the police had a suspect in custody, Juan-Emanuel Concepción, and that they were seeking the gun as evidence against him.

"That's what I mean," Flynn said, "no fun."

"No *gun*—but it says you do have a suspect in custody. How did I miss that?"

"I don't think it got a lot of coverage—too late for the dailies, I guess. . . ."

"How come *you* didn't tell me."

"Well, it was sort of an empty victory for various reasons and now it's even emptier."

"Why?"

Flynn looked at his watch. "This time around, Juan-Emanuel *is* gonna make the news. It's almost eleven—"

"Oh, shit. I think I did hear something about it but the name didn't mean anything and I didn't . . . Is *he* the one that escaped from court today?"

"You got it."

"What a bitch. After all that investigation . . ."

"I wouldn't mind talking about something else."

"There's only one silver lining to all of this."

Flynn looked incredulous.

"I can go back to old 'Nine-two' Street and let you have your beloved Anastasia Suite."

"What makes you think that's a good idea?"

"The guy's too busy hiding out to worry about some witness. He probably never goes out of the house, wherever he is."

"Forget it. This isn't just one guy—it's a whole network. Before he escaped, he told us quite a few things this network is not happy that we know. They're a bunch of extremely bad guys with all kinds of devious ideas about how to get what they want. It wouldn't be smart at all to assume they forgot about you."

Lauren looked anything but happy.

Flynn still had the *Westsider* clipping in his hand; he got up and put it on the round table with her briefcase. Then he went back to the futon and looked at it, head to one side, pretending puzzlement. "Excuse me, ma'am, d'you know how this thing works?"

Reflexively, she got up. "What? 'Ma'am' again!"

"I mean, 'miss'—give me a hand, miss, okay?"

Laughing, they put the futon in its bed mode, then Flynn reached out and drew her to him. He rolled up the hem of her red polo shirt and kissed her midriff. He undid her jeans and kissed her just above the top of her polka-dot bikini pants. Feeling her tremble, he picked her up and laid her on the futon bed. He stretched out next to her and brushed aside her hair just a little so he could kiss her neck yet still feel her hair on his face. She inhaled deeply and pressed her body against the length of his.

"You can change the subject," she said, undoing his belt buckle, "but not permanently."

The touch of her cool hand destroyed his ability to focus on anything else. "What subject?"

"My place—I miss it. I want to go back soon."

Saturday, October 19, 1985

Flynn threaded his way through the carnival of dubious characters who occupied Forty-second Street. The prostitutes, pimps, and transvestites; the larcenous dippers, hooks, and stalls and God knows what else—no single specimen could surprise him, but seen all together, they looked, as Jesse would say, a sight.

For once Flynn got to the gym at a reasonable hour. Salsa had just arrived, too—they'd have plenty of time for a workout. When Flynn came down from the locker room, he joined the kid in front of the mirror. Salsa's expression looked uncharacteristically serious.

Flynn started breathing deeply from the belly. He let his arms hang and concentrated on letting go of the tension in his shoulders. *Forget,* he told himself, as he always told the kids he trained. Forget everything except standing here in your body, he would tell them. This ain't the competitive part. Just for now, never mind that Gordo's in the wind and everything else.

Flynn and Salsa started the boxer's bounce, an easy little shuffle on the balls of the feet. Two minutes of that and your pulse starts to pick right up. Then the stretches—upper body, groin. Then the arms—small circles forward, then back; finally "windmills": big circles.

"Remember," Salsa broke the silence, looking at Flynn in the mirror as they began the second set of small arm-circles, "remember you was lookin' for somethin' last time I saw you?"

"Right."

"Didja, um, look where I said?"

"You bet."

"Find it?"

"No, we didn't." Flynn looked at Salsa in the mirror.

Salsa frowned. "I heard it was definitely supposed to be there. What about the owner of it, did he say where it's at?"

The gun-in-the-sewer tip might well have been planted by Viera, Flynn thought, especially since Salsa was still in one piece. As for Gordo, Salsa had brought up the subject himself. Flynn began to wonder if Salsa even knew the perp had escaped. "He told us about his childhood and his mom and all, but he didn't say nothing about the sewer."

"The boss and Monte talk about that guy a lot. Sounds like *they* wanna get ahold of him."

Flynn kept the windmills going, getting the distinct impression that this time it was Salsa who was looking for information.

"He ain't movin' from where he is—why couldn't they?"

Salsa stopped doing the exercise and shook out his arms. "That's gotta be sixty windmills." He frowned again. "I guess they ain't heard from him since a little after you got him—Monte keeps tellin' *me* to find him."

Salsa definitely wouldn't be telling Flynn where to find Gordo—because Salsa didn't know. And he was a lot more uptight about it than he was willing to admit. But why...?

"Okay, let's see how you look in the mirror. *Concentrate.* Look yourself in the eye—that's who you're fightin' right now." Flynn concentrated, too. Watching Salsa's technique intently, he allowed his mind to empty, except for the hypnotizing image in the mirror. The kid's work was uneven, punches savage but often lacking control. The reason why Salsa wanted to find Gordo, whatever it was, had put real fear in his eye. Only that once, years ago, had Flynn seen Salsa in terror. Why should finding Gordo be so important—even life-or-death? Flynn actually thanked God he don't know where Gordo was, because no way could he have told Salsa.

The bell rang. Salsa let his hands fall to his sides and sent Flynn a "What gives?" look. Usually, Flynn would make comments off and on through the round. Flynn handed him a water bottle. "Your timing's been better than it is today. A lot better. You kept your balance good—but you're kinda pushin' your punches—where's the snap an' pivot? You gotta make each one count, y'know. I ain't seen you like this before, like somethin's really buggin' you. More than buggin' you—scarin' you."

Salsa kept silent and avoided Flynn's eye.

"Fair enough; that's what boxin' is supposed to help you with. Just remember this—when you feel scared is when you need the control *most*. You gotta hold *on* to the technique, not let it go. You let go a little—next thing you know, it's all gone. Then you're sunk. If you lose it, you lose."

Salsa looked subdued.

Flynn kneaded the tense muscles behind Salsa's neck. "C'mon—deep breaths, pal. You got the stuff, all right. Everybody hits a rough spot. Let's do some combinations now. Ready?"

Saturday night, October 19, 1985

As soon as Flynn put the key in the lock at Lauren's apartment that night, he sensed something peculiar. He stood to the side of the door and leveraged it open with his outstretched arm. All the lights were on. Most of the floor space in the small living room was taken up by suitcases. Flynn walked in, pulling the door shut after him.

Kitchen light also was on; the Saturday papers lay on the counter. Everything might be all right, but the act of walking into an apartment that had suddenly become an unknown quantity made his adrenaline rush. He braced himself for disaster as he went to check the bedroom and bath. Nobody, and nothing looked wrong.

Just as Flynn reentered the living room, the front door opened. Flynn took a giant step back toward the bedroom, his hand going to the gun on his hip. Lauren walked in with a bag of groceries. "Oh, hi," she said.

"Oh, hi, yourself."

"Don't give me a hard time, okay?"

"What I said still goes." He was yelling without meaning to. "You're not *safe* here."

"I'm fine, thanks. Really." Her voice stayed normal.

"Look, there's nothing in it for me to keep you away from your place. Except to keep you in one piece, which—I plead guilty—matters to me."

She ignored his concern. "Mentally, I'm already in six pieces. I just need to be *here*. So I'm here and that's got to be that."

"Your living here right now is like living in enemy territory. It's like—driving drunk. A bad risk not worth taking."

Lauren plopped down in the big chair and folded her arms. "I just went to the supermarket and back; everything seems just the same except Abdul's place is empty. I absolutely refuse to give in to an overreacting cop. That's what it is—overreaction. I just won't let that rule my life."

She seemed out of reach of reason, and now the big chair was Flynn's enemy instead of his ally. "There's no such thing as overreacting if you know what goes on out there. How many different ways do I gotta tell you? What'd you do, leave your brains at the office yesterday or what?"

"I wasn't aware that my *brains* had ever attracted your notice."

That was about the only dumb thing he'd ever heard her say. But if that's what she really thought, it made it kind of tough to go put his arms around her. Talking didn't seem to be getting them anywhere either.

"I noticed your brains, all right. Only the *last* time I looked, they worked. And by the way, if you're gonna stay here, you better tune up those eyes and ears, too."

She picked up a suitcase and walked out of the living room.

"Hey, look—"

"Never mind, I can't hear you," she called from the bedroom.

"I guess not," he said to himself as he turned and walked out of the apartment, pulling the door shut behind him.

* * *

F. X. Flynn's was the only place to go to end a day like this one. Uncle Jack and his Saturday-night customers would help cushion the shocks.

"Well," Jack said eagerly, "what's goin' on down in your neck of the woods? How's the colleen—and the boxing star?"

Flynn leaned his elbow on the bar. "Good news is out of style. You don't wanna hear."

"Hey"—Jack poured his nephew's tonic water—"what's a bartender for? If nobody cries in their beer over here, I'm done for."

"You twisted my arm, Jack. I think maybe I do need a listener."

"That's better."

"I went to the gym this afternoon to coach Salsa—the kid's falling apart. He acts like somebody's threatenin' him, but he won't talk about it and I can't protect him anyway, as long as he works where he works. He ain't about to jump ship; the kind of money he makes already he won't make as a fighter for a long time, if ever."

Uncle Jack nodded sympathetically. "Somethin' else besides the kid?"

"Lauren. She's in danger, too—and I can't protect her either. She can't see the risk she's taking no matter what I say. We went three rounds on that tonight and we didn't shake hands afterward. She said—Oh, the hell with it—the point is, the way we left it, communications are totally down."

"That you can fix." Jack looked serious. "Take a little work, maybe. But the kid... don't sound too promisin', I gotta say."

Flynn sipped his tonic water and mentally sidestepped Jack's opinion about Salsa, but he didn't argue. Instead he said, "And to complete the whole prize package, I bet you heard about the murder suspect—'Gordo'—who walked outta court? None other than the perp in our latest homicide."

Jack whistled.

"*Plus* he's the only existin' witness with a reason to testify against Salsa's boss—the deadliest scum in Manhattan North. This most-wanted Gordo has now disappeared off the face of the earth. The Two-nine squad room is not a happy place—and we got two of the worst months of the year comin' up. You know it as well as we do: When the holidays start rollin' around, people get in family feuds or they get mad over money.... Next thing you know, somebody's cut up or shot up."

Jack poured a refill for his nephew. "Maybe this year'll be

different. Goodwill to men and all that. Anyways, why doncha start by straightenin' things out with Lauren. If you *want* to, you'll find a way."

"I can't see a way."

"Go home and sleep on it."

Flynn tried to follow his uncle's advice, but when he opened the futon and lay down, her fragrance surrounded him, keeping him awake for hours.

Monday, October 21, 1985

Flynn came up out of the subway on Monday morning, confident that his luck would change with a new week. Nothing had prepared him for the unpleasant surprise that greeted him—literally—at the top of the stairs.

Somehow he had managed to forget that the pleasant nip in the morning air meant election season was about to heat up; now he was reminded, in spades. City Councilman Oscar Rafael, genial in an iridescent brown suit, stood at the subway entrance pressing the flesh and handing out Oscar Rafael flyers to a captive audience of commuters.

Rafael, who obviously didn't recognize his Enemy-of-the-Barrio Number One, extended his hand cordially to Flynn.

"Hello, Councilman, I'm Lieutenant Flynn, Two-nine Detective Squad." He ignored Rafael's hand.

Rafael squinted at Flynn, who could see that somewhere in the politician's head some bell rang, but here, on a campaign hustle at a subway stop, he couldn't place Flynn's name. Sometimes it suited a politician's purpose to support the police, and when it suited Rafael's purpose, he did. This cop had insultingly refused his handshake, however. Giving his attention to the next group of downtown-bound potential supporters, Rafael absently handed Flynn a flyer.

Flynn tore it in half and walked up Broadway, passing the mix of Korean groceries, run-down shoe stores, and new yuppie restaurants. The image of Rafael clouded his outlook, but he remained ready for his luck to change.

Flynn went to the coffee room for his ten-o'clock refill and had just poured it when he felt a presence behind him in the doorway. He turned, expecting a squad member, but found himself face-to-face with a sour-looking Zachs. For once, Flynn was prepared with a full cup of hot coffee. He took a hurried sip, almost burning his tongue. "Morning, Cap."

Zachs folded his arms and leaned against the far wall. Flynn stayed on his feet, too.

"I'm gonna get right to the point, Andy. It looks like the Chief of D *read* that letter Oscar Rafael sent. I guess the chief's still talkin' about it with this one an' that one before making a final decision—but meanwhile, I got the transfer papers on my desk."

Flynn took a swallow of coffee. The searing heat didn't go down any better than Zachs's news. "Where's this transfer supposed to be to?"

"The One-oh-seven, October twenty-eighth."

"Well, I ain't just packin' up and gettin' on the Queens train. I got a week to fight it."

"Look, this wasn't my idea. But I did warn you—one more drug bandit dead or alive don't mean nothin' to nobody. Even that newspaper dealer the neighborhood got so worked up about—when's the last time you heard his name since the collar? Most of the time, property's what gets people upset. Carlucci understands that. How come you don't hear what he's sayin'? Before you came in, he ran this command fine—didn't make no waves at all."

"And tryin' to put a guy like Viera out of the homicide business is what you call makin' waves, I guess. If it happened to put him out of the coke business at the same time, who's that gonna bother? I hope not Oscar Rafael; I *hope* not the Chief of D."

"Viera is a job for Narcotics, as you well know. Or you should know, I told you enough times. Let 'em do it."

"I'm holdin' my breath, Cap, honest. Thanks for givin' me the word about the transfer. Don't say good-bye yet—I got another round or two before I'm outta here." He looked at his watch—1032 hours and his bad luck hadn't changed yet.

When C Team came on for the night tour, they found out from A Team about Flynn's impending transfer. Pastore, Mazocek, and Urquhart made no move to go home. Pastore had been in a deepening funk anyway, since Gordo escaped. (He'd interviewed each of the thirty-seven defendants who had been with Gordo and the shoplifter in the court's holding pens. A few tips had surfaced; none panned out.) Cooch strongly suggested that C Team calm down and get to work, but neither Obie nor his partners showed the least inclination to open a file or lift a telephone receiver.

"That's it," Obie told Flynn. "The minute you leave, I put in my papers and go home." Neither Reynolds nor Taylor had anything funny to say. And as usual when anything big hit, B Team was off—so of course O'Levy missed yet another Event.

"Look," Flynn said to the rest of the squad, "like Cooch says, this ain't the time to lose it. That'll just give 'em more ammunition and make 'em think Flynn's transfer is a done deal—which it ain't. Like I told the captain, it's too soon yet to count me out. Anybody who's bettin' against me might be makin' an expensive mistake."

"All *right!*" Taylor said. As the unrest slowly settled, the men made an honest effort to go about their business. Flynn headed for the coffee room and Taylor followed.

"You goin' to the gym now and work with the champ, or what?" Taylor asked his friend.

"The champ's in some kinda trouble I can't get him out of. How come it all hits the fan at once, anybody ever tell you?"

"I thought that's the way it's s'posed to go down. I never heard of one problem at a time, myself. You goin' to the gym anyhow?"

"Yeah—soon as I find a picture of the Chief of D to paste on the heavy bag." Flynn smashed an imaginary bag.

"And after the gym what's happening?"

"In my condition, I can't think so far ahead—why?" Flynn picked up his coffee mug and sank into the nearest chair.

Taylor busied himself measuring out coffee for the next pot. His back was to Flynn. "Well, I was thinking about takin' you up on that standing offer of yours, y'know, if it still stands...."

The offer to take Jesse to an AA meeting had been standing so long, Flynn had almost forgotten about it. He had never pushed it because you couldn't push anybody into AA. For better or worse (you could look at it either way), Jesse hadn't hit bottom—no drunken catastrophe had pitched him down that well of panic that makes people grab for the Program like a lifeline.

Taylor still had his back to Flynn. "I know today ain't Wednesday, when you usually go," he said.

Flynn never stopped to wonder why Jesse suddenly chose to bring up the subject at this particular moment. "No problem—I'm gonna call the hot line. There's probably a half a dozen Monday meetings in Manhattan alone. All we gotta do is choose."

When Flynn finished his workout at the gym, Taylor was waiting downstairs in the car. They had chosen a Harlem meeting, which turned out to be held in a cramped meeting room above a storefront church. On the peeling wall behind the leader of the meeting hung a well-worn white banner with the AA Twelve Steps lettered in black. The leader announced that the group was celebrating the sobriety anniversaries of members who'd stopped drinking in the month of October—any month of October, from a year ago to decades.

The cops listened to the sagas of four men and women, each of whom had dragged themselves out of the most sordid garbage heaps and gone on to make a lot more of themselves than they might have if they had never started drinking at all. Flynn had attended plenty of AA meetings and plenty of inspiring ones but none to compare with this—because it had the feel of a revival session, the speakers' voices lilting like a gospel preacher's, with the volume lowered maybe but just a bit.

He thought about his own sobriety anniversary in April. About Father Dunne's "goon squad" whisking him upstate to "The Farm" eight years ago, when, as the First Step says, his life had become unmanageable. Flynn had proved he could fight bad guys and win, but all the while he had been losing against some nameless thing, inside. He'd tried dousing it with alcohol; he thought it worked fine. But the time had come when without a few belts nothing seemed to work.

By the grace of Father Dunne and AA, he was sober now—one day at a time. It had been years since he had to struggle not to pick up a drink, but even so, one day at a time was still how it worked. The last couple of weeks had set some kind of record for everything going down the tubes all at once. Maybe Jesse's timing wasn't so bad.

"Did I ever tell you," Flynn said later on as he and Taylor walked to Taylor's car, "about one famous meeting in Saint Patty's basement? I don't know what the hell I said that night, but afterwards this woman took me for a walk—a short one, like about a hundred blocks: Washington Square and back. I swear I didn't say nothin' specific, but somehow she got the idea that on my own, I would've walked into the nearest bar. I would have, too."

"Yeah?" Jesse said. "When was that?"

"Oh, I was already a sergeant in the Bureau. Kenny Nolan was long gone to California—I didn't have no friends to speak of except in the program. I guess I'd been sober about a year."

"Some hot meeting tonight," Jesse said, "hallelooo-ya!" He beeped the horn for emphasis.

Silently, Flynn wished the beep meant Jesse accepted that alcohol was corroding his life. "You walked into a great one," he said aloud. "Those people are inspirin'. It's enough to give strength to a ninety-seven-pound weakling. I gotta admit, we ain't got that same rhythm downtown."

Taylor laughed. "No shit."

"Well, we got all the rest of the good stuff. But don't take my word for it, check it out." The night's speakers had given Flynn a real shot of strength. If they could fight those demons and win, he could damn well beat this bullshit political transfer. If he didn't, what the hell kind of example would that set for the squad?

"Are you plannin' to go to your meeting Wednesday?" Taylor asked casually.

"Yeah—but tomorrow I'm goin' over to see the Chief of D and tell him what he can do with his transfer. Or rather, Rafael's transfer."

"I'll drink to that," Taylor said, and beeped the horn again.

Tuesday evening, October 22, 1985

He had never thought about it before, but now Flynn could identify with how a hunted perp must feel when he gets somewhere that feels safe. After his audience with the Chief, the refuge Flynn needed was the gym. When he walked in off Forty-second Street, the long, dingy flight of stairs never looked better. The locker room smelled comfortingly foul as he changed his clothes. And the five-o'clock racket—this was the gym's busiest time of day—was exactly the noise he wanted to hear.

He joined the crowd on the floor and did some deep breathing, eyes shut, not expecting to be able to forget this day—just hoping to get some air in his lungs. As he went into the bounce, he saw Brooklyn Charlie coaching Jemal at the other end of the loft. Jemal, the ace! He had won his PAL bout. Fantastic! Flynn was ready to take attitude lessons from Jemal and every other winner in the room.

He bent over from the waist to loosen up his arms, shoulders, upper back. Staring at his boxing shoes on the scarred floorboards, he was thankful again to be nowhere but here. Straightening up, he did lunges to stretch the groin muscles. He rushed through the small arm-circles, triceps burning, and began the windmills, glad to activate the tense muscles above and below his shoulder blades.

Then it was time to face himself in the metal training mirror. Usually, he had no trouble with this—in fact, really enjoyed imagining an opponent and coming up with the strategy to deck him. But now, just as he'd told Salsa, he had himself to fight. After waiting around headquarters all afternoon, he had said what he had to say to the Chief of D while the Chief of D sat there and looked through his mail—and now the Chief of D would do whatever he would do, no telling what.

Well, not quite now—not till the end of the month. *Bing, bam*—Flynn jabbed and followed with a right at his own chin. He crouched, bobbing around, waiting for an opening. Nine days—*pow*. Nine days of limbo, something Flynn had never been good at. He feinted with his eyes first, bounced energetically as if he were getting ready for a big one—then he pulled the fake punch and caught his opponent off balance with the real one, right above the heart. *Unh!*

Limbo, yeah, nothing but limbo for miles in all directions. Flynn had Gordo to find. How could somebody so fat just disappear? *Whoosh*—Flynn's uppercut went wild and missed—leaving him wide open. He had Lauren to worry about, in more ways than one. Whoops—the bastard saw the hole and slipped one to Flynn's gut. *Whomp!* He gasped for air. God willing, he wouldn't have to send the whole squad to boot camp for a week to whip them back into shape. *Ba boom*—Flynn's one-two connected with the other fighter's chin and the side of his skull. Flynn kept after him, driving him toward the ropes. And God willing, Salsa is absent from the gym today simply because he is doing his roadwork, and we won't have to drag the river for him. *Bing, bam—bing, bam. Bong!* The bell signaled the end of this one and none too soon.

Flynn sucked on the water bottle, feeling a little relief from all the tension. His goal was to get here every other night this week, go for a run in between, and get to an AA meeting every night, too. He was coming to understand that he better not try to coast through this round with life or he'd wake up flat on the canvas. He moved over to the heavy bag and started working it. It always felt like some big son of a bitch who just keeps leaning on you.

"Andy!" Brooklyn Charlie made his way through the jungle of sweaty bodies. "What the fuck is this rumor—it's all over the city that you're goin' to *Queens?* I heard about it in the Brooklyn morgue, for chrissake."

"Good news travels fast, somebody said." Flynn battled the heavy bag.

"When it comes to gossip, cops are nothin' but a bunch of old ladies. It's a fact of life, right?" Charlie's mustache bristled with outrage.

"Well, if you hear that from any more old ladies, you could point out that I'm not gone till I'm gone."

"They're all havin' shitfits, I don't have to tell ya. Everybody's disgusted as hell. It's gotta be political. What else could it be? This is the way the PD treats a guy who does miracles?"

"I appreciate the support, I mean it. But like I said, they can wait awhile before they get upset."

Charlie wouldn't be appeased. "In private industry you accomplish something like you did in the Two-nine, you're a fuckin' millionaire—not transferred to the boonies."

"Yeah? So maybe I'll retire and go work for one of those corporations where they got a Department of Makin' Waves."

Charlie broke up.

"When they start one of those, pal, we'll both get rich."

That kept Charlie laughing. Finally Charlie said, "There's a lot of people who'll be glad to hear this whole transfer thing is just horseshit. All I gotta do is tell one guy and it'll get around. Of course, there's a few people who'll be disappointed."

"Those people's problems ain't gonna be solved by my goin' to Queens anyway, but I guess they don't see it that way."

"You're *not* goin', you said," Charlie protested.

"Not if the PD knows what's good for 'em. Which mostly they don't. Maybe they'll surprise us this once."

"Meaning?"

"Meaning..." Flynn stepped back from the heavy bag and went in search of his skip rope. "Meaning"—he began skipping at a gradually increasing pace—"I told the Chief of D that the guy behind this political puppet show is the king of coke in Manhattan North. Who happens to be pissed at the squad 'cause when some drunken Colombian popped a customer in the king of coke's 'legit' music club, we investigated the case and made a little noise in the club. Maybe even a little extra noise since the king of coke is also the known homicide prince of the Two-nine and we're lookin' to get him his due for some time now. Narcotics tries but they ain't collared Viera in years. He just ain't around when they raid. Somebody's talkin' to somebody."

Charlie looked inquiringly at Flynn. "You said 'puppet show'?"

Flynn nodded. The skip rope sounded like *d'dum, d'dum, d'dum*.... "I told the Chief of D," he went on, "that the community really ain't gonna be thrilled if they find out a major drug dealer is movin' detective commanders around like puppets. And as I was leaving the Chief's office, I told him he knows as well as I do that this kind of show has a way of attractin' bad reviews."

"That's gotta work," Charlie said, crossing himself, "it's gotta. Right?"

"It's a shot." Flynn skipped at top speed till the bell rang for the end of the round.

"Yeah." Charlie nodded. "Well, I better go, I'm gonna get creamed in traffic. See ya soon."

"I'll be here tomorrow. Five o'clock." Flynn toweled the sweat off his face and chest and walked over to where Jemal was doing sit-ups. "Way to go, champ—congratulations!"

"Thanks, boss."

"I hear you got a lotta respect."

"Yeah, they see me comin' in my royal-blue shorts, I say a few magic words, Ali style—they just never recover." Jemal didn't break his sit-up rhythm. "The *mind* is a tricky thing, huh, boss?"

"So I hear." Flynn laughed.

Jemal glanced toward the door of the now-empty gym. "By the way, how's that foxy lady? When she comin' over for another boxin' appreciation lesson? She learn fast—gonna be a referee anytime now."

Flynn enjoyed the image of Lauren wearing a bow tie, separating a couple of heavyweights. "I'll tell her you said so, that'll get her attention for sure." Worth a try, he thought—the mind is a tricky thing.

Saturday afternoon, October 26, 1985

On weekends, you'd always be in good company at the boxing club: nothing but hard workers and guys with a fight coming up. Flynn had worked out faithfully all week, as he'd resolved, and had gone to a string of AA meetings. To say he felt better might be an overstatement, but at least he didn't feel worse. That was saying quite a bit considering that limbo seemed to have swallowed up both Gordo and Lauren. On the plus side, the squad was pulling itself together.

And one other big plus—here comes Salsa, walking into the gym at the regular Saturday time, in one piece and looking like his old confident self. The problem, whatever it was, must have blown over.

Salsa did his warm-up moves and all his stretches as smooth as silk. When he was ready to go to the mirror, Flynn asked, "What did you and Charlie practice last time?"

"Right up da middle"—Salsa imitated Charlie's Brooklynese—" 'one-two, one-two.' "

"Left jab–right cross?"

"Nope—left jab–straight right."

"Okay, let's see how it looks in the mirror. If you got it, we'll add a number three...."

Salsa practiced the combination several times.

"Okay, *mira.*" Flynn guided Salsa's left glove till the arm was fully extended. "Don't pull it. Follow through all the way. And watch out your right hand don't drop or you're wide open to his left." He strapped on a pair of hand pads, held up his hands surrender style, and let Salsa punch at them instead of his own reflection in the mirror. "Nice—much better. Keep 'em coming, pal. Push him back with that jab. Yeah, that's it. More!"

When Salsa had the one-two to Flynn's satisfaction, Flynn said, "Now, add the left hook; you can go for the chin or the body. See?—you're back on balance. Nice work."

As the session wound down, Flynn asked where Jemal was today.

"He took off, I bet," Salsa said. "He could—he fought good and he's the new hero of the gym."

"You just keep up like you're doin', do what Charlie says, you'll be the next one," Flynn said. "Any day you'll be signing up for a smoker yourself."

Neither of them so much as mentioned Gordo's name. Could Salsa have managed to track him down? If Viera had learned his ex-dealer's location, the body could show up anytime...showing beyond a doubt which side Salsa had chosen. But Flynn didn't have time to let that tale tell itself. He had to find Gordo—alive.

Monday morning, October 28, 1985

Lauren woke up early and caught the red-eye subway to work. For once she got a seat, but she had trouble concentrating on her Monday *Times*. After having spent a couple of happy hours on Saturday afternoon browsing among the junk-laden tables of a neighborhood street fair, she had come home to find a disconcerting message on her answering machine. Andy's partner, Jesse Taylor. He was sorry to miss her but would call her at the office first thing Monday—something important to tell her.

Close as Andy and Jesse were, Lauren didn't think Jesse would have called because Andy had a heartache—even if by some chance he had one. And if Jesse had wanted to relay an urgent bulletin about her safety, he'd have been more persistent. Still, even without knowing him, she thought his tone had sounded serious.

She'd sighed as she unwound the layers of newspaper from her street-fair treasure, an art deco sugar bowl from the ocean liner *Coronia*. Until the message from Jesse, she had been pretty good about derailing thoughts of Andy. He had created his own space in her life and filled it; now that space was empty. In her mind she walked past it, looking the other way. Sort of like trying to ignore the Grand Canyon.

But as for the space she lived in, that was something else. It was hers and it was *her*. She needed it and she filled it all by herself. Even if she had been in danger, she had no intention of taking a... live-in bodyguard. Her last affair, with David, a married colleague, had worked because it kept her living space free. It was a much more manageable affair than her romance with Andy—but Andy made her feelings for David seem... thin. Lately, even since the fight with Andy, she'd been evasive with David. Next to Andy, he looked kind of tame. She had sighed again, washed the sugar bowl, and filled it while fantasizing a nice long voyage on the *Coronia*.

Now, after a restless Sunday—she had even looked up Jesse's phone number, knowing perfectly well cops didn't list their phones—she hoped he would call before her boss decided to request the favor of her company for a two-hour discussion. Her boss's office was next to hers and closing her door was a futile gesture. She closed it anyway and sat down at the counter she used as a desk. The leaded-glass panels on either side of the door diffused both light and privacy; anybody passing by could see whether or not she was there.

Deliberately, she paged through the sheaf of background material attached to the Calendar of applications for special land-use permits to be reviewed at the staff meeting that afternoon. She put the papers aside. She had all this covered—what else had she been doing here till seven o'clock Friday and eight Thursday? *Next* week's Calendar was the problem, but she couldn't find it in her interoffice mail. She fidgeted, not wanting to leave the phone....

Nine twenty-five. She grabbed the phone on the first ring.

"Lauren—you got a minute? Jesse Taylor. I'll talk fast, while I'm still alone. Your friend and mine doesn't know I'm makin' this call."

Taylor told Lauren that the PD had a transfer pending for Andy—a disciplinary action taken because he got on the wrong side of a drug lord, a well-connected drug lord.

"The one with the club on Columbus Avenue?"

"Right."

"God, what a story. We could get it on page one tomorrow and they'd...yeah, they'd find some other way to get Andy, eventually, wouldn't they?"

"You obviously know how the game is played," Taylor said. "But I thought of another angle that maybe we could work—that is, if you want to help."

"What can I do?" Lauren heard herself answer.

"Only the community's got the clout to reverse this with no down side. The brass don't like to buck the community. So—"

"When is this transfer effective?"

"A week from now, Flynn will be in Queens. 'Darkest Queens,' as Billy Reynolds would say. This is one place even you never heard of. They don't need land-use permits out there 'cause the precinct is mostly desert. 'Fresh Meadows' is just a name, see?"

A knock on Lauren's door cut off her laughter. She waved at the boss's secretary's silhouette, visible through the leaded-glass panel. "Oh-oh, they're paging me. The Community Council board meets this Thursday. I'll make some calls first. The board should write a strong letter of protest, right?"

"That's it."

"And *if* I can get a majority in favor, we send it to...?"

"I'll write up a list and leave it under your door at home, how's that?"

"Great. Wish me luck, Jesse. I'll definitely need it."

Lauren hung up the phone, grabbed some papers, and showed up in the corner office.

Early morning, Tuesday, October 29, 1985

"You gotta watch it around this place," Monte told Salsa as they made their way out of the Grantley Hotel at about four-fifteen A.M. The sky was still dark and no one had replaced the hallway light bulbs or the ones over the entrance door.

"Wow, it's cold out here." Salsa blew a big breath into the air to see if he could see it. He could.

"Listen, *papá,* I'm tellin' you a good story: This guy who lived here was walkin' in one night late, like now. Somebody threw something *big* out the window and just missed the guy. He didn't stop—he was too scared. They found this black garbage bag on the sidewalk, so heavy the super got nervous and called the cops. When they opened up the bag, they found a dealer inside, chopped up in pieces."

Salsa looked over his shoulder. "That happened here? When?"

"Maybe five years ago."

"So you knew him! You know all the dealers."

"I figure he had to be visiting that night, checkin' out the hotel or something. I know four dealers around this place, they was all still alive after the garbage bag thing."

"Juanito, he was here already?"

Monte unlocked his blue Chevy and replied that Juanito, Viera's outlet in the Grantley, was already there. Once inside the car, while Monte drove, Salsa sat back with his accounting system—a roll of adding machine tape he kept in the glove compartment. He read off the night's activity: what they had delivered to whom, how much they had collected from whom, what was left to do. He wrote it all in pencil on the tape in some kind of scratches nobody else could read. Finally he produced his little calculator, ran the totals so far, and read them out.

"Muy bien!" Monte said, opening up the Chevy in the empty darkness of Riverside Drive. "The boss likes your work, he told me. We're gonna forget that business about Gordo's gun. 'Cause we think anybody can make *one* mistake, if they learn from it. We know you learned where you're supposed to listen and where you're supposed to talk. As long as you got that straight—you got a future with Irish Luck."

Thursday evening, October 31, 1985

As one of a dozen vice presidents of the Precinct Community Council executive board, Lauren had limited power, to put it mildly. Further, being a white person and living south of Ninety-sixth Street put her at a disadvantage compared to the black and Hispanic vice presidents from poorer areas to the north. Ever since the Council's minority-group members had launched a successful drive to elect more of their own, nobody could make a motion and take the outcome for granted. Power was so evenly balanced that every vote was a cliff-hanger.

Though the minority board members basically supported the police, they were concerned that their neighborhoods usually got less attention from the cops. They were also quick and militant when they believed that a black or Hispanic individual got what they considered too much police attention—in the form of brutality.

Lauren had managed to phone four vice presidents whom she felt she could count on, including one Hispanic woman, and they all had promised to try hard to make the meeting. A fifth, an executive Lauren had met at a few meetings, was out of town, but his secretary said he might return in time. Lauren left a long message on his answering tape at home. *If* all five showed up, plus herself, she'd have six votes.

The board secretary and the treasurer attended meetings but were unpredictable as voters. The president, a Latino, could cast the deciding vote in case of a tie. Lauren decided to call him before the meeting as a courtesy, but she waited till the day of the meeting so he would have less time to round up "no" votes if that's what he wanted to do. After speaking to him, her prediction was the same as it had been before—he could go either way.

Riding the subway from her office, she drafted the letter of protest against Andy's transfer. Dinner would be a chocolate bar again; she had just enough time before the seven-thirty meeting to stop and grab one at the drugstore. She whizzed up Broadway, feeling sentimental as she passed the ice cream place where she and Andy had started to become friends. She wondered whether he loved her, whether he *could* love her.

Irrelevant, she told herself; he loved his job and did it—heroically. That was the right word, even though it didn't mean Superman. Her eyes burned. No tears at the meeting, she warned herself—get mad instead. As her letter said (in polite language), instead of the recognition Flynn deserved, his superiors were giving him shit. This transfer not only disciplined the lieutenant unfairly, but would deprive the community of his expertise—and discourage others from aspiring to topflight work like his. In the letter, Lauren didn't refer to the Tabu Club incident that had been the immediate cause of the move against Flynn.

Lauren seated herself as near the board president as possible. She wanted to ally herself symbolically with power. Her four VPs had kept their promises to show up but no sign of the traveling executive.

Old Business seemed to take forever; finally the president asked for New Business and recognized Lauren. She reminded the board of the murdered Hispanic boy whose killer had been apprehended by the "hundred percent squad" lieutenant and his detectives upstairs. Now, she said, she had to tell the board bad news. Bad for the squad, bad for the precinct. Speaking forcefully yet clearly, she reported that the police brass had decided arbitrarily to transfer Lieutenant Flynn. She proposed a protest by the executive board and read her letter.

When she finished, a hand immediately shot up: Mrs. Berry, the well-to-do senior citizen. In her opinion, the squad badly needed a change of leadership; she thought the lieutenant's transfer "perfectly appropriate." The board should not waste their pressure on this matter.

Lauren watched the faces around the table at Mrs. Berry went on. She went on and on, and too bossily, alienating people who potentially agreed with her. The board secretary spoke next; an attractive white woman, very pro-police, she did not like Lauren. Her support of Flynn came out lukewarm.

So far, no consensus. Then came a young man, Hispanic, who spoke passionately about the squad's abusive treatment of Hispanic guests at the Tabu. "Unjustified, intolerable police behavior." He said the incident was typical of Flynn's squad—no wonder Lauren had failed to tell the board what had prompted the transfer. He accused the squad's black/Hispanic detective of acting particularly vicious toward Hispanics—and called him a "real Uncle Tomás." Lauren saw that this accusation disturbed the two black board members who could usually be counted on to vote with the speaker.

Lauren's ally, Conchita, raised her hand. She had once been the victim of an assault, she said—the squad had been courteous as could be. Terrific! They had arrested her attacker and helped her press charges. Justice had been done; even though it had been a long haul in the courts, the squad made it as painless for her as they could. They had fine leadership and nothing should be changed; she would like to make a motion that Lauren Daniels's letter be approved as read—and sent. Lauren smiled as another ally spoke up, seconding Conchita's motion.

Someone wanted to change some language in the letter, but the chairman said that couldn't be done unless Conchita's motion was defeated and a new one put forward. The chairman asked whether board members would prefer a secret ballot. Anxious to get home, the members chose a show of hands. The two blacks supported Flynn but the board secretary didn't; otherwise, no surprises—and no majority.

Just as the chair cleared his throat to announce his deciding vote, the muster-room door opened and the traveling executive rushed in. With apologies to all, he said his plane had arrived late but he wanted to exercise his right to vote on the proposed letter about the squad lieutenant.

"You haven't heard the discussion," the president objected.

"But I'm familiar with the issues or I wouldn't be here," answered the executive.

The president asked the secretary to read the motion, then asked the executive, "All right, how do you vote?"

"In favor of the protest letter," he said firmly.

Monday night, November 4, 1985

"On the house!" Uncle Jack announced, not for the first time that evening. A contingent of F. X. Flynn's Monday regulars eagerly celebrated along with Andy Flynn and his friends anything and everything the cops wanted to celebrate.

Jesse Taylor raised his snifter and toasted Lauren again. "This one's for her—cool under fire: Miss... Lauren... D.!"

Flynn gazed into his glass of tonic, his cheeks flushed as if he'd been drinking booze.

"I thought the two of you was, uh, not seein' eye to eye," Jack said to him.

Taylor answered, "Whatever they are or ain't, the lady did the right thing. Y'see, Jack, it was nobody but Miss Lauren who gave those board members what for and got 'em to put the heat on the brass. Wrote a hot letter and sent it to all the slimy politicians, too—I happened to see a copy upstairs in the Borough office. It was radio*active.*"

"When you put the heat on the brass, y'know what happens?" Reynolds leaned confidentially toward Jack.

Uncle Jack knew more or less what to expect from Reynolds, who didn't mind admitting he'd seen the business side of a bar himself. "Sure do," Jack bluffed, "but go ahead an' tell me anyway. I'm a bartender."

"When you put the heat on the brass, it melts."

"Okay, pal"—Flynn grimaced—"let's talk about something you're better qualified to discuss."

"That could be a lot of things," Reynolds pointed out.

"Of course," his boss said, "but what would be first on the list?"

"Females."

"Good. It's twenty-two oh five hours—d'you think Miss D. is home yet?"

"Stop right there, boss. Lauren ain't 'miss'; Jesse got that wrong, too."

"Well, 'ma'am' is out."

"Ma'am! You gotta say *Ms.* to the Lauren type: smart, single, over thirty. Repeat after me, *Mzzz*. Just takes gettin' used to."

"In your expert opinion, would you say Mzz. Daniels is—"

"That's easy: maybe."

While everybody at the bar laughed, Flynn went to the pay phone. Lauren's voice answered him on tape. Only one ring—she probably hadn't come home yet, or even picked up her messages. Flynn left a message saying he missed her and hoped to talk to her soon.

He returned to the bar, mulling over whether Lauren was the type to let her answering machine take calls when she was in. He realized how many little things about her he didn't know but would like to. He knew the big thing—what she'd done at the Council board.

"How you doin' down south in homicide city?" One of the regulars interrupted Flynn's thoughts.

"Workin' hard." Flynn nodded at Taylor and Reynolds. "I got the best outfit in the five boroughs. I don't know how much use they're gonna be tomorrow, though." He cleared his throat. "The A Train is leaving at twenty-three hundred hours; two stops only—Upper East Side and Sunnyside, Queens."

"Get on board," Uncle Jack sang, "get on board..." His gospel delivery got a hand from Taylor, who requested one more Rémy for the road.

By the time Flynn had pried his friends out of F. X. Flynn's, driven them home in Jesse's car, and made it back to Times Square on the pokey IND line, the night people had taken over. The drizzle deterred nobody from whatever they were up to. What he could disregard in daylight as a colorful sideshow looked nothing less than sinister now. He walked purposefully.

Light showed under the door of the Anastasia Suite but didn't alarm Flynn. His place was well protected against burglars, not because he had much to lose but because he disliked the idea of someone's messing up the place and selling his personal stuff to buy a fix. He was so certain that he'd left the lamp on, he ignored his gun in its holster and unlocked the door.

Curled up on the futon, a newspaper beside her, Lauren dozed. The sight of a burglar would have been easier for him to deal with. He sat down next to her, tried to breathe, and smoothed her hair away from her face.

His touch woke her. "Hi," she said, "I, um, called the squad but missed you, and I—wanted to say congratulations." She pointed to a bunch of keys on the little table. "Still had your keys…"

She wore office clothes: a red fall suit, silk blouse.

"Would you be—more comfortable with your shoes off?" He touched the dark-green leather of the left one.

"Thanks."

He slipped them off her feet, got up, and went to the little table, absently placing the shoes underneath it as if out of habit. "Listen," he began from across the small room, "maybe your ears were burning before. People drank quite a few rounds in your honor tonight." He paced as far as the front door and leaned against it, arms folded. "I'm knocked out by what you did. Not just how but why—I guess that part is sort of a—mystery."

"How was a lot harder than why."

He went over and sat next to her again. "Why?"

"I didn't see why they should ace you out of a job you are fantastically good at and happen to really care about, if I could do something. I was just lucky it *worked.*"

"I think you know what you're doing—which makes it a lot easier to get lucky. Jesse is very impressed; they all are."

"What about the mystery—have I cleared that up?"

He took her hand. "Women usually don't get what the hell I see in this job. Why I keep coming back for more. It don't make sense to them, but I—I'm glad you put it together. I guess I still don't understand how come you're different…." He looked at her. "But I'm glad you are."

"I don't know the *reason* either."

"Maybe the reason don't matter." Flynn and Lauren reached for each other and kissed for quite a while. "Ms. Daniels," Flynn said eventually, "would you like to share the Anastasia Suite, humble though it is, with me? For—a while?"

"Live together?"

"Right."

"Maybe we could—try it."

Tuesday afternoon, November 5, 1985

Cooch glanced at the logbook and stuck his head into the squad room. "Your 'homicide specialist,' Reynolds, signed out and never signed back in," Cooch heckled Flynn. "Destination illegible."

"I think he's across town," Betty Dominic said, trying to be helpful.

"When he comes by," Cooch growled, "tell him I'll see him later."

Betty stood up and darkened her shiny lipstick in a mirror she pulled from her desk drawer. "It's sixteen hundred hours, Sergeant. Bye-bye, see you tomorrow."

Flynn said Billy probably went out to vote. He imagined Reynolds in the steam room at the Y. Envious thoughts rather than disciplinary ones resulted. Something to clear his head was exactly what Flynn needed, too. If he closed his eyes for longer than a blink, a collage of Lauren filled his mind. Lauren curled up on the futon in her red suit. Lauren taking off the silk blouse. Lauren this morning standing on the downtown subway platform while he stood across the tracks on the uptown side. Later on, he would help her move some stuff—enough to seal the living-together decision before she could back out.

As Cooch revved up to start grumbling where he'd left off, the phone rang; Flynn took it.

"Lieutenant! I know it's your voice. *Qué tal?*"

"Hey, Carmel—great to hear yours. *Qué tal* yourself?"

"Wonderful, wonderful. I'm so happy; *Mami también.*"

"Things going good for you up in the Heights, huh?"

"Well, it's okay. *Mami* likes it. But we want to thank you about Salsa's boxing, he's so *busy* with it—it's good for him, I think. No?"

"Sure—healthy, and he can handle himself if he ever gets in a little spot. He's workin' hard and that's good, too: for his head, you know."

"Oh, I hope very much! Of course, we're going to see his fight in that church. I look for you there? Okay?"

"Definitely," Flynn said as if he knew what she was talking about. "Then we'll catch up on everything."

"Okay, Lieutenant Flynn. Thanks again—bye."

"Take care, Carmel."

So Salsa had a fight scheduled and he was keeping it a secret. His first match. Flynn figured Salsa must want to surprise him. Okay, he'd be sure to act surprised when the time came. Next month probably. He and Lauren would go watch Salsa fight; she would get a kick out of that.

"Marty, I'm gonna make coffee," he said; "can you use a cup?"

Cooch looked up from his paperwork long enough to say yes.

Flynn came out of the coffee room with the two brimming mugs and almost bumped into Captain Zachs.

"Cap! Just made a fresh pot, you want some?"

Zachs declined. "Did you hear the early returns?"

"No. Be right with you. The sergeant ordered coffee. I gotta deliver it hot, or no tip."

Once the captain had disappeared into his own office, Cooch looked up at Flynn. "You planning an insanity defense or what? They couldn't quite dump you in Queens, but Bellevue ain't gonna be no problem."

"Thanks, Marty. I'll be okay in the morning—"

"Get in there"—Cooch gestured toward the captain's office—"but make it a short visit!"

"Ten-four."

Flynn stood in the doorway facing the captain, who chose not to skip a beat. "The polls are still open but Councilman Rafael is reelected. By a landslide."

"Yeah, the victory party was supposed to be at the Tabu, the story goes—only Viera canceled when he found out Rafael couldn't eighty-six me."

"You're a million laughs today. However, it's probably true about the party. But Irish wouldn't cancel. He ain't gonna let up on you and he's gonna make sure Rafael don't either."

"If I was Viera, I'd play it the same way," Flynn said. "He knows when we catch him, he's gonna get heavy time. If he was *really* smart, he'd retire to Ecuador next week."

"If he does, how you gonna clear all those homicides he did?"

"If he goes for good—everybody and his brother would give depositions and the city would be rid of that snake."

"Very touching. Now let's get serious. We're all entitled to one miracle in life and you just had yours." His voice boomed. "It's a fuckin' miracle you're not in Queens, but from now on anybody in this squad better say *pardon me, please* when they put cuffs on a Spanish person."

Flynn frowned in spite of himself.

The captain stood up in slow motion and leaned deliberately across his desk. "Next time they write a transfer for you, it's gonna stick. Remember who said so."

"I hear you, Cap."

Obie waited for Flynn in the back of the squad room by the file cabinets. "Lieu," Obie said, "forget the blarney. Last I heard, God's in charge of miracles—even in the Two-nine."

"You sure of that?"

"If there was a change in the miracle procedure," he laid the brogue on extra-thick, "they would've interviewed the Pope on the news. Now the transfer's KO'd—so what's got to you today, anyway?"

"I'll be all right in the morning."

Obie turned around from the file drawer to take a better look at his boss. He moved his glasses from the top of his head to his nose and peered. "Eyes a little glassy, balance is off. How's the appetite?" He didn't wait for an answer. "None of my business, but you look like *cupid* flew in your bedroom window and poured *love potion* in your ear. The tour's over—maybe you should go to the gym and work it off."

Midnight, Tuesday, November 5, 1985

Mia Greenfield regretted having missed the better part of summer in the city. Empty streets, laid-back people, light clothes, open shoes. She always wore open shoes as late in the season as she could—they kept the pressure off her bruised ballet dancer's toes. Mild weather the past couple of days had put her back in sandals and thin little socks. Today she wore a boat-neck jersey dress striped in black and white with her tan leather Cherokee sandals. The horizontal stripes flattered her slight dancer's figure, and the color combination looked good with her blazing red hair—and the black and white didn't make her freckles stand out. After rehearsal, she'd buttoned a bright-green cotton sweater over the dress and walked to a nearby cafe where she and a group of her friends usually hung out for a while before going home. She wore a gold neck chain and the 1940s watch her parents had given her when she'd been hired to dance in the corps of the Plaza Ballet. On her shoulder she carried a bulging zippered tote with a wide strap—an overnight bag, just about—made of black nylon and silk-screened in white with the elegant Plaza Ballet logo.

Mia took the Broadway subway uptown to her Eighty-sixth Street stop. The subway line that ran under Central Park West left her a little closer to her building, but the walk along the park to Eighty-ninth Street was lonelier than on Broadway, where coffee shops and delis stayed open late. People went in and out, keeping the street busy.

For the first time since she had started dancing professionally at age sixteen, she had recently begun to *feel* a little bit like the person audiences saw on stage. When she looked in the mirror now—as she and the other dancers compulsively did throughout their daily classes and rehearsals—she glimpsed that person who was not only lithe and technically strong but who could radiate confidence. In the past she had seen only the "defects," the "room for improvement." Finally, she felt ready to give up dissecting her talent and to find the freedom to grow.

Ironically, if she hadn't come so close to the edge of self-destruction, she wouldn't have been able to come back. By last June she'd had a heavy cocaine habit—so heavy that she had been dealing to support it. She'd been warned by the ballet company that she was barely meeting her obligations.

Somehow her father found out and spirited her off to a New England treatment center. There she had the luck to find a counselor who really understood her—who had been like a "mirror," letting her see herself and her talent without the help of the drug.

It had seemed impossible, but she had started to let go of the crutch. She was excited and caught up in the process of building emotional strength, hoping to bring it somewhere near the level of her physical strength. She had begun to put space between herself and coke. She...

"Hey, Mia!"

The familiar voice called to her from in front of the restaurant on the corner of Eighty-eighth Street. Nobody but Walter would be out making social calls at this hour. She noticed that he still carried the same Gucci attaché case. Mia took a deep breath and reminded herself that she had nothing to fear from Walter except his drug and she had that under control.

"Hi, Walter."

He fell in beside her as she continued up Broadway. He always wore these million-dollar Italian suits and silk shirts and tonight was no exception. This suit was light colored, as they usually were, even in winter.

"How's the high kicks, Miamor?"

"Oh, I'm not a Rockette, you know."

"Ballet dancers don't kick?"

"Well, they do, but it's not the same thing."

"I never saw you dance." He sounded as if he didn't believe she really did.

"All you need is a ticket, Walter, and you can certainly afford one. The season starts soon—middle of this month."

"Speaking of money—"

"We already did speak about it two weeks ago." Mia turned the corner and began walking east on Eighty-ninth; Walter turned with her. "When I came and met you at Trax, I told you I'd pay you what I owe and I will. My loan's coming through this week."

"I was thinkin' about it, Miamor. You gotta be crazy to take a loan and pay interest. Do it my way, it'll be a lot easier. I got a nice package of perico for you—a big one. One more deal and we're even. You can make it all up in one shot. Take you about a week, for chrissake—instead of all those bank payments. That'd take *forever.*"

"I don't know," Mia said. He was right about one thing: It would be wonderful to get it over with and not have to think about him every month for six years when she made a bank payment. But selling? Her stomach churned. She didn't even want to have the stuff in her hands again.

"You'll get all your money at once," Mia said, "the bank is my problem—don't worry your handsome Latin head about it."

"I got it right here for you, Mia. You don't have to *use* it to sell it. It's better if you don't use it. After we're all squared away, I'll give you a bonus package. Do whatever you want with it, it's yours."

She was tired; in less than a block, she'd be home; she just wanted to end the conversation and be rid of him. She sighed but didn't say anything.

"I don't want to do this in the street," Walter said, sensing his advantage. "You can never tell who's gonna come ridin' around the corner. Come in here."

The streetlight spilled onto the crumbling brownstone stoop, and at the top, Mia could see a metal door surrounded by cement, filling in the rest of what could once have been a nice entry.

"In there?"

"Yeah, the door's open." He put his hand on her elbow and led her up the steps. "See?" Walter pushed the hollow-sounding metal slab and it gave. When they were inside, he slammed it shut. Chunks of plaster littered the floor of the entryway. A huge hole in the wall gaped where the mailboxes had been.

Instead of stopping as Mia expected, he walked her toward the back of the narrow hallway. She could hardly breathe the close, musty air. The windows must be all plugged up—it was much hotter in the building than outside.

"What are we doing?" Mia coughed and shook her head. "It's unbelievable in here." She pulled away from Walter and turned back toward the door.

Walter reached out and regained his grip on her arm. "Forget that, Miamor, you're staying with me." He tightened his grasp painfully, then pushed and dragged her over to the stairs.

"I'll take the coke, Walter. Okay? Now let go!" Her voice stayed just under a scream. She couldn't wrench free of him. When her ballet bag got in the way, he tore it off her shoulder, breaking a strap, and hurled it into a corner near the door. She figured that was okay—she could fight better without it and she could grab it on her way out of the house. But Walter kept his grip on her, steering her toward the stairs.

"Let go—"

Suddenly he banged her buttocks with his attaché case. "Shut up or you're really gonna get hurt." Her socks were no protection for her sore toes; she stubbed them excruciatingly on the bottom step and stifled a moan.

"I warned you not to give me trouble, didn't I?"

She knew that if she didn't start up the stairs, he'd push her again, she'd fall forward, and do some damage to her legs, too. She'd get out of here somehow, but it would be easier to fight him off where she had more room.

On the way up, she wondered if he had a gun. If he did, he'd already have threatened her with it, she decided. At the top of the stairs she turned suddenly and tried to knee him in the groin, but he dodged.

"Cabróna!" He didn't give her time to try again but bashed her shins with his attaché case, forcing her backward to an old mattress that lay rotting on the floor. A partly punched-out window let a bit of grayed light into the room. Walter shoved her chest with the flat of his hand so she lost her balance and fell onto the mattress. Then he took a big folding knife out of his pocket and opened it fast.

"Take my advice, Miamor, stay put," he said.

As soon as I catch my breath, Mia thought, I'll scream, then he'll let me go. "What's this shit, Walter?" she gasped. "I said I'll take the coke, so—"

"I changed my mind," he said. "I want you to take *more* than one package." He opened his attaché case, then the big plastic bag of white powder, and scooped up a thick line on his knife. "You got a good market there and I want you to deal for me steady, like before. I'm gonna convince you—sit up now!" He held the knife over her breasts; his hand was steady and none of the powder fell off the blade. "Sit up!"

Mia sat up fast, screamed, "No!" and knocked the knife to the floor. Her right hand began to bleed. Walter socked her in the jaw and when she fell back, slapped her face hard, stunning her. Then he retrieved the knife. When he had it in his fist, pointing down, he said, *"Shut* your fuckin' mouth." He tore Mia's sweater open, ripped the neckline of her dress to expose her left shoulder, and began methodically cutting a series of bloody lines on the skin. The pain revived Mia. "No, no-o-o—stop cutting me!" she screamed.

"I told you—*shut up*. I'm done with that. That mark means you're workin' for me—for good. And if you're workin' for me, you're layin' down for me—so let's have some fun." He grabbed her dress and started cutting downward from the middle of the neckline. Mia screamed again, louder. The jersey fabric stretched, resisting Walter's knife.

"Help, someone help me!" her voice echoed in the empty building. She flailed at him with her hands, bloodying his silk shirt.

Walter's knife cut through the dress into Mia's flesh, just below her rib cage on the left side. *"Please help me,"* Mia screamed again. *"Help—he's killing me."* She leaned forward and twisted from side to side, trying to sit up despite her bleeding wounds, but Walter yanked off her underpants and rammed into her, pressing all his weight on her. She sobbed and scratched his face, mixing his blood with her own. When he came, he bit her right arm; her shriek bounced off the walls.

As he smoothed his bloody shirt and zipped up his pants, she continued to yell; he picked up the knife and jabbed her in the groin. "Stupid fuckin' bitch," he shouted before he ran down the stairs.

His eyes were used to the darkness, but he couldn't locate her bag. He almost fell over it. The bloody knife still clutched in one hand, he ripped open the ballet bag zipper and rummaged through everything, dumping tights, socks, and sweaters all over the floor. Finally, he found what he was looking for—a small pink nylon pouch containing a change purse, keys, her address book. Dropping the pink pouch, he pocketed the address book along with the thirty dollars from her change purse.

He could still hear her yelling; he might bump into some asshole outside.... He lobbed the knife far into the rubble-filled room to the left of the front door. Then he kicked open the door and ran to Columbus Avenue, where, within three minutes, a cab stopped for him.

Mia's screams continued, more audibly now, through the door that Walter had failed to close all the way.

"Columbus Avenue and Nine-oh Street in what borough?" the 911 operator asked the night watchman of St. Gregory's, a church that backed up on the building where the attack took place.

"Manhattan."

"I don't have the address," the operator complained, "the house number."

"I don't either—put the call over with what I gave you!" The watchman hung up hard. He went out to the street and jogged up and down, listening. Finally, he reentered the church and walked out onto a catwalk in the rear. The screams seemed much closer.

Police Officer Elvia Tierney had been taught that emotion has no place at a crime scene—and that the first official acts there can make or break a case. She remembered the exact words from her class notes: *Good judgment gives way to confusion. The turmoil of personal feelings is reflected in the handling of evidence—and eventually, in unsatisfactory courtroom testimony*. When Officer Tierney's flashlight caught the young woman fallen on her back, bloody from the waist down, the officer paused on the threshold of the room and took a very deep breath.

Her partner had the radio. "Tell Central we got a bleeder," she told him, "we need a bus. And let's really try to keep out everybody but the sergeant till the detectives come. This room is too damn small—there won't be any crime scene left if a whole bunch of cops pile in here."

She wanted the scum who did this to be locked up forever. She walked around the edge of the room and crouched down, directing the flashlight beam at the blood-soaked mattress and the girl. She looks like a crushed bird, Tierney thought.

The paramedics came running up the stairs. Tierney's partner used his light to point out a roundabout route to the victim, to avoid disturbing the litter on the crime scene floor. One of the paramedics carried oxygen equipment, which he set on the floor at the head of the mattress. He delved into his pack for compresses to stop the bleeding. The other paramedic shook his head gloomily. He knelt down and reached for the girl's left wrist.

As Tierney watched, the medic kept hold of the wrist and looked at the victim's eyes.

"Can you see?" Tierney asked.

"Yeah," he said. "Better have your desk call the medical examiner."

Early morning, Wednesday, November 6, 1985

On top of everything else, this was Obie's case—he was up. He told Cooch that the DOA, a young white woman on Eight-nine Street, might be a celebrity. Even if she ain't, Cooch said, Obie should call Flynn. Let him decide if he should come in or not.

Obie was truly sorry he had answered the squad room phone—five minutes later, the Nightwatch squad would have handled the case, for tonight anyway. Obie figured that Flynn had his lady with him, but even if not, a homicide wasn't gonna be great news. As for what Flynn would do, you didn't need a crystal ball: grab a cab and meet them at the scene.

"If I knew I had to guard a DOA tonight," Police Officer Tierney told Obie and his bosses when they came upstairs, "I would've asked for a different one. She can't be more than twenty years old."

Tierney told them how a watchman had hailed the radio car, saying he'd heard screams coming from the rear of a house on Eight-nine. Even though Central gave the job as Nine-oh Street, the watchman had been right. Obie took down his name. Tierney gave him the medics' names, too.

"Was it you who told the desk the deceased might be famous?" Flynn asked her.

"Yeah. I think she's a ballet dancer—look at her body. She's so thin but yet she looks strong. Even if she is a dancer, that don't exactly make her famous. But..."

Obie's mouth went dry. His forehead sweated.

"It's just a guess, Obie," Flynn told him. He turned to Tierney. "Detective O'Brien's daughter is a dancer."

"Officer"—Cooch claimed Tierney's attention—"did you see the knife or whatever the perp cut her with? What about ID?"

Flynn borrowed the officer's light and squatted down by the

body. Obie supposed that most of the wounds were too bloody to read, but Flynn said, "Maybe a razor; a knife more likely."

"Ain't no knife in this room," Tierney said. "I went over it with the light. No ID neither—just a bunch of old porno mags. But—"

"A knife might be anywhere in the building," Obie said. "If it is, Emergency Service will find it."

Flynn looked at Tierney. "But what?"

"I noticed somethin' on the floor, looked like cocaine powder. There was so little, but it was too white not to see it."

Obie said if it was coke, maybe it had nothing to do with this case.

"We'll make sure CSU looks for it," Flynn told Tierney. "Thanks for rememberin' that."

She looked at him. "I got a few things to say to that jury that a picture can't tell."

"Don't worry," he assured the cop, "we'll get him and you'll be first on the stand." He used her light to scrutinize the girl's clothing and body. "Did anyone move her?" he asked.

"No," Tierney said.

Finally Flynn stood up, pulled a notebook from an inside pocket, and began to write as he narrated to Obie: *semen traces on left thigh, defensive wounds on both hands, series of superficial knife (?) cuts on left shoulder, toes badly bruised. Profuse bleeding from body wounds.*

"You gonna do the notification, Lieu?" Tierney asked when he was through.

"Nobody to notify till we get an ID."

"Let us keep the flashlight a little longer," Obie said. "I thought I saw somethin' downstairs."

Silently, Obie picked up the dancer's garments one at a time from the filthy hallway floor, folded them, and stowed them in the PLAZA BALLET bag. He showed Flynn the torn place at the end of the bag where the strap had been attached. Flynn went out and flashed the light on the stoop, but the steps were too beat up for signs of a struggle to show. He checked the outside door for bloodstains but saw none. CSU should dust it for prints, he told Obie and Cooch.

Cooch said the change purse was empty—no ID, no money.

"The ballet's gonna know somebody's missing," Obie said; "they practice all day, every day." As he folded a sweater, something fluttered to the floor.

"Mia Greenfield, Seventy-six West Eighty-ninth Street," Flynn read off the envelope. "She lives less than a block from here."

"Let's go over," Obie said.

"Yeah," Flynn agreed, "but it's too late for the canvass; we'll do it when folks are awake and talkative."

"The watchman," Cooch said, "he must still be on duty. I'm gonna stop by the church."

"What's in the letter?" Obie asked Flynn as they walked up the street.

"No letter, but the return address on the envelope is Dr. Greenfield in Traverse City, Michigan."

Obie sighed. "It won't hurt to wait a couple of hours before we call."

The three-story brownstone building at Seventy-six West had come back from its boardinghouse days, Obie noticed, but not all the way back, like some of its fancy neighbors, to restored stonework and folding shutters in the windows. "Somebody gave it the white-paint treatment and raised the rents," Obie said.

"Looks kinda strange in the dark—pale." The label by the bell for Apartment 2 said Clarence/Greenfield. Flynn rang, waited, rang again. No response. A light rain began to fall.

The PLAZA BALLET bag weighed on Obie's shoulder. He shifted it.

"Let's find Cooch," Flynn said, "we'll catch up with the roommate in a few hours."

At six-thirty, just before tiptoeing out of the Anastasia Suite, Flynn set the clock radio so Lauren would wake up to an all-news station. Every twenty minutes or so, they would report the latest West Side crime—the savage stabbing and probably sexual assault of a young white woman on the edge of fame. Once Mia Greenfield's relatives had been notified and the details could be released, media interest would go off the charts. In the meantime, Flynn was sure Lauren would figure out why he had disappeared.

When he was married, his wife had followed his sensational cases so she could talk about them at the office and with her clients. Lauren *was* different. She was amazing, he decided as he locked all the locks and left her. Flynn became aware that this new homicide could be some kind of acid test; if the squad did clear the case, that wouldn't necessarily add up to a "pass" for him.

Wednesday, November 6, 1985

Obie had slept in the dorm and was waiting for Flynn. He'd bounced right back—pretty good on four hours' sleep. You had to bounce back, couldn't lose your objectivity. The fresh coffee had just finished dripping when Flynn arrived.

"How are you, pal?"

"Well, I called the morgue, Lieu."

"When's the autopsy?"

Obie blanched. "Not till tomorrow, oh nine hundred. I'm gonna skip this one and let Detective Defina be my eyes and ears if she can do it. She knows what she's doin'."

Flynn knew that Obie should go, but he said, "Okay, but someone from the squad's gotta be there. We'll send Billy. Did Defina say they're gonna do fingernail scrapings and all the smears?"

"Yeah. The ME who went to the scene detected some white granular material stuck to the blood of the wounds. It ain't been tested yet, but his guess is the same as Tierney's. Defina's gonna make sure they order drug tests on the deceased, too."

"What's your guess?"

"Why guess? Either way, it's bad news. Even if Mia Greenfield was a cokehead, she didn't deserve that death. If Mia was usin' coke or if she wasn't, I'd say Barbara O'Brien would be as safe in the PD as in a ballet company."

"If she wasn't your own kid you'd say, 'Keep an open mind.' Like you usually do."

"Yeah," Obie admitted, "this don't help. It's oh six-thirty hours in Michigan; I'm gonna call the Traverse City cops. I'm gonna ask 'em to call me right back after they make the notification. Then I'll reach out for the Greenfields."

The phone on Flynn's desk rang: Estrelita said Jesse had heard the news report and was on his way in. Flynn called Reynolds and woke him up. "Put on your suit and come on over," he advised, "we got a heavy. Look at the *News,* page three." Then he checked Information listings for Greenfield and Clarence at 76 West Eighty-ninth Street and got the number—the same for both names. When he called it, an answering machine offered to take messages for Heather and Mia.

The rest of C Team had signed in. Flynn sat down with everyone and went over the homicide so far, including what the watchman had told Cooch.

"The roommate's name," he concluded, "is Heather Clarence; looks like Heather didn't sleep home last night, but we're gonna keep tryin' to reach her."

Then Obie walked into the bosses' office. "Y'know," he said, "when I told Dr. Greenfield about my daughter bein' a dancer, too, he said he was always against that career 'cause he knew the physical demands was too much. But then, he says, kinda like he was talkin' to himself, that he never realized the mental demands might be even worse. I asked him what he meant; he says he's too upset to go into it. 'Well, did she have any problems that you know of?' I says. 'Because if she did, it helps the detectives to have that information.' He said just some medical problems, dancer's injuries."

"Yeah?" Flynn looked at Obie. "Sounds like he—"

"I didn't push him for more now. Most parents don't know their kid is usin' till it's too late. I figure we got other ways to go into it and we can always come back to him. I told him nobody in the city could give this case the kind of attention it's gonna get from us; well, he did say thank you, but he goes, 'Whatever happens, you can't bring her back.' I says, 'Relatives usually feel better when the perpetrator is brought to justice.' No reaction like, 'Give it everything you got.' Nothing like that. All he says is, 'I wish we could just have a nice service and leave her in peace.' I says, 'I understand how you feel,' and I warned him he's gonna hear from the media. That didn't seem to affect him one way or the other. He don't have no plans to come east; I told him we'll release the body as soon as we can and he can call us anytime."

"Sounds like we're gonna want to call him. If he knew Mia was using drugs, we should know that. If it's something else he doesn't want to talk about, we can't let him off the hook on that either," Flynn said.

"Are you suggestin' I let somebody off the hook, Lieu?" O'Brien had the same look in his eye as when somebody mentioned Queen Elizabeth.

"Even the best of us, which is you, might not be able to keep from reacting like a human just at the wrong moment, Obie, but we can backtrack if we have to. Right now, let's get everybody on the road." Flynn was gambling that Obie's discipline would override his abused pride. "Jesse'll get on the 911 tapes because there was quite a few callers who heard screams," Flynn continued. "C Team guys and Reynolds start the canvass. You gotta talk to Ninetieth Street, not just Eight-nine. From what the watchman said, he could hear the screams better on Ninetieth."

Before leaving the bosses' office, Reynolds showed Obie where the *News* mentioned "Det. First Grade Paul O'Brien—Lieut. Flynn's most senior investigator."

"This would be the case," Obie grumbled, "that lands my name in the paper."

"It's a first?" Taylor asked incredulously.

"Maybe one other time."

Reynolds read aloud the bit at the end about "Flynn's ace Two-nine squad and their 100% reputation for solving homicides."

"Ace, huh?" Taylor snorted. "Let's get *outta* here before the captain gets a look at that."

Flynn's phone rang. Reynolds hooted and Taylor pushed him out the bosses' office door. Taylor stood there, looking expectantly at Flynn, who managed to get his arms into his sport jacket by switching the receiver from one hand to the other.

"Yes, Chief—good morning."

The Chief of D's tone was conciliatory. "Well, it's probably a good thing the community lobbied to keep you right where you are, Andy. This Greenfield case is the kind of thing you can handle and they know it."

"Myself and O'Brien are just leavin' for Manhattan Cultural Center; we got a lot of people to talk to there, I'm sure."

"Yeah, well—this one's a heavy, a real big one. As soon as the media put out that the deceased was a ballerina and all, you know we'll be hearing from the mayor. There's gonna be a lot of noise, Andy; we'll be under big pressure. Not just from the precinct, either—citywide. So let's see your 'hundred percent squad' show their stuff—right?"

All of a sudden the Chief decides "a hundred percent" comes in handy, Flynn noticed. "This ain't the kind of case where anybody's gotta scrounge for motivation," Flynn told him. "Some butcher destroys a young person with a beautiful future, everybody's in early."

"Great! Anything special you need, you let me know—okay?"

"Like you said, Chief, we got the stuff: motivation—that's at least half the battle; experience and skill—that's the rest."

"We-e-ell then, that *News* reporter picked the right word, didn't he, 'ace'! Go for it!"

"Thanks for calling. I'll be sure and tell the men what you said."

* * *

Miss Rosemont, assistant to the general manager of the Plaza Ballet, invited the cops to sit down in her reception area while she gathered some material for them. They watched her manicured fingers pull papers in quick succession from various files, align them neatly, and hand them to Obie in a sturdy folder. She included a list of all the dancers in the company. A biography of Mia and a glossy head shot. A schedule of the fall season with all the ballets to be performed by date, together with a cast list showing which dancers were assigned what roles. Obie marveled at Miss Rosemont's organizational flair and Flynn backed him up.

"Precision is not only for the dancers," she answered, turning back to her computer monitor. "We must keep the environment purring along so they can concentrate on their art. Petty distractions are stressful, so why not eliminate as many as possible." She smiled. "I try."

"We also need a list of all the people that the dancers cross paths with during the day," Obie said. "The tech people, wardrobe, orchestra, maintenance. Sort of a tall order, but important." Obie was thinking of the musician who'd been raped and murdered by a stagehand a few years earlier. In that case the body had been found right on the Cultural Center premises.

"I'll ask payroll to help you with that," Miss Rosemont promised.

"Right now, as we speak"—Flynn's confidential manner included her in the work he and Obie were doing—"detectives are going from door to door, talking to residents in the buildings near the crime scene. It's tedious but there's no way to predict who might have some piece of information. Well, we need to do the same thing here, starting with the dancers. Can you suggest some central place where we can find them?"

Miss Rosemont got up from her well-organized desk. "I'll take you to the Green Room," she said, "they all go in and out. If you'll wear your badges, they'll know why you're here. And everyone will help in any way they can. They all spend hour after hour together, day after day. This is a terrible jolt for the whole company."

"As you know, Mia's parents are not planning to come east from Michigan," Flynn told Miss Rosemont. "And so far, we haven't located her roommate. But we do need someone who knew her well to identify the body, today."

Miss Rosemont supposed that she would be the logical person to go to the morgue. "I knew her quite well—and there's no one else to do it," she said, "story of my life."

* * *

"I've been to the recitals for years," Obie told Flynn as they settled on a worn couch in a corner of the still-empty room, "but I never saw a class. I'll say this, though, it boggles your mind to see this waif walk out of the house in rags—seriously, rags, with safety pins for decoration—and come out on stage lookin' and dancin' like heaven's own angel. I got a feeling what we're gonna see in here is real, professional rags."

They saw faded pink tights and black ones washed to gray, worn with bloomers over them. Skintight bodysuits with holes "mended" by safety pins and worn under baggy sweat shirts with more holes. Scarves. Leg warmers stretched to thigh-height or bunched up at the ankle. Hair twisted into odd shapes and held by odd-shaped clips, or worn in a bun pierced by pencils. Strong, muscular legs and delicate hands. Prominent cheekbones, pale mouths, and exotically colored eye makeup. And the ever-present huge nylon or canvas bag.

Tears blurred the eye makeup colors as the dancers talked to Flynn and Obie about Mia. They talked about her "long line" and her "extension"; the natural way her dancing seemed to grow out of the music. And they talked about how hard she worked, richly deserving the roles that had just recently started coming her way, the first step toward a promotion. And since then she had worked harder, never becoming temperamental or conceited.

For all the hours the dancers had shared with Mia, they had little to say about her life after work. Most of us don't *have* much of a life after work, one after another explained. Each time Flynn or Obie would ask a dancer if Mia could have had an enemy, the notion was rejected. Obie or Flynn would point out that Mia knew the city, had lived here for several years while attending the company ballet school—did she seem like someone who would willingly walk into a boarded-up building with a stranger?

No, the dancers said, but they all insisted that Mia was admired and adored by all who knew her: the murderer could only be a stranger.

Obie's mood did not benefit from seven hours behind the scenes at the ballet. "I got a feeling this is a clear-cut case of what-Daddy-doesn't-know-won't-hurt-him," he told Flynn on their way back to the squad. "They all look like they could use a good meal—three times a day. Besides, I can think of more inspiring ways to spend a Wednesday than bein' stonewalled by three or four dozen porcelain dolls who could all be your daughter, from the back at least."

"Stonewalled is right," Flynn said, "we should've brought charmin' Billy. But you know who those porcelain dolls remind me of?"

"Who?"

"A bunch of cops in a station house where somethin's goin' on. Nobody's about to give up the one—or rather, the ones—who did it." He pulled the Chrysler into the parking lot behind the Two-nine and both detectives got out.

"So accordin' to Andy Flynn," Obie's voice rose, "Mia Greenfield wasn't the only one usin' drugs. Is that how you see it?"

"It is likely—"

"That's premature, goddamn it. Keep an open mind, will ya?"

"*If* it turns out that I'm right," Flynn placated, holding the station-house door for Obie, "this case will get it out in the open. Something positive out of Mia's death."

"If it turns out that you're right, Mary Maureen Healy O'Brien is gonna raise hell in a manner previously unknown in the history of Queens housewives," Obie predicted.

Flynn tried another tack. "Maybe the canvass was more productive than we were."

This time the look in Obie's eye said, "It wouldn't take much," but he kept his mouth shut.

Betty Dominic brought Flynn six phone messages. The top one said call Detective Defina in the A.M. or try tonight at home. "The rest is media," Betty said. "They all wanted to talk to you about the 'ballet dancer case.' She was a dancer, the girl who got stabbed to death?"

"With the Plaza Ballet." Flynn hung up his jacket and rolled up his sleeves.

"The murders are all sad in a way," Betty said, "but this is worse. A dancer seems like—more alive, you know?"

Neither Flynn nor Cooch answered Betty; fortunately, Obie was out of earshot in the coffee room. "Anyway, Lieutenant, I told the reporters you'd be back later. I gotta leave, it's sixteen-ten hours already."

"The *News* called back again," Cooch told Flynn. "Your 'old friend'?—says he's gotta talk to you before his deadline." He opened a desk drawer. "ESU brought this." A photocopy of both sides of a Buck knife with a stained five-and-a-half-inch blade.

Obie walked into the bosses' office, looking relieved. "I spoke to Heather Clarence: sounds like she's holding up. I don't think it hit her yet. She said try to get there before six so she has more time to talk to us." Obie saw the photocopied knife on Flynn's desk. "Mother of God," he said under his breath.

"I need a cup of coffee," Flynn said. "Let's hear how everybody made out and then we'll go see Heather."

Taylor had the 911 data. "The first calls came at oh oh twenty-six and oh oh twenty-nine; calls kept coming till oh oh forty-three," he said. "Out of fourteen callers, six gave names; I'm gonna hook up with all of 'em tomorrow."

"Okay." Reynolds looked at some notes on a steno pad. "Several people on the block saw a figure running east on Eight-nine Street after the screams started. But not immediately after—like around ten minutes, they estimated. She must have struggled with him before he booked. Witnesses all say he was a white male; some say dark hair, some couldn't tell; all say light-colored suit. We're not lookin' for some skel—he's well dressed. Probably in his twenties."

Obie broke in, "The dancers told us she 'didn't have any enemies' so she couldn't know the guy. From that description, he sure sounds like someone she could know. An acquaintance, even a friend."

"How fast can a friend become an enemy?" Taylor asked himself aloud. "Hypocrisy is an art, Machiavelli says. Especially in a competitive field like that."

Cooch cleared his throat. "If this is a drug-related homicide—and let's face it, that's how it's gonna come out—she knew him, all right. Ninety-six percent of victims and perps in drug-related homicides knew each other—latest figures. Hit 'em with *that.*"

"Okay, Marty—thanks," Flynn said.

"Go ahead, Billy."

"Height: you name it. Some people told us he's tall, about my height, thin build; some say 'average.' Several people mentioned he was carrying a briefcase-type thing or attaché. One witness said when he looked out and saw the guy, he thought of a commuter running for a train. At first he didn't associate this 'commuter' with the screams—with a crime—because, you know, it didn't fit."

"Nice work. You told that witness we may want him to testify?" Flynn asked. "This could be a first—a perp who's gotta come into court wearin' jeans and an old undershirt to look innocent for the jury!"

"If we ever get that far." Cooch looked at Reynolds. "Where's the paper on these witnesses?"

"Reports are all in your IN box, Sarge, waitin' for you to sign."

Cooch had no intention of demeaning himself by looking in

the IN box, and Reynolds, counting on that, could just as well be bluffing.

Flynn held up the photocopied knife. He read aloud the ESU sergeant's note, which said the knife had been found in the rubble in the front room on the parlor floor, west of the stairs. Partial prints had been lifted from the knife and sent to Latent; a blood sample had been sent to the lab.

Taylor wanted to know about the white granular stuff found at the scene. Not tested yet, Flynn said. He turned to Billy. "Make sure to check on those tests when you're at the morgue tomorrow. The autopsy is at oh nine hundred and I gotta have Obie workin' with me. Detective Defina's expectin' you."

"How long has it been?" one of Obie's partners wondered aloud, "since we was lookin' for a *white* perp?"

"Not that long," Taylor answered, "you forgot about Franny, the young lady who killed her pot connection."

"Okay," Obie's partner said, "but who are we lookin' for here—a white, well-dressed *what?*"

"That's the right question, pal," Flynn said. He noticed Taylor giving him the fish-eye.

Obie looked up. "How come we didn't talk to any *male* dancers, Lieu? Where were they?"

"We'll audition 'em all," Flynn said. "Tomorrow. Unless Heather recognizes this description tonight and we're headin' straight for Central Booking."

The men shook their heads and grinned at the boss's latest flight of optimism. As they all straggled out of the bosses' office, Taylor buttonholed Flynn. "I think I heard a word at AA that fits what's going on here. 'Denial.' "

Flynn sighed. "Okay. Obie is denying that drugs could be widespread in the ballet company because he's worried about his daughter, and I am enabling him. But not for long. We're both gonna get a good night's sleep and face the music—"

"Tomorrow? Why, Scarlett, honey—welcome to the Big Apple. What happened to Andy 'Every-minute-counts-in-a-homicide' Flynn?"

"I *need* Obie on this investigation—if he jumps ship—"

"You don't need him to blow this case."

Reynolds yelled out of the coffee room, "Hey, this is your life—Channel Two."

Five men made a capacity crowd in the coffee room. Cooch stayed away. The five-o'clock news led with the ballet dancer case. First videotape of the brownstone on Eighty-ninth Street, with crime-scene tape stretched across the bottom of the stoop and an

Emergency Service truck parked outside. "Police spent hours in this abandoned building today, searching the rubble for clues," the reporter said in voice-over, "but if the house has been used by drug addicts as a shooting gallery, as is likely, that most certainly would complicate the task."

"How about that!" Obie looked at Flynn. "Maybe coke has nothin' to do with *this* case."

Now the reporter appeared live on camera, standing outside the ballet stage door in the Cultural Center. Two dancers wearing blue jeans, baggy sweaters, and dirty sneakers spoke tearfully of Mia and her talent. The reporter asked, "Mia Greenfield was scheduled to dance on opening night, wasn't she?"

"Yes, she'd been chosen to lead the corps de ballet in *Rubies,*" one of the dancers replied, turning away from the camera in tears.

"Two weeks from now, when the Plaza Ballet opens the 1985–86 season with a gala benefit," the reporter said, "their performance will be marked by a special quality of grief for the talented corps de ballet dancer Mia Greenfield, victim of a brutal stabbing and, police tell us, sexual assault. She was twenty years old. Her promise will never be fulfilled."

The anchorwoman asked the reporter whether Mia was a New Yorker. "No, she was from Michigan—but she had studied here at the company school for three years before joining the corps last fall."

The anchor faced into the camera. "Ballet lovers and all New Yorkers are grieving about this tragedy tonight."

Reynolds looked at Obie. "That's how those dancers dress? Some glamor!"

"The audience sees the glamor," Obie came back. "For the dancers, it's a lot of work, dangerous hard work, like buildin' bridges or somethin'. Lieu, you ready?" he prodded.

"Gettin' my coat."

The phone rang on Flynn's desk.

"I only got time for one question," he told his friend at the *News,* "shoot."

"Any leads?" the reporter asked.

"Directions. It would be more accurate to say we're working in a couple of directions, which is good progress. More than a dozen people called 911 when they heard the victim's screams—we're extremely grateful to them and to everyone who has come forward to tell us what they heard or saw."

* * *

Heather Clarence let the detectives into the floor-through apartment. Obie introduced himself and Flynn to the tall young woman. On a first impression, she looked severe in her black skirt and white blouse, but that changed when you saw the hairdo—a long, dark braid down her back. Her skin was without color except for vibrant red lipstick. Blue eyes, rimmed in red.

Propped against the wall next to the front door stood a large musical-instrument case. "You're a musician?" Flynn asked.

"I play the cello in Broadway musicals—I'm in the orchestra of *Big River*. I'm due at work pretty soon; that's why I can't spend too much time with you right now." She saw the ballet bag on Obie's shoulder and the tears started.

"Oh, God. This is so—dreadful. Did she—"

"Sit down, Heather," Obie said. "Go slow. We'll just do whatever you can, for now." He took the high-backed chair next to the hand-me-down couch. Flynn scanned the comfortable clutter around him. A scarred upright piano, a music stand with classical sheet music, a table by the window covered with last Sunday's *Times*. Posters for the Plaza Ballet and several Broadway shows taped to the walls.

He walked over to Obie and Heather. "I'll only confuse the situation if I butt in. Just one thing—did the two of you share a bedroom or did Mia have her own?"

"Mia sleeps in that one." Heather gestured to the left of the front door.

"I'll go look around in there; maybe something will give me an idea. We're kinda in the dark, so far."

The small room had an almost spartan feel to it. A study in pastel blue, it could have been the room of a younger girl—except for its neatness. Flynn stared at the room; one look at this would have Obie on a stretcher, but Obie should see it; he might catch something Flynn missed. He almost wished he himself could be in the chaos of a crime scene instead of here. You started an investigation with a couple of facts about a corpse. As you progressed, the person came alive; became someone you could almost talk to. In the end, sometimes you had to bury someone you liked. He moved slowly, reluctant to get this close to Mia. And to be the first to disrupt the fine order that stood for her life.

The closet contained very simple clothes and a pair of blue jeans for every day of the week. In the chest of drawers, Flynn found piles of practice clothes. A few of them seemed hardly worn; most looked just like the 'professional rags' that he and Obie had seen on all the dancers in the Green Room. At the foot of the bed, Mia had a cardboard carton full of pop sheet music and a collection of jazz records.

Several pairs of pink pointe shoes, mostly dirty and ripped, hung by their ribbons from the ladder back of the chair in front of the desk. Two brand-new, perfect pairs occupied the chair seat along with glossy ribbons not yet attached.

Visible through the glass doors of a cabinet over Mia's desk, some books of poetry, *Jonathan Livingston Seagull,* and many more books about ballet. A shelf stuffed with ballet programs. A family-group picture in which she seemed to be about twelve years old. Inside a drawer, Flynn found a scrapbook with many empty pages and a few clippings not yet pasted down. On the desk surface, a Metropolitan Museum of Art date book lay open to the current week. Flynn recognized the names of the ballets that Mia had been scheduled to dance in. Other than those, he saw few notes as he flipped quickly through her last weeks.

Glossy photos of ballet performances took up much of the room's wall space. In one photo, Mia and a partner danced alone on the stage.

Flynn gathered up the calendar and the scrap book and returned to the living room. The ballet bag sat unopened on the floor between Obie and Heather. She talked about her friendship with Mia, as Obie probed about her roommate's career, boyfriends, hobbies, habits.

"Last night," Obie said, "would she have been at Manhattan Cultural Center into the evening?"

"Definitely. They go on and on, rehearsing."

"Would you know if she had a date afterwards?"

Heather said she and Mia could hardly keep track of each other because Mia was gone all day and until late at night. Even on Sunday, Mia usually took class. On Monday night, Heather's show and the ballet both were dark, but Heather usually spent the time off with her boyfriend. Once in a while, Mia would join them for dinner.

As for last night, if Mia had followed her usual habit, she would have gone with other dancers to a place called The Barre for something to drink. They got VIP treatment there, because where they went, the ballet fans followed. It wasn't likely that Mia had a date, but if she had, Heather wouldn't know.

"Which dancers was she friendly with?"

Heather had probably heard the names but couldn't remember any right now.

"What did she like to drink?" Flynn asked.

"Oh, white wine or a draft beer." After the dancers left The Barre, Heather explained, Mia would take the subway home, the Number One train, because she thought walking up Broadway was the safest route.

Heather had dried her tears but now started to cry once again. "Did she have her keys? I keep imagining that she got to the door and discovered she had lost them and turned around to—and if I'd been here, she wouldn't—"

Obie looked at Flynn and reached for the bag. "I remember the keys bein' here, don't you?" He unzipped the zipper and sorted through till he found keys. "She had them, Heather. Don't blame yourself, now. You couldn't have prevented this."

"But you're helping us figure out who was responsible," Flynn said. "Take a look in the bag, please—something just might remind you of something we haven't talked about."

Heather unpacked everything that Obie had folded and tucked away. "Oh—you wanted her dancer friends' names. I'll know them when I see them in her address book. Red leather, exactly the same as my own. She liked mine so I gave her one.... She always had it with her. Did you see it in here?" As the detectives watched attentively, Heather went through all the pieces, reaching into sleeves and tights in hopes that the small address book had worked its way in somewhere.

"Come on," Obie said as Heather looked up miserably from the last piece. "We'll give you a ride to the theater."

Flynn drove down Broadway, past Manhattan Cultural Center. At Sixty-third Street, Heather pointed out a place just in from the corner. "The Barre Cafe," she said, "where I told you the dancers go for drinks after work."

"Thanks," Flynn said, "that's good for us to know. Do you happen to remember," he asked offhandedly, "Mia ever going on the wagon, or, like—making up her mind to quit drinking for a period of time?"

"Well, she—" Heather seemed confused. "No. Why would she, because it wasn't a problem, you know. For her, two drinks was a lot."

When traffic backed up in the Fifties, Flynn put the Chrysler's siren on and sped the last ten blocks to the theater. Obie helped Heather out with her cello. "We're very sorry, about... everything. You know if anybody can find this—animal—we can. And when we do, we'll put him in a cage and keep him there. We're gonna stay in touch with you." He gave her a business card. "And here's where we are if you need us."

When he got back in the car, he asked Flynn, "Where are you goin' with the booze questions, Lieu? What's booze got to do with this?"

"Maybe nothing," Flynn answered, "I gotta sleep on it. And tomorrow we'll take a fresh look at everything. With *an open mind,* like you always say. Okay, pal?"

"Yeah."

Flynn said he would skip the gym tonight. "Nobody but mice left in there at this hour, anyway. I'll walk from here, Obie, I can use the exercise."

"It ain't safe, I don't have to tell you." Obie took Flynn's place at the wheel.

"It's a jungle," Flynn agreed, "but it's my jungle. Say hi to Maureen—but like the judge says, 'Don't discuss the case.'"

"In thirty-two years I haven't talked about a case at home. It's against my goddamn religion. You don't suppose I'm gonna *start* with the homicide of Plaza Ballet dancer Mia Greenfield. But I can't stop anybody from watchin' the news, can I?" Obie stepped on the gas and roared off.

Flynn felt as if he were digging his own grave. Nobody, not even Jesse, could do a better job than Obie on a case like this—*if* he kept his distance. But Jesse was right: You couldn't use up time fighting that battle. And Obie hadn't begun to fight.

As he walked, Flynn wondered what Lauren had heard or read by now. He had no doubt that she'd have something to say about the "ballet dancer murder." Disappointingly, he didn't find her in the Anastasia Suite. Nor did she answer her office phone. He made fresh coffee, put his feet up, and wondered where she was.

Then he wondered which of the ballet company's hundred or so dancers had been with Mia at the cafe last night and whether the same waiter that had served her group would be there tomorrow night. Someone, undoubtedly himself and Obie, would have to retrace all her steps from the moment she left the theater.

Midnight, Wednesday, November 6, 1985

Viera introduced Sami Fuego's second set and decided to unwind for a few minutes with the live music of a great group. He would just sit and listen to "Siempre Tu" all the way through. Latin music–lovers filled the Tabu dining room from the best tables all the way back, but the bar had some places. No sooner had Viera settled down with a fresh Bailey's on the rocks than Monte came upstairs and occupied the next barstool. Ramón hurried to fix his martini, placing it within easy reach on the bar, but Monte ignored the drink.

"Siempre tu...," the audience sang along, and Sami held out the mike toward them.

"Boss."

The trombones blared and the congas thundered and the heel of Viera's sleek loafer thumped the rung of the teak barstool. Monte saw that short of pulling a gun, he would not get the boss to pay attention. He waited uncomfortably for the long number to end. When it finally did, Viera applauded enthusiastically and took no notice of him. At last, Monte stood up and jogged the boss's elbow. "I gotta see ya, Irish. Sorry—this can't wait."

As Sami announced the next number, Monte followed Viera down the stairs to the office.

"What is it?" Viera asked sharply as he sat down.

Monte took a breath. "You heard somebody took out a dancer last night in a squat?"

"What about it?"

"I had a call from Chino just now. From what he said, it sounds like he did it. She—"

"Maricón! That asshole lost it and now we lose the organization's key salesman." Irish Luck's main growth area was the high end of the market, and at the moment Chino had a lock on those people. Viera got up and paced around, sat down again, and pounded the marble slab. "This is the kind of trick that makes the cops launch manhunts. I can't believe he's the one. Are you sure? I thought Chino was cool."

"Yeah, he did it, and she was a mess when he got through. What a dumb move. He said she—"

"I don't give a fuck why he did it. All that matters now is damage control—that's it. Chino *must* keep every customer satisfied but he also must *not* get picked up. Do you know where he is?"

"He's gonna call me back."

"That creep could really mess us up. Tell him no coke unless he gets out of circulation fast and stays out. Period. But as soon as he's set up, you're gonna get him three telephone lines under a legit business name and a good courier to deliver his orders. Everything fail-safe. Chino's customers must get Chino-style service, whatever it costs, until you find his replacement." In the past,

Monte had scouted competitors, looking for a rival upmarket dealer to lure away, but he had found nobody with a following to compare with Chino's. "Try harder this time—you got me?"

Thursday morning, November 7, 1985

The call had come into Luna Car Service at six-thirty A.M., a little later than usual; Luna sent their regular driver to collect Viera at the Tabu and take him home. "Good morning, señor—are you okay? You look like maybe you been workin' too hard."

"You might be right, Pepe. Last night was rough."

"Everybody in my cab talk about one thing all night. I guess you heard about it—that murder—the dancer? On the news and in the papers, they don't leave it alone."

"I heard about it all right and I'm sick of it already. Just another murder—why are these idiots so excited?"

"You mean the TV and the papers? Because it's so tragic, señor—a young dancer, she's a big loss. And she floats up to heaven, a beautiful picture in the mind, making people cry when they watch the TV or read about it. Also there's the cops. That makes excitement, too."

"Cops?"

"In the paper." Pepe held the wheel with one hand and reached for the copy of the *Daily News* that lay on the seat next to him. He held it up. "Yesterday the story is pretty small, page three or four, and they don't say nothin' about she's a dancer. Today, it's the front page and stories all over the inside about her family, her life—"

"What about the cops?"

"Oh, yeah, they keep telling about this detective who got the case; him and his squad, they're famous for getting all the murderers. So he's gonna get this one for sure, this guy who stabbed the beautiful—"

"You remember the cop's name? Was it Flynn?"

"*Sí, sí, señor*—that's it! You know this famous cop?" Pepe could not have sounded more impressed if Viera had known Geraldo Rivera.

"I do know him and you are lucky that you don't. Believe me, he's pure poison. He pushes his men to go after Spanish people and torment them. This community won't tolerate him much longer. You'll hear his name again soon enough—when we run him out in disgrace."

"Sí, señor." The car pulled up in front of Viera's Riverdale *alcázar*. *"Buenos días."*

Sunday morning, November 10, 1985

A soft breeze blew in the window behind the futon and across Flynn's forehead, waking him. "God," Lauren whispered, "it's like May."

"If it was May, then 1985 would be finished—history—whatever way it turned out. Nice thought." Since the night of the Greenfield homicide, they had sometimes been asleep together but until now, Sunday, never awake for a real conversation.

"I have another nice thought. . . ." Lauren smoothed her thin nightie demurely and then pressed her not-quite-naked body to his completely naked one. He could feel the general softness of breasts and tummy but no details. He reached around, ready to slide his hand under the nightie in back, but she was too quick. Grabbing the hem on either side, she pulled the nightie taut against herself.

But now that her hands were busy with that, he could use his on the front of her, stretching the nightie fabric across a breast with one hand and caressing with the other—broad, molding strokes of the palm, then fingers teasing through the thin fabric. "I love this nightie," he said.

Before long, her grip on the nightie relaxed and he rolled it up, bit by bit, to her shoulders, covering her body instead with his own until he found his way inside her. As they moved together, her fragrance bloomed and he inhaled it greedily with each deepening breath.

"You even smell like May," he said when they finally lay still. "Where've you been lately—like the other night, the one after the homicide?"

"Wednesday? Well, we have a hearing every other Wednesday. It lasted late, then I went to dinner with one of the planners and we talked shop—some neighborhood stuff he's working on. Sometimes I miss knowing the ins and outs of the kind of project that won't make headlines but means everything to the people right there. That's why I like the Precinct Council, you know—it gets my feet on the ground; we're not there to talk about the crossroads of the world, just my streets, my block."

"But now you're the one who could put that kind of project—more or less any project—in the headlines. Right?"

"What makes city-planning headlines is what the mayor and my boss decide should make headlines. The public knows what they want the public to know. Mostly."

"Mostly? Keep talking."

Lauren smiled. "Well, I know where the bodies are buried and once in a while I might have given a reporter an idea—and that can make things even more interesting than usual."

Flynn whistled. "You're talking serious power. Not exactly like my job."

"The scale is different. With you it's one-on-one. But it's life and death—what's as powerful as Mia Greenfield?"

"Yeah," he said, and looked at the clock, "Mia." The phone began to ring.

"Lieu." Obie's voice sounded flat. "Sorry, but I can't back you up after all. Maureen is—upset—'cause it's the last day of my swing *and* it's Sunday. She—"

"It's okay, pal. I'll just take it slow today. The two of us will get together tomorrow and go from there. Make sure you take her to Mass—it's a nice day for it. And out for lunch; someplace different for a change. I'm buyin'. We gotta get Maureen back on our side, right?"

"Thanks, Lieu."

"Have a good one now."

"Whew," Lauren said, "doesn't sound so good."

"You got a good ear. Today I can go to Manhattan Center and do what I gotta do. No problem. What's not so good is that Maureen is totally freaked because their daughter is a ballet dancer, like Mia. Maureen is always puttin' the pressure on Obie to retire—but now he's in almost as bad shape as she is over this case and she's pressin' harder than ever."

"Will he give in?"

"I don't know. But I do know it's not the same squad without Obie."

"Well," Lauren said, "one day at a time, huh? Maybe I'll make some coffee."

Flynn went and stood under the shower, imagining that the water could wash away the garbage in his brain and wishing he could make a long speech to Lauren in which some of what he felt about her would somehow get said.

* * *

Flynn showed his badge to the security guard at the stage door and pinned it through the corduroy of his jacket so he could make his way through the backstage halls. Surprisingly, Miss Rosemont's chair stood empty and her clean desk showed that she wasn't just off somewhere for a few minutes. Flynn did see lights on through the open door of the general manager's office. He knocked on the doorjamb and stuck his head in.

"Yes, Lieutenant, come in. I'm Susanna Sherman." The petite, gray-haired woman offered him a firm hand. On the wall behind her hung a huge color photo of that Christmas ballet with a cast of thousands—*The Nutcracker;* Flynn now knew its name. Otherwise the office looked ordinary.

"Lieutenant Flynn, Two-nine Precinct. Looks like we both got work to do on this nice spring Sunday."

"Our season starts any minute. The dancers work Sundays at this time of year. Sometimes I do, too, because you don't get many outside interruptions; easier to concentrate. Sit down, if you like."

Flynn smiled and used the chair back as a prop instead. "This is an interesting world, all new to me."

"And?"

"It seems extremely—complex. I find it's tough to figure out what's inside the heads that go with these fine-tuned bodies. I don't like to admit it because that's my job, that kind of figuring out."

"Of course these aren't 'average' people, I agree, but I think you overstate the case. Dancers are long on discipline and self-denial; in return for the sacrifices, they get applause and roses as well as money. They consider it a fair exchange. That's not so very complex."

"'Lightness of heart,'" Flynn quoted, "'a mind without shadows...' Less than a year and a half ago—when Mia Greenfield graduated from the Plaza Ballet School—*New York* magazine said that about her dancing. Tell me, because you're familiar with this special ballet world, how an angelic creature like that could end up in such horror?"

"We're all baffled, Lieutenant Flynn." Miss Sherman sighed. "And rather terrified."

"I wish that were true—both of those." Flynn turned on the half-smile and a cool hazel glance.

The ballet's general manager picked up a pair of reading glasses and tapped them impatiently on a stack of papers. "You think someone knows who killed Mia and won't tell you. That would be amusing if it weren't—"

"Not *who* killed her, but *what* did. I think all of you know damn well what did it—and you *should* be absolutely terrified that the same tragedy will happen to other dancers. It is true that you're terrified of one thing—facing what's going on here."

Flynn gestured at the *Nutcracker* photo. "Behind the pretty picture there's an ugly one. Interesting subject for an exposé, but that's not really my department. I'm looking for the 'who,' that's all. And nobody here is helping. It's making a tough case tougher—and it's not making me look too kindly on—"

"I gather you wouldn't spend your Sunday in my office unless you thought I could help. So what exactly...?"

"My partner and I have talked to three-quarters of the company, Miss Sherman, and not one single person admits to knowing Mia more than casually. Yet I know for a fact that she frequently went out after work with a group of dancers. More or less the same group, time after time. Nobody even admits to being part of that group. I have confidence that you can and will give me the name of at least one dancer who was close to Mia, who knew her well."

"I do know of one, Rachel French."

"If I could have Rachel's picture and her bio, I'll go away and let you work."

Miss Sherman went to her assistant's files and gave Flynn the material.

"Wish me luck," he said.

"Of course I do."

Monday, November 11, 1985

"Nice, pretty all-American type," Obie said, adjusting his glasses for another look at the head shot of Rachel French. He and Flynn sat in the Chrysler rereading Rachel's bio. "Now, Mia's the midwesterner, right? But she had those kinda European-looking features, could've been Irish with that red hair. Her friend is a brunette from Atlanta. Compared to Mia, she's little—five foot four."

"Southern girls like to talk, don't they?" Flynn put the NYPD plate on the dash.

"Let's hope," Obie said as they left the car.

They cooled their heels in the Green Room most of the

morning with nothing to do but say hi to dancers they'd already interviewed. Obie saw Rachel walk in the door, her arms swathed in a peculiar-looking garment. You couldn't miss the detectives with their central location in the room, but Rachel seemed oblivious. Another dancer hailed her and they began a long conversation on a couch in a far corner. The detectives waited some more. At last the conversation ended; the other dancer left Rachel occupying a corner of the couch with her feet up on the couch back, eyes closed.

Flynn and Obie could go over there and shift from one foot to the other, or they could move furniture. They chose to pick up an armchair and set it down by Rachel's couch. Obie sat on the seat, Flynn perched on the arm.

"Is that her—Rachel French?" Obie stage-whispered.

"Absolutely," Flynn whispered back. "Look at those perfect insteps!"

The long, dark eyelashes flicked up; a pair of special-effects green eyes looked warily at the detectives.

Obie folded his hands on his knee in his most fatherly pose. "We only need a few minutes, Miss French. We're investigating the murder of Mia Greenfield. Now, myself and Lieutenant Flynn, we'd like to ask you, since you knew her well—"

Tears welled up and overflowed the special-effects eyes. Flynn leaned forward and offered a pocket-size package of tissues. Rachel accepted. "I *can't*. I just can't talk about it."

"But we know you must want to help us apprehend the—"

More tears, shaking sobs. "The what? The werewolf who—Please—" She shook her head back and forth. "I can't."

"There now," Obie said. "This wasn't a werewolf-type thing, you know—comin' outta nowhere."

"It was a man," Flynn said, "and Mia knew him."

Rachel fell apart. She opened her hands helplessly and shook her head again. "Sorry. I want to help but don't know any—when I think about it, I'm just a—mess. Really—sorry."

"We're sorry, too, Rachel," Obie said softly. "I got a daughter myself who's gonna be a dancer. All we want is to catch the creep and put him away. The faster we move, the better chance we got." Obie stuck a business card on Rachel's ballet bag. "We're waitin' to hear from you, okay? As soon as you feel better, just call us."

"It's important," Flynn told her.

On the way uptown in the car he said to Obie, "Some eyes, huh?"

"Yeah."

"Good actress, too."

"I wouldn't say that."

"She's got no idea in the whole wide world how this happened to Mia?"

"I wouldn't say that, either." Obie sighed. "But she *was* a good friend of Mia's and she's takin' it hard."

"If anybody can make her feel better, Billy can. *And* get us some answers. This is a Reynolds job if ever there was one. What about Maureen, by the way? Is she feelin' better? Hope you bought her a super-duper lunch."

"We just went for a little ride since it was such a nice day; found a new place out by Sea Cliff. Don't worry—I'll hit you up later. It's good we got away, sort of a minivacation."

Flynn hoped that the minivacation had calmed down Obie's wife, but he didn't push it. "I could use a burger," he said, "what about you?"

"Let's go to McDonald's—we deserve a break today."

"Right—in this *case.*"

At almost 1400 hours, traffic in McDonald's had thinned out. Flynn and Obie sat by themselves in the front window overlooking Broadway. Their little wood-grain plastic table groaned under the Big Macs, the fries, and the large Cokes. Obie took a long swallow from the red-and-white-striped container. "I forgot to ask you what you were gettin' at with Heather about Mia and the booze," Obie said.

"What if"—Flynn doused his fries with ketchup—"what if Mia was usin' coke. Say she was, but she stopped, went for rehab and stayed the course—they'd advise her not to drink either. It's like in AA they say, 'You can't be high and sober at the same time.' Same idea if you go off drugs. And I wondered if that's what happened—she's in recovery from drugs, doesn't drink anymore either. But Heather couldn't say Mia went on the wagon without spillin' all the beans. Then, remember when we talked to the waiter at The Barre—"

"He told us she was drinkin' seltzer and stuff lately, not booze."

"Exactly."

"It's plausible but it don't *prove* she was on drugs. But okay, let's say she was—let's even say she had a 'slip' and that stuff at the scene does have somethin' to do with her. It certainly don't prove half the ballet company's on drugs. I don't see that."

"Then why do all the dancers stonewall? And when I let on to

Miss Sherman that I know damn well the company has a major coke problem—which I just might expose—why does Miss Sherman cave right in and give up Rachel French?"

"Because the company knows *Mia* had a coke problem. The murder is bad PR and drugs make it worse—they're afraid if it gets out that Mia used coke, everybody's gonna think what you think: The company's all full of cokeheads. They don't want us gettin' a false picture 'cause if we do, so will the media."

"Obie, for pete's sake—are you doin' PR for Plaza Ballet or workin' on a homicide?"

Obie put down his half-eaten burger and stared out the window toward the display of magazines on the busy corner newsstand at Ninety-sixth Street and Broadway.

Flynn pushed aside the ketchupy mass of half-eaten fries. "You *can't* let it screw you up that Barbara is a dancer, too. That's got *nothin'* to do with this—nothin'. I need you on this goddamm case as much as I always do if not more, but you ain't *here.*"

Finally, Obie looked at Flynn. "I gotta think about that, Lieutenant. *If* it's true that I 'ain't here,' then I might as well give Maureen what she wants and be *there*. More in touch with the family—'specially Barbara. Like Maureen says, Barbara is eighteen, two years younger than Mia. While there's time, I need to—"

"But Barbara has lived in New York City all her life. Not Traverse 'City' where you can't get streetwise 'cause there's not enough goddamn streets. Barbara comes from a good home and she's too smart to get fast-talked into drugs. She's not Mia."

"There's nothin' wrong with Mia's home, either, and Mia was no fool. What a load of horseshit. It's that *job* and the temperament it takes to do it; Mia had it, and so does Barbara. I know my daughter."

"While you're on this case, just pay attention to the facts of this case. If you can't do that—"

"I always did do that. Maybe more than I paid attention to my kids. Maybe I'm gettin' my last chance to make a difference—to Barbara, at least...."

"That's what Maureen says, I bet." Until now, Flynn hadn't regretted anything he'd said, but he dearly wished he could take back that last desperate shot.

"Puttin' in the papers takes a while," Obie said. "Might as well get started."

"What happened to 'gotta think about it'?"

"I just did."

Late afternoon, Wednesday, November 13, 1985

Every newspaper in town had run a photo of the white brownstone where Mia had shared the second-floor apartment with Heather Clarence. Next to a dazzling picture of Mia in costume, the *News* had shown one of Heather in a plain black dress, playing the cello. Now she answered the door, barefoot and wearing a neat white shirt with a pair of jeans. Her long straight hair hung loose. As before, red lipstick lent her heart-shaped face its only color. "Hi, Lieutenant Flynn. Come in."

"Thanks, Heather."

"I was expecting Detective O'Brien, too."

"He wanted me to tell you hello for him; he did a day tour so he went home at four." In fact, Maureen had called in sick for him. " 'Tell Heather to keep her chin up,' he said."

The shape of her face made the chin a focal point. It quivered a little. "Well, I am trying," she said, reaching into her shirt pocket for a tissue. "Anyway, please sit down wherever...."

He chose Obie's chair, the high-back one. Opening a brown envelope that contained the Metropolitan Museum calendar he'd taken from Mia's desk, he said, "Here's what I wanted to look at with you." The book slid out.

"Her calendar. Oh, did you find the address book?"

"Not yet. It could still turn up. Let's work on this—I think it might take us somewhere. Okay?"

Heather dabbed at her eyes. "Ready."

"Let's just start with this month and work back. Mostly, it's the ballets she was scheduled to perform in, starting with the nineteenth. There's a note here, 'Thxgvg—tkts!' "

"Yes, she was planning a fast trip home to Michigan; she hadn't been back for a while."

"And here, on Friday she says 'PU loan $—ChemBk.' Why did she need to borrow money?" Obie had talked to the bank; Mia's application for a five-thousand-dollar personal loan had been okayed, based on her employment status. Of course, the bank had no idea what she intended to use the money for.

"I didn't know she had applied, or why she'd need to get a loan. I'm really surprised," Heather said. "She didn't mention anything to me about a money problem, and we were close enough that she would have."

To Flynn's ear, Heather's surprise sounded real. He would keep the tone of it in mind, use it something like the answer to a control question on a polygraph test, and compare it with any other "I didn't know"s or "I don't know"s he might hear from her. Flynn scanned the fall weeks on the calendar. "Nothing, no dates, just like you said to Detective O'Brien. Okay, here, Saturday, October nineteenth: 'Walter—Trax.' "

"She must have gone to the disco after rehearsal."

"Ever hear of a Walter?"

"I think so."

Heather's answers had turned short and sweet; she'd stopped volunteering any details. "What did you hear?"

"He wasn't—you know, someone she was interested in beyond a date or two."

Flynn pretended to be satisfied and moved on. "How about this September sixteenth: 'H & B'...?"

" 'Heather and Brian'! She came out to dinner with us that night. Just a little Italian place we like. Nice crowd, good pasta. She and Brian got along great—he's Irish, like Detective O'Brien. And you—right?"

"Uh-oh, this cello business is just a cover. You've been to detective school."

Heather laughed. "If you really want to know, I guess I have a thing about Irish men."

"We'll come back to that. Meantime, I won't say a word to Mrs. O'Brien."

"Promise?"

"Sure." Flynn felt flattered that the striking twenty-three-year-old would flirt with him. But he wasn't going to let it distract him from a key interview. He looked down at the calendar and turned pages. "She seems to have spent Labor Day weekend with 'Brad'...?"

"Oh," Heather said, "that's her brother. He's interning at a hospital up in Boston. I never met him. He's the only person in the world with a worse schedule than Mia's, but he did have part of that weekend off so she went up. Said she had a great time, met some nice people, and was looking forward to going back there on tour with the company."

Obie had reached Brad at the phone number provided by Dr. Greenfield. The brother had been groggy with fatigue and overcome by grief. Obie had kept the interview short and said he'd call again. Flynn flipped back through the summer weeks as if they didn't matter. "Nothing written here at all—we can skip this for now.

"How about—Monday, May twentieth, 'party—Rachel'...?"

"May what?" Heather leaned over to look at the page, brushing Flynn's hand with her own as she found the entry. "Oh! Rachel—she's another dancer, a pretty good friend of Mia's, I think. One of the crowd that hangs out at The Barre, in fact. Rachel probably knew about a party and Mia went with her. Must not have been that great or she'd have said something—I don't remember any glowing reports."

Heather seemed in no hurry to move her hand away from his. Flynn *was* flattered, tempted to respond. But Lauren's image appeared in his head. One woman at a time, he told himself—especially if the woman is Lauren. That she managed to find space for herself in his life blew his mind. The big question was, could he do what he had to do and still be with her? . . . And right now, how could he get what he wanted from Heather? Flynn didn't have to be Billy Reynolds to borrow what he needed from Billy's MO.

He gave her the half-smile and kept his tone light. "But look, there's something else: 'Walter' again—six or seven times . . . and we missed this—he's here in May and June pretty often. I thought you told Detective O'Brien *and* me, Mia wasn't dating—yet she saw this guy a lot."

"Well, I don't think those were *dates*. Walter was just a . . ."

"Friend?"

"More or less. I don't know, really."

Flynn's mental polygraph superblipped. "Walter who?"

"I don't know his last name."

That one rang true. Flynn turned back to those empty summer pages. "Not a thing, all this time?" He gave Heather a puzzled, frustrated look.

She avoided his eye. "It is strange, because she was . . ." Heather couldn't find a way to end the sentence.

"Suppose I told you that whatever Mia might have done, we don't want to judge her at all. That the only thing we give a damn about is locking up the scum who destroyed her. Period. Would you believe me?"

"Okay." Heather sounded as if the idea was welcome but might not be a real possibility.

"It's the truth. No one wants to put her memory on trial." Flynn turned the summer pages again. "If I was up against a wall and had to take a guess, I'd say . . . I'd say that Mia was away last summer at a rehab, kicking her coke habit."

Tearfully, Heather nodded yes. "It worked—she came back

and she stayed clean. I know she did. She said she felt great about her dancing, better than ever."

"What she did takes a lot of strength, and the people who love her can be proud of her."

Tears ran down Heather's cheeks.

"What else can you tell me that could help our investigation?" He patted her shoulder. "Don't hold back, it's okay."

"Before she went away, Mia was...she was dealing, too. I never saw drugs, but I did see quite a bit of money in her room sometimes. And Walter left a lot of messages on the tape."

"You think he was her source?"

"Well, it seems like he must have been. I know he wasn't anything else to her." Heather had regained control.

"How about his last name?"

"He always just said 'Walter.'"

"What kind of a voice?"

"He tried to sound suave, but he was pushy—like 'You better call when I say to or I won't be around.' I heard a slight accent."

"What accent?"

"I'd say Spanish."

"Good—that's a real start." Flynn exaggerated to encourage Heather to keep trying to remember things. "Are you heading for the theater now?"

Heather shook her head, causing the fall of long hair to swing seductively. "It's still early."

"I'd keep you company"—Flynn flashed the half-smile—"but I got a witness waitin' for me. If you think of *anything,* even something that seems silly, you pick up the phone and let us know. Right?"

"I will."

Thursday morning, November 14, 1985

Obie walked into the coffee room where Flynn was getting a refill. Neither one had yet spoken to the other since the McDonald's disaster, but Flynn was working up to telling Obie what he had learned from Heather. If Obie wanted to retire, Flynn couldn't stop him, but the Greenfield homicide was still his case. Obie sat down at the table, shuffled the papers in front of him, and adjusted his glasses.

"Ready for some coffee?" Flynn asked.

"Thanks. Betty just handed me these—the test reports."

Flynn pulled out a chair and sat down.

"Lieu"—relief lit up Obie's face—"the stuff on the floor and all was coke. But she tested *clean*—no drugs or alcohol either."

"Well, we're gettin' somewhere. That fits with what Heather said yesterday. She sends her regards, by the way—she's into Irish guys an' she loves your brogue."

"Never mind the blarney, what'd she say that goes with the tests?"

"She said that Mia was clean since the summer and dancin' like never before."

"Since the summer?"

"She spent most of it in rehab up in Rhode Island. She visited Brad over Labor Day. And she was fine ever since."

Obie sipped his coffee thoughtfully. "She went through all that hell and survived so some ape could cut her to pieces. You can't really blame me for wantin' to retire, can you?"

"No."

"But I won't."

"You sure?" Flynn didn't smile.

Obie looked surprised. "Why d'you ask?"

"Because of something else Heather said."

"Yeah?"

"Mia didn't tell Heather, but she wasn't really tryin' to hide it either. For whatever reason—to support her habit or because she was bein' manipulated by somebody or both—she was dealin'."

Obie flinched as if someone had hit him. "Supplyin' the other dancers..."

Flynn kept going. "She couldn't hide the messages from her connection on the answering tape. And she had a lotta twenties lyin' around, sometimes fifties. Remember that 'Walter' in Mia's calendar? That's the same name on the tape. Heather says she never met him, but she's sure he's the connection."

"Mia had a date with him last month, it's on the calendar, right?"

"Exactly—the nineteenth. And when did she apply for that loan?"

"Monday the twenty-first.... She owed this Walter creep five thousand bucks and *he killed her before she could pay?*"

Flynn shrugged. "He was probably high, got paranoid.... You got the autopsy there, too?"

Obie pushed the papers across the table and changed his seat so he could look over Flynn's shoulder.

"See this?" Flynn pointed to the ME's drawing of four parallel lines. The caption read, "Stab Wound D, series of similar superficial incised wounds to left shoulder."

For the moment, Mia's violent death was reduced to technical words on sheets of paper, part of the puzzle that might help Flynn and Obie comprehend the killer.

"He made these precise cuts sorta like a monogram thing. Probably was doin' his macho number—with the rape, too—tryin' to get back his control, but she didn't go for it. She resisted—and she was no weakling, thin as she was." He turned back to the first page of the report. "'Five seven, a hundred and five pounds.' The ME goes on for half a page about her 'well-developed musculature.' She didn't just disintegrate at the sight of his knife, she *fought*. Here." He found the detailed "sharp force injury" descriptions of the cuts on Mia's hands and arms. "She fought and I'd say he went off the deep end."

"Wait." Obie reached over and turned the report's pages. Toward the end he located what he was looking for. He pointed out the phrase to Flynn: . . . *no needle tracks or wrist scars found.*

"Good," Flynn said.

"If she was dealin', then when she straightened out—her customers all hadda find a new source," Obie speculated. "Walter lost more than just her; he must've been pissed about that. What in hell did he gain by killin' her?" Obie shook his head. "Since when do we ask rational questions about the likes of Walter?"

"He wasn't all the way out of control, though."

"Like he made sure he didn't leave her address book behind. So, if that's the scenario, this operator Walter is makin' sure some dancers out there can still feed their habits. If they don't OD, they could end up in the morgue just like Mia."

"Why do you think the ballet brass don't look out for these kids—try and help 'em?"

"I seem to remember they had a star a few years ago get hooked. After that, they started urine testing—but only if they had a problem with a big-deal dancer. The company's just watchin' out for the box office, that's all they can handle. Besides there's always a good supply of new dancers comin' out of school. Lieu, I'm not gonna retire, but you owe me one. Okay?"

"Sure, what?"

"Soon as we drop off Walter at Central Booking, I want you to find a reporter who can tell this story and do it justice—about the beautiful illusion out front, but backstage, the dancers become victims while the ballet brass go around like a bunch of goddamm ostriches."

"You bet, pal." Flynn put the autopsy pages in order and gave them back to Obie. "Now, about this Walter..."

"Right away I can think of somebody who might know of him," Obie said. "I'll reach out."

Flynn thought of Salsa—and Salsa's boss. He was convinced that Salsa would know—and hoped to hell he didn't.

Late evening, Friday, November 15, 1985

As Rachel French came toward him, Reynolds noticed her eyes right away. Special effects, just like the boss said—green eyes, wide-set and bright. Too bright, maybe? "Hi. I'm Detective Reynolds. Here—I got it." She let him take her ballet bag. He slipped a protective arm around her, guiding her out the stage door and making a quick reverse right away from Broadway onto the side street. "How about Knight's?" He ducked his head to make eye contact. "It's not too fancy, but at least we won't have to yell to hear each other."

"No one from the company goes there; I won't see any familiar faces."

That was what he wanted; at The Barre, her buddies might wander over to check out who she was with. "Great. 'Cause I'd like to try and keep all your attention on me."

She wore a long skirt, fitted at the hips, and a suede jacket that weighed nothing and seemed about to melt under his hand. Earlier in the evening, the temperature had dropped below forty for the first time all season; they hurried in the door of Knight's. Reynolds took her to the last table against the brick wall, out of the way.

Under the suede jacket she seemed to be wearing several layers of T-shirts in various colors. Not quite the "rags" Obie talked about but a different look, all right. One he hadn't come across before. "Sure you don't want something to eat?" he said as their beers arrived. "Thanks for meeting me."

"I know I wasn't very helpful the other day in the Green Room—the detectives were sweet, but I—I'm having a really hard time with this. I still can't believe anyone would kill Mia." Rachel dug several tissues out of her bag, dabbed at the wild green eyes—and, Reynolds noticed, blew her nose as discreetly as she could. "I just couldn't talk about it right away. I was closer to Mia than anyone in the company."

"Then I know you can help." Reynolds sat facing into the room but he concentrated completely on her. "Everybody will feel better when we get Mia's killer. We're workin' every angle we can, as fast as we can. It's been a long time since the whole city got so caught up in a homicide. Detective O'Brien—he's on the job thirty-some-odd years—that's a lot of cases. This is the first one that's got him talkin' about leavin'."

"He mentioned that his daughter is a dancer."

"Been dancin' since she was seven. He told her—'get out of New York or quit ballet.' She just got a job with the Pennsylvania Ballet, I think. Anyway, this is a big case for us, all around. I hope you'll tell me everything you can think of about Mia. I've got all night—the mayor said take all the overtime you need." She liked his joke.

"Seriously—I don't want you to leave anything out, even if seems to have nothin' to do with this investigation. Or if you think it could be embarrassing." He'd been told that dancers had been known to perform with a broken bone in the foot, the same as an injured athlete would finish the game. He believed that their faces would show the kind of tension he saw in Rachel's now. He continued softly, "We don't care about her morals. We wouldn't tell her parents. All we care about is finding out who hurt her. Nothin's immoral next to that."

Rachel nodded.

"If you've been feelin' like you want revenge—"

She nodded again, vehemently.

"—just give me all the help you can. Start with when you met her."

"She quit high school to come here on scholarship—to the company school. That's where we met."

"What year was that?"

"In '83. The next year, they put her in the corps de ballet and boom! The critics are picking her out and going nuts. They were right, too—she had everything!" Rachel looked sadly at Reynolds, not flirting. "I don't know if you know ballet. . . ."

"Let's say I got some catching up to do. I certainly never thought I'd meet a ballerina."

Rachel smiled. "An emerging ballerina, I hope. Little girls in school dream they're ballerinas, but it takes more than pointe shoes and a tutu and even good technique. Mia was well on her way. This season she was going to dance a lot of little stepping-stone parts; by next spring she would've been promoted to soloist. After all that comes premier dancer."

"I wonder if even the real ballet fans know all the ins and outs of your world. Do they?"

"Like what are you thinking of?"

"Well, I guess they realize dancing is long on hard work and a lot shorter on glamor than it looks. But could any outsider begin to guess the pressures that someone like Mia was under?"

Rachel was too smart or too wary to pick up on suggestions; she wouldn't fill in the blanks for him. He backed off for the time being.

"How about her roommate, Heather, how did they hook up?"

"Heather's old roommate was a pianist who sometimes played for our classes. She was getting married and Mia moved into her old room. In '84—June, I think. The summer before we officially joined the company. We got to know each other that summer. We actually had time to ourselves—even spent a couple of Sundays at Fire Island. Of course we took class every day, but that was it. I sometimes miss that freedom but Mia didn't seem to need it. She just wanted to dance and she always loved New York."

"She was ambitious?"

"Driven."

"And she was gettin' where she wanted to go?"

"Yes, she was."

"Ballet is very competitive, lots of jealousy?"

"Worse than the opera. It's just built into the system and the ballet dancer mentality."

"Did Mia have any enemies at work?"

"People do have to fight for position unfortunately and some of it's just politics. But mostly your weapon in the ballet wars is yourself—your talent, your body."

"I guess that's the kind of thing I was trying to get at when I was talking about pressures. If you must really look perfect, *be* perfect—"

"Well, I'm not sure but I think that there you're fighting—yourself. I *am* sure that those pressures don't end up with someone going after another dancer in the middle of the night, in some sleazy building and—stabbing her."

Rachel's account squared with Heather's. Reynolds had also wanted to test out on Rachel the theory of Flynn's that though Mia's killer knew her, knew her routine, he had not been another dancer. Reynolds ordered a third round of beers; Rachel didn't seem to have any trouble keeping up with him.

"Was Mia seein' anyone? Boyfriend?"

"Dancers socialize with each other, the musicians, other people in the same world. No one else understands the hours. Heather's a musician herself. Anyway, Mia wasn't serious about anyone and she didn't go outside the circle."

"She could've been dating a male dancer and it went bad."

"She wasn't."

"We have the first name of someone that we know for a fact she knew but who doesn't fit anywhere." Reynolds took a sip of beer and kept his tone casual: "Musician in the orchestra? No. Stage crew? No. And not a dancer either. This name ain't on any of the lists. But maybe you heard Mia mention it—the two of you spent a lot of time together. It's a chance."

Rachel shredded the tissues in her hand. "Well, maybe..."

"The name is Walter."

"Oh, I think she met Walter through some musician." The voice sounded too bright, the words came too fast. "She went to a big party once with Heather—mostly people from one of those shows Heather plays for. I seem to remember Mia met him at that party."

"You weren't there?"

"No."

"But since then you've met this Walter."

"Um, a couple of times, I guess."

"Can you describe him?"

"He's Spanish but he doesn't exactly look it—his skin is too fair. He's on the tall side—around five eleven. Wears fancy suits."

Reynolds remembered witnesses on Eighty-ninth Street commenting about the suit. "Mustache? Beard?"

"No. Maybe because of his gringo image."

"He wasn't a boyfriend of Mia's?"

"No, he wasn't."

"But we know she saw him often. So that leaves some kind of a business relationship. Maybe he had somethin' she needed. Something a lot of dancers need—like drugs." He wondered if a coked-up dancer could still do those tricky steps.

"I never knew what he did for a living." Rachel tried to take a swig from an empty beer glass.

Reynolds would have been surprised if she hadn't lied. On the other hand, she didn't seem to be trying very hard to be convincing. Most likely, as sometimes happened, she wanted to confess. He ignored his thirst and sat like a statue for half a century until Rachel finally had to look at him. "Walter was makin' out good with his ballet customers; he won't let all that profit go just because his distributor is dead." Reynolds reached over, gently took the shredded tissue, and put it in the ashtray. "I think he's gonna look you up, Rachel. What are you gonna say when he does?" Where was the sparkle now? He saw nothing but misery in the beautiful green eyes. He took her hand and held it sympathetically.

She grasped his hand tightly but looked away from him. "I'll say, 'Walter, *amigo*—let me have a gram.'"

Monday afternoon, November 18, 1985

A Team was almost out the door but Flynn asked them to stay for a short meeting. C Team was coming on. Cooch and Taylor were there; Reynolds, too. For once, nobody had to send out a search party for him. The minute the whole bunch had squeezed into the bosses' office, Cooch launched a preemptive strike.

"You probably noticed when you signed the log"—he got up from behind his desk—"today's the eighteenth." He dismantled his IN box in an elaborate, fruitless search. He scanned the faces. "*Whatever* you do between now and the end of your tour tomorrow, I *want* those *updated memo books* on my desk. Be advised that there will be *no* grace period next month or any month thereafter. I don't care *who* you are. 'Homicide specialists' are not exempt from keeping up-to-date memo books. Tie a string around your prick so you won't forget—if it's not on duty elsewhere." He focused on the wall directly above Reynolds's head, closed his eyes, and allowed a blissful expression to settle on his face. Mazocek chortled.

Cooch's eyes snapped open. "Another thing: Most of you have active burglaries, assaults, harassments—whatever: *non*homicides—that have not been reviewed yet. With me. For some cases it's gonna be three weeks any minute, for others—already *over*due. I strongly advise you to make an appointment to see me on those cases." He scanned the faces again and sat down.

Flynn leaned against the wall behind his desk. "More often than we would like," he began, "record keeping can make or break a court case. Besides—when we clear this Mia case *and* Frostbite and come up with a hundred percent for '85, as you well know, we're gonna put in for that unit citation again." Murmurs of approval. "Well"—he maintained a straight face—"before they send out to the printer for that plaque, they're gonna send somebody up *here* to check all our penmanship, grammar, you name it." Bursts of laughter. Taylor slapped his thigh.

"You're gonna *wish* I was kiddin'," Flynn predicted. "Also, a memo book is kinda like a progress report, which on this job ain't such a bad thing to have around. So please—comply with the sergeant's requests in a timely manner and be *sure* to be neat. Obie, speakin' of progress, I guess I would've heard about it if anybody got a lead on 'Walter'?"

"It ain't what you'd call a common name, but so far we're drawin' a blank. Don't ring a bell with nobody."

"What about the champ?" Taylor asked Flynn. "He could've come across Walter someplace."

"I went to the gym day before yesterday, lookin' for him," Flynn said. "Wasn't there. We might have to leave a message at the Tabu."

"Looks like Walter's the one we want, all right." Everyone immediately looked in Reynolds's direction.

"I took Rachel French out for a beer Friday. She knows Walter—met him through Mia. She didn't have a last name but she gave me a description." He repeated what Rachel had said. "I was hinting around that Walter might be callin' her soon; well, it sounds like he already *did* call her and now he's her connection. I'll be seein' her again for sure, and so I didn't really grill her right off. She's kinda jittery but she'll help us—no problem. Just gotta take it a little bit at a time."

A series of expressions flickered across Obie's face like movie images, but he only said, "We got a good description now and he don't look like your average Spanish pusher. Narcotics has gotta know him. I'm goin' right over there."

"Dynamite," Flynn said. "And thanks, Billy." Cooch found some papers on his desk that needed immediate perusal.

Pastore cleared his throat. "Boss, I started thinkin' about Gordo again. Tell you the truth I had *dream* about him."

"Did he give you his location?"

Pastore grinned. "He was just gonna carve it on a piece of birchbark for me and I woke up. But I gave Levy a call and he said Gordo was on his mind, too. I know we hadda put him on the back burner 'cause of this Mia homicide, but Franco said, what if Gordo goes on a fuckin' diet—then we'll never find him. Okay with you if myself and Franco keep workin' it on our own time? Maybe he'll show up at his sister's for Thanksgivin' or something—"

Mazocek interrupted. "Hold on, Ronnie—I'll look up that address for ya." Everybody laughed.

"Wait a minute"—Flynn was impressed—"you're plannin' to sit on Gordo for *Thanksgiving?*"

"Maybe we'll catch him before—we got ten days yet."

"Beautiful," Flynn said. "You got my blessing. Meeting's over. Thanks a lot." Pastore zipped into the squad room and Flynn heard him on the phone with O'Levy.

"Hey, you got the job! We can start anytime—even tonight. I'm swingin' out tomorrow till Friday.... Uh-huh. Great! That way when I get off tomorrow, we can start right in on the first subject."

Early evening, Tuesday, November 19, 1985

"Hiya, Franco!" Pastore stepped into Levy's Varick Street loft and paused, surprised by the big open space and the windows all around. Sort of the other end of the world from his own Staten Island colonial ranch. "Boy, this is real different."

"Before we go, how about a quick drink, Ronnie? And I'd like you to meet Joyce."

"Sit down." Joyce Levy smiled. "Good to see you. What would you like?"

Pastore sat in a funny-shaped canvas sling chair. "Maybe a Coke if you have it, with a little bit of rum? Just a little or I'll never get out of this chair."

Joyce said, "I think they designed them that way on purpose in the fifties. We found them in somebody's attic and Franco fell in love."

"Rum an' Coke," Levy said, "the same as Ronnie's. Thanks."

Joyce served the drinks in old soda-fountain-style Coke glasses. "You can pass these back and forth," she said, offering mixed nuts in a heavy glass dish

In a mild daze, Pastore helped himself and handed the dish of nuts to Levy. He mentally composed his description of the whole setup to Kitty. He looked at Joyce. "You must think we need our heads examined to be workin' on our own time."

"If so," Levy said, "she can do the exam herself. She's gettin' a master's in psych, in case I never told you."

"Child psych," Joyce told him.

Pastore's wife had the two kids but not the degree; she was doing pretty good on her own.

"But," Joyce said, "there's some kinds of craziness that keep you sane, if you see what I mean." She bent down and kissed her husband on the cheek. "Don't overdo it, though. I'm going back to my midterm paper. Good luck tonight!"

Kitty Pastore had no midterm paper to occupy her evenings and she liked to spend a little time with her husband, if he wasn't working nights, after the kids went to sleep.

"Got the list?" Levy asked.

Pastore took out his notebook and flipped through it. "Benny didn't visit his partner in jail—that wasn't very nice," he said.

"I think they had a marriage of convenience, you know" —Levy paused for rum and Coke—"after Abdul got killed, Benny probably figured he better go in the wind, and from then on it just wasn't convenient to show up at Rikers for dear old Gordo. Or maybe he was just doin' better without Gordo...."

"So other than the sister and Counselor Britton, Gordo had two—count 'em—two visitors."

Levy laughed. "Wonder why he was so popular."

"This doesn't make any kind of sense: *Ada Fernandez from Uniondale, Long Island.*"

"That's like hick city, right?" To Levy, anything east of the East River Drive deserved that label.

"Meaning we gotta borrow a van or a pickup to go sit on Ada's house. So who's left for tonight?"

"Henry Medina, Avenue B—Alphabet City. We could take my car—it's nondescript enough so they might not make us before we find a parking place. I checked the two names with BCI: nothing on Ada but Henry came up. He didn't get caught the last few years, though." Pastore handed Levy an ID photo. "Sort of a younger, poor man's Viera."

"It ain't everybody who smiles for the Central Booking camera. Since Henry was nice enough to visit Gordo in jail, maybe Gordo returns the favor now that he's on the loose. Might even drop in on Henry this very night...."

Pastore hoisted himself out of the fifties chair and followed his friend downstairs. It occurred to him that he was officially off duty; he loosened his tie, folded it, and put it in his pocket as he got into the driver's seat of his '79 Ford.

"What we need," Levy said as they parked by a meter on Avenue B and Thirteenth Street a few doors from Medina's building, "is Jersey plates. That way they'd think we was buyers."

Pastore was about to object that as buyers they could be expected to stick around for all of ninety seconds when he noticed a white Mazda cruising slowly west on Thirteenth. It had Jersey plates. Levy saw it, too. As the Mazda neared the corner, the driver's window rolled down, attracting the attention of a black guy in overalls and an engineer's cap who hustled over from the curb, removed a handful of tiny plastic vials with colored lids from under his cap, and held them out for the driver to see. Framed in the car window, a pair of white hands flashed some bills. From the curb, a second black guy in corduroy pants and a white sweatshirt caught sight of the money and went to the car. The driver gave his cash to Sweatshirt while Overalls handed over the crack, completing the deal. When Overalls went back to his old position on the sidewalk, a guy in a red golf sweater emerged from a nearby doorway and gave Overalls fresh stock to put in his cap. Pastore nudged Levy and pointed. "Hey, there's another player on that stoop."

"Yeah," Levy said, "must be the lookout up there. They got this down to a whole science. Y'know, Gordo might not feel at home around here—not his product."

"And so far Gordo is an inside man," Pastore pointed out.

"Okay," said Levy, "here's the deal.... Medina sees a future in crack; why should the blacks get a monopoly—we're just as handy with a frying pan as they are."

"That's how they make this stuff, in a *frying pan?*"

"According to Katz, the Street Narcotics guy, first they fry it then they freeze it. When they break it up into little pieces, it goes 'crack'! Like peanut brittle. Anyway, Medina takes advantage of Gordo's iffy status to make him an offer he can't refuse: Set up an indoor franchise in this area. Introduce the product to the hip downtown crowd. Charge a little more than on the street but it's worth it for the privacy. They cook up the stuff right there in the kitchen, for a start. Medina pays the overhead; Gordo gets a good hideout, plus his cut."

"Sounds perfect," Pastore said. "If I was Gordo, I'd grab it."

"He probably did. I bet he's in there right now."

"Well, who's gonna relieve him?" Pastore worried. "The boss? Somebody's gotta give him a break or he ain't gonna *come out.*"

Pastore and Levy waited for Gordo that night till after midnight, but he didn't come out—or go in, either.

Midnight, Wednesday, November 20, 1985

"How perfect," Rachel said as she and Reynolds entered the Italian restaurant. She told Reynolds she had danced her very first demisolo in tonight's performance of a ballet with an Italian name. "Most nights," she said, "when the curtain comes down—so do you. You kill yourself to dance perfectly but even when you do, only the star gets a bouquet; everybody else just goes home to a hot bath."

She didn't seem to be down tonight. She raved about the pasta, though she ate less than half, and she loved the Gavi wine that the waiter at Solamente suggested. "Delicious for a warm November night," she said. Reynolds had heard that cocaine increased your alcohol capacity. He did wonder if any of her good mood had to do with being with him, but he had his own little wine buzz on and didn't dwell on the question. And even though she herself was a tourist attraction in places like The Barre, his suggestion that they eat where the law enforcement notables hung out obviously made a big hit.

"No atmosphere," Reynolds had warned. The restaurant—located near the courthouse—had simple decor, mostly gray; a vase full of rust-colored chrysanthemums on the bar provided the only bright spot. Rachel's dress was almost the same shade. Ribbonlike strips of the fabric crisscrossed up the front between her small breasts and tied behind her neck. The color of the dress brought out auburn lights in her dark-brown hair, Reynolds noticed. Her green eyes fascinated him.

She disagreed with his definition of atmosphere. "Oh, it's the people that make this place." Like the tableful of assistant district attorneys that Reynolds discreetly pointed out, celebrating a conviction with a couple of detectives. When the check came, Rachel disappeared to the ladies' room and came back radiating enthusiasm; it struck Reynolds that they were surrounded by people whose job was to lock up coke dealers, including beautiful ones. Well—she was only a user as far as he knew now.

On the way uptown, he put a tape in the Firebird's deck and didn't drive too fast. He chose the East River Drive, guessing their destination was probably his place—rather than hers, south of Manhattan Center on the other side of town.

"Mmmm, great sound," she purred. "I wish someone would set a ballet to a medley of old blues." She let her head rest against his shoulder. "A Billie Holliday suite...why not?"

"Little nightcap?" he asked. "What do you like?" The silhouette of the United Nations secretariat building loomed—they were nearing the East Forty-second Street exit.

"Amaretto."

"Got any at home?" he asked.

"Ummm"—she seemed to look through her liquor supply—"I think I'm out."

"Well, I'm in good shape—brand-new bottle."

He whizzed past the exit and soon they were leaving the Drive at Eighty-sixth Street.

Reynolds lived in a huge high rise on Third Avenue. As the elevator climbed twenty-nine floors, he told Rachel that his older sister, who liked to spoil him, had found the studio apartment a few years back. A designer friend of his sister's had even spruced it up without charging an arm and a leg.

Rachel said the black-and-white scheme felt calming. Then she gazed out at the spectacular nighttime cityscape framed by the big windows along the end of the room. "I bet," she said, "there's more lights on after midnight here than anywhere." Rachel turned away from the view.

Just behind her, closing off the studio's sleeping el like a room divider, stood an upright piano. Reynolds watched her take a quick peek around it at the king-size bed with the puffy, bright-red quilt. She sat down on the piano bench, opened the cover, and doodled with the treble keys.

He brought her drink and sat next to her. The recessed light over the piano caught the auburn in her hair. "Go ahead and play if you want," he said, "nobody complains."

"How about a little 'Chopsticks' duet?"

"I think I can handle it."

They played the silly tune in perfect sync for almost ten minutes, gradually upping the tempo by unspoken agreement until she attempted to play and drink at the same time, missed, and gave up, laughing.

"Someone is about to complain," she predicted; "the neighbors expect better things from you." She closed the piano cover. "Mia liked to play show tunes on the piano and listen to jazz. A couple of times that first summer, we went to the Village. She said New York could give you anything you want. The city can double-cross you, too—she found that out, didn't she? Everyone's in a funk now, dancing without her...."

Reynolds had not been in any rush to talk about the case, but she brought it up herself. He turned around on the bench and leaned back against the piano. "Walter called you lately?"

"Forget it; I shouldn't have said—" She moved close to him.

He put his arm around her. "Why don't you quit while you're still ahead?"

"If I tell you why, you'll..."

"I'll know—that's all. Nothing will be different, okay?"

"It's—too *late* to quit. I'm already into him for too much."

"What do you call 'too much'?"

"Mia owed him five thousand dollars, but most of it was my tab and he knows it. So he—" She swiveled from the waist and put her arms around his neck. "You don't want to hear the sordid details," she said, then kissed him.

Her intensity surprised him. Somehow he didn't expect such strength from her small body. The kiss was long and eager. When they finally paused, he kissed her cheekbones, her eyelids, and swept her up in his arms.

The city cast its glow, lighting the night sky and spilling in through the windows onto the big bed. Reynolds untied the bow at the back of Rachel's neck and she let her dress slip to the floor. She stood facing him, wearing a tiny pair of bikini panties, busying her fingers with the buttons of his shirt, then the pants zipper. As he pressed her to him, she moved against him, getting the feel of his skin. He pulled her down to the bed with him, exploring her body with his hands and his mouth.

She moved on top of him and helped him enter her as she looked into his face and then closed her eyes, responding strongly to the quickening rhythm of his thrusts, her breathing becoming deep sighs, then short cries, and after he flipped her under him, thrusting harder, at last a long ohh. The glow of the city dappled their bodies, entwined on the pin-striped sheet.

Thursday afternoon, November 21, 1985

Obie was going out the squad room's swinging doors as Reynolds was coming in. Reynolds gave a jaunty salute and kept going. Obie stopped halfway through. "How's that girl?" His glasses glinted like a warning sign, or so it seemed to Taylor, who watched from his desk.

"Oh," Reynolds said, "the dancer? She's doin' good. She remembers you mentioned Barbara when you guys talked at Manhattan Cultural Center."

Obie started to ask another question but changed his approach. "Take a look on the boss's desk."

"You came up with something on Walter?"

"Photo: Walter *Torres*—street name, if any, unknown."

"All right!"

"Billy, from what you said at the meetin', the girl sounds like she needs help. That's what cops are for—remember all that stuff you heard in the Academy?" Obie turned and went through the swinging doors, on his way home.

The next time the doors swung open, O'Levy breezed in. "Jesse," he said, "somebody tryin' to confuse us with this weather, or what? Next week's Thanksgiving and it's fuckin' seventy-seven degrees out."

"Why?" Taylor answered. "We're confused *enough* already."

Reynolds and O'Levy stood around in the back of the squad near Jesse's preferred desk. The three of them pored over the ID photo of Walter Torres.

"All we need now is someone to wear a wire—get some audio on him," O'Levy said.

"We'll get it," Reynolds assured him, "only a matter of time till Rachel cooperates."

"Obie said the dancer that Billy's workin' needs 'help' and Billy should give it to her," Taylor informed O'Levy, and waited to hear what turn the conversation would take.

"Hey—I do the best I can with what I have," Reynolds said.

"Well, take it easy, lover boy"—O'Levy grinned—"you don't want any vital parts to burn out."

Now it was Flynn who came through the doors. "Nobody in *this* squad is burning out, I hope."

"Least of all," Taylor clarified, "the part of Billy's anatomy that O'Levy's concerned about."

"Damn right I'm concerned," O'Levy insisted. "Great natural resources gotta be conserved."

"Boss," Reynolds said when the laughter died down, "the story on Rachel French is that she's in debt to Walter. She told me that last night. She says Mia did owe him five grand and it was mostly for *Rachel's* blow—a fact that Walter made sure to let Rachel know that he knows and he don't plan on forgettin'. Between her coke habit and the five grand, she was an easy mark. He needed a new distributor at the ballet company and it sounds like she's got the job, whether she wants it or not. We gotta get him outta circulation, that's the best thing for us *and* her."

"You saw the Torres picture," Flynn said. "Took Obie all week in Narcotics files, but he found the skel. That's all he is—a skel in a fancy suit. And *guess* who Narcotics says he works for."

"Irish."

"Okay," Flynn went on, "think you can get Rachel French to work with us? Would she wear a wire?"

"That's where I'm lookin' to go. So far, so good."

"Keep goin'," Flynn said, and turned to O'Levy. "What's doin' in Alphabet City?"

"You'll be glad to hear," O'Levy began, "that the hot drug down there is crack. That stuff's sellin' as good as up here—maybe better. Any hour of the day or night."

"I've heard better news," Jesse said. "If Cooch was workin' now, he'd tell us it's ninety percent stronger than powder and you get high in four to six *seconds* instead of ten minutes. Fifteen minutes later, you crash like a Mack truck. We ain't gonna *recognize* this town six months from now, let alone keep the lid on it." Before Flynn could comment, Taylor switched gears and asked O'Levy, "You think Gordo's holed up in Loisaida?"

"In where?"

"Say it yourself," Taylor suggested, "you'll get it the first time."

O'Levy curled an imaginary mustache and said, "Lo, eee, zahd—uh!...means Lower East Side. Hey, that's all there is to it? Gimme another lesson, Jess."

Taylor pointed at Reynolds. "Flaco—opposite of *gordo.*"

O'Levy sucked in his cheeks and his gut: "Flaco." Then he stuck out his belly and ballooned his cheeks, "Gordo."

"Muy bien," Flynn said, *"pero dónde es Gordo?"*

O'Levy indicated the tender condition of his rear end. "Pastore and me, we're sittin' on the addresses of those two kind souls who visited our boy at Rikers. We was on Avenue B Monday night, Tuesday night, yesterday, and today. *Nada.*" He showed off.

"Nadie," Taylor corrected. "Nobody."

"Nadie," O'Levy repeated. "We been strikin' out on Avenue B. Next week we're gonna' try exotic Uniondale, Long Island, where Gordo has a female pal with no record."

"You're gonna need some kinda cover out there."

"Well, first we thought we'd be Avon ladies, but then we figured that'd take too much rehearsal. So instead Ronnie got a pal of his to lend us a pickup and we're gonna 'landscape the street.' We got it all worked out."

"That's good—get some exercise. 'Conserve our great natural resources!' What about Gordo's sister, though?"

"He can't pass up her cranberry sauce and turkey *chicharrones,* can he? If we ain't got him by Thanksgivin', you know where to find us on turkey day. East Elmhurst."

"East Elmhurst, Uniondale, Loisaida..." Reynolds had the last laugh. "Jeez, O'Levy—if it wasn't for Gordo, look what you'd be missin'!"

Saturday, November 23, 1985

"The only good thing about a rainy day," Lauren said as she opened her eyes, "is that my hair curls. On the other hand if it's too cold out, then it won't curl anyway."

Flynn hiked himself up on his elbow. He squinted at the mass of honey-blond hair on the pillow. "According to the curl-o-meter, it's not too cold out. By the window method, it looks like your standard lousy November day. Saturday, in fact." Maybe he would finally make it to the gym, see how Salsa was doing. He curled a lock of her hair around his finger, liking the silky feel of it.

"Congratulations," Lauren said. "I saw a quote from the Chief of Detectives saying you have a suspect in the ballet case."

"Must be tryin' to keep the PC happy, who's tryin' to keep the mayor happy. I'll pass the congratulations on to Billy Reynolds. He got himself a ballet dancer of his own, a friend of Mia's—and she's the key."

"What about Obie?"

"He's a trooper. Hangin' in."

"Did your suspect know who he was killing?" Lauren wanted to know.

"Yeah."

"It takes a special kind of monster to kill a ballet dancer? How do you see his 'profile'?"

"A guy with access—a crude street mutt in disguise, dressed up smooth so he can move in the better circles. A drug dealer who totes around a kilo or two of cocaine in an attaché case. He's fancy-lookin' outside and scum clear through."

"Ugh." Lauren shivered and tugged at the covers. "Maybe it's a good idea not to trust anyone in this city."

"Sounds like you been taking lessons from that famous philosopher Jesse Taylor. Myself and Jesse ain't in total agreement on that subject."

"He might be right."

"He might be. But I know you're not on his side."

"How do you know?"

Flynn took a chance. "Because nobody who's on Jesse's side

would ignore a real, honest-to-God threat to her safety and tell some cop he's just overreacting. Would she?"

"Look—let's say it is a 'real threat'; maybe I can handle that better than this now-you-see-it, now-you-don't terrorism kind of shit."

"I like your description and here's what I think: That stuff's too heavy for anybody but the experts—Jesse's the leading expert—and they pay a price for being good at it."

"Like what?"

"Like living in fear."

Lauren closed her eyes. The rain spattered the window for a few minutes. He picked up the edge of the sheet and saw that she was wearing his favorite nightie.

She turned on her side, facing him. "I'm going to the office, but if you have time to play, I could put it off a little while."

Flynn felt the pressure of the case. He *had* to see Salsa, who would be at the gym today for sure, training for his smoker. The question was, *when* would he be there? Flynn couldn't risk missing him. Lauren smiled, waiting. Flynn said, "I'll find some time."

"No taxis, right?" Lauren said. She looked ready for anything in a pea jacket and jeans tucked into her knee-high boots.

"Of course not, it's raining." Flynn walked her to the subway. "You look handsomer than ever in that turtleneck sweater." She kissed him good-bye. "Give my regards to the champs," she yelled just before she disappeared into the raunchy Times Square station.

Flynn bounded up the dilapidated gym stairs toward the locker room; he stopped and surveyed the almost empty boxing floor. A grand total of one trainer and three guys working out had the whole club to themselves. Two of the fighters sparred in the ring under the manager's watchful eye; the third, Salsa, bullied the speed bag, his back to the doorway where Flynn stood.

Flynn went upstairs and changed into a pair of gold Everlast trunks and put on his white high shoes. His boxing gear was about the only clothing he shopped for with any kind of attention. The stuff Tracy had picked out had long since bit the dust, and he had never spent much time thinking about what he wore to work. And since the divorce, when he wasn't working, mostly he was at the gym. Well, maybe now he should at least take a look at his turtleneck sweater supply. He was pretty sure he had an L. L. Bean catalog somewhere.

He grabbed a T-shirt, a skip rope, and a towel and went to the gym. Salsa beat a quick tune on the speed bag. "You got that good," Flynn said as he walked around to where Salsa could see him.

"Hey, A-Train—where you been!" Salsa grinned the same old Salsa grin.

"I was here last Saturday—didn't see you."

Salsa just said, "Guess you're tied up all the time with that ballet murder, huh?" He finally quit the bag, breathing hard.

"Yeah, it's a heavy case," Flynn admitted. "How many rounds you hit on that baby?"

"Five."

"You're keepin' your hands up just like you gotta do in the ring and you got the rhythm—that's the ticket for the speed bag."

"Now I'm gonna skip some rope," Salsa announced.

"I can take a hint," Flynn said, reaching for his own rope. "I guess we got enough room, for a change. What happens to all these macho guys when it rains? Do they melt or what?"

"Not me. I don't. I gotta keep pushin'."

"How come?"

"Brooklyn Charlie, he said I could sign up for a smoker," Salsa blurted. "It's comin' down the road fast."

"All right! When's the big night?"

"In a month from today." Salsa picked up his rope. "You comin'?"

"Are you kiddin'? Lauren's gonna leave me if she don't get to see one of her champs in the ring."

That settled, the two of them skipped rope in silence. Flynn worked up to a good clip but soon reverted to a pace he could maintain—he didn't want to give out before Salsa had skipped enough to make it worthwhile. *D'dum, d'dum, d'dum, d'dum*...Salsa finally showed signs of flagging.

"Nice work," Flynn said, slowing to a halt.

Salsa went another five skips or so for good measure. "Well, I been here since noon—did the whole thing; I'm ready to pack it in."

"Okay—say, how's your stomach muscles doin'?"

"I do plenty of sit-ups, sometimes even more than Brooklyn Charlie says."

"Hold on a second." Flynn walked across the gym and came back carrying a medicine ball. He stopped a few feet from Salsa. Gripping the heavy ball against his midriff, he demonstrated: "You catch it here, see? You gotta tense those muscles before it hits. All set?"

Salsa looked intrigued. *"Vaya!"*

Flynn hefted the ball. "Tense up!" he yelled.

The impact took Salsa by surprise. *"Coño!"* He almost dropped the ball but managed to recover.

"Over here." The ball came and Flynn's years of practice stood behind him. "See what I mean? I bet Charlie'll work this with you some more. Sit-ups probably ain't enough, especially for you. You gotta watch your body—they're gonna go for it every time, 'cause you're tall."

"I'm gonna stay outta reach." Salsa danced around Flynn in a circle pattern.

"Most of the time," Flynn agreed. "But somebody's gotta catch up with you sometime. Right, pal?"

"Work on the gut!" Salsa drummed on his midriff with his fists. "Okay, Lieutenant Flynn. You gonna hang around here or you want a ride somewhere? It's still rainin', y'know."

Flynn let himself look astounded, to Salsa's obvious delight.

"I got a company car—so I can work separate from Monte. We can cover more bases workin' separate. I got a yellow Wrangler Jeep."

Inside, Flynn's reaction was more than astonishment—he warded off sensations of defeat. Promising boxer though Salsa might be, he still saw boxing as just a sideline; he was more and more caught up in the main event—Viera's world. Flynn's efforts were only reaching him on the surface. But Flynn didn't like to lose—especially not to Irish Viera. He went into a boxer's bounce. "When you are *the welterweight champ,"* he said, "you'll drive a yellow *Jag*. Gonna give me a ride in that?"

Salsa laughed.

As long as Salsa inhabited that world, Flynn would give him chances to betray it. "By the way"—Flynn kept up the bounce—"we're lookin' for a big-name Spanish coke dealer named Walter. Know him? Ever hear of him?"

"'Walter'..." Salsa looked blank. "That's his street name?"

"As far as I know."

Salsa shook his head. "Nope, never heard of nobody like that. Don't remember runnin' into him."

"Maybe you still will."

"I'll look out for him," Salsa said.

"Well, I better put in some more time here today," Flynn said, "or I'm gonna start comin' apart at the seams, y'know? See you later, okay?"

"Keep punchin'!" Salsa headed for the locker room.

Midnight, Saturday, November 23, 1985

Rachel's West Side walk-up reminded Reynolds of the ones where many of his friends from P.S. 60 had grown up. East Side or West, the layout stayed the same; the rooms stayed about the size of the inside of a Checker cab. On the other hand, Rachel could afford to live here alone on her salary as a corps dancer.

"Beer?" Rachel called from the kitchen. "Or there's a little of this and a little of that in the cupboard in there. No amaretto, though."

"Beer's fine."

She settled down with him on the huge, odd-shaped leather couch that took up the longest wall of the living room.

"Hey, this is more comfortable than it looks." Reynolds shed his shoes and stretched out with his head at the narrow end of the couch.

"A present from Daddy." Once in a while, like in "Daddy," he could hear Atlanta in her speech. "He custom-designed it for a penthouse and ordered an extra that ended up here. We had fun getting it up those stairs." She sat cross-legged, her bare feet with their bruised toes tucked under her and her back against the wide end of the couch. Reynolds flashed on Mia's feet as he had seen them at the morgue. The sight had not made him eager to watch a ballet.

Rachel wore a loose army-navy-store sweater and dancer's tights; she had twisted a green bandana like a rope and tied it around her head, hippie style. Even in that getup, she sparkled. He wondered again how much of the sparkle was the drug.

"I danced a new part tonight, in a new ballet. Except for Mia not being there, it felt great. My body really knew it all—and for once my head didn't get in the way."

Reynolds decided to go for broke. "I guess that's the upside of coke—what's the downside?" He took a pull on his beer.

She shrugged. "It's too expensive."

"Did Mia quit because of the expense?"

"Her father made her. Mia's old ballet teacher came to New York for a visit...she must have told Dr. Greenfield what was happening and he just came and got her. No advance notice."

"Okay, he got her into the rehab—but she stayed clean on her own, didn't she?"

After a moment, Rachel said yes.

"The company had nothing to do with it?"

"No."

"They gotta know what's going on."

"They do. They threaten you about lateness and not meeting your responsibilities, but they never ever mention drugs. The message gets through: 'Just don't let it get out of control. If your dancing's good, that's what matters.'"

"Mia left her habit in Rhode Island. You said she was never dancing better than when—"

"When she came back she was just... in a, a state of grace. It was so beautiful to see. That fucking son of a bitch Walter. I have fantasies about booby-trapping his BMW."

"Sounds like you came to the same conclusion as we did about him."

"In the beginning when we first knew him, he was sort of a friend. 'Mr. Bountiful.' That ended a long time ago. Now I hate the sight of him."

"Well, you could make your booby-trap fantasy come true. All you gotta do is fly him to Beirut—car bombin's against the law around here. What color BMW are we blowin' up?"

"Burgundy." Rachel smiled unhappily. "Even if I could get away with it, I couldn't kill him. I need him."

"There's other dealers."

"The only thing good about Walter is the quality of the blow—and he's never out of stock. It's always the same top grade. That's—you know, his macho thing: He's got the best and he's got it on hand. He told me he'd never sell that new stuff—crack. 'Low-class shit.' Did you know that some dealers cut the powder with some kind of poison and your leg can swell up to twice the size? I couldn't take a risk like that. I want what Walter sells."

"Rachel, you know we're gonna lock up this sleazeball for what he did. ASAP. And I've got something better for you than booby-trapping his car." He had her full attention.

"Meaning?"

"A way you can get back at him for what he did to Mia—and what he's doing to you."

"I *can't*. I—"

"Like I said, we're *gonna lock him up*." Reynolds pushed himself up to a sitting position and faced her. "But we need your help. In fact, we designed the plan around you."

Her amazing green eyes fastened on him. "What plan?"

"We need him to make statements to you that incriminate him in the murder. The plan is—we wire you so what he says gets recorded on tape. With the recording as evidence, we can arrest him."

"He hardly ever mentions her."

"What does he say when he does?"

"'You owe me what Mia owes me'—that kind of thing."

"That's a good opening. You just lead him a little further."

"I'm a dancer, not an actress. He'll know in two seconds and that'll be the last thing on the tape before he—"

"First of all, you're a performer—you know how to keep your cool. Undercover cops have to *learn* that. Compared to most people who end up wearin' a wire, you got a big advantage."

He moved next to her on the couch and looked into the green eyes. "I'm not saying there's no risk at all, but I wouldn't put you in real danger. And neither would Lieutenant Flynn or Detective O'Brien. We'll be close by, listening to everything that's bein' said and taped. You got a back-up team just like a regular police undercover, except it's the best team in the business. You know? *The best.*"

Rachel bent forward over her crossed legs, the top of her head touching the couch. After several minutes she sat up straight. "Billy, he's a crazy mad-dog killer. If I try and do this, I'll never live to see him in jail. I know it."

Reynolds saw that he couldn't take it further—not tonight anyway. He put his arms around her and comforted her as best he could.

Monday night, November 25, 1985

Rachel told herself she was taking a cab home from her meeting with Walter because it was cold out—she would never get accustomed to New York winters—not because she was nervous. Why be nervous about a package the size of a small sampling of some delicious French cheese from Zabar's. No one would mug her for three ounces of cheese. And no one had reason to guess she had three ounces of cheese hidden in her ballet bag, much less thousands of dollars' worth of cocaine.

She tipped the driver and asked him please to wait until she was inside the building. Her head whipped around as she crossed the sidewalk: not a soul in the street. Her fingers battled with the key to the outside door; she took so long about it that the driver gave up and zoomed off in search of a new fare. The door swung open at last, and propelled by anxiety about that three-ounce secret wrapped in a pair of white tights, Rachel ran up three flights of stairs.

Once inside her apartment with the door locked, she almost relaxed. She pulled the shade on the tiny kitchen window that looked out on a minicourtyard and across to other kitchen windows. She plopped the bag on the kitchen table, hung up her parka, took off her sneakers, and ran a bubble bath. The water pressure was not great in the old tub with the bear-claw feet so you had to plan your bath ahead. She had painted the tub's toenails magenta and they continued to amuse her. Her own toes had enough trouble without any polish, and dancers were forbidden to paint their fingernails because from the audience their fingers would look shorter.

Standing on a chair, she reached a shelf in the bedroom closet where she kept the scale that Mia had bought. Rachel had the scale because Mia said Heather would know Mia wasn't going in for alchemy or something; no use shocking her roommate. Rachel carefully climbed down, clutching the scale and the box of weights.

She put the scale and the weights on the kitchen table and opened her ballet bag. She unrolled the white tights and hefted her "cheese" in its neat plastic wrapping, imprinted with a shamrock. Walter had previously given her a supply of shamrock-printed mini-Baggies that were marked ACCEPT NO SUBSTITUTES. "No charge for the bags," he had said. "Use 'em. People remember packaging—like the Tiffany blue or the Gucci buckle." He'd also given her some little green plastic shamrocks with a half-gram scoop in the top leaf. "Girls like these." He held a Baggie full of them between his thumb and forefinger and let it drop on the table in front of her.

Rachel had set out the Baggies next to the scale, along with a list of nineteen sets of initials and the quantity requested for each. She had three orders for ten grams plus her own; six orders for five grams, and ten orders for one gram each. Walter would take in $6,050, less her ten-percent cut, which would just about cover her personal buy.

She hurried into the bathroom and turned off the taps, admiring the mound of bubbles and inhaling the warm, rose-y fragrance. She looked in the mirror, turned back to the tub, and scooped up some suds. Looking in the mirror again, she created a suds crown and posed with a regal carriage, arced arms framing her head. "Introducing *The Snow Queen!*" A sad fairy tale with a beautiful heroine—everything a choreographer needs, except the Tchaikovsky score. So it'll never be a ballet.

Back in the kitchen, she placed the "cheese" on the scale, and on the balance, a fifty-gram weight plus three tens and two twos. The scale seesawed and failed to balance. The weights were too heavy. Rachel gritted her teeth and removed a two-gram weight;

the balance improved. Off came the other two-gram weight—in a second, the scale leveled. *Four grams short.*

"Rot in hell, Walter," Rachel said. The weights banged as she swept them off the scale onto the table. She measured out a gram of coke into a Baggie and dipped two lines from the gram onto a pocket mirror shaped like a pair of lips. After inhaling the lines through a small straw, she marched into the bathroom, dropped her clothes in a pile on the floor, and sank into the tub. Eyes closed, she was treated to a Technicolor version of the bombing of the burgundy BMW, complete with flying body parts.

Late afternoon, Tuesday, November 26, 1985

Right away, Taylor's bad-news antenna quivered.

Cooch, instead of just yelling to Flynn that he had a phone call, had got up from behind his desk and stood in the doorway between the bosses' office and the squad room. "I didn't know you knew somebody at Internal Affairs," he said. Cooch's intense interest in the subject just about made his spiffy gray hair stand on end.

"I don't." Flynn stayed where he was, at the desk next to Taylor's.

"Yeah," Cooch insisted. "The guy says 'tell him it's IAD—but it's a friend, not to worry.' "

"No name?"

"Nope."

"Another one of life's little mysteries." Flynn got up and went to the phone.

Taylor slipped into the coffee room and came back with a flimsy excuse to eavesdrop. He delivered the mug of coffee to Flynn's desk. From what Taylor gathered, Flynn apparently did know the guy, "Moe" something, but they had been out of touch. Whatever Moe was doing in IAD, Flynn spoke like he wasn't going to hang up on the guy. Taylor got the impression he'd only been doing it for a few months.

"A forty-nine on who? Reynolds?" Flynn didn't actually say "you gotta be kidding" but that was the tone. "And it says?"

All three people in the room concentrated on Flynn's conversation. Taylor kept half an eye on Cooch's face.

"Of course there's a 'link,' " Flynn protested, "that was his assignment: Get to Walter through French. She wasn't talkin' to nobody with a shield till Reynolds—"

The IAD guy's question made Flynn reach for his coffee.

"Women trust him. What can I tell you? I don't know what his secret is."

Cooch muttered furiously to himself.

"Obviously *I* trust him." Flynn drained his mug. "Okay, but looks are deceiving—he's clean. Absolutely no question. And he knows what happens if he slips. I'll tell you somethin' else, Moe, we couldn't get nothin' on this Walter mutt till Reynolds started workin' the girl. Even now we're takin' the photo around... zero. Seems like Señor Walter never gets outta that maroon BMW and gets down on the street. Anyway, if IAD gets nervous 'cause somebody dropped a dime on Reynolds, I'll tell 'em what I just told you. And I appreciate your reachin' out."

Taylor had looked sideways at Cooch when Flynn said "dropped a dime." Would Cooch have gone that far?

The sergeant looked as if he were going to burst unless Flynn hung up the phone in the next ten seconds. Flynn was in no rush.

"Uncle Jack's been askin' for ya," he told Moe. "When are you comin' up to the bar?"

Taylor clutched his head at this blunder. You better be pretty fuckin' grateful to invite a shoofly to a cop bar.

Flynn recovered neatly. "Uncle Jack says, 'Tell Moe to get himself a goddamn transfer an' we'll give him a big racket on the house." He swallowed hard. "Damn right it's a good offer—that's why I'm passin' it along. Thanks again, pal."

"Y'see, Andy?" Cooch jumped up and paced out the office door and back. "What've I been tellin' you all this time. That lazy fuckin' wiseass idiot ain't no harmless clown. He's worse than worthless—he's six feet of sheer trouble. Trouble runs in his *veins* and when IAD pokes a hole in him, *you* are the one that's gonna bleed. You could lose too much blood to survive. I must've told you four hundred and eighty-three times, but now you heard it from the authorities: Dump Reynolds. Before it's too late." Cooch looked as if he'd just got off a soapbox in the old days of Union Square.

Taylor heard the squeak of the swinging doors, and before he had time to wonder who it might be, Reynolds waltzed by on his way to check his messages. He shuffled the contents of the minilocker and closed it. A handmade sign pasted on the locker door read BILLY THE KID.

"Speak of the devil," Taylor said as Reynolds signed the log.

"Hiya pal." Flynn looked glad to see Billy. "Pull up a chair."

First, Reynolds pointedly deposited his memo book in Cooch's IN box. "Sorry it's a little late, Sarge. Had a lot to say."

Before Cooch could respond, Taylor said, "Oh, boy! Soon as you're done, Sergeant, I gotta read the good parts."

Everybody but Cooch cracked up.

Reynolds rolled a secretarial chair into the bosses' office and sat on it backward, resting his arms on top of the backrest. It had been raining all day but he was dry from his wing-tip shoes to his slicked-back hair.

"Listen, pal," Flynn said when he stopped laughing, "somebody dropped a dime on you."

Reynolds looked startled.

Cooch had his file drawer open and was checking the alphabetical order or something.

"I got an old buddy just went to IAD," Flynn went on. "He told me unofficially: Narcotics was tailin' Walter and they bump into Rachel—she's with him. They already know him but she's new, so they figure let's see what she's all about. Next thing you know, she hooks up with Detective Reynolds. Presto—you are 'linked' to Walter."

Reynolds pointed at the memo book in Cooch's IN box. "Whenever I have contact with Rachel French, it's in my activity log."

"They got her at your *house.*"

"Right. I sometimes entertain girlfriends at my house. She'd think it was kinda strange if I didn't."

"Granted, but IAD thinks it's kinda strange that you do. They're jumpy—I mean more so than usual—'cause of the big bump in drug activity; there's big bucks, easier bucks than ever. Face it, they're lookin' for cops to go bad—"

"She doesn't use controlled substances in front of me."

"If they want to get you—for failure to take police action or for any damn thing they dream up, they'll do it. My old pal Moe couldn't do a thing."

"Lieu, I'm workin' *her,* not IAD. I gotta pay attention to her if I'm gonna get the job done. The bottom line is, you gotta trust me."

"Andy"—Cooch cleared his throat—"did you by any chance know that in the first ten months of last year—I'm quotin' the *Times*—five hundred and fourteen drug-related complaints were made against police officers...."

Taylor hummed a little bit of "Nice Work if You Can Get It" as he sauntered into the bosses' office. Then he said, "Some people sure do get the plum assignments. How's it goin'?"

"It's goin'...nice," Reynolds said. "I don't need to snort coke...to have a good time. I'm doin' okay." He looked at Flynn.

"She's gonna set Walter up. It's just a matter of time till she gets her head around the idea."

"Great," Taylor said, "but the boss is sayin'—the bottom line is, you gotta watch your *rear end*. Now more than ever."

"I *am* watchin' it." Reynolds got up and shimmied it as he rolled his chair out the office door.

"Good thing Obie is off tonight—he probably would've lost his sense of humor," Flynn said. He looked thoughtfully at Taylor. "If you were bettin' on Billy, would you bet with Marty or with me?"

"Billy the Kid..." Taylor hummed a little bit of "Back in the Saddle Again." "He does like to shoot from the hip and he's *wise*—that's what drives Cooch up the wall most. Billy might leap before he looks, but not into a drug situation. When push comes to shove, he knows what's good for *him*. So...I'd bet with you."

Wednesday morning, November 27, 1985

"Amarillo," Salsa specified. "*Por favor*. I like *yellow* rice with my eggs and beans 'cause it looks good with the eggs."

"Okay, señor," said the cute waitress in the purple sweater. "I can tell you're not any old *arroz blanco*." She laughed and her dangle earrings jingled. Salsa and Monte had breakfast at Las Flores off and on—if they didn't see too many taxis outside, they'd stop in—but in all the times they'd sat at the long counter, Salsa couldn't recall ever having been served twice by the same waitress. When the one with the earrings brought the food, Salsa asked her name.

"Tina," she answered.

"How long you been workin' here?"

"Now and then for a year, a year and a half."

Monte devoured his eggs, ignoring Salsa's conversation.

"Last summer?" Salsa persisted. "Didja work here in August?"

Tina said she couldn't remember; her memory didn't work good so early in the morning.

Salsa attacked his breakfast for a couple of minutes. Then he said, "You must've heard about the arrest even if you wasn't workin' that day—when they collared Rico at breakfasttime, just like now?"

Tina woke right up. *"Ohhh, sí! Qué dia! Ooooh!"*

Salsa ate his beans with satisfaction.

"So fast," Tina said, "we didn't really know what happened till it was all finished. You was here, too?"

"I was outside—just comin' down the street to get somethin' to eat and zap! Right in front of my face they did it. I saw it good. How about that!"

"Ooooh!" Tina batted her eyelashes like mad as she turned to the taxi driver down the counter who'd been trying to give her an order since Salsa started talking.

Monte was busy with his toast, spreading the melted butter around. "Rico is finished." Monte smiled a big smile over the slice of toast. "Locked up without bail. We ain't gonna see him around here for long enough. Luzan is up a creek—don't have nothin' but beginners on the payroll and still no manager. The cops did okay on that one, *verdad!*"

"Sí." Salsa mopped up the last of his eggs. "They could be workin' on an encore, too...."

Monte stopped chewing in the middle of a mouthful. "Yeah?"

"Lieutenant Flynn, he's lookin' for some Spanish dealer with a gringo name—'Arnold'? No, no—'Walter,' that's the one. I figure it's gotta be somethin' to do with that ballet murder."

Tina came over and put fresh coffee in the steam machine for Salsa's and Monte's free second cups.

"Mucha' gracia'," Salsa said. "You know, I like your earrings a *lot*. You like salsa music?" It poured from the Las Flores kitchen radio around the clock.

She gave him a sexy look. "It all depends who's playin'."

Monte paid the ten-dollar check and left a ten-dollar tip.

Tina tossed her head, making the earrings jingle. *"Gracia'!"*

Before Salsa left Las Flores, he got her number. "One of these days," he said, pointing out the window at the yellow Jeep, "I'll take you for a little ride...."

The custom horn on Salsa's Jeep had three notes that sounded like a Latin trombone: *Dah doo dah*. Salsa hopped in, fired up the engine, and hit the horn as he cut his wheels away from the curb. Monte watched the Jeep take off down the block and then punched in the boss's home number on the car phone. Irish must be just about to Riverdale, by now.

Nobody but El Grande and Monte had the phone number, so Viera took whatever calls came in when he was there. The number rang six times.

"Sí?"

"It's me, boss—got something for you. Somethin' big."

"Vaya!"

"That cocksucker in the precinct is lookin' for Chino; sniffin' around, gettin' close. Sounds like Chino's a suspect—"

"Puta madre! We can't relocate him again. Those upscale cokeheads of his will just find some other dealer. They want *service*. We should have made Chino train a partner in the beginning. Now we're in a fuckin' corner. We gotta get the cops to lay off—*forget the whole thing,* you know? No other way to handle this."

"I got just what we need."

"I'm listening."

"Remember when Salsa got the Jeep and Ramón organized that party for him?"

"Sí."

"Salsa snorted a few lines and he started talkin' about Flynn—Flynn this, Flynn that, Flynn got a chick in the neighborhood—"

"Eso es! Perfecto. Get somebody on this *fast*. We might not have much time at all."

"No problem, boss. Sleep tight."

"Adios."

Late afternoon, Wednesday, November 27, 1985

"Lieu"—O'Levy signed in—"you oughta go see Macon Place. You won't find a neater street in all Uniondale—well, one side of it. And Ronnie's got fireplace kindling for the whole season."

"I hope you took pictures."

"You're right," O'Levy said, "shoulda brought the Polaroid."

"Well, what's with Ada?"

"Not home—she ain't a housewife, it turns out. This little kid comes walkin' down the street yesterday, sort of a *Peanuts* type. He says, Mrs. Fernandez, she's a cook in the city. Ronnie says, where in the city? The kid says, Colonel Sanders. So, Ronnie asks the kid, 'Don't she have no day off?' The kids says, 'Yeah, Sunday, but she goes to church.' So then I butt in, 'No school today, huh?' The kid does this realistic coughin' fit; 'I'm sick,' he says. I jump back, 'I don't wanna catch *that*. But I'm lookin' for Mrs. Fernandez's friend, Mr. Concepción—he's a big fat guy. You seen him lately?' The kid says no, he don't remember a big fat Spanish guy around here, 'ever.'"

Flynn couldn't help laughing, despite the negative outcome.

"Anyway," O'Levy concluded, "in case we don't run into

Gordo in East Elmhurst tomorrow, we'll probably got back to Uniondale on Sunday and clean up the other side of Macon Place. Gordo could've got born again and now he goes to church with Ada."

"I don't think landscapers work Sundays," Flynn objected.

"Boss"—O'Levy shrugged a shrug he hoped was worthy of the great Jewish comics—"if detectives can work on their own time—why not landscapers?"

"You fellas are too much." Flynn chuckled. "Let's hope you get roast Gordo in East Elmhurst. If anybody deserves it, you do."

"Watcha doin' for turkey yourself, boss?"

Flynn looked blank. "Jeez, I didn't even work that out. Lauren must think I got lost. Thanks, Franco—I better give her a buzz at the office."

Flynn and O'Levy both looked at their watches and saw that the time was after 1700 hours. Flynn picked up the phone and dialed. At first he looked surprised, then less and less thrilled as he got nothing but rings on the other end.

Finally, he hung up. "I'm goin' to the gym, Franco. With any luck, somebody'll knock some sense into me."

O'Levy grinned. "See ya later."

Early evening, Wednesday, November 27, 1985

—whisk (for gravy)
—sharp paring knife (for chestnuts)
—recipes: cranberry relish, chestnut stuffing
—small roasting pan

Lauren had not exactly been shocked to discover that Flynn didn't own a roasting pan, large or small. On Tuesday night she had planned her Thanksgiving-for-two menu. Rummaging around his kitchen, she had figured out what she would need to borrow from her own place to put together their first ever home-cooked dinner. And a surprise, to boot. She rather enjoyed the gamble—would Andy have to put down the carving knife and race to a crime scene? What the hell—she was cooking for the pleasure of cooking; eating would have to take care of itself.

She had the list in her raincoat pocket and a shopping bag to carry the roasting pan. Having left work "early" (five o'clock), she would still have time to drop off the roaster at Andy's and do her grocery shopping over there on Ninth Avenue.

A head full of pleasant details left Lauren little room for brooding about Abdul as she passed his still-empty shop. She also managed to sidestep any feeling that by living with Andy she was being disloyal to her well-loved neighborhood. All that would keep for another time.

Ignoring the sweatshirted figure poking some kind of a pipe into the garbage cans on the sidewalk next to her stoop, she climbed the familiar brownstone steps. She had never become accustomed to the homeless who dotted the city streets, but their presence no longer startled her. When she heard the man's breathing and felt him standing close behind her as she unlocked the front door, it was much too late.

"In!" he snarled. "Keep y'mouth *shut* or I'll use this right now." She felt a sharp point jab through her raincoat into the back of her waist. *"Keep* movin'," the voice said. *"Up!"* Her heart pounded as she climbed the two flights of stairs. When they reached her apartment door, she felt the cold metal of a knife blade press against the side of her neck. *"In!" Why* had she ignored him on the street? Too late. Panic took root in her and began to spread. She tried to counter it, telling herself this was one of those "push-in robberies" they talked about. Nothing to do with Flynn.

Now the man shoved the door shut behind him, keeping the blade pressing on the side of her neck. Almost no light spilled in the living room windows from outside.

"What do you want?" she asked in the darkness. She saw a man's shadow, the pipe thing down by his side—and the silvery gleam of the blade up high, near her face.

"Pay attention, you fuckin' cop lover—tell Flynn to dump the dancer case or his *next* case is gonna be you." The pressure on the side of her neck became a sharp pain, and then something heavy smashed into the side of her head, making an unbearable noise. She reeled, the ache in her head ballooning, and felt herself hit the floor. Hanging above her, pulsating in the dark, the indistinct face framed by the sweatshirt hood and the pipe shape again, a blur arcing toward her.

Wednesday night, November 27, 1985

"She's roughed up," O'Levy had said on the phone, "but her X rays are all negative." He didn't yell this time. "Maybe she'll have a scar but no broken anything. The neighbor knew Lauren wasn't around; all of a sudden she hears loud thumps, and she called 911 right away. I'm comin' to get you, Lieu."

"She was mugged!"

A dial tone had answered him. O'Levy had already hung up.

The windshield wipers swished monotonously as O'Levy drove uptown.

"What scar?" Flynn asked him. "Was she mugged or what, tell me."

"He cut her—here." O'Levy indicated the side of the neck, close to the collar bone. "Not real deep, luckily. Like—a warning kind of thing." The words tumbled out.

Flynn let out a long, slow breath and rubbed his temples. "A warning."

"The guy told her to tell you to get off the ballet case."

"Cocksuckers," Flynn raged. "What fucking asshole figures we can be bullied off a homicide with a personal threat?" The next thing Flynn said was, "Wonder what she went home for anyway...."

"She said she wanted to pick up some recipes and her roasting gismo—pan. I guess she was gonna spring it on you—candlelight Thanksgivin'."

"Christ. That's what I get for forgetting Thanksgivin'."

"It's rainin'," O'Levy pointed out unnecessarily as they pulled up to the hospital. "I'll wait and run you back."

After five years in the precinct, Flynn could almost find his way blindfolded through the twists and turns of the St. Luke's emergency-room complex. He went right to the emergency head-nurse's office.

"Flynn, you phantom—where've you been?" Kim Manley asked.

"Lately we seem to be skippin' this stop. Every time I get to a scene, the victim is DOA."

"Well, you're here tonight."

"I'm off duty—and the victim this time is a friend. Lauren Daniels."

The head nurse consulted her clipboard. "Any idea what time she came in?"

"Something like six-thirty."

"Okay, here she is—'H'." Manley got up from her desk and came to the door. She was noticeably taller than Flynn. "Straight ahead to the EXIT sign"—she pointed—"then left. Third door in from the corner." She gave him a mock-flirtatious wink. "Come by more often when you're off duty, why don't you. Don't wait for an emergency."

Any other time Flynn would have winked back. "Happy Thanksgivin'," he said.

Lauren was asleep on the gurney in her office clothes, her face pale, dressings on her head and neck. Honey-blond hair spilled across the pillow. Flynn took her hand, waking her.

She opened her eyes and made a chagrined face. She squeezed his hand but said nothing.

"Hi." He leaned over and kissed her lightly. "You're okay?" he coaxed.

"Getting there. Happy Thanksgiving."

"What hurts?"

She touched the dressing on her neck and he felt the reality of the threat. Saw it staring him in the face.

"Want to get out of here? Will they let you?"

"I don't know—they didn't give me anything to sign."

"But how do you feel? Ready?"

"Let's see." She leaned on him as she eased up to a sitting position. "A little shaky but I can make it."

"Detective Levy—"

"Nice man."

"Yeah, in fact, he's waitin' outside to give us a ride—it's rainin'." Flynn picked up the *Times* that had slipped to the floor next to the gurney. "Okay, take it easy while I go see about your paperwork."

After Lauren had signed the release, he took her raincoat off a chair. "Slip into this." The slash in the back of the coat shocked him all over again. He guided her through the corridors, out to where O'Levy waited, and put her in the Thunderbird's backseat. He sat next to her.

"Sorry about your Thanksgivin' dinner, folks," O'Levy said, heading down Columbus. "I'd say come have dinner with us, but me and Ronnie got a date with East Elmhurst—we're sendin' the wives to the in-laws'."

"East Elmhurst?" Lauren came across like she wanted to sound fine. "Can't be a vacation—must be work."

"We're lookin' for a fugitive and we hope he's gonna show up at his sister's for turkey."

"Gordo?"

"Who else." O'Levy double-parked in front of Lauren's house.

"How could Gordo let an eating holiday go by?" Again, Lauren made like her old self. "If you can wait till he's full, the arrest will be a cinch."

"Or Plan B—borrow the turkey, put it on the backseat and he'll hop right in the car," Flynn added. "I can see it now."

"Plan A, Plan B, I got it all down," O'Levy confirmed.

Flynn clapped O'Levy on the shoulder. "Happy Thanksgivin', Franco, and tell Ronnie the same. You guys are absolutely the best." He helped Lauren out, keeping his arm around her.

"Thanks for everything, Franco," she said. "Good luck in East Elmhurst."

Lauren looked apprehensively at the garbage cans next to the stoop. "He was *right there,*" she whispered, "and I didn't give it a thought. That's what I get for not living in fear."

"Shh. It ain't your fault," Flynn said. "Don't blame the victim."

When she unlocked the outside door, he slid in ahead of her. "I'll go up first."

She handed him the keys. He unbuttoned his trench coat for easier access to his gun and stretched out an arm to keep her behind him. At the top of the stairs, he unlocked the door fast and swung it open faster, stepping back. Nothing.

He led her in to the big armchair in the living room. "Sit here for a second, okay?"

She sank into the chair without taking off her raincoat. Flynn toured the other rooms and came back to her. He sat on the ottoman. "All clear," he said, "for now."

"For now." Her voice was tired but not too tired to convey the protest.

"Franco told me what the guy said to you. We gotta take the bastard at his word. So, before you were just a risk because of Abdul—now it's because of *me,* too. That means you can't stay here *or* stay at my place. I want you to go down to your friend Cary's—first thing tomorrow. You'll be fine in Battery Park City till we make a collar in the ballet murder. We're gettin' there, you know."

Lauren looked at him. "You found out his last name?"

"Yep."

"Well?"

"Well, he's not exactly holding open house lately, but even that ain't what's stopping us; we could find him. We just need some more evidence to back up our theory. The DA likes evidence."

"Sounds like 'don't hold your breath.'"

"We are *workin'* on it. By the time you and Cary run out of conversation topics, the guy'll be arraigned and you'll be back in the Anastasia Suite."

"They're closing in... I'm on the run." She shuddered.

"You just take sensible precautions, that's all."

"A prisoner in Liberty Vistas." She grimaced. "Ironic twist number one."

"There's more? Let's hear the rest."

"You might not like them."

"Try me anyway."

"Here goes: My lover is a cop who says he's not Superman but who's into playing bodyguard. I want a *lover,* not a bodyguard—"

"But—"

"Surprise, Andy! They're not the same thing. Here's the next twist: One day I suddenly wake up in dire need of a bodyguard—otherwise known as 'police protection'—*because* my lover is a cop. Now what do I do for a bodyguard?"

"Let's say you're right—a lover and a bodyguard ain't the same thing. Then what's the problem? Even if I'm a washout as a bodyguard, you still got a lover."

"A lover who's always chasing after that hundred percent. If you ask me, it's not the Holy Grail."

Flynn got up and paced the few feet of floor space available. He stood in front of her, feeling like the defendant in the case. "No, it ain't the Holy Grail, but it's more than a number: you can't hit a hundred percent without lockin' up a lot of killers! And a hundred percent keeps us goin' when there's nothin' to go on. That means something, too." He sat down on the arm of the chair and massaged the tight muscles behind her shoulders. The white dressings accused him, in particular the one on her neck. "Before I... cared about you, nothing mattered but the job—the big hundred percent. I've got a hell of a lot more to fight for now—an' I ain't plannin' to lose."

She sniffled and swiped at her tears as he helped her out of the armchair and to bed.

Thanksgiving afternoon, 1985

"This is the place?" Pastore asked, not cracking a smile.

"Looks familiar," Levy answered, "but—maybe we got the wrong day."

They stared at the two-family house where Gordo's sister lived, barely distinguishable from its neighbors set among the leafless November "gardens" and driveways of the East Elmhurst development. Without a doubt, nobody home.

"Well, they could've gone to..." Pastore looked once more through his binoculars at the empty rooms.

"It's sixteen forty-five hours; they gotta come home by midnight."

"Okay, let's say they cut short the turkey fiesta and get back here by then. Let's even say Gordo went where they went—why should he come back here with them? I'd give you a hundred to one he won't."

Flynn had told Pastore and Levy to take the Chrysler and do the Thanksgiving job on department time. Pastore was scheduled to work the four-to-one; Levy had switched tours to hook up with Pastore. Levy looked out on the scruffy landscaping. "Shit," he said, "this fuckin' street is a mess. We could've brought the pickup truck and made ourselves useful at least."

"Uh-uh," Pastore said. "Landscapers do not—repeat, do not—work Thanksgivin'. Somebody would've figured we was up to somethin'."

Levy disagreed. "Everybody is too busy eatin' turkey to worry about a couple of oddball landscapers. Nobody would give a rat's ass anyway unless Gordo was around."

"And he ain't." Pastore sighed. "You won't believe what Cooch shared with me the other day."

"A statistic."

"The FBI has *a hundred and fifty thousand* fugitives on file; every month, they get a thousand more." He adjusted the car seat backward a bit. "Might as well have some leg room—we're gonna be here awhile."

"What's the point? You said yourself, the chances—"

"What would Obie do? What would the boss do?"

"What anybody with a brain would do—go eat!"

"Right!" Pastore said. "Except my in-laws are better at barbecue than turkey, if you know what I mean."

"Oh, yeah? So you don't have to go there till next summer. Meanwhile, Yonkers is turkey city." O'Levy smacked his lips. "We got plenty of time to go eat and be back by midnight. You hungry?"

"Now that you mention it." Pastore pulled the seat upright and gunned the Chrysler.

Monday night, December 2, 1985

Even on a Monday night, Jed's Montparnasse was full of sleekly dressed East Sixties types. Each of the three times Rachel had to meet Walter, he sent her to a different glitzy East Side bar. This one boasted 1920s-style decor. Everybody in the place except Rachel wore huge shoulder pads. Relieved of her jacket by the coat-check girl, she now had nothing on her thin shoulders but a sweater. Despite the coat-check girl's best efforts, Rachel held on to her ballet bag. She scanned the crowd—no sign of Walter.

A woman whose square-shoulder black jumpsuit made her look six feet tall loomed over Rachel. "Looking for Walter?" If she had added "little girl," Rachel wouldn't have been surprised.

"Yes, thanks."

The woman took her through the bar to an equally crowded back room and beyond it to a door marked PRIVATE. She let Rachel in and left. The office had indirect lightning and office glitz instead of bar glitz. Walter sat tilted back in his chair with his feet up on a cream-colored wooden desktop that set off his mirror finish tan loafers.

Rachel sat down on the edge of an office chair and forced a smile. "This place is you, Walter. Stop shopping and take it."

"Maybe I will."

She unzipped her ballet bag and handed him the brown envelope. Inside it she had put three white envelopes, one for each buyer category, marked with the number of buyers and the cash total.

Walter took his feet off the desk and sat up. He counted the bills against the total written on each white envelope and then shuffled the money, concentrating on getting it all in a neat, sharp-edged stack. The he picked up the stack and struck her across the face with it. "You owe me three bills, you cunt. What kinda shit are you trying to pull on me?"

Rachel touched the stinging welts on her cheek. "I ordered three ounces but the bag was four grams short. I weighed it when I got home."

"On what," he sneered, "the bathroom scale?"

"On the same scale Mia used—she kept it at my place."

Walter played with the stack of bills, reshuffling them, and brandished them menacingly. "She had that scale fixed—she told me she did."

Rachel hadn't cried when he hit her—now the tears came.

"Yeah," he said, "your girlfriend shorted you, the whole bunch of you."

Speechless, Rachel shook her head no.

Walter came out of his chair and at her so fast she only had time to cover her face. He swiveled her chair on its casters and smashed her against a low bookcase, shins first. She hit the edge of the shelf right over the bone where there was no cushion of flesh at all. When she screamed in pain, he slapped his hand over her mouth and held it there. "You listen to me, cunt. Don't fuck around with my business. I'm not gonna be so nice about the bucks you owe me, after all. Why should I? I need bread just like any businessman. I'm gonna call in that loan early—and till you pay it off, I'm raisin' the interest: seven percent over prime."

Rachel sat hunched over her legs and said nothing.

"You got a problem with that?" he yelled. " 'Cause if you do, we can handle it. I'm givin' a party next week for some friends of mine. The ten best. You can come, too—and *work* off some of your debt right there." He grabbed her chair and dumped her out of it. "Get the fuck outta here *right now*. Before I break your poor little ankles."

Wednesday morning, December 4, 1985

Apart from the wonderful harbor view from Cary's place, Lauren really had no use for tower living in the wintertime. Battery Park City didn't even have its own newsstand yet. No sooner had she settled in among the bankers and stockbrokers at Liberty Vistas than she found herself missing the shabby coziness of the Anastasia Suite. Thinking about Flynn had made her head ache more than her bruises did. Changing the dressing on her neck kept the thug's threat fresh in her mind. She had stocked up on aspirin and escaped to the office, where she spent Thanksgiving weekend at her desk, catching up.

The towers of Liberty Vistas put her off, but the neighborhood—

the southern tip of Manhattan with its "Olde New York" crazy quilt of streets with names instead of numbers—had always attracted her. The planners hadn't spoiled Battery Park City by imposing a strict uptown-style grid on the landfill, so walking to work from Cary's—and often back—diverted her and promptly became a habit. The only disadvantage was that she arrived at the office without having read a page of news.

Lauren's boss had turned up about noon two days in a row, so this morning she expected him on time. She dashed into her office and without even hanging up her coat, opened the metro section of the *Times*. Nicaragua and the Philippines could wait; for her the day had to start with city news; she needed it like some people need morning coffee.

Upper Westsiders Rally to Decry Murders, Drug Trade. Page B1.

More than any group in the city, Upper Westsiders were notorious for angry civic meetings. Some people Lauren knew in the area made a way of life out of these events, managing to squeeze in at least one for each day of the week. That the *Times* had sent a reporter to this meeting and put his story on page one of the metro section was news all by itself.

By Peter Euston. The byline helped explain matters. Peter Euston and a bunch of other *Times* reporters lived in the neighborhood; you couldn't walk down Broadway on a Saturday night without bumping into a couple of them. If they felt strongly about a subject, it stood a good chance of becoming a story. The *Times* had carried page-one articles about Abdul's murder as well as Mia Greenfield's. Of course, all the papers continued to play the ballet murder case, but only the *Times* had covered Abdul's violent death. There's always a private story behind the public one, Lauren thought as she began to read.

> More than 300 Upper Westsiders, reacting to two recent drug-related murders in their community, jammed the community room of a local church Monday night for an emergency meeting with police and government officials.
>
> The community members aired their anger and disgust at drug violence and their fear of "becoming a statistic" themselves. Politicians, out in force, promised to manipulate budgets and pressure city, state and federal governments to respond. But most of the two-and-a-

half-hour meeting's controversy swirled around the police officials who attended.

Lauren hurriedly skimmed the piece. The neighborhood regulars had certainly turned out—and Peter Euston captured the whole cast of characters. Lauren knew most of them, including the woman who had chaired the meeting. Euston quoted Judy Stine, activist organizer of a drug-watcher group:

> "In the old days, we all knew someone who had been mugged by an addict or had their apartment burglarized. We wondered when it would be our turn. And pretty soon it *was* our turn. Now most of us know someone who's been *killed* in this drug war. Probably everybody in this room knew Abdul Mahmoud; some of you knew Mia Greenfield or saw her dance. Which one of *us* is the next statistic?" Ms. Stine challenged the overflow crowd.

A vocal opposition wanted no part of drug watching; Lauren knew their hard-nosed spokesman, too.

> "We should fight, all right—fight to make the cops do what we pay them to do: Get rid of the pushers and the drugs. I heard that Abdul Mahmoud went to the cops for help with the dealing on his corner and got too little, too late. It's the cops' job to catch murderers, not ours," Steven Thompson contended.

The Community Council board secretary, the blonde who didn't like Lauren, jumped up to defend the police:

> Rhoda Kling identified herself as a member of the Precinct Community Council board. Ms. Kling said, "The police of our Two-nine want to help. They are out there every day for us. Show up at Council meetings and give them your support! They really need it now—the other team has more players and bigger guns. These druggies don't follow the old rules—pretty soon, more cops will be getting killed themselves."

Next came the precinct commander who touted the special antidrug force that he himself had set up. Peter Euston quoted:

> "Since February, Sgt. Mel Katz and his men have arrested 375 low-level dealers and customers," D.I. Payne said. "Of course, every one of 'em was back out on the street before the arresting officer got

done with the paperwork. There's gridlock in that court system. Murder suspects even *walk out of the courtroom right under the judge's nose*. We're makin' the collars, but it's like shovelin' sand against the tide.''

Then Katz had his say:

''In Bolivia today, the only crop they're growin' is coca. The federal government's gotta step in and stop this *over there*. We're seein' a 'new, improved' cocaine drug now—crack,'' Sgt. Katz warned. ''It's the wave of the future and it's gonna give us all trouble—more trouble than we ever had.''

Katz's job might be low-level dealers, Lauren thought, but he could see the big picture.

The name Oscar Rafael jumped out at her from Euston's piece. Euston quoted him on his recent fact-finding mission to South America:

''You don't know how to react when you see those poor peasant farmers in Peru and Bolivia finally enjoying a better way of life. There's no way whatsoever to get countries to stop growing the crop,'' City Councilman Rafael said. ''What we need is a meaningful program to educate young people that drugs are a terrible, terrible disease that will kill you.''

Lauren skipped ahead:

. . . many area residents demanded information about the November 5 murder of ballet dancer Mia Greenfield. Manhattan North Det. Capt. Joe Zachs said the homicide unquestionably is drug related because drugs were found at the crime scene. The detective captain referred to Sgt. Katz's team: ''They are our first line of defense against the so-called low-level trafficking where major violence often starts brewing. But when we have a homicide in this precinct, Lieut. Andrew Flynn and his squad are responsible for apprehending the perpetrator. Many of you have heard of the squad's terrific hundred percent homicide clearance record last year and the year before. Lieut. Flynn is here to report on the progress of the Greenfield case.''

Clever Zachs, Lauren thought—he had left the impression that "Katz's team" might somehow have prevented the homicide, but now Flynn's hero squad would come riding over the hill and rescue the community from its terror. Zachs drove a neat wedge between Katz's group and Flynn's. And if the ballet murder should remain unsolved, people would definitely know who to blame.

Lauren's eye jumped to the next mention of Flynn.

> Lieut. Flynn said the two recent cases followed "the drug-related pattern of the vast majority of homicides in the area." He said his detectives were making progress in the Greenfield case, but he offered no details because the investigation is "at a sensitive point." And he praised community cooperation in the 29th Precinct. "When you and your neighbors hear screams in the middle of the night, you don't think about goin' back to sleep—you reach for the phone to call 911. When detectives show up at your door, you don't hide. If we ask you to testify, you don't hide." Lieut. Flynn told the group he anticipates an arrest in the "brutal murder of a talented young dancer in the near future."

Lauren's headache came back instantly. She threw the aspirin bottle in her shoulder bag and dashed down the long hall toward the ladies' room, hoping for a few more minutes' grace before her boss appeared. Rival notions battled in her brain. Flynn seemed staunch and brave, a bold risk-taker. He had to keep pursuing Mia's killer, catch him—and show up Zachs and the rest of the cheap-shot brass. And, of course, free his lover, Lauren Daniels, from the threat of harm.

She gulped water from the COLD faucet to wash down the aspirin. Then she fished in her bag and, watching her progress in the mirror, began to darken her blond lashes with mascara. Flynn also seemed like a headstrong optimist. He believed that people would follow his brave example because it was right—even if it put them at risk. What "protection" could he or any cop offer? Rhonda Kling had it right: They were all more and more vulnerable themselves.

Lauren realized that if she wanted a shield to hide behind, she had better not look to Flynn. But if she needed a chance to test her ability to manage without one—he had unintentionally given her that. Apparently, she welcomed the test. Why shouldn't he understand? And if he could—what then? "You still have a lover," he said. She blinked back tears. But what could she and Flynn give each other? She glanced in the mirror; the mascara she had just applied had started to run.

The ladies' room door opened. "Oh, there you are!" her boss's secretary said. "He wants you, pronto."

Wednesday afternoon, December 4, 1985

After Walter beat Rachel, she asked Reynolds to come and stay with her. Reynolds said he would see what he could do.

"All in a day's work, right?" he said to Flynn, who agreed that for Reynolds to be attentive to Rachel at this time might be good for the investigation. Just in case Flynn needed to reach Reynolds, he would find her phone number in Reynolds's message box. "Eyes only," Reynolds told his boss, hoping that Flynn would not see fit to give access to Carlucci.

Playing nurse didn't bother Reynolds at all. His patient detested staying home from work, however, and sometimes could get cranky. She brooded about the *Nutcracker* ballet that was starting its run tomorrow; she had been given a good part and she wanted to dance it.... This morning she had said she knew she would feel better if she could sew the ribbons and elastic on her pointe shoes. So Reynolds had taken a ride to the theater to pick up a week's supply of the made-to-measure satin shoes—a dozen pair.

Along with the shoes, he brought back some basic groceries, a fifth of amaretto, and a bunch of roses. Rachel was in the tub when he returned. The bubble-bath foam was breaking up so she must have been soaking awhile. The steamy room smelled sweet. He held out a small glass of amaretto and she reached for it, destroying what was left of the bubbles.

"Mmm." She tilted her chin up to swallow, showing a fragile curve of neck and breast. "I hope the lieutenant doesn't miss you—I feel so spoiled with you here"—she smiled guiltily—"and it feels good."

"The lieutenant sends you his best wishes. In fact, they're waiting for you in the other room."

"What's waiting?"

"I told you—best wishes from Lieutenant Flynn."

She laughed. "I give up—but whatever it is, I don't deserve it. The *Nutcracker* opens tomorrow, I have a role debut in a lovely part—and I'm not rehearsing." Tears replaced the laughter. "I can't bear not to dance Dewdrop."

"I've heard of *Nutcracker*—kid stuff, right?"

"Balanchine said that the most important part of anyone is that which remains from childhood."

"Balanchine?"

"The great master of twentieth-century ballet. When we dance, we're like the colors on his canvas, portraying his vision."

Reynolds retrieved the amaretto glass, finished the last drop, and set the glass on the sink. "You can't rehearse with your legs all smacked to hell."

"People dance on *broken bones*—the same as athletes. I called and said I'm coming—but I *don't know if I can do it.*"

He looked through the bath water to the black-and-blue mess that Walter had made of her shins. "Your bubbles have had it but your towel is warm." He snatched the white towel off the radiator and held it open for her. "Want to lean on me?" He stooped so she could put her arm around his neck and put some of her weight on him.

"Okay, straighten up," she said; she kept her legs at right angles to her body, and as he stood up, she came right out of the tub, toes pointed, everything dripping. He wrapped her up in the towel and kissed her as if he had just rediscovered kissing.

Before the back of her neck had a chance to dry, they were in bed. She slid her hands up under his T-shirt and he stopped kissing her long enough for her to slip it off.

He always went for thin girls, but Rachel's body felt different. Her ninety-five pounds were really nothing but bone and muscle. Underneath the seductive curve of thigh, he could feel the toughness that helped her dance like a feather in the wind twelve hours a day—not including the performance.

"Hide me." She drew her palms along his back, telling him she liked the idea that a spider on the wall would see nothing of her but her hands and her hair on the pillow. His pleasure in her body always seemed to surprise her.

He must have dozed off after they made love; when he opened his eyes, he saw her come into the bedroom carrying the roses in a pitcher.

"Are these the best wishes from Lieutenant Flynn?"

"Some are, some are mine."

"Pink." She buried her nose in them. "My favorite." She set the roses on the dresser. "Thank you both." She sat on the bed and kissed him. "I called the doctor and he said maybe he can fix me up so I can rehearse."

"Now I know how an athlete's family probably feels: So you'll go out there and play—but will you come back in one piece?"

"I always have before."

"This is a different kind of injury," Reynolds pointed out. "The Walter kind."

"Did you think I forgot that?"

"Well, I haven't even heard you say a bad word about that scum."

"You still might." She stood up, rummaged in the closet and the dresser, collected a pair of jeans, a T-shirt, and couple of sweaters and put them on.

Reynolds reached for the phone, dialed his number, and listened to various young women say, "Hi, Billy!" on his tape. He hung up, telling Rachel, "The message is: 'Drive Rachel to the doctor.'"

"And over to the theater afterwards?"

"You got it. I guess you want to take the shoes back there." She had told him about the dancers' using their time in the dressing room to sew the endless pairs of pointe shoes.

Rachel retrieved Reynolds's clothes from the floor and put them neatly on the bed. "Walter's sitting there knowing that sooner or later, I'll have to call. Well, he's right. But next time I see him will be... different."

"I sure as hell hope so." Reynolds played dumb, waiting to see if she had changed her mind about helping the squad. "I bet he doesn't give a shit if you dance Dewdrop or not."

"No—I mean, how about... could we talk to Lieutenant Flynn about that 'wire.'"

"Ten-four." Reynolds grinned. "As soon as you stop limping, we'll see what he says." He wondered, as he pulled on his clothes, how fast Rachel and her customers would go through her last coke buy. A week? Shit—that would be almost halfway through the month of December.

Wednesday afternoon, December 11, 1985

Betty Dominic redid her lipstick and smiled at herself in her makeup mirror. From where Flynn, Taylor, and O'Levy sat in the back of the squad, they could see Cooch heading for Betty's desk. Zoom. Would he make it before she jumped up at precisely 1459 hours? Cooch's wavy hair gave his head that aerodynamic look. He screeched to a halt.

"This is one of those days"—Betty looked wistfully out the window at the flat, gray sky—"when you never know if you're gonna get rained on or not. If I leave now I could—"

Cooch stood in her way. "In those files of yours, I never know if I'm gonna find what I'm lookin' for or not." He held out a slip of paper. "Now, I want this case on my desk when I come back Saturday—I'm workin' nights."

"It'll be there, Sergeant." She tucked the slip into the corner of her desk blotter. "Don't worry, okay?" She scooted around him, grabbed her coat, and skittered down the aisle to the minilockers. She threw a note in the locker marked BILLY THE KID, then whooshed back up the other aisle and out the swinging doors with her coat still half on and half off.

"For a change, that girl is right," Taylor said. "You never know if you're gonna get rained on or not."

"We ain't gonna get rained on again by Gordo." O'Levy grabbed his umbrella, opened it, twirled it over his head, and struck a Gene Kelly pose. "We *are* gonna smoke him out. Down at the courthouse yesterday, I happened to go to the men's room and who should turn up at the next urinal but Stanley Britton, Esq. 'Counselor,' I says, 'how's your client?'

" 'Which one?' he says.

" 'The fat one that walked right out of Judge Belk's courtroom before he even got arraigned.'

" 'Haven't heard from him,' Britton says.

" 'That's not nice,' I told him. 'Very ungrateful to someone who's so *good natured* about losing a defendant at the first court appearance. If all your clients went in the wind like that, you'd have to put the key in the door.'

"He goes, it's not a problem—most of his clients ain't clever enough to do what Mr. Concepción did. Uh-huh, I says, that's exactly why they get themselves a clever defense attorney who knows all the *ins and outs*. I had him, right? What could he say, 'Nah, I'm just another one of the dummies.' Anyway, Gordo's gonna show at Colonel Sanders sometime soon, I *know*. And we're gonna be there when he does."

"Good, old-fashioned detective work," Cooch said, "that's what you and Ronnie are doin'. I'd say we got another shot at that fatass joker. But that Walter. Forget rain—we're gonna get *pissed on* by him, I guarantee it." He looked at Flynn. "So what's the story with that dancer Reynolds is workin'? I'm willin' to believe he's bustin' his balls for once—but where's the results?"

While Cooch was busy listening to O'Levy, Reynolds came in and examined the top layer of geological sediment in his minilocker. Flynn saw Billy reach for the phone on the nearest desk, dial a number, and listen silently for a minute or so. Then he hung up and joined the group sitting in the back of the room. "What's doin', pal?" Flynn asked him.

Reynolds made a thumbs-up sign. "We're in business. Rachel has been out of contact with Walter ever since he beat her, but she just got hold of him—she's been tryin' for a few days now—and she's gonna hook up with him to get her next consignment. They're on for Saturday night, after her performance. She's ready to wear the wire. We can't wire her till after the show, so the timing could be a little tight. But if we can put that together—we're set."

Cooch noticed that it was after 1630. He signed the log, put on his trench coat, and disappeared out the swinging doors.

"How's Rachel doin' since Walter went after her?" Flynn asked Reynolds.

"She stayed out a day and a half. Then she got a doctor to shoot some local anesthetic in her legs and she went on. This week she don't need the anaesthetic. Just puts on a half inch of makeup to cover the bruises."

"Did you talk to her before now about wearin' a wire?"

"Yeah. I asked her about it a while back but she was too scared—plus she says he's the one source in the world that don't cut the drug with stuff that could really mess up the dancers. That ain't the *reason* he keeps it pure—he wants to be kinda the Tiffany's of blow, she says. It's an ego thing. Anyway," Reynolds continued, "I don't know if Rachel was more scared of him or of losin' the source, but now she ain't thinkin' about any of that. If he had just cheated her, she might've swallowed it, but the physical thing got to her. She started askin' me to tell her what he did to Mia."

"Did you tell her?" Taylor asked.

"I told her enough."

"Saturday's still a long way off," Taylor said, "but when it gets here—who is she gonna go with?"

"I think he means is she still gonna be able to manage those fears you mentioned," Flynn said, "both of them. How far gone is she as a junkie?"

"How do you measure that before it's so obvious you trip over it? So far she's a junkie who does what she's gotta do. I don't see her stayin' up all night and she shows up for work. But I'd say she ain't on the dot all the time, either, like she was before."

"There is a way to get an idea where she's at with the drugs," Taylor said. "It's basic but it ain't simple."

O'Levy was absorbing every word of the conversation while

trying to look as if he'd heard it all a million times. Flynn figured O'Levy had been within sight of a dead junkie once or twice but didn't know many live ones to talk to. But everybody wanted to hear Jesse's test for a junkie you could count on in a tight spot.

"Basic but not simple . . . ?" Flynn prodded.

"Yeah," Taylor said. "Does she lie? You know, junkies can get so they don't even *know* when they're lyin'. No excuse, but the concept of responsibility goes up in smoke."

"Think about that, Billy," Flynn said, "and then let's talk. Meantime get started on that wire."

Saturday night, December 14, 1985

Rachel had given Reynolds a good seat for the *Nutcracker*, but he came late and stood restlessly in the back of the orchestra. The waltz music—now that he heard the piece, it actually sounded familiar—announced the Flowers.

A dozen ballerinas floated from the wings; Rachel followed, her green eyes bright, her smile looking strained to Reynolds's eyes—off somehow. The ballerinas stepped up to twirl on their toes but Rachel's right foot buckled and she fell. Reynolds felt as if someone had punched him in the gut. She recovered quickly, her face paler than the white costume, and finished the piece, but without ever rising all the way to her toes. It looked to him as if her right shoe would not support her.

As soon as the "Waltz of the Flowers" ended, he made his way to the stage entrance. The security guard greeted him. At first, Reynolds waited alone in the hallway, leaning against the cinder-block wall. After the curtain calls, the crush of fans and friends moved in. Rachel usually didn't linger in the dressing room, but tonight the corps dancers began to trickle out and she did not come.

Reynolds had just decided to go backstage when the guard caught his eye and beckoned to him. He held out a small envelope.

"He canceled," her note said. "Don't wait. Call me tomorrow. Love, Rachel."

As prearranged, Reynolds called the squad from a pay phone in the street to say he was on his way uptown. The receiver felt cold in his hand and the wind whipped up the trash in the gutter; it was mid-December, all right.

"We'll meet you downtown," Flynn said.

"No, wait for me at the squad," Reynolds told him. "We're off—at least for tonight."

Instead of asking a lot of questions, Flynn just said, "Too bad. Are you okay?"

"Come to think of it, I been missin' Uncle Jack," Reynolds answered. "What if we meet at Flynn's and I fill you in up there."

"You're on."

Reynolds felt in his trench-coat pocket for Rachel's note. He remembered how pale she looked after her foot caved in. For once he didn't feel so smart. He wondered if she was lying about Torres's canceling.

Early morning, Wednesday, December 18, 1985

When Walter canceled on Rachel, it had dissolved her last shred of doubt about helping the police catch him. Now it was time. She thought she saw Billy and the other detectives in a Chrysler parked at the intersection across St. Nicholas Avenue, but she couldn't see their faces well enough to be sure. Gritting her teeth, she entered the Harlem bar, La Puerta del Sol. She blocked the sour smell of old liquor out of her nostrils and breathed through her mouth, wishing for one of Walter's glitzy places.

Walter sat on a barstool near the far end. She focused narrowly on him, screening out the other faces and ignoring the hissing, kissing noises that followed her. The bar went on forever. Unexpectedly, he got up and came to meet her before she reached the halfway point. Normally, he just waited for her to come to him. His cream-colored suit needed a pressing.

"*Adios,* Chino," the bartender yelled after him.

"Green Eyes"—he smiled his charming, good-customer smile—"let's take a ride tonight."

He better have her coke in the car, Rachel worried. She had planned on having her little conversation with him in a quiet booth with the table safely between them. She still had no clear idea what she would say to get him to admit killing Mia.

Walter struck a macho pose with his feet planted wide apart and jerked his head toward the door behind her. She turned and walked out ahead of him, conscious of the minitransmitter taped in the small of her back. She wore two sweaters tucked into her jeans and the suede baseball jacket over them. High, soft suede boots didn't hurt her toes. As always when she came from the theater, she carried her ballet bag. She hesitated on the sidewalk but didn't dare to look across the avenue to see whether the Chrysler was still there. Billy had said the detectives would hear and record whatever she and Walter said—as long as they remained within about four blocks of her transmitter. But they were counting on a conversation in a bar—would traffic noises interfere?

Lieutenant Flynn, Detective O'Brien, and Jesse Taylor, the Spanish-speaking black detective, all had been waiting for her and Billy at the office where she was "wired." Lieutenant Flynn introduced Rachel to Taylor's partner for the night, an undercover narcotics officer called Nanette. Taylor and Nanette's car would follow closest to Walter's; if he happened to see them, he wouldn't take them for cops. If Rachel was in danger, to alert the detectives she would say the code word *sweetheart*.

"Let's go," Walter prodded.

The BMW sped uptown in the sparse after-midnight traffic on the parkway. Below, the Hudson River ran thick and black. Twinkling lights on the George Washington Bridge outlined the long curves of the span against the black sky.

"Walter, I'm tired tonight. What's this ride, all of a sudden?"

"Check out the bridge, baby—look how pretty—that good old GWB. We're going up that way, turn on a few lights of our own. Don't worry, I'm gonna wake you right up. Wait and see."

Oh, God—if she got high, would she be able to do what she had to do? At 158th Street, he drove around to the southbound side of the road, pulled off, and parked in the shadows. She could barely make out his face. Out of the corner of her eye, she saw another car park farther north, but it didn't look like a Chrysler. She had forgotten what kind of car Taylor would be driving. Walter finally passed her the mirror with two neatly formed lines on it. "Just for you, Green Eyes." The powder sparkled pure white. Rachel held the mirror so that her hand shielded the coke from his view and sniffed, doing almost all of one line.

A barge slid by on the river. "Look Walter—a ghost ship." She giggled nervously. He turned his head and she bent over the mirror, faked a deep sniff and flipped the powder into her palm. She wished she had something in her ballet bag to dump it in. Well, she could just put it in her jacket pocket and empty it out later.

"Feeling fine, right?" He pocketed the mirror and moved toward her, his hands going to the front of her jacket, tugging open the zipper, reaching inside. He held her around the rib cage, gripping tight on either side as he bent his head and covered her mouth with his, probing roughly with his tongue. Thank God the wire was taped low, just above the end of her spine. He seemed not to care whether she kissed him back; she just held herself still, the small of her back tight against the car seat. When she felt a hand on her leg, she actually welcomed it: This was safer. He fondled the soft suede of her boot, taking a deep breath and letting it out hot on her neck. His fingers rubbed and squeezed their way upward—robot fingers, hard, thorough.

"Coño! What the fuck is this?"

Up above on Riverside Drive where the Chrysler waited, the three detectives started at Walter's words. Flynn radioed Taylor and the undercover Nanette, parked within sight of the BMW. "He might have made her, Jesse. Move up—see what's happening."

Flynn, Obie, and Reynolds sat out the silence.

"Highway Patrol car got in the way," Taylor finally radioed back.

Rachel watched the blue-and-white police car disappear from the rearview mirror.

"Go to bed, you motherfuckers," Walter muttered. He stepped on the gas and moved smoothly out, keeping his speed just under the limit as he took off downtown.

She saw no other car that might be her backup. Suppose she had to say *sweetheart* right now?

"So, Green Eyes"—he drove with one hand and put the other on her thigh—"you got a blade in that boot of yours."

"I need it. I get home late from the theater every night. My neighborhood's not safe; it's deserted. So I keep the razor on me and I use it for cutting the blow, too."

"Passing One two-five Street, Lieu," Taylor radioed.

"We're a few cars back," Flynn answered, "and we got him up on the wire again. Must not have made her after all."

"He's still got time," Obie commented under his breath, but Flynn caught it.

"Yeah, I see him!" Taylor's voice came in clear as a bell. "He's slowing down—heading for the Nine-six exit, looks like. I'll pass him up and come back."

"Okay, let's not all leave the road together."

As Flynn's Chrysler left the parkway at Ninety-sixth Street, the detectives spotted Walter's BMW in a secluded parking area jutting over the Hudson. Just north of it, yet out of sight, was another, similar, area. Flynn radioed Taylor to pull in there. The Chrysler turned onto Riverside Drive and parked right next to the highway exit at Ninety-fifth Street.

To Rachel's left, a stone wall ran along the edge of the park; she could make out some kind of an arched opening in the wall. On her right, only water. Walter had left the engine on; maybe he didn't plan a long stay.

"Now we got some peace," he said, "nobody to bother us here." He moved closer to her. "Green Eyes, you know I'm still holdin' that big loan of yours." His tone of voice seemed copied from a TV mafioso. "You still got to pay back what Mia owed me."

Good that he had brought up Mia. "I don't see why I have to make up Mia's debt. I'm selling plenty for you, Walter." Rachel convinced herself that Billy's car was somewhere within range of her transmitter.

"This is the last time I'm gonna go over it. You got to pay Mia's debt on account of most of what she owed me was what *you* owed her. So you owe me, you gonna pay me. Got the picture now?"

"I am paying you, as fast as I can—it's the best I can do."

"No, it ain't—you gotta use less and sell *more*. She gave me that same shit, trying to con me. Didn't do her no good at all, did it."

"Because you—you killed Mia."

"She wasn't doing *nothing* for me. This is a business—I got people to pay, too. Nobody gets a free ride—not me, not her, not you. But I told her we could make a deal and now I'm telling you the same thing: Give me what I want, I'll forget about the money. But she was stupid—she wouldn't pay me, she wouldn't lay down for me."

He jerked open Rachel's jacket and pulled at her sweater. "Better give me what I want, Green Eyes. Don't be stupid yourself."

Rachel couldn't help it, she recoiled. Walter's hand came up under her chin, knocking her head back against the window, hard.

"She started giving me trouble—'getting tough.' So I told her again: 'You owe me money, you're mine: I put my own mark on you.' Like this... Watch—" A blade gleamed in the darkness, like the flickers of light on the river.

"What are you doing! Take that knife away!"

* * *

"Andy," Obie yelled, "he's gonna cut her!"

"Jesse, let's go," Flynn radioed.

"She must be okay," Reynolds broke in, "she didn't give the signal."

"Billy, for chrissake, he's got a knife on 'er," Obie growled. "She could've forgotten what to say—"

They heard Walter's voice again: "You owe me money, Green Eyes—you're *mine*. You got that? I'm the boss. You gonna get tough with me, now? You end up like her."

"No, no—sweetheart, I got it. I do. I'll give you what you want."

"Okay, Jesse—let's move!"

Rachel heard a car go by very fast on the highway above and then thought she saw faraway headlights flash in the rearview mirror. In a matter of seconds, a car—maybe the same one—zoomed up behind the BMW. Both front doors flew open and Taylor and Nanette jumped out, guns drawn.

As Walter stamped on the gas, she saw the Chrysler come speeding up the exit ramp of the parking lot the wrong way, heading directly for Walter. He swerved, bashing the Chrysler's left fender. "Fuckin' cops never arrested me yet," he yelled. "Gonna lose 'em this time, too." The tires squealed as he threw the BMW into reverse, but the engine stalled.

Rachel fumbled with the lever that would open the door, but Walter locked his arm around her neck, tightening his grip, making her gasp. With the other hand, he pulled a gun from under the seat.

"You're stayin' with me, Green Eyes, you're my ticket outta here." He pushed her ahead of him out of the car, his gun in her back. But with detectives blocking both escape routes, where could he go? Nowhere but that archway in the wall. He saw it. Taylor and Nanette stood only a few feet in front of her and Walter. Rachel shivered in the cold night. She looked over her shoulder at Billy, Lieutenant Flynn, and Detective O'Brien, watching from a few feet behind.

Walter started to pull her toward the archway. *"Fuck off or she's dead!"* he screamed. Rachel could make out a sagging iron gate set into the stone arch.

Flynn motioned for everybody to move back a few steps; they kept their guns trained on the target. "Lieu," Obie said, "that's the old Penn Central tunnel. Nothin' but tracks and a lotta trash. There's an opening at One oh three Street and one at Eight-nine."

Walter fired a wild shot, pushed Rachel through the tunnel opening, and disappeared after her into the darkness.

"Listen, boss"—Reynolds turned to Flynn—"no sweat—I been in there before."

Taylor had pulled up the Thunderbird by the arched opening. He kicked the iron gate; it swung inward with an earsplitting creak.

Walter shouted something but his words got lost in the echo. Flynn heard a single gunshot explode in the depths of the tunnel.

"He's headed south, boss," Taylor told him.

"Nice work." Flynn radioed a 10-85, ordering backup from uniformed patrol to cover both ends of the tunnel.

"We can go in and get the drop on him before he hits that exit at Eight-nine," Reynolds urged.

Flynn told Obie and Taylor to ride up to 103rd Street. "Make sure nobody else goes in there. Next thing you know, we'll have cops shootin' cops. Nanette's comin' with us. When Rachel gets out of there, she might need some female company."

In the Chrysler's backseat, the reels of the Kel set receiver steadily revolved. Nanette turned up the volume.

"Jesus, Walter—where's the tunnel going?" Rachel's panicky voice. "Can't see anything."

"Shut up. Just walk, it's gonna end and when it does, we're out and no cops."

"God, it's pitch-black in here. If I trip on something and sprain my ankle—"

"Shut up or I'll break your feet and leave you here for rat food." Sounds of breathing and footsteps.

"I can think of people I'd rather be with in a dark tunnel," Nanette said to the men in the front seat.

"We gotta go around," Reynolds reminded his boss. To reach the tunnel, Reynolds remembered, they had to be on the northbound side of the highway. Flynn floored the accelerator, heading for the next northbound access at Seventy-ninth Street.

No gate at this tunnel opening, just a yawning, black hole.

"All set?" Flynn asked Reynolds.

"Let's go."

"Easy does it," Nanette said as Flynn and Reynolds got out of the Chrysler.

"You bet," Flynn answered. If only they could take Walter alive, Flynn was sure Walter would try to save himself by giving them Viera. But Flynn kept his wish to himself; they had to shoot to kill or risk ending up dead themselves.

Reynolds borrowed a flashlight from a patrol cop.

"We gotta hug the wall," Flynn said as he and Reynolds approached the tunnel entrance. Soon they were moving silently in the total darkness, elbows touching, stepping gingerly through the refuse by the side of the track. They advanced a few feet, paused to listen, heard nothing, and edged forward again, conscious that the slightest noise could bring death. Again they stopped, hardly breathing. An animal scuttled by.

Walter's voice: "Move it! We're gonna be outta here pretty soon."

Flynn went closer to the wall, nudging Reynolds to follow. Impossible to judge the distance by the sound in the disorienting blackness, yet he felt they must be right near.

The cops waited. Silence. Then approaching footsteps. Reynolds seemed about to move toward the noise; Flynn's arm held him back. The footsteps came closer, just a few feet. Now Flynn poked Reynolds.

Reynolds held the flashlight so that no light would spill on himself and switched on the beam for a split second—barely long enough to catch Walter and Rachel, not more than five feet away. *"Coño!"* Walter shouted and spun toward the light, momentarily forgetting Rachel, who pulled away from him as darkness surrounded them again and Flynn emptied his .38 into the dark tunnel, aiming first by sound and then, as his ears rang with the gunshots, by instinct and his impressions of the muzzle flashes. Walter's gun fired once, then clanked on the rails. Again Reynolds flicked on the beam. Walter's body had pitched backward, bloodstains spreading on the jacket and pants of his cream-colored suit. As Flynn warily approached the fallen coke dealer, Reynolds kept his gun and the light trained on Walter, watching for the slightest movement. Flynn used his foot as a lever, turned Walter on his face, and handcuffed him. He wasn't gonna be much use in nailing Viera.

"Billy?" Rachel's voice was weak; Reynolds caught her just as she collapsed.

Late afternoon, Thursday, December 19, 1985

"Buenos tardes, señor."

"How's business, Pepe?"

"Oh, it's a good day, señor—the people they talk to me while I drive and I don't get bored. Only when I'm in between passengers, you know, I got to play my radio. They don't put no radio in the car except to tell me the addresses, so I bring this one." He held up a bright-red transistor set. "No, for me a good day is when everybody talk."

"They tell you their business, like in a barbershop?"

"Oh, no, señor, not in the car. Here they talk about the current events. The mayor, the city, the guy that tear down the hotel in the middle of the night because the law say he can't tear down his hotel." Pepe laughed. "Now you see it, now you don't. That made a very good day, too. It's amazing—when something big happen, everybody want to talk about that. Nothing else."

"That is amazing."

"I guess you know what everybody talk about today, señor."

"No," Viera said, "I just woke up. What's big today?"

"You kidding, señor, you really don't know?"

"Verdad!"

"Wait—I turn on the all-news, they give the big story every twenty-two minutes!"

". . . Ten-ten WINS News. Police officials report an end to the manhunt for the killer of ballerina Mia Greenfield. WINS reporter Janet—"

"What did I tell you"—Pepe punched the steering wheel—"that's it right now!"

"The violent death early last month of a twenty-year-old dancer in an abandoned building devastated the city. Today detectives at Manhattan's Twenty-ninth Precinct told reporters they had been seeking a suspect—reputed cocaine dealer Walter Torres. They say Torres abducted Mia Greenfield on her way home from the theater on November sixth, then sexually assaulted and stabbed her to death. Sergeant Ray McCullough, a police spokesman, said detectives have an incriminating tape naming Torres in the Greenfield murder. As police closed in on the suspect early this morning, he fled—taking another ballet dancer hostage. The chase ended with Torres dead of police bullets. His hostage, identified as Plaza Ballet dancer Rachel French, was treated for shock at St. Luke's Hospital and released. This is Janet Galotti, Ten-ten WINS News on the Upper West Side."

"So," Pepe declared as he pulled up to the Tabu Club, "that is how it ends, the story of the beautiful dancer and the guy who cut her in pieces. That famous detective, I guess he got his man." Pepe looked in the rearview mirror and saw Viera's eyes glint with fury.

"Five weeks and Flynn can't find a murderer," Viera sneered, "so the mayor gets mad. You shouldn't be surprised Flynn found a

Spanish guy to shoot and faked some kind of a tape. I told you before: He's poison and he will answer for his crimes against our community. Next time all your passengers talk about a big story, it will be the story of our victory over Flynn. He will go, I promise you."

"Sí, Señor. Hace un buen día."

Ramón rushed to open the Tabu's front door, admitting Viera in a blast of arctic air. Monte had been in the bar for almost half an hour, drinking and pacing around, cursing under his breath. Now the boss comes in with this terrible expression on his face. He and Monte just sat on their barstools, not saying a word. Ramón hurried to fix Viera's whiskey and a fresh martini for Monte; he put the drinks on the little tray, ready to take downstairs. He thought of offering to carry the drinks down to the office but was afraid to speak. When the time came for the storm to break, he sincerely wanted to be somewhere else. He picked up his knife and started on the lemons.

The boss and Monte both grabbed their drinks. They didn't look like they were going *nowhere*.

"Chino was supposed to be holed up, doing business by courier. I'd like to know how the fuck he got his ass in the street." Irish sounded as icy as the wind outside.

"I gave him the rules, boss, but I couldn't lock him in. He got himself screwed up with a ballerina again; must've had some kind of a complex or something. I never heard of that in my life. The only thing he did say to me—'It's a dynamite market, Monte.'"

"So it blew up in his face."

"That fuckin' copper set him up. I sure wish you woulda let me—"

"I'm ready now—but he's gotta see it coming. He's gonna be sorry he didn't pay attention."

"Caramba!" Monte jumped off the stool and raised his glass, sloshing the martini around. "With one hand I'm gonna get you the replacement for Chino and with the other—"

"We're gonna do it, all right. We'll fuckin' wipe him out."

"Are you leavin' this to me?"

Irish got a faraway look in his eye. "I got a few ideas—I gotta think about it some more. It so happens I owe this sucker for a long time—even before I know you. I want Flynn to die a couple of deaths while he's still alive. He'll be in such bad shape he'll be *dreamin'* of the final one and we'll make sure his dream comes true."

"You want special—like a Colombian necktie?"

Ramón had never seen Monte so intense. Just then, Ramón heard footsteps on the back stairs and Salsa came into view, dancing along the bar. The boss looked at Salsa and then at Monte and said, "Gotta be better than that. I told you—I want to get to Flynn's head—first."

"Gimme an example," Monte said.

"Send him on a nice little goose chase with his men."

"Like the gun in the sewer!"

"Yeah. And—make him wonder if somebody he trusted fucked him over. He won't know, just wonder."

Monte looked antsy but the boss ignored it and went on, "We're gonna cut the ground out from under him a chunk at a time. He'll be *grateful* to fall in."

Thursday night, December 19, 1985

Lauren's friend Cary was busy packing in the other room. Off to St. Moritz for the Christmas "hols," as she called them, Cary had talked Lauren into staying on at Liberty Vistas while she was away. Cary said she'd feel better knowing someone would be in her apartment. Lauren surprised herself by not putting up much resistance despite the fact that there was no one in her own place.

Now that Mia Greenfield's killer had come to a bad end thanks to Flynn, Lauren's life could go on more or less as before. *It's over,* she told herself, and realized that for Flynn "it" would never be over. She felt fatigued. She could put off going home for a while. Cary's building had a concierge in the lobby at all times.

Lauren had changed since she was assaulted. She evaluated strangers who came near her, avoided deserted streets, didn't assume that a garbage picker was only a garbage picker—and on and on.

She curled up in the corner of Cary's beige linen couch and clicked on the TV remote to see what the ten-o'clock news shows would do with the story of Flynn's triumph.

She didn't wait long; the story led the hour-long program. Over the anchor's left shoulder, the Ballet Murder logo—a pointe shoe juxtaposed with a bloody dagger. "Walter Torres, the man police say raped and murdered ballerina Mia Greenfield, died early this morning of gunshot wounds inflicted by the police." The anchor's image blacked out, replaced by a head shot of the startlingly handsome Torres with his eyes closed—a Polaroid photo taken at the morgue. Torres's picture remained on screen, joined by a publicity photo of Mia Greenfield in a ballet pose; the camera zoomed in on her delicate facial features.

Next, a reporter on videotape stood near the entrance to a tunnel under Riverside Drive, showing where "police say hours of surveillance ended with a hair-raising chase in this old railroad tunnel—and finally Torres's death." A tape of the afternoon press conference at 1 Police Plaza—the Chief of Detectives congratulating the city on ridding itself of a vicious drug dealer and killer. The department believed Lieutenant Flynn acted properly in regard to the shooting of the suspect, he said, but the incident would be subject to consideration by the Firearms Discharge Review Board.

Standing in a row of cops behind the Chief was an unsmiling Andy Flynn with an older man that Lauren was sure must be Obie and a thin, jumpy type who couldn't be anybody but Zachs.

"And now," the anchor announced, "correspondent Jay Clark with Mia Greenfield's father in Traverse City, Michigan." The dignified-looking Dr. Greenfield said he was grateful that the killer wouldn't destroy any more lives and content that the family had been spared a long and difficult courtroom trial. "God will try Walter Torres for what he did. We are satisfied to have that be the end of it, even though of course we can never accept Mia's loss." Jay Clark asked if the Greenfields blamed drug-plagued New York for her death. "We don't expect to go there anytime soon," the doctor said in a bitter voice.

"Thank you, Jay," said the anchor in a somber tone. Over a publicity photo of another dancer, the anchor concluded, "Taken hostage during Torres's flight was dancer Rachel French, a friend and colleague of Mia Greenfield. Rachel French did not suffer any serious injury in her ordeal, but she declined to be interviewed by *The News at Ten.*"

Lauren wondered about this other dancer; she wondered about dancers and drugs—the glaring connection that the report failed to acknowledge. And she wondered how Flynn was doing.

She pushed the buttons on Cary's sleek white telephone, zapping the TV volume as she waited for the phone to answer in the Anastasia Suite. The butterflies in her stomach fluttered when she heard him. "Andy? It's Lauren. Congratulations."

"Hey, great to hear from you. How're you doin'?" His voice was warm.

"I'm happy your ballet murder is cleared. But I just saw you on the tube at the press conference and you didn't look so thrilled. What's that 'Firearms Review' business about?"

"In this case, nothing. Just a formality."

"So is anything wrong?"

"Not really..."

He sounded glum to her. "But?"

"You won't believe this—if I could've taken that animal alive, I would have—but it was him or us." He laughed. "Since we couldn't have both, we settled for our side."

"That's a blessing. Would he have told you something useful if he had lived?"

"Guys facin' twenty-five to life usually like to talk. I doubt if he would have gotten much of a deal, but maybe we would've gotten somethin' useful on Viera. Anything on Viera would be useful; we're still sittin' with zero."

"And it's the middle of December, so—"

"With the ballet case in the can, we're only missin' the double homicide. That Gordo is all we need to pin it on Viera and we *had* the big blob, that's what so lousy. Maybe he went on a diet and that's why he don't show up at any of his favorite chow-downs. My guys are gettin' fat themselves waitin' for him."

"How about advertising for fat Santa types? 'Earn big bucks'..."

Flynn managed a full-fledged chuckle. "And we'll call it the Santa Sting."

"Well, you sound a little cheerier now."

"Are you thinkin' of leaving Cary's? You didn't leave yet, did you?" He sounded tired, subdued. Almost as if he didn't have the strength to fight over this again, at least not now.

"Matter of fact, I'm still here. She's going on vacation and she asked me to stay till she gets back. After accepting her hospitality all this time, what could I say?"

"To tell you the truth, I'm glad you said yes. Viera probably was behind that beating you got and now his crew is minus one. Not just a grunt, either—we think Torres seems to have had the cream of the customers. I doubt if Viera is just gonna let bygones be bygones, you know?"

"I'm sort of stressed out; I wanted to stay here a little longer. I guess I need to be where I feel like—the princess in the tower. A couple more weeks should do it."

"I wish I was a better bodyguard, princess."

"Well, you told me yourself, with or without a bodyguard, I still have a lover."

"Easy to say. But what does that mean to you? What do I

mean? I really don't have a—clue." They both laughed, easing the tension a bit.

"I went for a walk on the Esplanade the other day and I was thinking about—that. All this windswept space down here sort of gets the cobwebs out."

"And?"

"I'll tell you—but not now. I'm not that great at heavy stuff on the telephone. Next time there's a quiet moment—okay?"

"I'll call you tomorrow."

"Good."

Friday morning, December 20, 1985

Captain Zachs let Flynn know up front that he, for one, disapproved of all the photos of Flynn in Friday morning's bundle of "ballet murder" news stories. "I remember telling you, *low profile* it!"

Flynn had looked at the *Times* on the subway; the paper ran a photo of the Chief of D at the press conference, with himself, Zachs, and Obie in the background—but the caption identified only the Chief and Flynn. Flynn could see what Lauren meant about his gloomy mug. To Zachs he just said, "Sorry, Cap—I don't know what pictures they could've used. I didn't have time to do any posin'. Unless you count the press conference."

The captain's phone rang and he retired to his office.

Taylor had overheard the whole thing. "You didn't expect a hero's welcome, I hope."

"Not even when we get our mitts on Gordo. Which we *gotta* do, pal. What's today—the twentieth? Where's Cooch? I gotta tell him—every tour from now till we get a better idea, somebody sits on Colonel Sanders."

"I'm gonna be somewhere else when you tell him that. He's gonna love it. He ain't in a great mood anyway. Didja hear where he was the other night while we was chasin' Walter?"

"He didn't mention it to me."

"Him and Claudia went to her branch store in Texas for a fancy charity affair."

"Texas! What's wrong with that?"

"The PD don't give no overtime for it."

"I know what'll make him happy." Flynn snapped his fingers. "He's supposed to be swingin' out Sunday. He can sit on Gordo himself, on overtime. Nights or days—his choice."

"That just might work." Taylor grinned. "A little fried chicken will do him all the good in the world."

"Lemme know when he turns up. I gotta get my coffee and give Ms. Daniels a call."

"Oh, ho," Taylor said, "patched it up, huh? Nothin' like a little fame to bring 'em around."

When the captain was out, his office was useful for personal phone calls; otherwise, privacy was at a premium. Flynn settled for Betty Dominic's desk in the far front corner of the room.

Lauren didn't answer her phone. Her secretary finally picked up and said that she wasn't at her desk.

"In a meeting?" he stalled.

"I don't think so, Mr. Flynn."

Flynn started to leave his number but the secretary said, "Oh, just a minute, I see her. Hold on now."

"Hi, Andy."

"How's it goin'?"

"Hectic. Everybody wants a Special Permit for Christmas. Want me to put your name on the list?"

"Well, maybe not on that list, but listen—Salsa's first fight is comin' up Monday night. He needs a cheering section and I'm organizin' it; I called you first. How about it?"

"Are you kidding—Salsa's first fight? Of course. D'you think we can get there from Battery Park City, though?"

Flynn laughed. "There's gotta be a way."

Sunday afternoon, December 22, 1985

As he drove the yellow Jeep over the Willis Avenue Bridge into the South Bronx, Salsa wished the Jeep wasn't so new or so yellow. It stuck out. As soon as he got off the expressway, he felt like he was on a lonely dirt road somewhere in Mexico and any minute the bandits would jump out. He hardly saw any people or cars up here on this freezing Sunday. What a graveyard.

He checked the map at the next streetlight... yeah, he seemed to be doing okay. The street should be coming up; take a right.... Steam poured out of the manholes. The building looked like it could have been a palace way back when—nicer than anywhere Salsa grew up—but it was wrecked now.

Nobody in this building could buy anything like the amount

of drugs in the package Salsa was carrying. Something else must be in the package.... He didn't really care. What mattered was that all of a sudden Viera had smiled and acted friendly when he handed it to Salsa. Until last night, the boss had kept Salsa in the deep freeze for ages.

He parked the Jeep, grabbed the bulky package, and hopped out. The box weighed more than any order he'd ever delivered. The icy wind made a storm out of the garbage in the courtyard.

In the lobby, a couple of dim bulbs hung by wires from the ceiling, but Salsa saw the shadowy stairwell and knew he would have to go upstairs blind. He felt in his pocket and hit pay dirt—a shiny black-and-gold Tabu Club matchbox. He opened the box so the matches fell out in his pocket; he pinched a good-sized bunch, held the heavy package under his arm, and struck the matches all at once on the side of the box. He carried this little torch in front of him up the narrow staircase. He wasn't about to walk into a dark elevator, not knowing who might join him.

As he got to the third flight of stairs, he made out two men on the next landing, blocking his path. They spoke between themselves but not so you could hear what they said. To retreat now, Salsa would have to turn his back to them, which was out of the question. Besides, he had to face the unknown just as he would at the smoker tomorrow night. He struck enough matches to cause a startling flare and kept going. When he reached the landing, the men let him pass.

By the time he found the right apartment, he had to wait till his heart calmed down. He was mad at himself for being scared. He could handle this. That's why he was boxing—so he could hang in and get through the fear. What would Lieutenant Flynn and Brooklyn Charlie say? He crouched in the stance he had practiced so often and closed his eyes even though the hallway was dark anyway. When he opened them, he was ready to knock forcefully.

Qué pasa? The door flew open and Salsa faced the biggest Spanish guy he ever remembered seeing, bigger even than the bouncers at the club. They guy had muscles like Mr. Clean but he had hair. The minute Salsa was in, the giant slammed the door shut. Salsa quickly handed him the bulky package; the giant squinted at it and motioned him into what must once have been the kitchen of the apartment. Now all that was left was a filthy sink. The giant dropped the package in there and disappeared for a long minute, coming back with a monster machete. Ignoring Salsa, he slashed at the package. Cardboard and brown paper fell away, revealing pile after pile of fifty-dollar bills.

Salsa knew that Irish didn't do any buy-now/pay-later drug deals, so what was he paying for with that mountain of cash?

"Feliz Navida'!" the giant boomed, handing Salsa five fifty-dollar bills for his trouble.

"Mucha' gracia', señor!—I guess you did Irish a good favor."

"Claro!" the giant boasted, "I made that fat guy into *chorizo.*"

Salsa tucked away his money carefully. *"Feliz año nuevo!"* he said, and beat it the hell out.

Monday night, December 23, 1985

Lauren chattered on about Battery Park City. Maybe she was a little nervous, Flynn thought; if so, she had company. He definitely was nervous. About seeing her, about how Salsa would fight.

"The developers of the apartment houses that are going up now"—she waved at construction sites to the south as they left Cary's lobby—"have to follow the BPC master plan, which calls for architecture that relates to the best residential traditions in the city."

Flynn looked back at the tower behind them. "So what happened to that one—it reminds me of Metropolitan Correctional."

"I see what you mean, but we won't tell Cary." Lauren laughed. "What happened is that this was part of the *old* master plan from the sixties; they junked that one before they got any further. The architects who did the new plan deserve a lot of credit."

"Okay," Flynn said, "but can they get us a taxi to Park and Sixtieth in time for Salsa's fight?" They had already covered quite a bit of ground, walking east.

"That's why BPC better not be boring to live in—once you're there you can hardly get anywhere else. Well, don't give up hope—at least it's not snowing like it was this morning."

"Here we go." Flynn hailed the cab that rushed toward them down Broadway.

In the taxi, Lauren asked who else would be part of Salsa's cheering section.

Flynn told her about his friend Brooklyn Charlie, about Carmel, "and maybe Jemal will show up. He told me you got the sport down cold and you could get hired as a referee in the near future."

"Maybe I'll have to go to a professional match first—what do you think?"

"My friends learn fast," Flynn said. "Most people who've been boxing the short time Salsa has would just be stepping into the ring for their first sparring session about now. And here he is with a real fight. He worked hard; let's hope he works hard tonight. When you got a real opponent all of a sudden—not just a sparring partner—it's easy to forget all your homework."

Lauren asked how Flynn knew Salsa in the first place; he told her the story of Salsa's stealing his stepfather's numbers money when he was eight years old.

By the time the taxi crossed Union Square to Park Avenue, Flynn felt as close to her as before. They sped along the avenue where sedately festive Christmas trees, their minilights twinkling, "grew" on the traffic islands as far uptown as you could see.

They got out at Christ Church. Flynn led the way to the side entrance of the imposing building that ornamented the posh street. "We're in the right place," Flynn assured Lauren, "this way to the smoker."

"It's in a *church?*"

"In the basement. This church has a whale of a basement, as you'll see. They even got space for the kids to change. Way back when, in the old neighborhood, I once had to put on my trunks in the confession box."

"Tall stories." Lauren smiled at him.

"Okay, I *almost* had to."

"It's okay—cops' tall stories are the best."

They walked two flights down and took a right turn. At the end of a short hallway by the double doors was the PAL ticket table. The ticket taker handed out the boxing "card," a photocopied sheet announcing eight fights for the benefit of Dennis Brennan, the police officer seriously wounded earlier that year in Harlem by a sniper's gun.

"Wow." Lauren took in the vast room, filled not only with smoke but with boisterous voices. Every other hand held a beer can. "Something tells me there's a few cops in here."

"Yes, *ma'am.*" He winked. "We gotta sit over this way near the aisle." He took her hand and walked ahead through the crowd, saying "hiya" every few steps. "Would you believe that on Tuesday nights in this very same space they put on one of the city's four-star AA meetings. That gets pretty smoky, too."

They settled down in their metal folding chairs and studied their cards. Salsa's bout came fifth, right after intermission; his opponent—Paul "Chopsticks" Cho.

"Salsa's a welterweight." Flynn spoke under the roar that greeted the appearance of the first pair of fighters. "The bouts go more or less in order of weight. These guys are featherweights—one twenty-five pounds, give or take. Then comes two lightweight bouts and one welterweight before Salsa's."

"Andy, look back there—I think somebody's trying to get your attention."

"Brooklyn Charlie!" Flynn waved.

"Looks like he's counting the house. I thought you were Salsa's trainer."

"No, I just turn up once in a while and confuse matters. Charlie's always there—steady."

The bell rang. "Here go these two little sluggers—they got three two-minute rounds. Let's see what they can do."

"I didn't know they wore headgear."

"'Cause you saw pictures of pros and they don't wear it. These are novices tonight, just a little way past green."

After two rounds Flynn said respectfully, "They're in shape. Who do you think's gonna win this war of attrition?"

"I'd say the one in the blue trunks."

"I'm with you; the other one—Camaro—looks like he might run outta gas."

Camaro's trainer dropped ice cubes inside the front of the fighter's trunks. "That's to wake him up," Flynn said. The other trainer did the same to the fighter in the blue.

As it turned out, Lauren called it. Between fights, Flynn explained about "boxer" and "infighter" styles and a little bit about strategy. When intermission came, Lauren had called all four bouts.

"Beginner's luck," she said.

"Don't be so sure, but anyway, don't knock it," Flynn told her. "How about a beer to keep you goin'?"

"Coffee," she said, "need a clear head."

"We'll be the only ones in the audience." As they made their way to the refreshment counter in the back of the room, cops caroused all around them, feeling no pain. "Look—there's Carmel sittin' right by the ring." Flynn caught her eye.

Carmel nudged the friend next to her, pointed in Flynn's direction, and jumped up from her seat.

He gestured for her to stay where she was, he would come

over. When he and Lauren had their coffees, they made their way through the crowd.

After Flynn had introduced Lauren, Carmel said, "And this is Tina, a friend of Salsa's."

Tina's jazzy earrings flashed. "Ooooh," she said, "so excitin', the fights! I only watch on TV before."

Lauren said it was her first one, too.

"It's almost time," Flynn said, "we'll find you later, okay?"

"Salsa and Tina are an item?" Lauren wanted to know.

"Stop the presses," Flynn said, "it's news to me. What's more, I think that devil has gone and fixed up Charlie with his sister."

He and Lauren sat down just as the far door opened and Chopsticks Cho paraded down the aisle opposite theirs, wearing purple satin trunks and a silk jacket with gold quilting. The Chinatown contingent all but set off firecrackers.

Then came Salsa and he was no orphan either. Brooklyn Charlie's cop network knew how to get out the vote, and the voters remembered that they were there for Dennis Brennan *and* Salsa Delacruz. Their favorite bopped on down to the ring as only Salsa could, impressive in a black robe and those hot-pink trunks.

Flynn put two fingers in his mouth and let out a piercing whistle. "At least he ain't up against a mick the first time out."

"Okay," Lauren said as the announcer introduced the two welterweights, "in the blue corner, Salsa, the lanky boxer; in the red, Chopsticks Cho, the slugger—right?"

The bell rang, as if to confirm Lauren's report.

"Damn, just look at those smart kids," Flynn said. "Nobody's rushin' into nothin'. If you start out too aggressive, pretty soon you got nothin' left."

"Salsa's dancing in a nice circle, light as you please, and jab, jab, jab." Lauren beamed.

"But he don't jump—keeps his feet on that canvas."

"Oh-oh... Chopsticks is trying to keep him from finishing the circle."

"Okay!" Flynn yelled, as Salsa landed a nice one.

The cops let loose.

"Go, baby, go!"

"Stick him again!"

"He landed the first punch. That's good for your confidence and bad for the other guy's. But he lowered his right a touch when he jabbed and Cho slipped inside with a straight left—"

"And Salsa took it on the chin!"

"Not for long!" After Salsa's next jab, he whipped a left hook to Chopsticks' jaw instead of the straight right his opponent counted on. Salsa danced away. He kept up the dance, circling and using that left jab to measure Chopsticks and to give him some grief at the same time. Salsa had three or four inches' height on Chopsticks—Chopsticks kept looking to slip underneath Salsa's jabs and move in where *he* wanted to fight. In time he succeeded, landing a couple of solid body shots. With the impact of the blows, you could see the sweat fly off Salsa's shoulder.

"Stay on him!" Chinatown screamed.

But Salsa got Chopsticks in a clinch and bought himself some time. He only needed a couple of seconds; before the referee could separate the fighters, the bell rang, ending the round.

Brooklyn Charlie scrambled up to the blue corner with the stool for his fighter to sit on and the water bucket and sponge to cool him off. Salsa breathed hard, his back against the corner, his hands in the bright-red boxing gloves hanging down by his thighs. Charlie talked rapidly as he sponged and Salsa drank from the water bottle, listening to his trainer.

"Whew!" Lauren sighed. "I wouldn't exactly call this a day at the beach."

"Elbows in! Chin down!" Flynn saw the kid tighten up his form as if he had heard the advice. "Don't forget your ABCs," Flynn muttered, "he won't land no more body blows." The "boxing coach" looked at Lauren. "So now, ace, what's your call, if you can be objective?"

She shook her head. "Too close—for me at least. Really tough."

An aggressive Chopsticks applied pressure as the second round began... cutting off the ring, leaving Salsa with precious little room to dance out of reach. Then Chopsticks barreled in with a big left hook, but Salsa's feet saved him. Sidestepping Chopsticks' big one, he delivered a dynamite combination that left the Cho puffing on the ropes.

"Beautiful!"

"When he misses make him *pay!*"

The final two-minute round was a cliff-hanger. As the seconds waned, the three judges scribbled notes furiously. In the end they had only a little less trouble with the bout than Lauren did—calling Salsa the winner in a split decision.

The cops roared their approval. Carmel produced a pair of maracas and she and Tina shook up a storm. Salsa and Brooklyn Charlie yelled to Flynn to come to the ring, and the two coaches took turns shooting victory pictures of each other with the budding champ.

"Pretty neat work, pal!" Flynn said as he gave Salsa a hug.

Salsa thanked both of his trainers. *"You* got me started," he told Flynn.

"Well, don't you stop," Flynn answered, "you got a chance to make a mark with this, you know. We sure are proud of you." When he saw how pleased the kid looked, the thought of Sean flickered in Flynn's mind and his eyes stung.

"Lieutenant A-Train, you ain't leavin' yet, are you?" Salsa asked as the three climbed down from the ring.

"We'll wait for you—Lauren wants to shake hands with da winnah."

When they met in the hallway, Salsa was all snazzed up, toting his gear in a big black duffel. Carmel frowned at the welt coming out under Salsa's left eye, but otherwise she was in seventh heaven, beaming at her brother and everybody else.

"Congratulations, star!" Lauren said to him. "I guess we'll be going to see you at the Garden one of these days."

"That's up to my manager," Salsa joked, "he's gotta work all that out."

Everybody laughed and started toward the stairs. "Hold on," Salsa said under his breath to Flynn, "I got somethin' to tell you."

Lauren went on chatting with Brooklyn Charlie as Flynn and Salsa fell behind. Salsa frowned. "It's about that fat guy you been lookin' for all this time—wanted in the newsdealer shootin', right?"

"Gordo?"

"Same one Monte was makin' me look for, but he never told me why."

"Yeah."

"Well, I guess Monte must've found out where he was but didn't say nothin' to me. By the time I heard, it was too late. Somebody hit him."

"Where'd you hear that?"

"The boss sent me up to the Bronx yesterday, special—handed me this heavy mother of a package himself. Turned out to be a payment: The guy must've got ten grand. He opens it and hands me a big tip—braggin' how he did the job."

Flynn asked for the hit man's description and Salsa told him about Mr. Clean. He pulled a piece of paper out of the zipper pocket on his duffel bag. "I got the address where he was if you wanna look him up. It's real shit building—you need a flashlight."

Flynn thanked him and put the paper in his inside jacket pocket.

"Sorry," Salsa said as they went up the stairs.

"You couldn't help it," Flynn told him. "Thanks for tellin' me."

Everybody said good-bye in front of the church and Salsa's Jeep drove away up Park Avenue.

Lauren looked at Flynn. "Something happened that wasn't as nice as Salsa winning his fight," she speculated.

"Let's go have dinner and raise a glass to the winner, okay? The other stuff can wait."

"Okay."

Flynn snagged a taxi before they had even decided where to go. "Downtown," he told the driver, "we'll give you the details in a minute."

"Where to?" he asked Lauren.

"Have you ever had onion rings at the Moondance Diner?"

"Are you kidding?"

"They're the best in the city and the chili's good, too. Just what I crave after the fights. If we can't get a cab home, the subway's right there."

"Hey, these are the real thing," Flynn said when the waiter brought the hill of homemade onion rings to their booth.

Lauren munched contentedly. "Here's to you and Charlie," she said, "you obviously put a lot into Salsa."

"We're both hopin' he'll get enough out of the sport to give him another career option. A legal one. I guess I told you—he works for Viera. Well, he's a big success at it—been 'promoted' and everything. Any day now, he'll be makin' more than I do—and he's *nineteen years old.*"

"It's amazing you even got this far with him against that kind of competition. You must give him something he needs."

"Viera gives him a chance to get rich."

"But if he didn't need something besides that, he wouldn't have the bond with you that he has. Here's my guess: He wants what Viera has—but he wants to be *like* you."

"He's on the fence, that's for sure, however he got there. Which way he'll go is anybody's guess. Keep your fingers crossed."

"You were going to tell me some 'other stuff' later...?"

He looked as if he was sorry she'd brought it up, but he said, "Salsa heard that our witness against Viera in the double homicide—the guy who escaped from court—is dead. Viera had him hit.

Some Christmas present for the men who've been sittin' on this mutt since before Thanksgivin', even on their own time."

"Sitting on him?"

Waiting around in parked cars tour after tour, hoping he'll show up at one location or another. And if he's out of the picture, that's it for the famous hundred percent."

"I apologize for what I said about it," she interrupted, "that's not what I really feel."

He reached for her hand. "Okay."

Their waiter appeared. "How ya doin', folks? Need anything?"

"We're fine," Flynn said. The waiter glanced at their not-quite-empty plates and retreated.

Lauren twined her fingers with his. "The hundred percent, you were saying?"

"That it's not the main event. The main event is Viera, and who knows when we'll get another shot at that jackal. That's by far the worst part of this news." His hand tightened on hers. "For you, too."

"For me?"

"As long as he's in business, you need a bodyguard—and I flunked that one, remember?"

"But you said I still have a lover, remember? And that's what I want. Grown-ups don't have to hide behind somebody. Even female grown-ups—they can take reasonable precautions on their own."

"When you put it that way, it sounds kind of—basic." He looked surprised. "But not for cops. That's not the way we see it. If you can't be protective, what's left?"

"What's left may be about as romantic as an onion ring." She held one up to her eye like a monocle and looked at him through it, making him laugh. "Maybe I'm kinky, but what turns me on about Andy Flynn is he's somebody who's always trying to figure out stuff."

"Figure out people. That's what eighty, ninety percent of it is. And don't tell anybody I said so, but a lot of the time it don't come out as black-and-white as a cop would like."

"If it did, it wouldn't be real. Life-and-death is dramatic—*bam!*" She imitated an explosion with her hands. "But so are the day-by-day things: small but—telling."

"Yeah, they are. But I don't see—"

"Look, it's not the war stories—or even the tall stories. It's the teller I like."

Only *like?* he thought. Maybe there was something more than that in her eyes. Or was he fooling himself, seeing what he wanted to?

"There's a lot more to that guy than just a bodyguard," she said. "If you ask me, the princess-in-the-tower type would bore him to tears before he had time to turn around."

Rattled as he was by their conversation, Flynn could tell his reply was important to her. The trouble was, he didn't know what to say. Luckily, the waiter reappeared. Lauren smiled brightly. "Apple pie, please, with a scoop of vanilla."

"And for you, sir?"

"Coffee, please."

"I'll just get these out of your way, then?" The waiter reached for the plates.

"Okay," Flynn said, "thanks." He fiddled with his tonic-water glass till the waiter finally left with the dishes. Then he looked at Lauren and smiled the half-smile, hoping his confusion wouldn't turn her off. "I guess this is another example of 'not just black-and-white.'"

"What is?"

"Well—us. I don't know what the former bodyguard *does* with the ex-princess in the tower."

"Maybe the same thing she does with him: plays it by ear?"

The waiter came with the apple pie and ice cream and the coffee. "I brought an extra plate."

"Great," Flynn said. "When you get a chance, we'd like the check, too."

Lauren divvied up the pie.

"Does it matter if the ex-princess is still holed up in that tower?" he said, his fork poised. "Can they start anyway?"

She shrugged. "Only her body is still up there; in her head she's out of the tower. That's what matters."

"There's one other thing." He grinned at her. "Can they find a cab or will they take the train?"

Tuesday morning, December 24, 1985

An IRISH LUCK Baggie lay on the Formica-top table in the luncheonette booth, a token of frustration. Pastore had found the Baggie lying on the floor of the wrecked apartment at the address that Salsa had given Flynn. The Baggie—unused and in mint condition—suggested that someone connected with Viera's organization had recently been in the Bronx apartment. But by the time Flynn, Taylor, and Pastore bashed their way in, the place was empty. The three consoled themselves with coffee in the luncheonette just off the Grand Concourse. Taylor got downright sentimental about the boomerangs in the pattern of the Formica and made everybody promise not to tell O'Levy that he had missed a real fifties spot.

Flynn stood up, pointing at the Baggie. "Somebody's gonna try and buy a couple of grams off you, Ronnie."

Pastore blushed and laughed. "Fifty-five degrees on Christmas Eve!" He passed a paper napkin over his damp forehead and wrapped another one around the Baggie.

"I'm gonna reach out for Irene Defina," Flynn said, "just in case she's workin' today. If Gordo is somewhere in the morgue system, she'll know it."

The pay phone in the rear of the luncheonette looked about the same vintage as the rest of the place. Flynn slid into the old wooden phone booth with its glass-paneled folding door and rotary dial phone. He deposited a quarter and cranked out the number of the morgue detective's office. Busy. Busy. Busy again... By the time he got through, his dialing finger was numb.

"Don't tell me *you* got a DOA down here," Defina said when she heard his "Merry Christmas."

"Not a victim. I'm lookin' for a perp and a witness rolled into one—and I *mean* rolled. This guy's a tub. Remember the homicide suspect who waltzed outta court back in October—switched IDs with a goddamn shoplifter?"

"I wish I could forget."

"We heard he got hit—which is not exactly good news. He's the only mutt in New York with a motive to testify against the Two-nine's numero uno most-wanted. We been tryin' to nail this particular creep since I been with the squad. The thing is, we ain't seen the witness's body yet—maybe there's still hope."

"You want me to check through the paperwork on the recent DOAs? When did they say he got hit?"

"Sometime in the past week. In the Bronx, maybe. His name is Juan-Emanuel Concepción—street name Gordo, 'cause he's about five eight, two oh five."

"Got it. Can ya bear with me, though? It's busy season down here. What a mess!"

"When could you get back to me?"

"This afternoon maybe I can raise someone in the Bronx and see what the story is—will you be in the squad?"

"I sure hope so. I've had about enough action for 1985, I swear."

"Uh-huh," Defina said, "talk to you later."

Late afternoon, Tuesday, December 24, 1985

"Autumn Leaves" wasn't Viera's idea of Latin excitement, but Dave Melendez had made a Latin-market chartbuster out of the tune, and Viera had allowed himself to be convinced that Melendez would be a big draw for Christmas Eve at the Tabu. But now Viera regretted his decision, he told Monte as he stacked up the tape boxes in front of him.

"I can think of worse problems," Monte said.

"So can I," Viera answered. "El Grande called three times today. He's decided to send Miguelito back up here to hit a big narc, but he knows Miguelito will never make it through Customs."

"Right. If they get a blip on their computer, he's fucked. But El Grande must have ten other guys he can send and Miguelito can just stay home and relax for the holidays."

"Miguelito the pet son-in-law wants to come to New York for Christmas—period. So we gotta get rid of that worthless porter who squealed. Unless the cops can make a case against Miguelito, they can't hold him. We'll get Salsa to find out where Flynn put the porter."

"Lousy timing," Monte said. "Who's gonna organize the orders if Salsa is workin' on something else? He's better at this detail stuff than anybody in the place. We can't afford a backlog. Everybody and his brother wants to have a white Christmas; we got record-breaking orders."

"If we don't keep El Grande happy, a lot of our customers ain't gonna have a happy New Year after their white Christmas. Which could put a crimp in our festivities, too. Tell Ramón to send Salsa in here. And tell him I need a drink."

When Salsa stepped into the office carrying the tray of drinks, Viera thanked him in a hearty voice; Viera looked approvingly at Salsa's new yellow sweater. He raised his glass, "A white Christmas to all and plenty of Irish Luck in the New Year!"

Salsa joined the toast, holding up his bottle of Mexican beer. He didn't sit down until Viera told him to.

"I got a job for you." Viera leaned across the black marble

slab. "You're the only person who can do it and do it right. I know you're busy but this is urgent and I'm counting on you."

"I'll take care of it," Salsa said.

"Good." Viera sat back and folded his arms. He looked over at Monte, who folded his arms, too.

"That little porter who snitched to the cops about the guy who got shot on Saturday night of the Eldorado date...?"

Salsa nodded.

"We gotta get in touch with the porter. Find out where the cops took him. Exactly where—address, apartment, whatever we need to send somebody to... see him. Talk to those cop friends of yours and get the information. Pronto! That clear?" Viera stacked up all the tape boxes in front of him and knocked them down on the marble again.

Looking as if he was trying not to look worried, Salsa said it was clear.

"Vaya con Dios!"

Salsa went back downstairs to the order room that most of the Tabu employees didn't even know existed. Monte didn't trust very many people to work with the material. Salsa knew he was the best organizer-man Irish Luck had ever had. He usually liked these sort-and-label jobs; he'd just listen to the music coming through his phones and the work went fast. But now he couldn't concentrate. Irish and Monte had not reminded him that he was on trial, but they didn't need to.

Because Salsa was so good at this organizing stuff, they hadn't taken him apart for telling Flynn about the gun. But even so, Salsa knew that to Viera, it was the secret-secret stuff, not the organizing, that mattered. Salsa had the kilo packs and the pound packs sorted and ready to go into shopping bags labeled by street. He started labeling the shopping bags.

If he wanted Viera to keep promoting him so that in time he himself could live a Viera-type life, information would get him there. Salsa got a sizzle out of giving Flynn tips and locking up killers. Just like he got a charge out of the boxing that Flynn had put him on to. Why Flynn and Brooklyn Charlie took an interest in him, he wasn't sure, but he admired them. However, that wasn't enough—they couldn't take Salsa where he wanted to go. Only Viera could do that. If Salsa got the information about the porter and told Viera, that would be bad for Flynn and Nieves.... Salsa set about piling the packs of coke powder in the big brown bags.

Tomorrow afternoon, he'd be seeing Flynn; he better have this figured out by then.

Late afternoon, Wednesday, December 25, 1985

"Feliz Navidad!" Carmel opened the door to her mother's apartment for Flynn. She was the soul of Christmas in her green blouse, holly earrings, and nail polish the exact color of the holly berries.

"Y tu también," Flynn kissed her on the cheek.

"Mami had to stay in the store, she's very sorry," Carmel said. "Come in, give me your coat." She raised her voice. "Salsa—the lieutenant is here."

Salsa had his Walkman on with the earphones around the turtleneck of his electric-blue sweater. He and Flynn shook hands and hugged.

"Hey, champ—you ain't at the gym? What's the story?" Flynn teased. "And don't tell me it's closed today."

"I did my roadwork anyway," Salsa bragged. "How about some eggnog?"

"I like it without the rum."

"You got it." He went to the kitchen and came back with a glassful of frothy eggnog for Flynn.

"Terrific." Flynn sat on the chair at right angles to the couch where the brother and sister sat.

Carmel twinkled. "Santa brought you a new sweater, right, Lieutenant Flynn? Gray—matches your eyes. You could put this on, too." She held out a flat Christmas-wrapped box. "You're all set for winter."

"Hey, I was just tellin' myself what a nice Christmas this is. The best in years. Thanks for thinkin' of me."

"Salsa picked it," she said.

Flynn recognized the name on the box, a classy store on Columbus Avenue where he would never have thought of buying a thing. The wool plaid of the muffler had gray, navy blue, green, and white and a little yellow. "This is really nice," he said. "Between you guys and Lauren, my wardrobe is gettin' refreshed. I guess maybe it was time. Thanks a lot."

Flynn felt the soft wool, remembering the Christmas when Sean was nine years old—the last time the brothers had given each other a present. The soft material felt good. At the same time, though, Flynn held in his hand a little piece of Salsa's success in

Irish Viera's organization. Some things were coming out as Flynn would have hoped, but not others. He admired the muffler again, smiling at Carmel and Salsa, not finding much more to say.

Salsa saved him. "What about that Lauren? How's she doin'?"

Flynn rallied. "Great. We went to St. Patty's for midnight mass. *Very* nice. By the way," he teased Carmel, "I believe Brooklyn Charlie has been sighted simonizin' that Daytona of his, gettin' set for a trip to Washington Heights. Is that what you heard, Salsa?"

"Sí, señor."

"What about you, Carmel?"

"Carmel is goin' to the store to help Mami before Mami fall off her feet, that's all I know." She rushed out of the room and came back with her coat. *"Te veo más tarde."* She waved from the doorway. "Bye!"

"Well!" Flynn said, and he and Salsa laughed for a good minute.

"You wanna ride downtown," Salsa asked, "or you wanna take the *A* train?"

Flynn knew Salsa must be headed for the Tabu. "I'll take a lift to Nine-six Street—how's that?" From there he would ride down to Lauren's.

"Let's go." Salsa put on a leather bomber jacket that was new but was supposed to look old.

Before Flynn put on his trench coat, he wrapped the new muffler around his neck.

The wind whistled past Salsa's yellow Jeep, making conversation a problem except when he stopped for a light. Salsa chose Riverside Drive because it had lights, instead of the parkway. Whenever he stopped, Salsa asked another question. He started with "How's Detective Taylor?" After that he asked about the old railroad tunnel that had been in the news when Flynn and the squad tracked down the ballet murderer.

Flynn answered the questions and added, "I didn't have no choice about that tunnel, but do me a favor and stay outta there, okay? It ain't no tourist attraction."

"Don't worry"—Salsa laughed—"I got nothin' to do in the tunnel. Just curious. What about that hit man up in the Bronx? How'd that go?"

"We missed him." Flynn smiled a funny little smile that Salsa had seen before. "By the time we got there, he was gone."

"I guess if you're in that kind of work, you gotta keep movin'," Salsa said.

"That's it," Flynn said, "keep runnin'. Can't hide forever, though."

At the next light, Salsa said, "Can a good guy hide forever? Sometimes the cops hide witnesses, don't they?"

"To protect them, if they need it."

"Where do they put 'em? Out of town?"

"Out of reach. Sometimes you don't have to go real far to do that. Maybe just a hotel across town. All depends on the particular person and the case." Flynn looked over at Salsa and gave him that little smile again. He didn't ask why Salsa wanted to know.

They had stopped by the big church at 122nd Street. The light changed. Salsa figured he would only have a couple more chances to ask. That Nieves was a sad little guy. But he was nothing to Salsa—only to Flynn's work. How important? Salsa couldn't tell. If Salsa came back to Viera without the information, that would be important, all right. But if Salsa asked about Nieves himself—right away Flynn would know why. It was better for everybody if Salsa could keep the cop friendly.

At the next light, Flynn asked if Salsa had heard anything from Chopsticks Cho. "If I was you," Flynn teased, "I'd watch my step in Chinatown."

Salsa laughed but he was still thinking about the porter, hoping he was right not to push it.

When they stopped at Ninety-sixth Street, Flynn stayed in his seat. "You okay, champ? Got the Christmas willies?"

"Everything's cool."

Flynn opened the door and climbed out of the Jeep. The wind blasted up Broadway and into the Jeep. *"Te veo,"* Salsa called, his voice going thin.

The wind blew Flynn's black hair around as he waved goodbye. He wrapped his muffler closer. "Thanks again for the present," he yelled, and banged shut the Jeep's door.

With a blast of his crazy horn, Salsa drove off to work.

Early Friday morning, December 27, 1985

Viera wasn't sitting behind the black marble; he walked back and forth restlessly across the office. Salsa had never seen him do that. Monte sat in one of the leather chairs, cleaning his nails with an Irish Luck knife. Salsa thought about all the deliveries still waiting to be made and it was already two in the morning; maybe the boss would get this over with quick. Salsa had a suggestion planned—maybe the boss would go with it. If he could have asked Flynn, that would have been better.

"Where you been?" Viera asked Salsa. "I been waiting for you to come and tell me where we gotta go to find the porter."

"Makin' deliveries, boss." To help make the point, he had one of the big brown bags by his side. "I still got plenty backed up—all of Central Park West, yet. We gotta keep the customers happy."

"We also gotta keep El Grande happy—or there won't *be* any customers. What about the porter?"

"He's in a hotel on the other side of town."

"Good," Monte said, "we could go anywhere, but this makes it easier."

"What hotel?" Viera asked.

"Not like the Waldorf, a smaller one."

"Yeah?"

Salsa picked up the big brown bag. "I ain't got the exact name but as soon as I get my other work done, I'll make a search myself. I can find it easy."

"Your fuckin' cop buddy let you down!"

"I hadda be careful about askin' for complete details. If he gets suspicious, I can't never ask him nothin' again. I gotta build up slowly, then he'll trust me."

"He'll trust your fuckin' money. You just lay it on the line."

"Then he'd have to arrest me for tryin' to bribe a cop. It ain't worthwile—he wouldn't go for it an' I'd go to Rikers for nothin'."

"Even if he wouldn't, his men sure would," Monte objected.

"Not the ones I know," Salsa said, "and that's who I'd be talkin' to."

Viera went and sat behind the marble. "*Bad* news. Puts us in a tight spot with El Grande. I'm gonna try and wiggle out of this one, but it makes us look bad, all right. I told you I was countin' on you to produce"—he fixed his eyes on Salsa—"but you didn't."

Maybe I should have asked after all, Salsa thought. "I could start the hotel search now," he said, "and do these deliveries later on."

Viera gave him a cold look. "No. Make the deliveries—and make them in a hurry. But before you go, sit down with Monte. He's gonna give you one more job to do. And *this* time you better come through."

Round one for the gun, Salsa thought; round two for the porter. He had managed to stay in the fight. When the bell rang this time, he knew he stood to lose his job . . . or worse.

Early afternoon, Friday, December 27, 1985

Vinnie Falcone was totally pissed. He was so fucking mad he couldn't see straight. He should have never left Bensonhurst, let alone come all the way to some bodega in Red Hook to cop a buy off a fucking spic. The fatass spic actually stiffed him, which came as such a shock that Vinnie never even pulled his gun. He was going to have to go back to Bensonhurst with no coke and broke, too—bad enough—but then the Mustang ran out of gas. Vinnie didn't have no plastic on him; not even a lousy subway token.

What the fuck was he going to do for cash? He had a choice: sell his gun, or use it. Naturally, he used it; did a mugging in daylight. Next thing he knew, he was in some godforsaken station house halfway to the city. He called his lawyer and the son of a bitch said he'd be over "later."

When the detective threw Vinnie in the cell, he said, "Take a nap—there's two ahead of you." The detective was a sharp dresser, Vinnie noticed—dark shirt, light tie, light coat. Almost as sharp as Vinnie himself.

Vinnie had a clear view through the wire-mesh cell into the squad office; he saw a uniform cop walk in with a deli bag and hand it to the detective. "Two ahead of you" my ass. The detective was eating his fucking lunch while Vinnie sat in a cell and burned. He kept racking his brain for some information to trade for a lower charge—any charge that would get him less than seven years in the clink. Short of turning in his uncle the fence, he couldn't come up with a thing.

Finally, the detective unlocked the cell and walked Vinnie back through the main room toward a smaller office. The phone rang and another detective said, "For you, Mitch."

The sharp dresser handcuffed Vinnie to a long wooden bench. "Stay right here," he said.

More waiting. Where the fuck was the lawyer? Vinnie twisted around to look at the stuff taped on the wall behind him. That was when he saw the Wanted poster. At first he couldn't believe his eyes. That fucking fatass spic who stiffed him: Gordo. "Juan-Emanuel Concepción." Wanted for homicide! No shit.

Vinnie sighed with relief and relaxed on the bench. Beautiful. Two birds with one stone. He would tip the detective to Gordo—a fuckin' *homicide* suspect—and that would not only reduce Vinnie's charge all the way to a misdemeanor, it would fix Gordo's fat ass for stiffing him. What a fucking break!

Mitch and the other detective sat him down in the small office. "Like I told you before, Vinnie," Mitch said, "you got the right to remain silent till your attorney shows up."

"Nah—I got some good news for you, Detective."

"That'll be nice for a change." Mitch looked surprised, all right. "In fact, I'm not sure my heart can take it. So we better start with the bad news that *I* got for you. To begin with, four different witnesses came forward on the street this morning, sayin' they saw you do an armed robbery on Columbia Street, around the corner from the Union Street Citibank."

Mitch shuffled some papers and said to the other detective, who wasn't a sharp dresser at all, "Did you see where I put that thing, Scotty?"

Scotty pointed to a pad with handwriting on it. "Ain't that it?"

"Oh, yeah. Thanks." Mitch read off the pad what Vinnie had to admit was a pretty fair description of what went down.

Then Mitch said, "In addition, within half an hour of the crime, when the cops was bookin' you downstairs in this station house, two of them witnesses was here and positively identified you as the perpetrator of that same armed robbery. In other words, Vinnie—by the way, I got your sheet right here—since you ain't exactly a first offender, you are lookin' at quite a stretch upstate. You know that."

"I told ya, Detective, I got some good news for ya—an' for me. So willya please lemme give it to ya?"

The two detectives looked at each other and shrugged. Scotty said, "Why not, he asked nice an' polite."

So Vinnie said he could tell the detectives how to find a homicide suspect, the one on the Wanted poster right outside the office door. "He's a sittin' duck—all ya gotta do is pick him off and you're a hero."

"Hm," Mitch said.

Scotty went out and brought back three posters and stuck them in Vinnie's face. "Which one?"

Vinnie showed him Gordo's fat mug. Scotty took the poster over to the desk and showed Mitch.

Mitch smoothed the sheet of paper, stared down at it, and yawned a big yawn. "This mutt's wanted in the *city*. The Two-nine no less; fuckin' hotshots over there got homicide collars up the ying-yang. No good, Vincent. You gotta gimme a Brooklyn perp, man."

Vinnie's uncle popped into his head again, but before he had a chance to decide, the detective said, "Better yet, *South* Brooklyn—from this precinct right here. We got a terrific selection of uncleared homicides." He stood up. "No rush—look over your little black book or whatever. Maybe by the time your attorney comes, you'll think of somebody." He walked Vinnie back to the cell and locked him in.

"See you next year!" Lauren's colleagues had disappeared out the door at lunchtime. Lauren herself was winding down, enjoying the unusual quiet before the holiday weekend. Her desk was as clear as it ever got, her "priority" list in decent shape. Not taking work home, she enjoyed the novelty of locking away her briefcase in the cabinet.

Along with her view of the majestic courthouses, the privilege of a windowed office meant that she could look out and make an informed decision about whether or not to carry an umbrella. Earlier, it had snowed a little; now it was sort of misting. Not too cold. She looked forward to the walk to Liberty Vistas—she had yet to decide on the route for today; she had many streets still to explore. Good exercise, too. Most pedestrians had their umbrellas up—might as well take hers; nothing else to carry except her shoulder bag. Feeling really free—no demands on her, no plans—she slipped into the shiny black raincoat, closed her door behind her, and took the elevator to the street.

Monte had said last night that Salsa would do "that" job today. That was all he said. Salsa put on sneakers and comfortable clothes. "You better be able to run," Monte had just told him on the phone. "Come in right now, with the Jeep." He still didn't say what this was all about. Monte was usually asleep this early in the afternoon. Salsa left the gun behind; he figured if he needed it, Monte would've said so.

He pulled up to the back door of the Tabu and Monte came right out.

He came to the driver's side. All he said was, "Get over," and took Salsa's seat. All the way down the West Side Highway, Monte didn't say a word, just drove.

Till now, nobody had driven Salsa's Jeep but Salsa. He stared out into the mist on the river, watching the few sea gulls fly around. Monte went crosstown on Chambers Street. They parked on a quiet street, in sight of the huge building with the archway you could drive a car through.

"You're gonna do the job with this." Monte handed him a

switchblade. "When the person comes, I'll tell you. First you get her money, then you cut her. You gotta take her out—DOA. Irish don't want her goin' anywhere after this but the cemetery."

Salsa felt the smooth shape of the knife, heavy in his hand. He never really looked at it. A blond woman in a black raincoat came around the corner toward them.

"That's her."

The woman shut her umbrella. *Dios.* Salsa realized he knew the face—*Lauren,* Lieutenant Flynn's girl.

"I'm gonna follow you," Monte growled. "This job you're gonna *do.* No more second chances."

"I ain't never killed nobody"—Salsa swallowed his panic, thinking fast—"but *I* ain't scared." He gave a cold little laugh. "I been hangin' with *you* long enough to know the score, ain't I?" He stared straight at Monte with a look copied from Monte himself. "No way do I do it where there's people. I just keep her goin' till I see the best place." He shoved the switchblade into his pants pocket as if it were an old friend. "I can handle this job, no fuckin' problem at all. You want it done right, don't make me"—he narrowed his eyes—*"nervous.* All *you* gotta do is gimme enough time and keep back. Way back." He clenched his jaw, forcing the words through his teeth: "Don't fuck it up and blame me!"

Abruptly, Salsa turned his back on Monte and opened the Jeep door. He leaned forward, about to jump out—then pulled back and carefully tightened up his shoelaces. The block looked almost empty, but it was too soon to do anything—Monte was right there. Salsa stalled with the shoelaces till Lauren got near the end of the block.

"Don't you fuckin' lose her!" Monte snarled as Salsa leaped out.

He moved fast till he was about a half block behind Lauren. Then he saw her take a left, cross Chambers Street, and walk along the park. She neared the subway entrance—Salsa wished she would disappear down the steps but she kept walking downtown. She passed one old-fashioned building, then another, and cut across the park area, not rushing; he hoped for crowds to come out of nowhere and get in his way. Instead, there was hardly anybody in this park. He walked quicker again, catching up as she reached the street on the far side. He felt that she knew somebody was following her but she didn't try to look. He didn't look for Monte, either.

She stood waiting to cross the wide street; he got close enough almost to touch her.

"Lauren, *don't turn around.* It's me, Salsa. Speed up a little—like you're afraid to look back. Go where I tell you, do what I say. Please!"

He crossed behind her, walking slower, mist in his face, dropping back a couple of feet. The minute they got across he spotted the place. "Look! On your right—see that alley, run for it!" Near the west end of the alley, he dashed up to her, waving the knife, "Gimme that bag!" He grabbed at it. "Fight me, grab it back! Throw it at me *hard.* RUN!"

Running after her, he ducked to pick up the bag, missed it on purpose, and made another pass—enough time for her to make it out of there into a busy street. He wheeled and ran for his life.

Where was Monte? Gone! Running back the other way, Salsa turned to scan the length of the alley. Nothing moved. He heard nobody, not a sound in the mist. Hope made his heart skip; his sneakers took him flying down the alley past the blank backs of buildings. He heard nothing until a sudden fearful thump between his shoulder blades, a high-pitched pain, and then a deafening crash, the side of his face hitting the pavement. Dark silence.

Monte stepped around the trickle of blood to a trash can full of computer printouts and tore off a fistful of the computer sheets. He wrapped the knife in some of the damp sheets. The rest of the papers fell to the ground near where Salsa lay. Monte made sure no one saw him leave the alley.

Midnight, December 27, 1985

O'Brien's Law: Stay late to catch up on your paperwork—the phone will ring off the hook. Never fails, not even at one in the morning. Instead of going right home after the night tour, Obie planned to type up a few odds and ends. Might as well clean the stuff up and start fresh in the new year. Betty Dominic was long gone, of course; O'Levy and the B Team were in the field and Taylor had gone with them, so Obie was alone.

Right on cue: ring... ring...

The caller said he was Fleming from the Seven-four squad. Fleming sounded like he was in a hurry to get home. "We got an armed-robbery collar here, career criminal—claims to know the location of your homicide perp on the Wanted flyer. Uh, 'Concepción'?" Obie just listened, wondering if the detective was putting him on.

"This guy's story could be for real, then again..." Fleming covered the mouthpiece. When he came back, he said, "Look, his defense attorney just walked in, so—"

"Hey, thanks for reachin' out." Obie almost did a dance. "My squad commander should be here any second." He checked the time. Where the hell was Flynn? "Would you mind puttin' the attorney on so I can set somethin' up? Maybe we'll come by you instead of goin' to Central Booking."

After talking to the lawyer, Obie had trouble keeping his mind on his typing. Finally, the doors flew open and Flynn strode in.

"Wait till you hear this," Obie said before Flynn even had his trench coat off. Obie talked fast; at the end he said, "The defense lawyer was playin' it cute—said he'd wait around 'a few more minutes' for you to get back to him."

Flynn's finger was already on the phone buttons. "Look at the log and see where O'Levy went."

O'Levy, his partner, and Taylor had taken the Chrysler to Colonel Sanders on 125th Street. When Obie drove Flynn up to meet them, O'Levy almost did a dance, too. The Chrysler set a course for South Brooklyn; Obie headed back to the squad to finish his typing.

He sat down at the desk and thought of calling Maureen but decided she was already asleep. He promised himself he would leave soon—half an hour.

Ring... ring...

The caller this time was Flynn's girlfriend, Lauren. Obie had never talked to her before, but he had the feeling Flynn's taste in women had improved since his marriage ended.

"Lieutenant Flynn is out in the field—I think he went to Brooklyn," Obie told her. "Can I leave him a message?"

"Detective O'Brien, something really odd happened—I thought Andy would want to know because—"

"Well, if you want to share it with me, I'll be sure to let him know. What happened?"

"This is very hard to explain. I was leaving my office today and someone started following me. I knew it but I didn't look back; I thought I would play dumb and lose him. All of a sudden I hear him say 'just keep going—it's Salsa.'"

"Salsa? That kid boxer?" There could be plenty of Chinos or Ricos, but Obie doubted there could be more than one Salsa.

"That's right," Lauren said. "Andy took me to see him box this week. Anyway, Salsa *pretended* to mug me and then ran away. It was like—it wasn't his idea; he had to make believe. He didn't hurt me at all but—"

"You're sure you're all right? Absolutely sure?"

"Fine. Just—mystified. And the more I thought about it, the more I thought Andy should know."

"He'll know, don't worry. And he'll probably call you when he gets back. It could be late though. What's the number where you're at?"

She gave it to him. "Thanks, Detective O'Brien. I hope I'll get a chance to meet you one of these days."

"Good night. Don't worry, I'm writing down the whole story for Lieutenant Flynn and I'll put it on his desk before I do anything else."

Something did seem strange, at the very least, about the incident, but Obie couldn't quite see it as urgent. Not so that he would interrupt Flynn's investigation in Brooklyn. He left a typewritten note on Flynn's desk, and on the outside of the swinging door he taped a note in block letters that said, *Lieut. Flynn—look on yr desk.* Then he put away his reports and left.

Early morning, Saturday, December 28, 1985

The suspect from Bensonhurst had a lawyer who was obviously giving the squad in Red Hook a lot of grief. A royal pain. The suspect told Flynn he couldn't remember the "dumb spic name" of the bodega where Gordo did business, but when the lawyer finally gave the signal, his client coughed up a location. Since the suspect said it was an all-night place, Flynn and the others drove around the unfamiliar streets in the cold, damp night till they found it.

"We gotta be nuts," O'Levy's partner said, and Flynn had to admit he was right. At 0230 hours in this weather, not even beer was moving at the bodega called El Anzuelo. If some desperate cokehead did venture out, he sure wouldn't find comfort-loving Gordo standing on the corner waiting to sell him a tin.

The detectives started back to Manhattan, just as a cutting sleet began to fall. When Flynn parked the Chrysler in the lot behind the precinct, he was ready to call it a night. On the way upstairs to sign the log, he even thought about crashing in the dorm instead of going home. He pulled Obie's note off the swinging door and went to his desk.

Taylor signed out, not unhappy with another ten hours' overtime courtesy of that Gordo shithead, and looked over at Flynn. "Want a ride somewhere?"

"Look at this." Flynn held out Obie's typed message about Salsa and Lauren.

Taylor read it through. "Looks like Lauren is okay but what kinda weirdo stunt . . . ?"

"It don't make any sense. That's what bothers me. I think it's too late to call Lauren, though."

"The note says to call her."

"Yeah, but it's after three. I guess I'll take that ride." They went down to the street and got in the Lincoln.

"The tape deck's fucked up," Taylor said. "That must be why nobody tries to rip it off." He flipped on the radio, drove around the block, and started down Columbus Avenue. The streets were empty but slick with sleet. Taylor paid more attention than usual to his driving. He noticed that the radio wasn't doing much better than the tape deck.

Flynn reached over and twisted the knob. "Ten-ten WINS, it's three-twenty . . ."

Taylor went back to thinking about the road and his balding front tires; he was in no hurry to hear any news.

"Jess—they found a DOA tonight—in an alley down below City Hall," Flynn said. "Unidentified Hispanic youth, stab wounds in the back."

"Kinda different for that part of town. Down there it's usually muggers in the office rest rooms, stuff like that. Those streets are so deserted at night. . . . Well, I guess Sanitation must've found the body." He looked sideways at Flynn. "Okay, I know what you're thinkin', but—"

"Maybe I will call Lauren."

They were entering Columbus Circle. "You got a few phones on Five-seven Street, I think," Taylor said.

"Hope one of 'em is working."

"It's a disaster out there. I know a coffee shop—"

"That's okay, a little wetness'll wake me up."

"You look plenty awake to me." *Worried* was what Flynn looked. Taylor stopped at Fifty-seventh and Seventh, but the place he was thinking of was closed.

Flynn got out and hurried to the nearest pay phone; Taylor

saw millions of needles of sleet come slanting out of the sky. Lauren must be sound asleep—Flynn wasn't talking yet. When he came back to the car, he said, "Salsa was wearin' a sweatshirt from the gym; dark pants, she thinks." He fished in his trench coat pockets.

"Whaddaya need," Taylor asked, "more quarters?"

"I got a quarter—maybe some more small change in case I gotta feed it while I wait."

"You're gonna stand around in that mess and *wait?* For who?"

"Whoever's at the morgue. Joe Mahoney, I hope."

Taylor sighed and dug up some change.

For lack of anything better to do while Flynn was out at the pay phone again, Taylor fiddled with the tape deck. Every time he looked out through the busy windshield wipers, it seemed like Flynn was putting in another coin. Just waiting, not talking, he stayed out there a good fifteen minutes. Taylor swore at the tape deck. He looked out again in time to see Flynn hang up and trudge toward the car, head down. Taylor reached back behind the front seat for a roll of paper towels that was supposed to be there, on the floor. He managed to grab it and hand it to Flynn when he got in.

"Thanks," was all Flynn said for a while. He blotted the moisture from his hands, face, and hair.

Taylor put the Lincoln in gear, swung east to Second Avenue, and kept going south.

"Are you positive?" Taylor finally asked.

"It ain't likely to be some other Spanish kid wearing a Clinton Boxing Club sweatshirt right about where Salsa 'mugged' Lauren. Too much of a coincidence."

"Jeez," Mahoney said, "I was off Christmas week. I was supposed to take this week instead—I wish I did. I feel bad for you, Andy."

"Thanks. I'm lucky you're here."

"You wanna go over to the lab right now?" If he could have put it off somehow, he clearly would have.

"Might as well. You remember Jesse Taylor? I been workin' with him since Harlem."

After Taylor and Mahoney shook hands, there was nothing left to do but follow Mahoney to the lab area.

The essential last door was locked; Mahoney went looking for the attendant with the key and came back empty-handed, cursing.

But through a small window in the door, the gurney was plainly visible.

"It's okay," Flynn said. "We can see fine from here."

Mahoney said, "I gotta go back to the phone."

"Thanks again. We can get out the front way, can't we?"

"Right." Mahoney patted Flynn on the shoulder and left.

Taylor walked with Flynn over to the window. One side of Salsa's face had massive lacerations, as if he had fallen on his face. From where the detectives stood, they could see no other wounds. "Stabbed in the back," Flynn muttered. "They goddamn set him up."

"He couldn't play both sides; that's a full-time occupation and even then..."

"Viera wasn't in no rush. He waited till the kid thought everything was cool—and slaughtered him."

Taylor and Flynn stood by the little window for a few minutes, not saying anything.

"Come on, let's find some coffee." Taylor felt rotten enough himself. Flynn should get out of there.

"I gotta leave a note for Defina. I don't think I'm goin' to this autopsy."

"You don't have to, Andy. It ain't our case. Ann Street—that's the First Precinct."

Yeah—I guess I better find out who caught it. From where they sit, it probably looks like a dump job." Flynn scribbled a note and stuck it on the morgue detectives' door for Irene Defina.

In a corner of the hospital lobby, Taylor spotted a coffee machine. "Hey, we're all set." The sleet had stopped. Flynn and Taylor carried their coffees to the Lincoln and got in.

"Wonder what else that squad down there has on their plate," Flynn said. "Could be lots more important cases than some Spanish kid with no ID. Kinda reminds me of Pichón." He laughed bitterly. "And as far as I know, they're not goin' for a hundred percent. They're too smart to play that game."

Taylor said he wished he could trade in his coffee for a Rémy and soda.

Flynn kept on, "Something like this happens, you're a loser no matter how good you are. You're down for the count. I didn't think of that when I dreamed up this—contest."

"The opposition's playin' with no rules," Taylor conceded.

"When you're goin' for a hundred percent, every case is the same—a line on the chart. Los Primos, where their own relatives could care less, is the same as Pichón or Mia Greenfield or Abdul. Or Salsa? That ain't right. And an atrocity like Viera—who needs a *game* to make you want to put him outta business? All you need is what you feel." He crumpled his empty coffee cup.

"Feel? On this job?"

Flynn looked at his friend. "Viera is one you ain't gonna forget." He stopped thinking for some few seconds. He couldn't believe the kid was dead. "Hell, what am I gonna do about notifyin' Carmel and Mrs. Delacruz?"

"I'll stop by Nightwatch on my way home; they'll get the ball rolling. You gotta get a little sleep." Before Flynn could protest, Taylor turned on the ignition. "Home?"

"Lauren said to come over there whenever I got done. She probably wasn't countin' on four-thirty, but she did say she'd leave word downstairs."

Taylor drove downtown and then west. No radio played this time and neither he nor Flynn spoke. The streets were still slick but nobody got in their way. Try to do this trip in fifteen minutes at rush hour, Taylor thought as they rolled up to the towers.

"Thanks, pal," Flynn said, and got out.

His partner sat with the motor running and watched through the plate-glass panels of the lobby.

Flynn woke up the concierge and spoke to him, then turned and waved to Taylor.

Taylor pulled away. By the time he could get home to Queens, the sun would almost be up. He would drive around the tip of Manhattan and up the FDR Drive, keeping the dark water on his right—the Hudson River, then the East River. He'd just empty out his mind till he had to talk to Nightwatch....

The highway stretched ahead with hardly a taillight in sight. A Rubén Blades song, "Sorpresas," sneaked into Taylor's head.... *A veces hablar resulta escencial, pero otras veces es mejor callar porque a veces hablar resulta un error mortal.* "Sometimes talking can be essential, but other times it's better to keep your mouth shut—because sometimes talking can be a fatal mistake."

Flynn rang the bell expecting to wait a while, but Lauren answered the door almost immediately, wearing her red plush bathrobe. Whether she blinked out of sleepiness or because of his appearance, he couldn't tell. Standing in the luxurious living room, he saw himself on a raft in black seas.

"Give me your coat?" he heard her say.

He automatically gave her the plaid muffler with it, then

reached out and took it back. He put it on again and stood there, gripping the ends in his fists.

She stepped back, about to go and hang up his coat. Her arms were folded around it; she looked at him and seemed to hug the clammy coat tighter. "Salsa..."

"Somebody killed him."

She let the coat fall on the couch and rushed into his arms, crying against him. His eyes shut, he stroked her hair. The image of Salsa on the gurney invaded his mind, dissolving into that of Sean, calm-faced and handsome in an open coffin.

"You must be exhausted," she said.

"Not yet."

"Is it cold out?"

"I don't exactly remember. Windy, I think."

"You'll think I'm crazy—I'd like to go walk on the Esplanade. A short walk."

"Good. Maybe I'll get tired."

"I'll put something on." She picked his coat. "Want to give this guy time out? Your sweater and windbreaker are here."

He followed her into the bedroom and sat on the bed while she dressed. As he watched her, he remembered the feel of her neck just now under his palm and fingertips—the firmness of the bones and the tautness of the flesh. That Viera wanted to rob him of these, too, he had absolutely no doubt. Salsa had cheated his boss out of half his revenge; Viera would hardly let it go at that.

Flynn and Lauren startled the concierge as they walked out through the glass doors into a gunmetal-gray predawn. They walked north on the Esplanade, arms braced against each other's backs, into the wind. Neither spoke till they turned at North Cove, putting the wind behind them. "Tell me what happened—whatever you know," Lauren said.

"I only know one thing: Viera. You told me the 'mugging' happened in an alley?"

"On the south side of Park Row; I ended up on Ann Street when I came out of it."

"Salsa was found right there, at the other end of the alley. There has to be a connection between this phony mugging and Salsa's death." Screeching gulls swooped at the gray Hudson and soared at the gray sky. "Like I told you, Irish Viera owes me from way back. Walter Torres was just insult to injury. Same with the squad looking to nail Viera himself, which he knows damn well is top priority. He was thinkin' about the old days when he sent Salsa to—get you—and somebody else to get Salsa." Flynn felt Lauren's arm tighten. "Salsa didn't do his job; the other guy did.... A knife in the back and run."

Lauren brushed at her tears. "Salsa knew whose side he was on. You... succeeded."

"And that's why he died."

"I mean, he didn't always know. He found out—too late. Too late for him, but not for me." The tears streamed down her face. Salsa had played both sides, Flynn thought—and so had he. He had tried to offer Salsa the choice he should have given Sean. And Viera—it could only have been him—had forced Salsa to choose once and for all. Live or die by it. Maybe life would only let you play one side... choose up, stick with it, and take what comes.

Flynn stopped walking, turned into the wind, and held her. If not for her arms around him, he wondered if he might just have come apart.

"I'd like to tell you something," she said when she could.

"Want to sit on the bench over there?"

"Okay." They walked holding hands.

She sat down, turning to face him directly. "What if you catch Gordo? Will he stick by what he said about Viera and the double murder?"

"I think we'll catch him; but he won't come through unless his lawyer is very sure we have the goods. Anything Viera and his group can do to foul Gordo up, they'll try to do." Flynn made himself sound like a rational person concealing the dread inside. What would she tell him?

"What I said at the lineup was true—I couldn't tell which was LaPaz because I had never seen his face." The clear brown eyes looked into Flynn's. "I saw Gordo's, though, before I went down."

Flynn could only look and listen.

"If it turns out that you need my testimony to keep Gordo tied up, I'll do it. It's worth the risk to put Viera away."

He held her hand hard. "We don't know if it'll come to that. We do know the risk right now, the one you didn't choose and that got you knocked on the head not too long ago. That could have got you killed yesterday if it wasn't for Salsa. The risk with my name on it."

"I told you I can handle that."

"'Take proper precautions' like we said?"

"Yes."

"I want you out of here. But somewhere where you know somebody with a gun. Take some vacation time and get on a plane to Wyoming. O'Levy and his wife are out there skiing." Still holding her hand, he looked at his watch. "Let's go pack."

Tuesday afternoon, December 31, 1985

Maybe the bodega was named for Red Hook; then again, maybe it was called El Anzuelo because so many customers got hooked on the numbers game that had thrived there for years. In the two months or so since Gordo had walked out of State Supreme Court in Manhattan and disappeared, Gordo had been pushing his *azúcar* at the spot, the detectives heard. He seemed to have built a nice following for *his* product, too. The bodega was becoming a real supermarket.

Members of the squad had been considering these vital matters since Saturday night when they began staking out the store where, according to Vinnie Falcone and others, Gordo could regularly be found. The sixth consecutive tour of the stakeout would be over in ninety minutes and Gordo had not showed up. Flynn's men noted the wasted looks of some of the folks who did come by; waiting for Fatso was a neighborhood pastime.

This was the first tour Flynn had done in Red Hook, caged up in the squad's ratty Plymouth. El Anzuelo made him think of the good old days and Salsa's stepfather's bodega. He was thinking about Salsa anyway since he'd spent most of the last seventy-two hours talking about him. When he wasn't mourning with Salsa's family and Brooklyn Charlie, he was going over the case with people from the First Precinct squad. All in all, he was down. The way he felt now he wasn't so sure he would even recognize Gordo. Fortunately, Taylor and Pastore were with him, doing most of the work. Cooch and Obie would relieve them for the night tour.

"There's gotta be a better way." Taylor was skilled at surveillance but he never pretended to like it. "I can't remember when I had such a great time on New Year's Eve." Deliberately or not, he distracted his friend from his troubles.

Flynn came to life. "Maybe we can think of a better way."

"Matter of fact"—Taylor grinned—"I just thought of one about two seconds ago."

Flynn and Pastore both looked at Taylor, but Taylor kept his eyes on the bodega.

"Yeah?" Flynn prompted.

"I'm just gonna mosey right over there and play myself a number." Taylor reached for his steno notebook, ripped out a sheet, and tore it in half raggedly, still watching the bodega.

"What're you doin'—*he* writes the numbers slip."

"Take it easy. I'm from Detroit, you know, and in Detroit we do it this way. I hope you guys are watchin' that place 'cause now I got to write." Holding the steno book on his lap to lean on, he scribbled on the scrap of paper.

"You wrote more than a number," Flynn protested.

"Don't you *trust* me?"

Taylor opened the car door. "If this works, it shouldn't take a whole lot of time."

A few minutes later, Taylor was back. He handed Flynn the scrap of paper and kept an eye on the bodega while Flynn read, *"Dónde vive Gordo?"*

Pastore looked over Flynn's shoulder. "Jeez, Jesse, why didn't ya come out here with us sooner."

"The guy in the spot claims he don't know where Gordo lives," Taylor said, "but he says don't worry, Gordo's gotta come today because he ain't been around yet this week. The guy's positive he's comin' today—and when he comes, it's always 'right about four.'"

Just then, Cooch and Obie came around the corner from where they had parked the Thunderbird, strolling like they were early. Flynn motioned them to hurry and get in the backseat. Taylor kept watching the bodega while Flynn reported to the newcomers the bodega owner's prediction and explained what was gonna go down if Gordo showed.

"We got five men and two cars. Gordo saw everybody but Obie the last time we collared him, so only Obie can be visible. Park the Thunderbird right there by the store, put the hood up, and 'fix something'; Ronnie, you can be in the backseat readin' your paper...Jesse, inside the bodega. Myself and Cooch will go in the stores on each side, the cleaners and the Chinese take-out place."

"Sarge, don't you go readin' the menu," Taylor hassled Cooch, who ignored him.

"While Gordo's busy with a customer, the four of us grab him," Flynn finished. "If there's a crowd, we wait till he's down to the last one. Jesse's inside the bodega makin' sure nobody in there tips Gordo off; any other problem comes up, Jesse'll spot it."

The problem came up right then: Gordo was ahead of

schedule. They could see him about a block away, waddling fast toward El Anzuelo. The sweat suit of the day was baby blue.

Obie and Pastore had no time to get the Thunderbird; they had to go ahead with the Plymouth even though anybody half streetwise would make it for a police vehicle with their eyes closed.

Flynn, Cooch, and Taylor all had to cross the street in plain view; knowing that Gordo could look up anytime and make them—or somebody else could spot them, take them for narcs, and scream.

They had bulletproof vests in the trunk of each car but no time to get them.

Red Hook was ready to party and everybody wanted *azúcar*. Gordo had all he could do to keep up with demand, let alone watch out for cops. Just as the last customer paid for his tin, Flynn and his men moved in. Cooch and Pastore, worried about that nine millimeter, each pinned an arm from behind. Flynn's and Obie's .38s pressed through the sweat suit top to the soft flesh of the coke dealer's midriff. Cooch snapped the cuffs on.

As they hustled him into the Plymouth, Gordo snarled with rage.

"Never mind," Taylor told him. "If it was Viera that found you, you'd be in the river already."

"If you're gonna make a call, Gordo," Pastore said when they got back to the squad, "you better think hard about whose number you're gonna dial. Anybody mentions to Viera where you are, you'll never make it off Rikers Island—he's got lots of pals out there, you know."

What worried Flynn and the others even more than Gordo's safety was that Viera could learn of the arrest and go in the wind. The squad would have their witness in the Frostbite case—but no perp. And the man who had surely ordered Salsa's death would escape Flynn forever.

When Flynn reviewed Gordo's original eyewitness statement about the double homicide, he thought it looked good. If the ADA agreed, they could try to find Viera and grab him tonight.

Kevin Patrick sounded cranky. He didn't love New Year's, he said, especially if he had to spend it at his wife's boss's house. "What about you, Andy? You're workin'? What on?"

"Irish Viera." Flynn paused for effect. "And we're close!"

"You're kiddin'!"

"I'm not. We just picked up Concepción, the homicide perp

who slipped out of court a couple of months back. He witnessed the double stabbing that Viera and his lieutenant did last spring. Well, back when we had Concepción in here, he gave us a full statement—*eye*witness. Ready to testify—so it hadda be Viera who stage-managed Concepción's escape. Bottom line: If we can find Viera... can we go ahead and collar the scumbag?"

Tuesday night, New Year's Eve, 1985

The Gordo collar had convinced the men they were on a roll. At this rate, they just might lock up Viera himself. If they could find him. Maybe Taylor could finesse that job like he had the bodega owner in Red Hook.

Flynn sat at Betty's desk with his feet up, trying to relax. Cooch was busy in the bosses' office. The A Team men watched TV in the coffee room; they were into their second tour. Pastore, Urquhart, and Mazocek had been working since that morning—thirteen hours, so far. Obie typed like a banshee at one of the back desks.

Taylor came out of the captain's office and sat down in the chair next to Betty's desk. "I talked to Ramón; he says Viera is out at some party. I told Ramón, 'I hate that fuckin' Luzan'; I referred to Luzan's mother in ways that made Ramón drop the phone and I said I'd had enough of Carlos an' his rotten low-class crack. 'With Chino gone, now Viera needs somebody like me. I wanna sign up with Irish Luck for '86. *Right now.*'"

"Nice work." Taylor's drug-dealer bit tickled Flynn.

"It's good luck to sign up *tonight.*" Taylor played the hustler like a pro. "'I got big sales I could be makin' as we speak'—I laid on all that shit but it didn't work. Ramón is very sorry he can't help me out—he don't know where the boss is except he's at a private party. I asked him where's Monte and he says Monte's with the boss. 'Call back after New Year's.'"

"So what do you think?" Flynn wanted to see if Taylor thought the same as he did.

"He must've went in a Luna car like always. We gotta find out from Johnny whatsis."

"Estevez." Flynn held up his right thumb. "I'm with you. Let's have a little war council." Taylor went and stuck his head in the coffee room. The others came out and sat down at the desks around Obie. Cooch got up and stood in the doorway of the bosses' office.

Flynn explained what had to be done and why. "We might need a little leverage if Estevez don't feel talkative," he said. "Any suggestions?"

"Wire cutters," Cooch said. "Just unpluggin' the phones ain't enough; gotta chop 'em."

"Dynamite!" Pastore whooped.

Everybody cracked up.

"Easy does it," Flynn said. "You want to see if Emergency Service can let us have a couple of pairs of wire cutters for the night?"

Pastore was out of his chair before Flynn had finished his sentence.

Emergency Service had a tense situation with a New Year's Eve jumper at the George Washington Bridge, but Pastore chased down the truck and returned to the squad with three pairs of wire cutters. "I got 'em oiled good."

"Dynamite!" Taylor grinned and held out his hand. Cooch reached for the second pair and Pastore unselfishly gave the third to Flynn.

"Okay," Flynn said, "we don't know yet where we're goin' after Luna, but wherever, Viera and company's gonna be there. Everybody should carry an off-duty gun and the service revolver."

"And wear a *vest,*" Cooch added.

"Hey—we might need pictures later," Pastore said. He went to the files and looked up the only existing ID shots of Viera and Monte. The pictures were pretty dated—it had been too long since either one of them was arrested.

Nobody in the Chrysler said much during the short ride. When the detectives got out on 110th Street, Flynn and Taylor led the way into Luna's storefront. In the outer office, five female dispatchers were so busy talking into their headsets that none of them could stop to ask the cops what was going on. Behind a dusty glass window, the cops could see Johnny Estevez. He didn't look ready to spread out the welcome mat, but he stood up and went to the PRIVATE OFFICE door. As soon as he opened it, all eight cops shouldered their way into the narrow room, occupying what floor space was not taken up by the desk and file cabinets.

"Lieutenant Flynn, Twenty-ninth Precinct squad. Busy night, huh?" He leaned his elbow on top of a file cabinet. "This is Sergeant Carlucci"—Cooch nodded curtly—"and Detective Taylor."

Estevez sat down at his desk. In front of him stood a bottle of champagne and a half-full glass that he lifted to his lips.

Taylor addressed Estevez as Juan; skipping the good-guy stuff, he just gave Juan to understand in rapid Spanish what the cops wanted to know from him.

Estevez rubbed the stubble on his prominent chin and jerked it belligerently at Taylor. "Since when is there a law that says I gotta tell *anybody* where my customers go. You make me laugh," he said, doing so raucously.

Flynn's patience had died with Salsa. Without warning, he lunged at Estevez, grabbing him out of the chair and slamming him against the wall between the desk and the closest metal file. He spun the chair on its casters, picked it up, and smashed it down right between Estevez's expensively sneakered feet. "Listen to me while you still got ears. This is a criminal investigation and you're obstructing it. That's a crime."

Taylor looked at Estevez and nodded, reinforcing Flynn's point. Cooch and the other men shifted restlessly in the cramped space.

"No more garbage," Flynn said. "Where'd your driver take Irish?"

"Puta madre!" Estevez jeered. "You *finished* in this precinct. All the people that's waiting to get you—they gonna be glad to hear this story. I can't wait to tell 'em." He eyed his champagne.

"Stay in these streets with scum like you? I'm sick of breathing your air. They can send me to Peoria and I'll live happily ever after."

Estevez said nothing. Smirking, he reached over to his desk, topped off his champagne, and calmly brought it to his lips.

The noise of a file drawer sliding open was quickly followed by a horrendous crash as the cabinet fell crosswise in the narrow room. The rest of the files toppled over in succession; papers and odd and ends that had been left on top went flying. The men tromped around in the mess, not exactly tidying up. Estevez stood with one foot resting on the base of his chair and his drink in his hand, sipping.

Flynn looked at Taylor and Cooch; the three of them took the wirecutters out of their trench coat pockets, turned, and followed the others out the office door.

At 2240 hours on New Year's Eve, Estevez's five dispatchers had all they could do to keep up with the workload. Flynn, Taylor, and Cooch held a brief conference to decide the order of business; they pointed out certain phones. They opened and shut the wire cutters' jaws, testing. Then, with the other cops standing watch by the front door, the two bosses and Taylor each headed toward a previously designated phone and placed the phone wires in the cutter's jaws....

Estevez walked out of the private office, slamming the door behind him. "Irish went to the Waldorf at ten o'clock. That's all I know."

Taylor turned around with his wire cutters in his hand, their jaws still open, and waved them carelessly at the car service owner. "The Waldorf! What a crock! Like there's only two places to go for New Year's in New York—Times Square and the Waldorf."

Flynn and Cooch snapped their wire cutters open and shut, like a menacing rhythm section behind Taylor.

"If you're blowin' smoke to get rid of us, you're gonna fuckin' regret it *early* in the New Year," Taylor promised.

"I'm *tellin'* you he went to the Waldorf," Estevez shouted. "But it's a big place." He lowered his voice. "*Where* in the Waldorf ain't my driver's problem—it's yours. But I'm sure you cops will locate him—'early in the New Year,'" he mimicked.

Snap. Three pairs of wire cutters shut loudly. Flynn and his men ran out to the cars and piled in.

"The Waldorf is all we got," Flynn told Taylor as they took off downtown. "Just pray that's where he's at."

"Pray?" Taylor said. "Listen, I got a long list; this ain't the time to start on that."

"Relax," Obie said from the backseat, "I'll take care of it."

"Good," Flynn told him, "a minute of silence so Obie can get his thoughts together." Flynn tried to get his own thoughts together as best he could.

Taylor managed to keep still for an extra thirty seconds. "What if Estevez is tellin' the truth that Irish went to the Waldorf—but he's lyin' about the rest. He does know the location an' he's gettin' a message through to him right now. You can bet Monte never gets dressed without his beeper. We should've brought Estevez with us."

Flynn stepped on the gas. "You got a damn good batting average, pal—this time I hope you're wrong."

In her suite in the Waldorf Towers, La Dalia glowed at Viera. She had brought her eight top salesmen and their ladies to New York as a reward for their record-breaking sales performance in the months since they had started selling Irish Luck. "The music is wonderful—such a thoughtful surprise," she said. "And your fellow is a mind reader; he's playing all my favorites."

"Anything you want to hear, just tell him," Viera murmured. The voice of Tonia Reyes billowed out of the speakers that Viera's disk jockey had brought with him as part of an elaborate portable sound system. Not that the guests could do much dancing; the suite was too full of furniture, especially the living room. The disk jockey had set up shop in the west bedroom where a determined couple or two might yet succeed in dancing on the free patch of carpet in front of the deejay's outfit.

Viera's eyes caressed La Dalia's Carolina Herrera dress, emerald-green velvet molded to her figure. He had always liked her figure, and now that she had taken his fashion advice, he was beginning to like her better. As she tapped her foot and swayed sexily to the music, he put his arm around her waist. For a minute he forgot the roomful of party guests.

Her entourage also included her bodyguard and her houseman, Paco, a Filipino with a physique that qualified him to substitute on the bodyguard's day off. Now the houseman suavely carved roast pork and passed champagne, every muscle clearly outlined under his skin-tight black sweater. The handle of a small black .38 stuck out of his waistband.

In Viera's opinion, the houseman swung past Dalia oftener than necessary. "Your guy in the hall needs a break," Viera told her. "You better send your houseman to relieve him."

She sighed. "Paco is devoted—it's a rare quality. I have to handle him with kid gloves." She looked at her Cartier watch. "Eleven oh five—I'll send him after a while."

"Boss"—Reynolds was in the back of the Chrysler with Obie—"that hundred percent is gonna be a tight squeeze—we got less than an hour to collar Viera." The car streaked by the Park Avenue traffic islands with their cheery Christmas trees.

"If we're as good as we know how to be, we can do it that fast. But the main event now is Viera. We're gonna grab him if it takes till Thursday. Everything we ever did in three years all together don't compare to this one job: puttin' that animal in his cage."

"Dennis Viera, his dealers, and his drug," Obie spat out the syllables, "a scourge on this earth."

The night manager at the Waldorf, the tall, Waspy blonde, remembered Flynn and Reynolds right away. Especially Reynolds.

"How come you're workin' tonight?" Flynn heard Billy ask as

he and the blonde went off in a corner. Flynn didn't have to hear Billy's next line to know it was something like, "Too bad we can't both play hookey and go celebrate together."

Their conversation went on and on. "What the fuck!" Cooch fumed, upsetting the elegant couple emerging from Peacock Alley. Cooch checked his watch. "There goes our famous hundred percent—" Flynn was amazed to hear him mutter under his breath, "thanks to that clown."

Reynolds gave Flynn the high sign and Flynn went to join him.

"Beverly can get us the New Year's Eve reservation list for the Grand Ballroom and the Waldorf Towers guest register," Reynolds told him.

"Nothin' but the best for our subjects," Flynn said, *"if* they're stayin' here."

"I'll be right back, Lieutenant," Beverly sounded sincere, "I know you're in a hurry."

"She's in charge of the hotel for the duration?" Flynn asked hopefully.

"Her boss is in the Ballroom with his wife—off duty."

Beverly returned at 2316 with both lists. Pastore saw what she had in her hand and whistled.

"Yes, I'm afraid we have almost five hundred reservations in the Ballroom—and the Towers are sold out, so that's a hundred and fifteen suites." Beverly gave the lists to Flynn. "Why don't you and your men have a seat while you look at these." She nodded toward the seating areas in the main lobby, with their upholstered chairs. She looked at their collection of trench coats. "And you could check your coats till after the... operation."

"Good idea," Flynn said, "thanks for your help. Will you be back in your office?"

"Well, I hope nothing *else* comes up!"

"Detective Reynolds will keep you posted."

"Fine," she said, "see you later then, Billy."

"Sooner than later, I hope."

"Amen," Obie said.

The men split up the lists and began poring over them. "I can't believe we're here and O'Levy's somewhere else." Taylor flipped to the next page.

"Joyce is always such a pussy cat, but she put her foot down this time—decided she hadda go skiin' for New Year's," Pastore explained.

Quite a few Spanish names showed up on the Ballroom list. "I was thinkin' of takin' speed reading," Urquhart said. "Why did I put that off." He glanced unhappily at his watch.

"If they're in this fuckin' Ballroom," Cooch said, "we got a problem."

"Pretty tricky with all those people," Flynn agreed, "plus the manager's up there partyin' with his wife. But maybe we could—"

"Hold on." Taylor had the Towers list. "Diaz, D.—Philadelphia, PA. Cromwell Suite: thirty-six-ten. That's the only one I see. Unless Viera went to a gringo party, this could be it."

"Especially if they are havin' a party," Flynn said.

"We gotta talk to room service," Reynolds said.

"Somebody who's been waitin' on that suite tonight."

"Floor plan, keys," Reynolds said, "anything else?"

Flynn noticed the time. "Maybe I better go with you and think about what else we need on the way. Let's all head back there so we can make it around to the Towers entrance fast." They trooped westward toward the Park Avenue entrance, stopping to check the trench coats in a hurry. Flynn Cooch, and Obie went into the manager's office with Reynolds.

Waldorf Room Service was miraculously swift—but an old-time New York waiter and a young New York detective might not be the smoothest combination, Flynn decided when the guy appeared.

"Obie, you do the honors," Flynn said. Pastore handed Obie the pictures of Viera and Monte.

Before you knew it, Obie had the surly waiter on the cops' side and ready to do what he could to help. The waiter said, "Yeah, it's a party but not a big one—only about twenty people. They did order the gold service: all the hors d'oeuvres plates is gold."

"Is that right!" Cooch marveled.

The waiter said if there wasn't so much furniture in there, they'd be rattling around in that big living room. "They're drinking a lot of Waldorf champagne and piña coladas and eatin' hors d'oeuvres. They got the TV on—plus Spanish music tapes or somethin'."

"Did you notice any guns, by chance?"

The waiter looked as if he were asked that once a day. "Nah—didn't see none. But they got a real heavy sittin' outside the door with a bulge under his coat." He pointed at the location on Obie's coat where you could just about see the gun poking against the Donegal tweed if you looked.

Obie showed him the pictures of Irish and Monte, but the guy said, "Listen, all these Eurotrash look alike to me. It's New Year's, the place is full of 'em—didja' see all them flags outside? Gimme ten bucks for every guest with pointy shoes and a mustache, I could retire right now."

Obie laughed and clapped the waiter on the back. "That's what my wife's tryin' to get me to do. Retire right now. If she succeeds, I'll invite you to the racket."

Meanwhile, Beverly had given Reynolds the Cromwell Suite keys but she hadn't come up with the floor plan. Flynn checked his watch. He pictured Estevez calling Viera. He figured he probably should have sent somebody back to keep Estevez off the phone. Too late now. He checked his watch again. Finally, Beverly hurried over with the plan. "Misfiled," she said with a frown. At Reynolds's request, she penciled in a little map of the corridor.

Reynolds and Flynn looked at the plan. "Three bedrooms; living room is twenty-five by thirty, front door here, and there's also access to these two bedrooms from the hall." Reynolds referred to the corridor sketch. "We get out of the elevator here, we gotta turn this corner—from there to the door where the guy's sitting, it's a good twenty feet," Reynolds said. "How we gonna jump him without him seein' us?"

"We won't, we gotta fake him out," Flynn said. "Ask Beverly how fast we can get a couple of jackets like the waiter is wearin', a couple of those napkins they drape over their arm, and a trolley—we'll make like we're goin' in there for the dirty plates." Reynolds went to Beverly's desk and relayed the request.

She started to answer him but her phone rang. "Beverly speaking. Yes! Hi, John." Her face reddened: she looked at Reynolds and mouthed, "My boss."

Flynn had been watching; now he saw Reynolds begin to pace. Beverly didn't look happy. Finally, she hung up. Flynn went over to her desk.

"My boss is adamant"—she shook her head—"the chief of security has to go with you to safeguard property."

"I think we can live with that," Flynn said. Mentally he tried to figure out how this would work. "Anyway, we ain't ready to blast off—we need some waiter's gear."

Reynolds listed the items.

"Okay," Beverly said, and dialed a number. While she waited for an answer, she asked, "What about the chief, though?" Before Flynn could reply, her party answered.

"Billy," Flynn said, "tell her that as soon the waiter stuff comes, she can call him and we'll hook up."

Then Flynn and Taylor went through their waiter routine.

At 2332 hours, a breathless busboy rushed in, pushing a trolley with the waiter's jackets and the napkins.

Flynn and Taylor tried on the jackets over their bulletproof vests.

"What about the chief?" Beverly urged.

Flynn and the chief both knew that the police had the ultimate authority, but Flynn wanted the chief on his side. "You can beep him and say we'll hook up with him in the Towers lobby; we're leavin' now." Flynn aimed the trolley at the doorway. "By the way, did Billy tell you—we'll need to shut down all the elevators except the one we're using."

"If the chief doesn't veto it..."

"What a picnic," Taylor said to Flynn as they rolled the squeaky trolley over the deep, garnet-colored carpet toward the hotel's Park Avenue entrance.

Flynn raised his voice so all the men could hear him. "Everybody get ready to give the chief a big hello and a glad hand, right?"

Around the corner of Fiftieth Street, the Towers doorman eyeballed the eight assorted men, dateless on New Year's Eve. Two of them in waiter's jackets. Then he noticed the bulky bulletproof vests under their coats.

Beverly followed them into the Towers lobby. "Hi, Sam," Beverly said. "Happy New Year. Is the chief here yet?"

The brushed-chrome doors of the nearest elevator opened and a grim-faced man in a brown suit stepped firmly out, only to be closely surrounded by eight cops, all saying, "Hiya, Chief" and "Ready to start the New Year right?"

The chief looked desperately at the ring of faces around him. He did a sudden double take. "Hey, Obie—how's life treatin' you!" Relief showed in the security chief's expression and Obie's, too.

"Son of a gun—Ray! We're gonna start your year off right, y'know that? Got a minute? Lemme tell you about it."

The others stepped back, leaving Obie and Ray to confer. Flynn and the rest appreciated Obie's trusty old-cop network. Nobody appreciated the length of Obie and Ray's conversation.

Cooch nudged Flynn. "There's three fuckin' bedrooms?" he prodded in a raspy whisper. "One cocksucker hides out in there and we're good and fucked."

"That's why we show up while they're watchin' the scene in Times Square—nobody's gonna want to miss that," Flynn said in normal tones, as if it were gospel.

Cooch folded his arms on his chest. "There's maybe ten of

them and only eight of us. We gotta have backup, Andy. *If* none of the females have guns, we're still outgunned four, at least. You gotta assume they each got two guns, too."

"Maybe the Seventeenth could send backup in time," Flynn said, "it's a couple of blocks from here."

The men all looked at their watches. "We can handle it," somebody said. "Yeah, yeah," the others chimed in.

"I always heard that Irish didn't carry a gun," Pastore said.

"The Seventeenth is near but how much manpower could they have on New Year's Eve anyway. We're *in* Manhattan North—which is far..."

Flynn knew the men didn't want to wait for a slow backup. He also knew that it didn't make sense to tempt fate when Viera was the target. Cooch was right: there was every chance they'd need backup. At 2345 hours, Flynn used the Towers' concierge's phone to call in a 10-85 for backup.

At last Obie seemed to have appeased Ray, who authorized Beverly to hold up all but one elevator. Flynn shook Ray's hand and thanked him as they led the way on to the remaining car.

As the doors closed, Reynolds blew a kiss to Beverly.

Flynn and Obie stood on either side of Ray. Over the hum of the high-speed lift, Flynn said, "Obie must've told you what kind of scum we're tryin' to scrape off the face of the city with this operation."

Obie said, "I told him that we're tryin' to pull this off with minimum damage, but whatever happens, Viera's collar is gonna get so much media coverage that the hotel will give him a raise for heroism."

"I hope you got the right room," Ray said. "Sure, it's registered in a Spanish name and they got a lookout at the door, but that don't mean it's your guy."

The elevator opened at the thirty-sixth floor. Flynn and Taylor carried rather than pushed the trolley to keep it from squeaking. Once they had it in the hallway, they stopped to put on their waiter's jackets. The salsa beat came right through the Cromwell Suite walls. The cops' staging area was around the corner that was twenty feet from the lookout's chair.

Flynn pushed the trolley forward. He all but had it around the corner into the lookout's view when Taylor grabbed his arm. They heard the suite door open and Spanish conversation between two males. The voices rose and fell. "Sounds like the shithead at the door wants a break," Taylor said, "and the other one's tryin' to get out of doin' his share—'I got a girl all lined up for you—soon as she gets here, I'll take over.' That kinda bull." The lookout didn't go for it until the other one told him to fuck off, *he* would take the girl himself and let the lookout sit there till the sun comes up. That did the trick; the cops heard the suite door close and nothing more except a throb of salsa.

Flynn moved out with the trolley; Taylor talked to him in a mixture of Spanish and English: "Don't forget the ashtrays," he admonished, loud enough to be heard by the lookout.

Flynn said those gold plates made him nervous. Who was responsible if the count came up short?

"Don't worry," Taylor said, and added in Spanish this time, "just get the dirty ashtrays out."

The lookout had a glass of champagne in one hand. He waved the other hand angrily and glowered at Taylor. "What are you—loco! You can't go in there now."

Flynn and Taylor moved closer. "If we don't do the ashtrays," Taylor answered, "the boss is gonna do *us.*" He lunged forward, stuffing his table napkin in the lookout's mouth while Flynn simultaneously jammed his gun in the lookout's gut. They made him curl up on the trolley in the fetal position and wheeled him back around the corner where they pushed him through the already open fire door.

"See," Obie told Ray, "nice an' clean." Ray looked relieved.

"Dalia, what's wrong with your faithful servant?" Viera asked. "Paco should be pouring refills and picking up the dirty glasses, but he looks hypnotized by the TV, like the ball won't drop till he says the word. I don't think your doorman ever got his break either."

On the TV screen, the crowd in Times Square surged with anticipation.

Taylor, Pastore, and Reynolds had escorted the lookout down a couple of flights and cuffed him to the stair rail. "We debriefed him," Taylor told Flynn when he and the others returned. "He says the party hostess is a lady from Philly and Viera is the guest of honor."

Flynn told himself the backup would arrive any minute; he didn't want to look for trouble by delaying an operation that was ready to go. He peered around the corner into an empty corridor and gave the all-clear sign to the men.

At 2356 hours, Cooch unlocked the west bedroom door to the corridor; Ray, Obie, Urquhart, and Pastore caught sight of a complicated, flashy disk jockey outfit in the middle of the room. "No good," Cooch signaled Flynn, who stood by the suite's front door.

Flynn, Taylor, Reynolds, and Mazocek rotated from the suite door to the east bedroom door; Cooch and his crew moved over to the suite door.

Dalia called Paco over. He approached nervously. "How come you never relieved the guard like you was supposed to?" she asked.

"I asked him—he said he's fine; don't want a break."

Viera's eyebrows went a mile high. "We can't depend on a lookout who's half asleep. Relieve him right now—don't take no for an answer." He called Monte over. "Make sure Paco relieves the lookout. No more games."

Flynn unlocked the east bedroom; every light in the room was blazing. Through the open door from the bedroom to the living room, Flynn spotted Viera at least thirty feet away by a huge TV; a familiar-looking woman in a low-cut green dress stood next to him. Flynn and his crew would be seen the minute they entered the brilliantly lit bedroom.

Flynn saw Viera send Monte in the direction of the suite door, following a big guy with a black .38 in his belt.

"Ten—" shouted the TV announcer in Times Square.

Cooch and Obie were pressed against the corridor wall flanking the suite door, Pastore and Urquhart behind them. No time to get them out of the way before Monte and the other guy got there.

"NOW!" Flynn shouted to Cooch. He heard Cooch's crew kick open the door. A shot, then two more.

"OBIE!" someone yelled.

Viera disappeared from view as Flynn and his crew dashed through the bedroom. Champagne glasses flew through the air. Piercing screams from the females in the suite mixed with the uproar of the TV crowd in Times Square.

Flynn pulled up short at the entrance to the living room, scanning the chaos for Viera as Taylor and Reynolds and Mazocek ran past. Guns drawn and shouting orders, they fanned out to cover the party guests and get them all down on the floor where they couldn't do anything sudden. Among the couple dozen men and women all dolled up for New Year's—some confused, some resisting, some docile—Flynn saw no sign of Viera. The Times

Square crowd sang "Auld Lang Syne," while Latin music still vibrated in the suite.

Ray and Pastore were bending over Obie where he lay near the suite's main door.

"Get a bus!" Flynn yelled, and thought, shit, Obie's down and no Viera. This can't be happening. He could see blood seeping from a wound in O'Brien's stomach, below the vest. "Get a bus!" The squad had their hands full patting down two dozen people for weapons. "Ray!"

The security chief seemed to snap out of a trance. "Right."

A blast of sound, incredibly loud, drove everything from Flynn's mind. It pounded and pulsed, so loud it was painful, a physical force, enough to drive you crazy, and it didn't stop. Flynn fought it, no idea what it was, saw that the others were as bad off as he was, except for a couple of the male party-goers who took the deafening noise as a signal to make a break. Reynolds and Mazocek were all over them before they got two steps.

Flynn's mind reeled. Music! It was the damn Latin music amplified a million times. Speakers somewhere, but he didn't see them and the sound reverberated too much to find them that way. What about the source? That other bedroom. Got to get in there. Anything to stop the music that was clobbering him like a fast-handed middleweight.

Flynn reached for the doorknob, then braked. Maybe Viera was in there. Maybe there were guys with guns in there. He flattened himself against the wall and reached way out to turn the doorknob with his fingertips.

As the knob turned a shotgun blast ripped through the closed door, almost taking off Flynn's fingers as he snatched away his hand. Urqhuart returned the fire, emptying his off-duty gun into the door, ejecting the shells and reloading with a speedloader. The music continued to pound.

At least I got the right door, Flynn thought. He looked around the room. The party guests were all glued to the floor, heads covered. Even though the shotgun, targetless behind the door, was holding its fire for now, no one wanted to risk being ventilated by lead pellets.

Flynn motioned to Taylor to follow him and dashed for the corridor. Intent on keeping Viera from making a break, he didn't register the blue uniforms and guns of the backup unit until he was faced with a half dozen revolver muzzles aimed at his head. "Freeze!" the cops shouted at him. "Drop the guns."

"Flynn, Two-nine squad," he said, motionless while they

registered the gold shield. Taylor almost piled into him from behind.

"Sorry, Lieu," the uniformed sergeant said.

"No problem." Flynn took in the empty corridor. The door to the second bedroom was closed. Viera was still in there.... There hadn't been enough time for him to make it to the elevator or the stairway. Unless he'd fled before the shotgun blasted from the bedroom. It could be anybody shooting from in there.

"Tell Ray to seal the hotel," he said to Taylor, who sped back into the suite.

Flynn started to fill the sergeant in. The music that seemed to be shaking the whole hotel stopped in midbeat, leaving an abrupt silence.

Cooch appeared at the suite door. "The fuckin' speakers were holding up the bar—I ripped the wires out. The bedroom's covered. No action there."

Through the ringing in his ears Flynn thought he heard a noise down the corridor—a door closing. "Work with the sergeant," he told Cooch and dashed for the corner. No time to stop and explain.

There was an emergency stairway at the other end of the hall. Flynn tucked one gun into his waistband, shoved the door open, and went in fast. Nothing. He stopped to listen. He couldn't hear any footsteps on the stairs, but he wasn't sure how well he could trust his ears. He could feel his heart beating like after five miles of roadwork. He peered down the stairwell. Nothing that he could see. Up. Nothing there, either.

Maybe it was a suite door, he thought, not the stairway. Maybe it wasn't even Viera. He turned away from the stairs to open the door and rejoin the squad.

Something heavy crashed into him, ramming him against the door, knocking the wind out of him. An arm grappled under his chin. His gun clattered to the floor. Instinct turned him around, gasping, pulling at the arm as a knife came around to slash his exposed throat.

He warded off the blade and backpedaled, smashing his attacker against the wall. Twisted free. Blackness in front of his eyes, but he could make out an image of Viera lunging at him.

Flynn sidestepped the knife on the outside, still struggling for breath and vision; almost reflexively, his hard right found Viera's jaw. Viera bucked with the impact but recovered, dropping into a knife-fighter's crouch. A second knife materialized in his other hand.

Flynn, dazed, getting his breath back, tried to circle, warily facing Viera. He wanted to get into a position on the small landing where he had some room, where his back wasn't against the wall or the door. Viera sidestepped to block him, agile as something from the South American jungle. A knife flicked out and back, leaving a line of blood on the outside of Flynn's hand.

Flynn's eyes were locked on Viera's. He could feel the hatred flowing between them.

He was concentrating so hard on his opponent that the memory of the gun still in his waistband came as a surprise. But it was only a gun, not a magic wand. Reaching for it and pulling it out would occupy one hand and part of his mind. At this close range Viera's speed with a blade meant that giving him even a split-second's advantage could be a fatal mistake.

"I'm going to kill you, cop," Viera spat. "You're overdue in hell."

"Yeah? Let's go, Irish. I'm takin' you with me." Make him mad, distract him.

Flynn watched the rage grow in Viera's eyes, could almost feel the druglord's muscles tense. Yeah, Flynn thought: rush me, give me a chance to duck and get clear just for half a second....

The moment passed. Viera laughed hollowly. "You think I'm a dumb kid like your friend Salsa? I'm going to cut you so the devil himself won't recognize you."

Salsa! Now Flynn had to master his own surge of anger—in time to catch Viera's attack. The knives flashed. Flynn parried, using his forearms against Viera's and going for a clinch, but Viera danced out of reach, then quickly forward, opening a cut below Flynn's right eye.

The door thudded into Flynn's shoulder. Viera took the advantage, cutting him again, crowding him so he couldn't let the door open but twisting away when Flynn tried to grab him.

"Andy?" Taylor's voice behind the door.

"Jesse—block the stairs. Go around."

"Now I have to finish you fast," Viera growled, cocking his arm to throw one of the knives.

As Viera's arm swept forward, Flynn dove sideways for the stairs, rolling into a ball and covering up to protect himself as he bounced downward against the sharp edges of the stair treads. He crashed into the wall.

Ignoring the pain, he scrambled to his feet, yanking at his gun to pull it free of his belt. Viera was bounding down the stairs, almost on top of him, the remaining knife ready to strike.

Taylor appeared on the landing above, and as Flynn drew his own gun, Jesse's roared twice. The impact of the bullets tumbled Viera forward. He hit the wall next to Flynn, then slid to the floor, leaving a smear of blood on the wall as he went down.

Viera didn't look as if he was going anywhere in a hurry, but Taylor stood over him while Flynn went back to the suite to get a uniformed cop and send for another ambulance.

Walking hurt, but at least he hadn't broken anything. The cuts were beginning to sting and he was feeling a little light-headed. He hoped some medics had arrived by now.

Back at the suite, the uniformed cops had cleared the second bedroom and Cooch was organizing the arrests.

"The fuckin' cop shooter first," the uniformed sergeant kibitzed. Urquhart had the big Filipino cuffed behind his back and sitting in a deep easy chair.

"Right," Cooch said. "This guy next." He indicated Monte, who was under Pastore's care. "He did a double homicide back in March."

"I saw you collar him—" Pastore said.

"As the ball was goin' down," Cooch crowed. "Twenty-three fifty-nine."

The uniformed sergeant didn't get the significance. "What about the females in the bedroom?" he asked hopefully. "Collars for them?"

"Shit, hold 'em all," Cooch said. "We got enough drugs in here to charge an army. And don't forget that mutt cuffed to the fire stairs a couple flights down."

The hotel entrance was a maze of radio cars and ambulances, lights and cameras. A million curious bystanders milled beyond the yellow tape. Flynn sat still while a medic cleaned and patched up his cuts, but he refused a ride to the hospital. He wasn't going anywhere till he saw Viera securely on his way.

The stretcher came out of the elevator surrounded by medics and cops, Taylor in the lead. He spotted Flynn and broke away.

"Viera wants to talk to Monte."

"Last words?" Flynn asked.

"On his way out," Taylor assured him.

Flynn and Pastore walked Monte over there, then stood back. Taylor returned to his position at the head of the stretcher.

* * *

"Did you hear what he said?" Flynn asked later.

Taylor gave him a level look. "He made Monte swear to finish that *cabrón* Flynn, even if he goes with Luzan to do it."

"No shit?" Flynn said.

"No shit."

Friday, January 3, 1986

Murphy, O'Shea, Anastasio, Wilde, Berger, Marshall, O'Connor, Wilson, Reardon, Hurley, Higgins, Gomez, Barberi, Moriarty, Rosario, Ortiz, O'Holloran...

How many newspaper stories had Lauren read about the "sea of blue" at the funeral of one of New York's Finest? Now here she was, feeling like an island in that sea and the tide rising. During the funeral service, thousands of officers crowded the street in front of the church. Chatting, joshing, waiting. They surrounded Lauren with those perfectly pressed uniforms, with that litany of names printed on dull black tags and worn below the silver badges, over the heart.

Lauren looked up and saw other cops watching from the roof of the church. Inside, Flynn and the squad would be sitting in one of the front pews.

She would remember the drops of tepid rain that belonged in April, not January, the sounds of birdsong, of police helicopters, the silence of Maureen O'Brien and her daughters as white-gloved officers carried Obie's coffin down the stone steps and along the strictly drawn deep-blue lines. The lines of uniformed cops stretching for half a block in each direction. She would remember the trumpet player in blue perched atop a van, stinging the air with his "Taps."

She stood on the curb, now surrounded by civilians. "I hate to hear 'Taps,'" a man said, "it tears me up."

The coffin, covered in a green, white, and deep-blue police flag, had disappeared into the hearse. Blue-and-white police cars, red rooflights flashing, followed the hearse as it inched away. The kilted cops in the Emerald Society pipe band paraded, their bagpipes wailing "Going Home."

Sooner than Lauren would have expected or wanted, the hearse had slipped out of sight. The strict lines of blue relaxed; the rain subsided. More blue-uniformed officers poured out of the church, mixing with those on the street. Other cops wore suits, gold detective badges on their lapels. Lauren thought she saw Flynn with Jesse Taylor, already half a block from the church.

"Need a ride home?" someone asked her. She had followed the crowd to the first intersection after the church. The police car was marked "29." The Community Affairs officer of her precinct smiled out the car window. "I'm goin' to the house. Room for one more."

"Hey, I'm glad to see a familiar face—how are you, Buddy?"

"No complaints—except maybe the tour ain't over yet; still a few hours to go. Well, jump in!"

"Thanks—I'm not going back to Manhattan yet. Meeting someone in Kate Cassidy's." Lauren had the Rego Park address in her bag but not the street map that she'd carefully brought home from the office. She had only a vague notion how to get to the bar.

"Oho—bouncin' with the Finest, huh? Well, I'm tellin' you, jump in while you got the chance. Kate Cassidy's ain't around the corner, y'know. Queens ain't Manhattan."

She smiled. Two cops wearing "29" collar pins moved over to let her into the backseat. Parkin cursed the traffic, then slouched in his seat, stuck his elbow out the window, and went with the flow.

All the frills that F. X. Flynn's was missing, Kate Cassidy's had. Flynn admired them—which took some doing because the four-sided bar was chockablock with cops on all sides. On the dark, burnished wood paneling hung carved and painted wooden coats of arms representing the counties of Eire. O'Levy asked Pastore which county he thought the O'Levys came from.

Reynolds read aloud the hand-lettered sign: "An Irish toast—May you be in heaven half an hour before the Devil knows you're dead."

"Lemme tell you somethin'," Cooch said, "the devil's got *you* in the cross hairs at all times."

Flynn pointed out to Taylor that some of the windows in the bar had stained glass—in the shape of "KC" with fancy designs. Flynn thought that "FX" would look terrific in stained glass. Taylor pointed out that, unlike Flynn's, this place was a full restaurant, too. The dining room behind the bar was now filling up with cops holding drinks in their hands and talking about every possible subject except the tragic fate of Detective First Grade Paul O'Brien.

Kate Cassidy's two owners, retired from the force, had kicked off the afternoon with a round in Obie's honor. On such a day only five or six years back, Flynn realized, the bartenders—both had brogues—would have been serving nobody but men. Now there were quite a few females with .38s in their purses, bouncing around. And there was Lauren, who came out to the funeral on her own. She stood by the near corner of the bar, sipping vermouth the same color as her hair. Next to her on the bar, he saw a folded copy of the *News.*

Taylor nudged him. "I think you got a visitor."

Captain Zachs cut through the crush to where the squad members were standing. "So Andy," he said in a voice bigger than he was, "I gotta hand it to you fellas. You did it again—a hundred percent."

"We're not celebratin', Cap." Flynn spoke to the floor. "With Obie gone, we're down a million. How are we gonna make up a loss like that?"

"A great detective," Zachs agreed. "In all those years, maybe got his name in print once."

Taylor took his glass off the bar and drained it. "Back to the squad, Lieu?"

Flynn nodded. "Let's go."

In Kate Cassidy's parking lot, he and Taylor wrangled about who would drive the Lincoln; Flynn won. Taylor got in the front with him. Lauren slid into the backseat where Reynolds lost no time in joining her.

"Hey"—Flynn looked over at Taylor—"we gotta take that guy's mind off the pretty girl."

Taylor asked Lauren if he could please borrow the *News.* He put it in Reynolds's lap. "Read to us, Billy, lieutenant's orders."

"You're gonna be glad I accepted this assignment, I promise. Accordin' to William F. Buckley, 'communism is the principal agent of human evil, but there is a great deal of this that springs, so to speak, from the very soul of man, and it is everywhere—in Central Park, in the South Bronx, and in West Hollywood.' Wait—there's more news here than you might think. Buckley says that Idi Amin killed his wife and dismembered her, killed his son and ate his heart. On the advice of a witch doctor."

"Wait—some guy is gonna use the witch doctor bit in his insanity defense," Taylor predicted.

"Boss—your horoscope says, 'Stick to your present way of doin' things,'" Reynolds reported.

"What does yours say?"

"'Don't allow yourself to feel trapped in your job.' And for O'Levy there's a nice feature here on ol' Ricky Nelson."

"You missed this." Lauren reached over and flipped some pages.

"Hey, boss." Reynolds rattled the paper. "Your reporter pal got himself a column?"

"Yeah. What's he up to today?" Flynn asked.

"Umm..." Reynolds skimmed the column. "Coke dealers. Crack dealers. Somebody collared a grandmother pushin' crack. Homicide stats creepin' up..."

"I guess we know all that," Taylor said, "except maybe the grandmother caper, that's kinda new."

"I suspect," Lauren said, "that Andy's friend wants to make sure the mayor knows all that."

"Not a bad idea," Flynn agreed.

"Okay"—Reynolds cleared his throat—"here's how he ends it: 'The bloodstained map of Manhattan's Upper West Side bears witness to multiple homicides said to be committed in the normal course of cocaine business by Dennis "Irish" Viera and his murderous minions.

"'Viera's flagrant career ended in a pitched gun battle on New Year's Eve with detectives of the Twenty-ninth Precinct, aka *the Hundred Percent Squad.* The squad's Lieutenant Andy Flynn, long the drug lord's mortal enemy, has said that "scraping that scum off the face of the city" is a source of satisfaction to his men and to him.

"'Their arrest the same night of Viera's lieutenant Luis (Monte) Almonte, alleged knifeman in the gory double homicide last spring of two coke dealers, earned the Hundred Percent Squad their title for the third year running. The first—and no doubt only—such hat trick in police history.

"'But at what cost! Fatally shot in the battle with Viera, allegedly by one "Paco," a visiting coke thug from Philadelphia, was Detective First Grade Paul (Obie) O'Brien, age 62. Detective O'Brien, widely respected in the NYPD and a recipient of the police Medal of Honor, planned to retire soon to a house in Ireland. This morning, Flynn's 29th Precinct squad and thousands of other policemen share the grief of his wife, Maureen, and their two daughters, at the detective's funeral. The service takes place at 10:30 A.M., at the church where Paul O'Brien was baptized: Our Lady Queen of Martyrs, Forest Hills, Queens.

"'Afterwards, in perhaps the most poignant of all tributes to their brother—the first police office to die in 1986—the city's cops will go back to their commands with a strengthened resolve. In heroic challenge to the drug lords who are taking our streets, and killing *us.*'"

The Lincoln sped on. Each person in the car thought his own thoughts.

Heroic challenge. Flynn weighed the phrase as the skyline glimmered ahead. The reporter had got that just right. In 1986, a squad like Flynn's could and would give a hundred percent—and never even see over the top of their IN boxes, thanks to Luzan and his clones. Flynn slowed for the tollgate and drove into the tunnel to Manhattan. But there would always be the ultimate hero, like Obie, who would choose—or be compelled—to give even more.

Flynn let Lauren out in front of her office near the courthouses in lower Manhattan. She leaned down and kissed him through the Lincoln's open window. "Thanks for the lift," she said.

"Thanks for being there."

She started to step away, then turned back and smiled at him. "Where else would I be?"